4

Choosing Rachel

M.B. Smith

Your support and encouragement
mean the world to me. Thank
you <u>so</u> much ♡

~ MB Smith

To my father,

Whenever I voiced one of life's trivial inconveniences, you would always say, "I can't wait to read about this in your book one day."

This is what you meant, right?

(Also because anytime I mentioned Ryder, you said, "Ryder? I barely know her.")

TABLE OF CONTENTS

CHAPTER ONE

Rachel

4 Years Ago

Get yourself together. Your friends deserve this night. I internally chant this for the hundredth time tonight as I use my pointer finger to fix the smudged lipstick my last drink is undoubtedly responsible for.

I'm about to repeat the mantra, when a group of giggling girls burst into the bathroom, and it's time to quit my sulking, plaster on a smile, and go find my roommates in the busy club.

I shoulder past the girls who have had way more to drink than I have, and I can't help but be envious of the smiles and laughs that come so naturally to them when I'm straining to keep mine in place.

Maybe a few more drinks will help loosen you up.

I pop my knuckles and take a deep breath, like that will distract me from seeing alcohol as the answer to my problems. I like to think I drink a healthy amount for a twenty-two-year-old, especially considering my tendency to latch onto vices. Usually, I can channel those tendencies into healthy habits, like working out or taking on extra projects at work. Still, nights like tonight make the prospect of falling into drunkenness harder to resist.

What's it going to hurt? It's not like you have anything else to direct your focus on.

I know, somewhere deep down, that it isn't true. I have my job at the pub, where I'll take on twice as many shifts starting next week now that school is over for the semester.

And? My cruel mind asks. *What else is there?*

Nothing. That's what.

At least last summer, I had my internship to keep myself occupied. This year, I couldn't find one that paid, and now the rent that used to be split three ways will be all my responsibility. I can't afford to accept anything unpaid. Besides, the course credit was filled, so as great as it would look to have more experience on my resume, I don't technically need it.

I spot Shay and Rosie from across the crowd, standing at the bar with two guys I don't recognize. Their faces are bright, blissful even, carrying none of the anxiety and pressure that weighs me down like bricks stacked on my shoulders.

For the hundredth time, I tell myself that my feelings have nothing to do with jealousy or that I'm not happy for my roommates. After all, I've known they'll graduate this year and move on to bigger and better things.

I pull at my little black dress as I walk. The damn thing keeps riding up my thighs no matter how many times I pull it down, but as a ten-dollar thrift find, it feels like a waste to not wear it at least once.

I'll be the first to admit that it pales in comparison to Shay's electric blue dress with cutouts highlighting her petite silhouette or Rosie's burgundy silk number that fits her like a glove, but I feel far from insecure.

Even now, pushing my way through the crowd of the busy nightclub to get to the bar, I feel eyes roaming my body. My thick, jet-black hair falls in perfectly straight strands to my shoulder blades. It had taken forever to get it just right, but damn if it wasn't worth it. My dress, as annoying as it is to constantly readjust, suits my body type perfectly. It's a skin-tight piece with a halter top that dips into a V-neckline in the front. The heels are my favorite, though. With thin straps that wrap around my ankles like ivy, the golden heels pop against my black skin—boosting my confidence and height.

I hear Shay's laugh from a few feet away, and though the sound would be cringeworthy from anyone else, it's somehow charming coming from her. She tosses her head back, letting her loose curls cascade down her back in a motion that the man standing at her side seems enchanted by.

His tan skin practically glows in the neon lights, and his dark hair falls over his eyes and out of the man bun that is stylishly piled on his head. The burgundy flannel is unbuttoned just a few too many, and even though he's undoubtedly handsome, he's far from the clean-cut men that Shay usually goes for.

Rosie is just as enthralled by his friend, a man with dark hair buzzed short, an impeccable black suit, and cool blue eyes that are striking against the black he surrounds himself with.

When I reach them, I lay my nude-painted fingernails over Shay's shoulder and gently squeeze, waiting for the returned squeeze or gentle pats of her response.

"Who's your new friend?"

Her bright smile flashes my way, and she pats my hand twice, signaling that he's not a creep she wants to get away from.

I eye Rosie, who gives me a similar, *all good here*, nod.

"Rachel, what took you so long?" Even though Shay asks, she doesn't give me any time to answer. "This is Donovan." She points to Man Bun, and then to Blue Eyes. "And this is Kade. They've invited us to the V.I.P. section."

Of course, they did. And now you get to be dragged along as the fifth wheel.

I hide my hand behind my back to pop my knuckles, but paste a wide smile on my face.

"That sounds like fun!"

Rosie passes me a drink before she takes Kade's hand, and I start drinking it, despite knowing that it probably isn't the best idea.

I trail behind Shay, Donovan, Rosie, and Kade like a rejected middle schooler who didn't find a date to the dance. This thought makes me sip my drink faster than I usually would.

My mood improves when I take in the V.I.P. section of the nightclub. It's bigger than I'd expected. Much bigger. It takes up the entire second floor, which is only a quarter the size of the rest of the club, with a mezzanine surrounding it to overlook the other party-goers. The red velvet rope—I hadn't realized the cliche was accurate—is placed at the base of the staircase, with a bull-like man guarding it with crossed arms and a deep scowl.

I slow as we get closer, waiting for Donovan to start talking to the man, but there's no need. The guard only lowers his head before moving the rope and stepping aside for the five of us to go through.

I feel more eyes on me than before as we ascend the staircase, both by envious onlookers below and those sizing up the new arrivals from above. I don't pay them any mind, focusing instead on putting one foot in front of the other and doing my best not to fall on my ass in front of everyone.

We reach the top, and an unexpected ball of dread settles in the pit of my stomach when I survey the model-like women in designer dresses sitting with movie-star-worthy men in three-piece suits worth more than I make in a year. I never thought I was particularly insecure, but those feelings thrive in this setting.

I follow Shay and Donovan to a white, U-shaped couch against the wall, and—to my continued discomfort—we're not alone.

Two men sit on the couch, one with meticulously slicked-back hair, a matching beard, and an immaculate gray suit. The other man has dirty blond hair and a scar that stretches from his eyebrow to his chin in a horrifying and intriguing way. Three women sit around them, all in dresses that look better suited for lingerie magazines than in a public setting. Still, it's not like I'm dressed like Mother Teresa.

"Boys." Donovan gets their attention, waving toward Shay, who smiles like she got *him* into the V.I.P. section, not vice versa. "This is Shay, Rosie, and Rachel," he says, pointing each of us out.

Kade, who holds Rosie's waist, steps up on my other side, pointing to the men on the couches. He points to Scar Face first. "This is Tripp." His finger then slides to the other man, who looks much older than everyone else but is still at ease in the environment. "And this is Nicholas."

Tripp and Nicholas inspect the three of us, as if assessing if we're worth taking the place of their current companions. Although, with Donovan and Kade both holding my friends, I'm the only available option. I brace myself for their lustful stares, but after one quick look at me, their attention goes back to the girls draping themselves all over them.

Wow, you weren't even worth a glance.

As if I want to be ogled anyway, I remind myself.

Donovan glances around us. "Where's Ryder?"

The man he introduces as Tripp rolls his eyes as a busty brunette scoots onto his lap, trailing violent kisses down his throat. "Taking a call from Boss."

Donovan and Kade both move to sit on the couch, pulling my friends with them, so I follow. I sit on the edge of the couch, no doubt looking just as out of place as I feel.

Donovan laughs. "I swear all he does is work."

"Is this 'Ryder' a friend of yours?" Shay's head tilts to the side in what I'm sure is a practiced move, allowing her curls to cascade down her shoulder, leading right to her chest.

Donovan takes the bait, eyes falling to her breasts with a visible swallow. "Uh, yeah, I'm sure you'll meet him, eventually."

Nicholas and Tripp engage in a hushed conversation, treating the women hanging on them more like cute puppies begging for attention than actual humans.

When I go to take another sip of my drink, it's empty. I suppose it's a sign that I should slow down, but instead, I choose to take it as an excuse to go to the bar and get out of this awkward situation.

I raise my empty glass to my friends. "I'll be right back."

Rosie doesn't acknowledge me, and Shay gives me a quick nod, her attention returning to Donovan, who looks ready to take a bite out of her. I wish I didn't mean that so literally.

The walk to the bar is too short, and I sit on the white, swiveling stool as I wave to the bartender, who acknowledges me with a nod and a finger, telling me he'll only be a moment.

Not like anyone is going to miss you anyway.

I tap my nails against the counter to the beat of the music and resist the urge to look at my phone like an awkward teen with no one to sit with at lunch.

Finally, the bartender comes my way. "What can I get for you?"

I open my mouth to ask for a vodka martini when the bartender's eyes focus on something behind me.

"A whiskey sour for me and a glass of your finest champagne for the lady."

The deep voice is as smooth as the world's most luxurious silk and is the most inviting sound I've ever heard.

I don't recognize his voice because there's no way I would've forgotten if I'd heard it before. The husky, rumbling tenor is one of a kind.

I can *feel* his presence behind me, big and dominating, like a storm swirling overhead. It's not stifling or suffocating, almost alluring, like a juicy red apple that you can't help but take a bite of, though you know deep down that it's poisonous.

The bartender nods spastically, but I hold up a hand before he can fetch the man's order.

"Actually, I'd like a vodka martini."

The bartender's eyes flicker to the man behind me as if to ask permission to grant my request. I have no idea what he sees there, but he turns away without another look at me.

"Not a champagne girl?" The man's honey-smooth voice sends

pleasant shivers down my spine so intense that I can feel the tingles in each vertebrae.

The heat radiating off him covers my back like a blanket, and I resist the urge to lean into it.

I'm not a PDA person. In fact, it's why my high school boyfriend broke up with me, since I wouldn't hold his hand in public. So, needless to say, the fact that touching a stranger—who I haven't even laid eyes on yet—sounds alluring is not only disconcerting, but wildly intriguing.

For the first time tonight, I'm interested in whatever games my mind plays with me. What can there possibly be about a stranger that I will find the least bit interesting?

I straighten my back, inspecting my nails like they're fine jewels, just to give myself something to focus on.

"Just need something a bit stronger," I answer.

"Rough night?"

"Nope," I say, popping the P like I'm pulling a sucker out of my mouth. I wish I could say I was having a rough night, but the night itself has been great. It's just my general bitterness toward life that's ruining it.

"Celebrating then?"

This time I do send a look over my shoulder, but only far enough to see my friends. Shay is deep in conversation with Donovan, so close that their noses appear to be touching, while Rosie and Kade are openly making out.

"Yeah, I guess I am," I say as I turn back toward the bar.

"And what are you celebrating?"

I think carefully about that. The answer is the last day of classes, but it isn't for me.

"I'm just here with friends," I tell him. "They had their last day of classes today."

"But you didn't," he states, intent on reading between the lines.

"No, I didn't. I still have another year because I had to slow down my course plan to make time for my job."

My mood dips as soon as I say the words, ruining any progress I've made on masking the frustration I harbor for the situation.

It's not Shay or Rosie's fault I can't balance my finance courses and a part-time job at the pub.

Slowing my course load over another year hadn't been a difficult choice to make. However, it feels impossible now that my roommates have packed up their part of the apartment we've shared for two years. It's not even the loss of a friendship that tears me apart—we all get along, but none of us were looking for more than someone to share the rent with—but having to watch everyone move on without me while I struggle to make ends meet.

Shay landed a job as an assistant event coordinator in New York City, which pays almost nothing but gets her foot in the door, which is why her parents don't mind footing the bill for her living expenses. Then there's Rosie, who is planning the wedding of her dreams to her high school sweetheart and is hired by the private school she graduated from to teach Language Arts.

I'm happy for them. I really am. They've both worked their asses off and deserve this, but I can't quite hush the voice in the back of my mind that whispers I deserve it, too.

Thankfully, we're interrupted when the bartender returns with our drinks, and I'm thankful to see my martini and not a glass of champaign.

I accept it with a thank you. "Could you put it on my tab?"

"That won't be necessary," the man behind me says, authority dripping from the words.

The bartender nods before moving to serve the other customers at the bar.

"I appreciate the offer, but I don't need anyone buying my drinks." I raise my hand to flag down the bartender, but a big hand reaches out to stop me.

His palm, warm and calloused, encases my entire hand with ease.

I wait for the discomfort that physical touch always brings me, for the overwhelming urge to pop my knuckles or the intrusive thoughts…but none of it comes.

There's only the racing of my heart and the fascination with how my body and mind react to this faceless man.

His hand—the only part of his body I've seen—is dark-skinned, large, and capable.

Of what? I'm not sure yet.

He guides my hand back to the bar top with ease, and though I might've deemed the gesture demeaning any other time, it doesn't feel the least bit disrespectful.

If anything, there's something almost…attractive about how he holds on to me, like my hand is something to be cherished and protected.

"Please," he says, and he must have stepped closer to me because I can feel his breath skate over the shell of my ear. "They're on the house."

When my hand is firmly pressed to the counter, I expect him to let go, but he doesn't. His hand keeps its hold on mine, only shifting to clasp in more of an embrace.

"And why would they do that?" I ask, eyes never leaving our joined hands as I try to understand how my mind interprets this interaction.

But, for the first time tonight, that bitch doesn't say a word.

"Well, there ought to be a few perks when you run the place," he says absently, his finger rubbing slow circles on the back of my hand in a mesmerizing pattern.

With anyone else, I'd think they were putting on a show to impress me, but that's not the case here. There's no trace of boasting in his words, only the simple statement of fact.

"I suppose there ought," I answer, reaching for my drink with my free hand and willing it not to shake as I lift it to my lips.

"What's your name?" he asks, and the question makes me laugh, though the sound gets lost in the music and chattering voices around us. Still, I'm sure he can see it in the shake of my shoulders and feel it in the hand that still lingers over mine.

"What's so funny?"

"My hair and my ass," I answer with another round of laughter— an indication that maybe I've had a bit too much to drink.

"Excuse me?"

"My hair and my ass," I repeat. "That's all you've seen of me, and yet, here you are buying me drinks and coming on to me."

I can feel him closing in from behind, asserting his dominance in a way that should make me want to run.

But it doesn't.

His lips are so close to my ear when he speaks that his breath sends warm shivers through my body. "On the contrary, I've had my eye on you since the second you walked into this club. Your friends haven't noticed how you drop your smile the second they look away, eye the exit like it's a saving grace, and pop your knuckles to give yourself something else to focus on, but I have. I sent my friends to charm yours just to get you here alone. So yes, I am coming on to you. As for the drinks, well, those were on the house."

What the...

My body tenses at the confession, and though I briefly wonder if it's possible to slide past him and get the hell away from here, I'm not entirely convinced I want that. He's watched me all night and pulled strings like a puppet master to get me here alone.

"You realize you're admitting to being a stalker, right?"

"Why do I get the feeling that doesn't bother you as much as it should?"

Instead of confronting the answer to that question—which I suspect has the potential to land me in a psych ward—I finally give into temptation and turn to face the man that still gently strokes my hand.

Just as I suspected, I'm speechless.

He's a broad man, given a wide birth from everyone around us, and the air surrounding him is even bigger, the kind of force others unconsciously submit to.

He has black hair cut short, barely showing the tight, natural curls that outline his rectangular-shaped head. His jaw is surrounded by neatly trimmed scruff, and his thick lips pull into a smile at my appraisal.

The black slacks fit like they were custom made for him, and a light blue button-up stretches across his chest with its sleeves rolled over muscular forearms. A simple silver watch is secured around his wrist, the only accessory complimenting his attire, but he doesn't need extravagant accessories. Hell, he could be adorned in rags, and people would *still* part like the Red Sea for him.

There are a million reasons I should rip my hand away from his, grab my friends, and run out of here like a bat out of hell, but I don't listen to a damn one as I hold out my free hand.

"Rachel."

If I thought his features alone were disarming, his growing smile might very well have the power to rid the entire state of California of its inhibitions.

He lifts his hand from mine and accepts my handshake firmly.

"Ryder."

CHAPTER TWO

Rachel

4 Years Ago

Ryder pulls my hand to his lips to place a sensual kiss.

When his lips meet my skin, I gasp at the warmth it elicits, starting in my hand and spreading through my entire body until it feels like he's setting me on fire in the best possible way.

It's a foreign reaction that scares me as much as it fascinates me. I'm so invested in deciphering my own reaction that I forget I'm holding my martini, so when I place that hand over my now-racing heart, the glass falls to the ground. It shatters to pieces, drawing attention from all around us.

Ryder unhurriedly pulls his lips from my hand and straightens to his full height, unbothered by the broken glass or the alcohol that no doubt covers his shoes.

"Shit," I whisper, turning as much as I can on the barstool, but I don't have time to get the bartender's attention because Ryder uses his hold on my hand to turn me back toward him.

"Allow me," he says.

He lifts his hand, gesturing to the bartender, who must give some sort of response because Ryder nods, but I don't take my eyes off of him to be sure, and really, I don't care much.

All I care about is figuring out what exactly it is about Ryder's presence that calms my over-active mind and makes me respond in ways I never have before.

He's not even my type.

I don't have an extensive romantic history, but I've been known to go for the funny, lean, golden-retriever-energy kind of guy, a far cry from the man hovering over me now.

"May I?" he asks, holding out his other hand.

Surprising myself even more, my mind takes a backseat as my body nods its approval.

I reach out to take his other hand so he can help me down, but he moves it before I get the chance. I don't realize his plan until it's too late, and he's cradling me in his arms bridal style.

"What are you doing?" I ask breathlessly.

He gives me a look like carrying me was the most logical option, and I'm silly for even questioning it.

"Wouldn't want to ruin your shoes."

"It hardly would've ruined them."

"Humor me," he whispers, his voice low and smile sly.

I swallow and nod because what else is there to say?

We head toward the same U-shaped couches that our friends still occupy, and all of them are still trapped in their own worlds, just as I left them. When we get there, my friends spare a quick glance at us, seeming to dismiss Ryder and me as a pair of strangers. Both Shay and Rosie do a double take when they realize I'm the girl cradled in the man's arms.

Their eyes scream their question of whether this is something I want. I send them a reassuring nod, which, mixed with my growing smile, lowers their guard and piques their interest.

I rarely entertain the men who hit on me when we go out, let alone let one carry me.

I almost *wish* I could blame the alcohol for my strange reaction to this even stranger man since it would be so much easier to brush it off as a drunken hallucination, but I've sobered up since Ryder approached me at the bar and can say with certainty that the alcohol isn't responsible for a damn thing.

We take a seat on the edge of the couch, and Ryder sets me on his lap like it's only natural, when in reality, I've never sat on a man's lap in my life.

What scares me the most is that my reaction to Ryder isn't only a physical attraction—though there's no denying that I am physically attracted to him. My usually cruel mind hasn't offered a single snarky comment or intrusive thought since meeting him.

It's the first time I remember my mind being so…quiet.

I'm only this relaxed when I throw myself into work, or any chore that will distract my mind from itself.

It's been half an hour since we sat down, and though most of it has been spent in silence, absolutely none of it has been awkward. In fact, it's the most peaceful I can ever remember being. It's like Ryder's presence is enough to fill every space of my consciousness. We don't have to make out like Rosie and Kade or tell each other stories like Shay and Donovan.

We just sit together.

Maybe I had just enough alcohol to not feel the pressure of filling the silence, or maybe—and I'm starting to think it's more likely that— Ryder is just the kind of person you can sit in companionable silence with.

It's like a drug to an over-thinker, to simply sit in the arms of a man I barely know, who quiets my mind just by being here.

Besides, is it so bad to simply bask in the blanket of warmth his body provides? I certainly don't think so.

I never thought myself to be a particularly small person, but wrapped up in Ryder's embrace, I look almost fragile. There's something so inexplicably comforting about how his arm is snaked around my back, resting on the curve of my hip with a subtle but sure possessiveness. I let my forehead rest against his cheek, enjoying the feel of his lips brushing against my ear, though he doesn't speak.

I move to reach for my drink—a new one that he had brought to us since I dropped the last one—, but his long arm extends before I can, and the next thing I know, he's holding the martini to my lips. I don't protest or even question him when he places the cool glass to my lips and lifts. I tilt my head back and drink until there's nothing left.

He pulls the glass back, and I lick my lips, relishing how he tightens his hold on my hip. Then with boldness I'm not accustomed to, I press my forehead to him, barely brushing my lips over the tip of his nose.

I expect him to lift his head and kiss me, but he doesn't. Instead, I watch those lips pull into a taunting smile that has me pressing my knees together. I know my reaction isn't lost on him because his eyes flick hungrily to my legs before returning with an almost playful spark.

"Ask."

"Huh?"

He tilts his chin up, brushing my lips with his, but pulling away before actually leaving a kiss. "If you want something from me, you'll have to ask for it."

There's no way he can feel how his words make my heartbeat quicken, but the knowing edge in his expression makes me think he can. I'm not sure what his game is, but when I remember how his lips felt pressed against my hand, how the warmth had spread like a fire I'd been ready to burn in, I decide to play.

"Kiss me," I breathe.

And he does.

I'm not sure if I ever knew what it meant to lose myself in a kiss before now. It's not like I imagined it. The music doesn't fade, and the smell of vodka and sweat is just as pungent, but my sanity is nonexistent. I don't consciously choose to wrap my arms around Ryder's neck or part my lips for his tongue to slide against mine. It just happens. I can't remember a time I felt so alive. The way my body feels like it's being lit on fire and doused by water at the same time is something I've never experienced before.

I have no idea how long we kiss for, and I don't think the lack of time perception has anything to do with my alcohol consumption but rather the consumption of *him*.

"Rachel!"

Shay's voice cuts through the private bubble Ryder and I have created. I reluctantly pull my lips from his and look at my friends, standing with their dates for the night.

The dates Ryder sent them so he could get me alone.

"We're going to dance! Want to come?" Rosie asks, flicking her eyes between Ryder and me like we're a science experiment she's waiting to watch explode.

I think through the best way to decline without making them feel like I'm ditching them, but I'm spared the task when Ryder answers for me.

"We'll pass. You go enjoy."

I don't even watch my friend's reactions to his response before they walk away because the second Ryder's eyes lock with mine, I snap back to our private bubble.

"Unless you'd like to go with your friends?" he asks gently, but with a sureness that implies he already knows my answer.

I shake my head.

"Then what would you like to do?"

"I think you already know."

His eyes trace my body with unbridled lust. "I need to hear you say it."

"Why?"

The slowest, most sensual smirk lifts his lips, promising all sorts of mischief as he brings his hand to my face, rubbing his thumb against my bottom lip. "Because when I'm pounding into you tonight, and you're delirious from coming so many times, I want to know these beautiful lips demanded the pleasure."

Oh my...

My shoulders tighten, and my knees rub against each other as tingles shoot from the top of my head, down my spine, and gather at my core.

I can't explain why I do what I do next. I've never done something like this before, but maybe that's why it feels so liberating when I open my lips to take his thumb into my mouth.

His eyes widen, and his lips part to suck in a sharp breath when I look up with the most innocent expression I can muster as I flick my tongue against him.

He suppresses his growing smile. "I've got a rebel on my hands, don't I?"

He doesn't.

No one has ever described me as a rebel, and rightfully so. I'm a rule follower. I'm the girl who is home by curfew, studies for every test, and never skips school, even when all the other kids do.

But right now, with Ryder holding on to me like I am both precious and filthy, I want to be a rebel.

I want to be *his* rebel.

So, I suck his thumb even deeper into my mouth, rolling my eyes back and pressing my chest to his with a deep inhale, knowing my breasts are on full display. He takes in another deep breath, almost like he's in pain.

His hand, which holds my lower back, skims over my body. At first, I don't know his intentions, but he makes them clear by dragging his fingers leisurely around my front, brushing my upper thighs, and dipping beneath my dress.

I can swear my heart pounds louder than the music, and I part my legs to make room for his large hand, but he doesn't take the hint. Instead, his fingers remain on my thighs.

"Ah, ah, ah," he mutters. "You'll have to ask, Rebel."

Still sucking his thumb between my lips, I grind my hips against him in an attempt to convince him to touch me. I expect him to either give in or pull back.

He does neither.

With an expectant brow raised, Ryder pinches my thigh. It's not hard, but firm enough to elicit a surprised—and admittedly aroused—whimper.

"Try again, and this time use your words, or do you want me to continue teasing you in front of all these people?"

People? What pe—

That's when I remember we were still on the couch.

My eyes flash around us to find that—thankfully—our friends are all on the dance floor. The couch's location has hidden us from the majority of the V.I.P. section, so no one can see us unless they're within the area of the couch.

Still, I can't believe I forgot that we're in public. I went from despising PDA to practically begging to get fingered in a crowded room.

What the hell is wrong with me?

I release his fingers as embarrassment breaks through the haze like shattered glass. Instead of letting me go, like I expect him to in my flustered state, Ryder uses his newly freed hand to capture the side of my neck, lifting my chin with the thumb I so shamelessly sucked only seconds ago.

"Rebel," he says, a command in that low voice. There's power in that tone, like it can be used to bring the most powerful pleasure or excruciating pain.

This time, I don't even try to pretend.

"Let's get out of here," I breathe, widening my dark eyes. "I want you to fuck me, Ryder."

The smile that splits his face is the most handsome I've ever seen, but there's more than just excitement.

There's a pride, an awe, a promise.

Of what? I'm not sure, but I have a feeling I will find out.

CHAPTER THREE

Ryder

8 Weeks Later

"Sales have gone up by twelve percent in the last six months alone, and we can expect a similar rise over the next six months. I'd say we're looking at our most profitable year yet."

Paul, the club manager, beams like he's been awarded employee of the decade, but fuck if I know where he gets the confidence because it sure as hell isn't from Moreno's expression.

I look between Moreno and the club manager like two sides of a battlefield, only there's no wondering who will win.

Joshua Moreno is the boss of the Moreno criminal family, which reigns over the majority of the west coast. He took over from his father, Marcus Marsollo, and changed the family name when he learned his father was a prick of epic proportions. At twenty-four years old, he's the youngest American Mafia boss in history, but that hasn't hindered his influence from reaching every corner of this country and others.

Then there's Paul, whose last name I never bothered to learn because he is *that* insignificant.

The lack of suspense at the outcome of the meeting is boring as hell, and a striking contrast to the last time I was here.

This is the first time I've been back at the club since I met Rachel.

I didn't have anything to drink after that whiskey sour because I wasn't willing to risk forgetting a single second that I spent with her. From the moment I saw her walk inside the club, swaying her hips in that little black dress with heels and jewelry that glowed against her skin, I hadn't been able to look away.

She was even more beautiful up close—which I hadn't thought possible—with soft features, rounded cheeks, a small nose, and wide, full lips that would make any supermodel envious.

When I'd noticed her constant scanning for exits, I couldn't, for the life of me, imagine why she'd be so desperate to get away.

But then I met her, and she didn't seem so keen on running anymore.

Which only fascinated me more.

Even then, undeniably beautiful and as drawn to me as I was to her, the reason I couldn't keep my hands off of her all night long was something entirely different.

Watching her respond to just the slightest contact was euphoric. Seeing her reaction to the lightest brush of my fingers, the fanning of my breath over her neck, and even the gentle squeeze of my hand with hers was like getting high on the strongest, most addictive drug.

Then I kissed her, and the addiction etched itself into my bones like a constant buzz that I craved, even as I still held her in my arms.

Over the years, I've learned to recognize what women want from me, whether it be my money, power, or body. I'd been willing to bet that Rachel's desire would reside with the latter, but it hadn't.

In fact, it didn't seem like she wanted anything from me at all.

She was just as fascinated with her reaction to me as I was.

When she finally said the words, asking me to fuck her in that alluring-as-hell voice of hers, I nearly took her in the middle of the V.I.P. section.

Of course, I didn't, and instead booked a suite in the most luxurious hotel in the area.

I've had my fair share of memorable nights, but none of them compared to the one I spent with her. It wasn't just about how compatible we were sexually, either. It was how natural it felt to bathe with her, and how soothing it was to cradle her to my chest in the king-sized bed.

It made me think about things I never had before, like what it would be like to have that every night.

Needless to say, I didn't do much sleeping.

Moreno's scoff brings me back to the small, cigar-scented office.

"And how many, out of those six months, were we investigated for issues with the alcohol license and underage drinking?" Moreno asks with the same ease he'd ask about the weather.

Paul's smile falters as his fingers fidget with the hem of his blazer. I'd crack a smile at the bastard's lack of confidence, but it's more pathetic than it is amusing.

"Well, Sir," he starts, throwing glances to the door like someone could come in here and save him from this meeting.

For fuck's sake, he's acting like he didn't know this was coming for three weeks now.

"There have been a few run-ins with the authorities, but it's nothing we haven't been able to resolve. We haven't had a single charge brought against us, and I don't believe that will change any time soon." Paul places his hands on the desk between us, seeming at ease with his own assurances, and waits for Moreno's response.

I don't have to send a glance to my side to know that Moreno won't be letting him off the hook that easily. We sit in a pleasantly suffocating silence for nearly a full minute before Paul's fidgeting returns.

Silence is my favorite form of intimidation.

Those who are aware of its value aren't as susceptible, but those who aren't—like Paul—can't help their instinctive urge to fill it.

"But, of course, we'll double down on—"

The second I see movement in the corner of my eye, I act on instinct. I flick my knife out of my pocket and place it in the palm of Moreno's waiting hand.

We move in sync, which is the product of years of working together, and makes Paul's anxiety visibly spike.

Moreno takes one side of the desk, and I round the other until the poor bastard is trapped between us.

Paul faces Moreno, turning his chair back to me. His eyes bulge at the sight of the knife in Moreno's grasp as he expertly twirls it around his fingers like it's a measly pencil and not a weapon responsible for the loss of more than a few lives.

"Mr. Moreno," he says in a shaky voice. "I didn't mean—I never meant—"

"I like you," Moreno starts. "And I like what you've done with the club."

Paul's trembling lips pull into a timid smile. "Well, thank—"

Moreno's posture change is subtle, but I catch the order as soon as he sends it and grab both Paul's shoulders from behind, pinning him to the chair as Moreno leans forward, grazing the knife against the man's chin.

"What I don't like, however, is that I've spent more than that precious *twelve percent* sales increase paying off the local authorities to look the other way for your carelessness."

I can't see Paul's face, but I feel his shudders under my hands and wouldn't be surprised if he pissed himself.

Once again, Moreno uses silence, dragging the knife from Paul's chin, up his face, and down again. He's not pressing hard enough to break the skin, but he's got to be close.

"I-I p-promise it—"

With a flick of his wrist, Moreno nicks Paul's ear. It's a small cut, one that will have no impact whatsoever aside from a sting, but he still wails like Moreno cut out his face. I roll my eyes and release his shoulders with a shove.

"You have six months to prove to me that you can do your job without drawing too much attention. Think you can do that?"

Paul's answer comes between gasping breaths. "Y-yes, Sir! Of course, Sir."

An hour later, we're leaving the club and climbing into the car with a thoroughly scared Paul left behind.

"You're seeing her again?" Moreno asks, the distaste clear in his tone.

I shrug and busy myself scrolling through emails on my phone. My outside reaction doesn't show any sign of change, but based on the shit-eating grin plastered on Moreno's face, I'm not fooling him.

"That isn't an answer," he points out, helpful as a fucking Boy Scout.

"Yes, I'm seeing her again," I answer, carefully mundane.

"It's been two months."

"And?"

"Are you *dating* her?" Joshua Moreno says the word *dating* like there's battery acid in his mouth, and to him, the concept is about that pleasant.

The answer is, technically, no. Rachel and I have never had a conversation about putting a label on what we are, but in all honesty, we don't have conversations, period.

Our relationship—if you can even call it that—is one of friends with benefits...just without the friends part.

It's more of a routine.

When we have free nights, we spend them together.

This usually means cutting out of poker nights and clubbing with the capos to eat Chinese food on the floor of Rachel's cardboard-box-sized apartment as she puts on her favorite shows—which are exclusively true crime.

Yes, I see the irony.

There's very little talking during these frequent nights. No, *tell me about your family* or *what are your plans for the future*. Hell, there's barely even a, *how was your day*, though the silence never feels strained.

The pressure that most people feel to make conversation is absent from Rachel. She isn't like the women who have asked me to take them on extravagant dates or to meet their parents. I've been nervous about —albeit not exactly opposed to—the idea of Rachel asking for more, but she never has.

It makes me wonder how she sees me in that pretty head of hers. All she can know about me is that I run the club we met at.

And I can make her come four times in ten minutes with nothing but my lips—yes, a personal record.

We simply enjoy each other's company—and bodies—before I leave for the night.

I've even been careful to make sure that we use protection and don't fall asleep together—unlike our first time in the hotel.

Though it's been two months, and I'm positive we're exclusive— no, we never explicitly said we would be, I just know she doesn't have time for anyone else with her work schedule—staying the night seemed like crossing a line.

Moreno's face is scrunched up, likely from having said the dreaded D-word, and I laugh at the reaction.

"No, we aren't dating," I confirm.

"Then what are you doing?"

"Fucking," I deadpan. "And eating more takeout than I ever have before."

Moreno eyes me like he doesn't believe me, but I pretend not to notice.

"So, you'll come to the club tonight with the capos and me?"

"I didn't say that."

"Pussy-whipped," he mutters, and I promptly kick him in the shin.

Childish? Yes. Necessary? Also, yes.

"Fuck you," he grits, but the shit-eating grin is back in place. "I'm glad to hear it's nothing serious since we're leaving next week."

My head snaps up from where I've been checking my phone for a message from Rachel—there isn't one. "We're not supposed to leave for another month."

"The rest of the meetings will be virtual. We've been gone too long, and I'm ready to get back to L.A.," he says flippantly.

It's not like I think what Rachel and I have will last forever, but I never thought about the end for some reason. Hell, she probably thinks I live here in Sacramento. The subject never came up.

I know he's waiting for a reaction, so I don't give him one and instead message Rachel that I'll be over as soon as she's off work.

I stand outside Rachel's door with her favorite dish from a local burger joint, and dig into my pocket for the key she gave me a month ago when it became clear we'd be a steady lay.

I suppose I can see how it might look like we're dating.

I'll be the first to admit that the idea doesn't repulse me like I thought it would. Traditional dating isn't common in my line of work since most marriages are arranged to strengthen the family, but it isn't unheard of either. As Moreno's second in command, there aren't strict stipulations regarding my marital expectations.

I turn the lock and open the door, just as Rachel glides from her bedroom to the living room, wearing a light pink loungewear set. Her hair is braided down her back, and there's not a trace of makeup on her face.

Another fact I appreciate about Rachel is her authenticity. She's always dressed for comfort, and yet, she still is the most stunning woman I've ever met.

"What's for dinner?" she asks, coming to sit on one of the two barstools—the only seating in the apartment aside from the worn, red leather couch in her living room.

"Burgers, that okay?"

"As long as you got one with pepper jack cheese and extra pickles."

I place that very burger on the counter in front of her.

Correction: Rachel and I talk just enough that I know her favorite meal from every takeout restaurant within a ten-mile radius.

I take a seat beside her and let the television fill whatever need for sound there might be as we open the wrapping on our burgers.

Rachel straightens at my side so fast I look at her food to make sure nothing jumps out at her, but the food looks perfectly normal. Before I get to ask her what the hell is wrong, she's out of her chair and darting for the bathroom.

She doesn't bother to close the door as she falls to her knees over the toilet and empties her stomach. I stand up, ready to spring into action but unsure how to help.

I opt for getting her a glass of water.

"The smell," she manages to say between deep breaths.

I leave the glass on the counter and pack up the food before putting it in the building hallway. When I'm done, I go to her linen closet to grab the aerosol can of air freshener, then spray a generous amount of it. I even light the candle beneath the clock on her stove with the lighter in one of her kitchen drawers.

When the scent of burgers is eradicated from the vicinity, I take the glass of water, kneel at Rachel's side, and hold it out to her.

She doesn't move to take it right away and instead seems to be working to control her breathing. "How-how did you know where all that was?" she asks, not raising her head from where it rests against her forearm, the only thing separating her cheek from the toilet seat.

"I'm perceptive."

It's true enough. Plenty of people keep lighters in kitchen drawers and air fresher in linen closets. She doesn't need to know that I did a sweep of her apartment while she was at work a week into our fling. I decided against the background check, but I couldn't spend most of my evenings in her apartment without knowing for certain it was not bugged.

"How are you feeling?"

She shakes her head, finally taking the water from me and sipping from it cautiously. "I think I'm fine now. That was strange. I've felt fine all day, but nausea hit me out of nowhere when I smelled the food."

"Does this kind of thing happen often?"

"No, but—" She starts to shake her head but stops. Her expression, which had been shaken, but nonchalant, morphs into calculation.

"Rachel? What's wrong?" I ask, mental alarm bells blaring in my head at the sudden change in countenance.

She doesn't answer, and, for some reason, I get the impression that she's using all her mental strength to force herself to keep breathing. So, instead of forcing answers out of her, I pull us to our feet and strengthen my hold on her.

One of my arms is wrapped around her waist, anchoring her to me, and allowing me to feel every labored breath she pulls into her lungs.

Since Rachel doesn't say anything, I take a moment to appreciate how nicely she fits against me. She's laughably small in my arms, like a house cat curled up beside the king of the jungle. There's something so satisfying about how her entire body can be shielded by mine, how— even in this moment of distress—she leans into me like I'm the rock that'll ground her.

A woman, who I truly have minimal communication with, has me thinking about things I never have before, like size difference, compatibility, and *exclusivity*, which I've never wanted, let alone offered.

And yet, here I am, with the most beautiful woman, realizing that's exactly what I want.

My free hand lifts, brushing aside a part of her hair meant to frame her face but has fallen over her eye as she furrows her brow.

"What's wrong, Rebel?" I whisper.

The questions draw her eyes to me with a start, like she's forgotten I'm here. The look on her face doesn't change aside from the flicker of recognition, no doubt at the mention of the nickname I gave her the night we met but haven't used since. At first, I hadn't wanted her to think I was attached just because of some pet name. Of course, now I know she isn't the *attached* type.

When Rachel's lips finally part, my thoughts are solely focused on how full they are and how—yes, even after she threw up only a moment ago—I'd like to take that bottom lip between my teeth and bruise it before devouring her.

"I'm late."

"Late?" I ask with a lifted brow. "For what?"

Her eyes close with the realization that she'll have to be more direct. Resignation covers her features when she speaks the words she so clearly doesn't want to.

"My period, Ryder. It's late."

My hand freezes where it's placed against her cheek. My mouth goes slack. My chest constricts. My lungs burn with a held breath.

But that organ that I've never given much thought to, the one beating like it's trying to burst out of my chest, swells.

Fucking *swells*.

I've never associated that word with anything aside from injuries —of which I've had plenty—but right now, it's the only word that can describe the full, bursting feeling that's taking over my entire body, starting at my center and spreading through every nerve.

It must be taking over my mind, too, because I don't notice that Rachel is crying until her sniffle brings me back to reality.

"I think I'm pregnant," she whispers, closing any space between us and burying her face in my chest.

I have three realizations at that moment.

Rachel's tears are the worst sight I've ever seen.

Rachel clinging to me like I'm her lifeline is the best sight I've ever seen.

And most importantly, I have a reason to keep her tied to me for life.

CHAPTER FOUR

Ryder

Present

"It's been two weeks since the factory night, and we still haven't found any indication that Mason Consoli's efforts were supported by a leak in our supply chain. It's still early, so we'll keep looking, but we may need to consider that he really did have his own connections," Kade, our head of cyber security, says from my side.

Donovan sits in the seat that used to be mine—at Moreno's right hand—and Alec and Jay fill the seats on his other side. The last seat at the table is to Moreno's left and occupied by Elli.

She sends me sad looks from across the table, but other than that, no physical signs hint at the palpable tension weighing down the room. No one mentions why this meeting differs from others, but that doesn't make the reason any less suffocating.

Donovan shakes his head. "It wouldn't have been the most logical option. He was already balancing his work as a capo for the Consoli's and his undercover work for us. The chances that he had the time to find his own suppliers and funding are minimal."

If I wasn't sitting directly across from Elli, I might've missed her shoulders tense at that.

Elise is the only daughter of the late Gabriel Consoli of the Consoli criminal family. She's not only the newest Moreno capo but also Joshua's fiancée.

She's the first female capo of our family and any of the country's five major American Mafia families. The news of this recent development is still making its way to the other families, but so far, most aren't happy about it.

Considering the alliance we've established with Logan Consoli—one of Elli's older brothers and the newly appointed boss of their family—we're not worried about any wars starting over it.

What we are worried about is cleaning up the mess that was—as we've come to refer to it—the factory night.

Two weeks ago, Mason Consoli (another of Elise's brothers who worked undercover for the Moreno family to push his father out of power) lured both our families to a factory where he tried to kill us all in his attempt for a massive power grab.

His efforts failed but left us with two jobs. Find the traitors within each family who aligned themselves with Mason, and find out where he received his funding and supplies.

The Consoli family is taking point on the first task because Mason would've done most of his communication from their main base in Chicago. The Moreno family is taking on the second task since the factory he lured us to was local to Los Angeles, giving us reason to believe Mason exploited leaks from our bases to build his army.

"All I'm saying is that we may need to take a different course of action," Kade says.

"What are you suggesting?" Moreno asks with a frustrated edge.

It's the first thing he's said since this meeting started, and I have no illusions as to why he's brooding in silence.

It's because I'm here.

At the few meetings I've been invited to in the last two weeks, Moreno has rarely said a word and none directly to me.

Not that I can blame him.

"All we've done so far is look at each base's financial report as a big picture, and since that hasn't shown us anything useful, it might be time to dig deeper. We should schedule a trip to each base to get a closer look at how things are running. Being there in person might give us a better chance of locating these leaks."

Moreno rubs the spot between his eye with a sigh, waving to Donovan.

Don raises a brow, looking to me for translation. Not wanting to give it verbally, I gesture to my phone, hoping that's enough of an answer.

Only a second passes before Don seems to get it. "Right, yeah. Okay, let's get those trips on the calendar."

I lower my head in confirmation that he did fine, and his lips tilt in a small smile.

"We just need to make progress before Consoli does," Moreno says, dropping his fist the table with a thud. "Bastard can't finish before we do."

"Joshua," Elli hisses, "that's my brother you're talking about."

"As if I could forget," he mutters.

The Consolis and Morenos have been enemies for years. They are only recently on good terms because of Elli, but that doesn't mean Joshua and Logan are friendly with each other.

They are not.

I breathe a laugh at Elli's scowl, which is enough to bring back her smile. Moreno, on the other hand, looks at me for the first time since coming into this room, but it's only to send me a scathing glare.

"Let's go over the responsibilities one last time, and we'll be done," Moreno spits in a cold, detached tone.

The atmosphere shifts from tense to suffocating. No one dares look in my direction to associate the tension with its cause.

"I'll be taking over all underboss responsibilities," Donovan says with a hint of discomfort, and though I have no right to resent him for taking over the job that I've had for years, a small part of me can't help it. "Elli will take base management from Alec so he can oversee all security in my place. Jay will be running recruitment training, and Kade will retain all of his current cyber security duties."

Most of the capos nod their agreement, and though Elli rolls her eyes instead, she doesn't speak up about her frustration.

"Questions or clarification needed?" Moreno asks the group.

When no one speaks up, Moreno pushes to his feet, leans to kiss Elli just long enough to make everyone uncomfortable, then straightens.

"This meeting is over," he says before striding out of the room without a glance back.

The slam of that door echoes like the tragic ending that it is.

"When do you leave?" Donovan asks, and the other capos look at me expectantly.

I clear my throat. "Now, actually."

"What?" Elli's eyes widen. "I thought you weren't leaving until tomorrow."

"Since this meeting was pushed forward, I don't have a reason to stay. The car's all packed up."

The silence in the room carries a physical weight, like everyone has something to say, but no one can find the words.

Not that it matters. Nothing can change the situation. This is the way things are.

My goodbyes to Donovan and Kade are short and straight to the point, which I appreciate. It's when I get to Alec that my throat constricts.

Alec was named a capo at nineteen-years-old, the youngest in the history of our family. Now, at twenty-three, he's one of the best men I've ever worked with.

"You're the reason Mr. Moreno even considered me for a capo position," he says thoughtfully. "I owe you a lot."

The words hit me harder than I'll ever admit, and he lets me pull him into a quick hug. Alec is a good kid, arguably too good to work in this business.

"You earned your place here," I tell him, taking a step back. "You would've been made a capo either way."

He gives me a disbelieving look but doesn't bother arguing the point.

Jay, Alec's uncle, steps up next. He's the spitting image of his nephew—scruffy, dark hair, and green eyes—only older and heavy set. "Take care, Ryder."

"I'll see you guys soon," I tell them, though we all know it might not be true.

Then I watch as the men, who I see as family, walk out the door. At least I actually got to say goodbye to them.

I haven't talked to Moreno in weeks.

"He'll come around, you know. Eventually." I turn to face Elli, who's looking up at me with a mixture of anger and sadness.

I've known Moreno for most of my life, and he's only ever softened for the girl standing in front of me. For anyone else, myself included, the chances of him *coming around* are slim to none.

"His anger is justified. He can take all the time he needs."

Her sadness fades, and anger fills the void, creasing her delicate features with a glare. "You should've tried harder. You didn't even defend yourself."

"There's nothing to defend. I betrayed him," I remind her.

And I did.

Because when Mason Consoli launched his attack two weeks ago, he kidnapped Rachel and our daughter, Lyla, to use as leverage against me. I was forced to abduct Elli and take her to Mason, so he could use her as bait for both families.

If I had any other choice, I never would've done it, but I didn't.

Elli forgave me immediately and hasn't once held my actions against me, but Moreno was less forgiving.

A betrayal like mine should've ended with a bullet in my head—a fate I accepted when I made a choice to save Lyla and Rachel—but Moreno didn't kill me. It could be argued that he understands why I did what I did, but I know better. The only reason Joshua didn't give me the slow, painful death I deserve is that Elli never would've forgiven him for it.

So, instead of going to an early grave, I've been transferred to the base located in Sacramento. It's far enough away that Moreno will have the space he needs to not kill me, but close enough that I can return if needed.

It's also where my daughter lives, meaning, for the first time in her three-year-life, I'll actually be living with her.

I've accepted this punishment since there are fates far worse than banishment, but Elli isn't convinced.

"You only did it to protect your family. I don't understand why we can't just move on," she huffs, folding her arms—one of which is still bandaged from a wound she suffered the factory night—over her chest.

I know my insistence won't change her mind, so I take a different approach.

"This isn't just about what I've done. It's about spending more time with Lyla. She's been through a lot, and she's going to need the support of both her parents right now."

As I suspected, Elli doesn't argue this.

She and Rachel met a few days after the factory night and became fast friends. They talk often enough for Elli to know that Lyla has become overly clingy and anxious as a result of what she went through. Not even she can deny that my daughter needs me right now, which makes having to leave marginally easier.

The fight leaves Elli with a sigh.

"Just come back soon, okay? Joshua might be mad now, but it won't be long for him to realize how badly he needs you. When the chance comes, tell me you'll take it and come back."

I look to the same door I just watched my friends go through. The door that leads to the life of luxury and power that I've lived for years.

The door that leads to everything I've lost.
 This is my home.
 This is where I belong.
 And I'll do whatever it takes to get it back.
 I pull Elli into a hug that she returns.
 "Don't worry, Elli. I'll be back before you know it."

CHAPTER FIVE

Ryder

The drive takes me over six hours thanks to the traffic outside of L.A. and my pit stop, meaning it's after five when I finally pull up to the light wood and gray stone house. It's a modest, two story building with tall windows, some of which are missing the white curtains that would hide the piles of unpacked boxes from the street view.

Rachel and Lyla have been back for over a week, and upon their arrival, it became clear that it no longer felt like a safe place after having been kidnapped from there. So, the girls stayed in a nearby hotel while Rachel looked for a new house.

She found this house, a twenty-five hundred square foot house with a large yard and a few neighbors within walking distance. The last house had been isolated, a factor that no longer appealed to the girls.

Rachel wanted to pack up the entire place by herself, but I convinced her to hire a moving company with the reminder that it would give her more time to spend with Lyla, and she relented. Within the week, Rachel and Lyla left the hotel and moved into the new house, which I happily paid for. Normally, Rachel fights me tooth and nail before accepting that kind of money, but even she had to admit that giving Lyla a home she feels safe in was worth it.

A few cars are parked along the street, but none in the driveway, so I assume Rachel's is tucked away in the garage.

I throw my car into park, tossing the duffle of essentials over my shoulder and grabbing the bouquet of flowers for Rachel and sour gummy worms for Lyla that I picked up on my way over here.

I knock on the door, not wanting to put the flowers down to fish the key Rachel sent me out of my pocket. After a few seconds of silence, I knock again, this time leaning in to listen for any signs of life from the other side. I think I hear something resembling the padding of footsteps, but it's too soft to be sure.

When we talked over my plans to move here a few days ago, Rachel said she'd be home by five. So, why wouldn't she answer the door?

My instincts kick in as I slide the flowers to the ground, and take out the key from my jeans then the handgun from the side pocket of my duffle. I conceal the weapon at my side to not scare Lyla if she's inside.

The eucalyptus and mint mixture of Rachel's favorite candle hits my nostrils as soon as I push the door open and gingerly step inside. I pause at the door when muffled, overly expressive voices echo from somewhere in the house.

I leave my bag, the flowers, and the candy on the front porch and take slow steps down the hall. I cast a glance to the right, where the dining room is full to the brim with boxes, then to the left, past the staircase, where a mudroom shows the first signs of personalization with Lyla's purple raincoat hanging from the hooks against the wall.

I walk deeper into the house, and my shoulders relax when I realize the voices are undoubtedly a children's show. I turn the corner and peek into the living room, but the small figure in front of the screen is not my daughter.

It's a boy.

With another step, I'm about to call out to him when I notice movement to my left. My hand twitches to pull the gun out, but I refrain for the boy's sake.

A woman, likely late twenties like me, bustles around the master suite. There's classical music playing on a speaker in the room, blocking her ability to hear me as she unpacks a cardboard box, laying several sweaters in a neat pile on the bed. She lifts the now-empty box and turns on her heels, finally putting me in her line of sight.

Something tells me that if she'd been the one with a gun, I'd be dead.

The woman nearly jumps out of her own skin. Racing to turn off the music like it's personally wronged her, she places one hand over her heart and the other on her forehead.

"Oh my goodness, you scared the bejeezus out of me!" she says, her voice chipper and light like a bird. "You must be Ryder. Gosh, I completely lost track of time."

She's small, barely five feet tall, with short, coal-black hair shaved on the sides, leaving a flow of locks on top that curl over, falling to her ear. She wears leggings and a thick crewneck, stained with paint in a few places, with the sleeves bunched at her elbow. She has hazel eyes that are more green than brown, and the contrast against her dark hair is jarring in a way that, somehow, is both bland and intriguing.

She gets a hold of herself only a moment later, putting the box down and approaching me with an outstretched hand and a friendly smile. "I'm Meredith." She points past us in the general direction of the child. "And that's my son, Dominic."

The name clicks, and I release my hold on the gun that, thankfully, Meredith didn't even notice. Both Rachel and Lyla talk about Meredith and Dominic so often that I'm surprised I didn't put the pieces together myself.

Soon after Lyla was born, Rachel took her to a daycare that Meredith worked at, and they've been friends ever since. As far as I know, she's also a single mother and now works at a local nursing home. Since their work schedules often conflict, she and Rachel help each other with babysitting and housework, which is why I assume she's here now.

I take her hand, which is so small it might as well be a child's. "It's nice to meet you," I tell her, casting a look around the house. "I didn't mean to scare you. I was expecting Rachel and Lyla to be here."

She nods, brushing some of the dust from her leggings. "They'll be home in a bit. I believe Lyla's appointment went over, and then Rachel was going to grab dinner."

"Appointment?"

"With the child psychologist?" Meredith eyes me curiously like this is common knowledge.

It isn't to me.

We've known since the factory night that Lyla would need to talk to a professional, but considering the nature of the events, and the fact that no one involved was on the right side of the law, she can't talk to just anyone.

I'd planned to take on the job of finding a suitable candidate myself, but Elli was determined to do it. She said it was the least she could do to help, as if she was the cause of everything that happened and not a victim herself. She vetted and personally interviewed several specialists before giving Rachel and me Dr. Danver's number, an older woman willing to see our daughter off the books.

Why the hell didn't Rachel tell me the appointment was today?

"Right," I say like I'd only forgotten. "Would you happen to know which room is mine?"

"Of course! Let me throw my shoes on," she says, disappearing to the mudroom.

I decide not to ask why she feels the need to wear shoes around the house and get my stuff from where I dropped it at the door. I place the flowers and gummy worms on the kitchen counter at the same moment Meredith returns.

I'm about to head to the stairs when she strides right past me toward the living room. I'm about to ask where we're going when she slides the back door open, revealing the spacious deck and the structure built in the yard.

A few yards beyond the pool is a pool house, small by house standards but plenty of space for one room, which I'm sure is all it is. It matches the house down to its wood and stony exterior, even having four pillars with an overhead cover across the front, creating a porch-like effect complete with a swing. It's an impressive building, no doubt the most luxurious pool house available, but the realization of its purpose is like a slap to the face.

Rachel is kicking me out without kicking me out.

This is a three-bedroom house, meaning there's plenty of room for me inside, and yet, Rachel has me out here.

This is her loophole in our agreement.

Meredith hands me a key when we get to the door.

"I'll be inside finishing up Rachel's room. Let me know if you need anything!" she says with the enthusiasm of one of the cartoon characters her son watches inside.

I thank her and unlock the door as she goes back to the house.

I first notice a kitchenette to my immediate right and a white couch with two matching chairs around a flat-screen TV to my left. Past what I suppose could be considered a living room is a white barn door that's slid open, revealing the bedroom and the attached bathroom.

It's not a bad set up by any stretch of the imagination, but it's not in the same house as my daughter.

I spend the next twenty minutes making trips from the pool house to the driveway using a brick path around the yard to give myself something to do until the girls get home.

When all my belongings lie around the pool house, I drop into one of the chairs across from the TV and check my phone.

No messages.

Rachel could've told me she'd be late, but she only told Meredith, and I already know why. Rachel isn't a spiteful or even mischievous person. If she didn't tell me about the appointment, it's not because she's playing some game.

It's a simple message, given with pure intentions and unmovable certainty.

My house, my rules.

CHAPTER SIX

Rachel

"I sent Lindsey the details for next month's New York trip, so she can book the flight and hotel arrangements. Mrs. Caster has requested the Jones' account by the end of the day, and your joint call with Franklin Corp. had to be rescheduled for next Thursday at noon, but I already sent that to Lindsey, too," I tell David and place a stack of papers on his desk. "These will need to be reviewed before that call."

I look up from my tablet to meet his hazel eyes, creased with smile lines, staring me down knowingly. "Since when are *you*, my assistant? I have Lindsey you know."

"It's all Mrs. Caster's work, too. Besides, Lindsey's done a lot of covering for me these last two weeks. I owe her any help I can give."

David—Mr. Patel, as I'm supposed to call him in the office—was a fast friend of mine when I first started at Stanly CPA, Incorporated.

I'd originally interviewed for a role as a Staff Auditor, but because of a mix-up in HR, they offered me a position as Mrs. Caster's personal assistant. When I arrived at the office to talk about the offer, I was ready to decline. After all, I didn't get my degree just so I could get coffee and book appointments.

But when I got to the office to meet with Mrs. Caster and David—both Senior Auditors—I reconsidered. There is secretarial work, but they were mostly looking for someone to share their workload with. They could offer me a position that had the flexibility I desired as a new mother and still allowed me to do what I love.

The only downside to my job is that my title is still that of an assistant. David and I have talked about transitioning me into a Staff

Auditor role, but the timing never seemed right.

And considering everything that happened two weeks ago, it's not my biggest priority.

It had been tricky to explain that I didn't show up for work because of a personal emergency that then turned into a car accident that required time off. I only took a few vacation days and have worked the rest remotely.

David doesn't mind one bit as long as I get my work done, which I have. Mrs. Caster, on the other hand, cares.

She cares a lot.

And since I'm technically *her* assistant, she's the one I need to keep happy.

David ignores the stack of papers on his desk and sets his still-steaming coffee down. "How are you doing lately? How's Lyla?"

As a single, young, and brand new mom, I'd had a difficult time adjusting to working full-time. More than once, David caught me looking through pictures of Lyla and struggling to focus when I hadn't heard updates from the daycare. On a particularly difficult day during my second week at the firm, he took me out to lunch to help distract me and has acted as a sort of mentor ever since.

With anyone else in the office, I assure them all is well, and I'm fine, but I know that with David, I don't have to lie.

With a look over my shoulder that ensures Mrs. Caster is still occupied, I lower into the seat across from David's desk. "She's all right. I have an appointment with a child therapist today to see if that helps. Thanks for checking in."

He nods, then eyes me. "And you?"

"What about me?"

"You were in that car crash, too. How are you doing with everything?"

Aside from the constant fear of someone taking and harming my child? Or said child's inability to leave my side without having a meltdown?

I wave him, and the too-real thoughts off. "Oh, I'm fine."

He eyes me like he can read the lies all over my face, but we're interrupted by a shrill voice.

"Miss Lance! Miss—oh! There you are!" Mrs. Caster's heels click against the floor as she makes her way into David's office. She's roughly David's age—late forties—with a pinned-up, overly hair-sprayed bun, and bright lips that always match the color of her blazer.

Today, it's neon pink.

I shoot to my feet at her entrance.

"I need the Marshall Industries audit completed by the end of the day."

"Already done," I tell her. "Sent it directly to Mrs. Marshall with a full summary an hour ago. She's very pleased with our dedication to the tight deadline."

"Excellent, as always," she says with a nod of approval.

Mrs. Caster isn't a bad boss, not by a long shot, though her shrill voice and overbearing nature have given her a bad reputation. I'm sure the idea of working with someone so uptight would be a nightmare to most people, but not me. Mrs. Caster needed a P.A. willing to go above and beyond to complete their work and do so to perfection. I needed a job to be the vice that distracts my overly active mind.

It's a win-win.

In the last few years, my need for these vices has lessened—since motherhood is a never-ending job in itself—but it's never fully gone away. Between being a mother and Mrs. Caster's personal assistant, I've done a good job controlling the cruel thoughts.

At least, I was before the factory night.

Now, there's only one vice that keeps the darkness at bay.

"Did you already tell her?" Mrs. Caster asks David, who straightens in his chair.

"No, I was waiting for you."

I look between them. "Tell me what?"

David gestures to the chairs across from his desk, and I sit back down as Mrs. Caster does the same.

I shoot a quick glance at the clock. It's a quarter 'til four, and if I'm going to be home in time for Ryder's arrival, Lyla and I have to leave for the appointment now, but since it's my first day back in the office, I don't rush my bosses.

"Mr. Campbell will be announcing his retirement at the end of this week," David says.

The information, though new to me, isn't shocking. Mr. Campbell is the Audit Manager of our branch, and he's almost a decade past the normal retirement age. With a dozen grandkids from his five children, everyone assumed he'd leave years ago. We've come to realize, mostly from the lack of personal pictures on his desk, that he isn't much of a family man.

"Oh, really?"

He nods, gesturing to the woman beside me. "Mrs. Caster will be moving into the position at the end of next month."

"That's incredible!" I say with a genuine smile. "Congratulations! You've earned this."

And she has. Mrs. Caster is by far one of the hardest-working people in this entire office. A promotion is long overdue.

"Thank you, Miss Lance," she says.

"Mrs. Caster was asked to give her recommendation for who should take over her role, and she's named you as her primary candidate."

If possible, my eyes bulge even wider.

"What?" I ask, but they only nod. "I'm an assistant. I don't have the qualifications for this."

Mrs. Caster gives me a knowing look. "You know this role better than anyone else. You've been doing it, plus P.A. work for years. Besides, your work ethic and reputation speak for themselves."

"I—I don't know what to say," I practically breathe the words.

"Well, don't say anything yet," David says with a raised hand. "You have both of us vouching for you, but Mr. Campbell will be making the final decision. He's on the fence about having a P.A. moving into this position, but we talked him into giving you a fair shot. Over the next few weeks, he'll be watching your work to make sure you'll be a good fit when he leaves and she takes his position. Consider this your official invitation to the management dinner at the cooperate retreat next month. He's agreed to give his answer by then."

"The management dinner?" I repeat, sure I didn't hear him correctly.

The management dinner is a thing of legend around the office. During this dinner, the rest of the firm's employees typically enjoy a night of heavy drinking since all of their superiors are occupied. Everyone jokes about how they're having way more fun, but no one would pass up the opportunity to have a seat at that table.

"And if he decides against me?"

"Then you'll remain my P.A., and the position will go to another candidate," she tells me.

"We could still talk about moving you into a staff auditor role if you're interested," David notes.

So, this is my chance to get the kind of job I was after in the first place. If I don't manage to make this work, who knows when I'll get the chance again?

"I really appreciate this opportunity. Thank you for sticking your neck out for me," I tell them, meaning it more than they know.

"Of course," David says.

"There is one more thing." Mrs. Caster sends a pointed look over her shoulder, and I know what she'll say before she does. "I'm sure I don't need to remind you that this is not a workplace suitable for children?"

I turn to see my three-year-old daughter standing on the edge of my cubicle, clutching her doll to her chest as she stares at Mrs. Caster and me with wide, curious eyes.

"It's only been two weeks since the accident, and Lyla's still having panic attacks at the idea of being separated from me," I explain. "I understand this isn't the most professional option, but I haven't let it affect my work."

"Unfortunately, it isn't your work that's being affected by this arrangement."

I follow her eyes to where several co-workers stare at my daughter in confusion, some even leaning toward each other to whisper.

I'm about to remind Mrs. Caster that other people's lack of control over their focus isn't my problem, but she doesn't give me a chance.

"I know you're only doing what's best for your daughter, and I think that's what every mother should do. However, I feel the need to be frank with you—this won't look good when Mr. Campbell starts watching your work."

I nod. "I'll figure something out," I tell her, though I have absolutely no idea how I plan to do that.

"I'm really optimistic about Lyla's mental state. Regarding trauma for a three-year-old, she has a healthy understanding of what happened. It's a sign that you and her father explained everything well to her."

I know the words are supposed to be comforting, and, in a way, they are, but the all-consuming guilt that wracks me every time I think about what my three-year-old experienced a few weeks ago can't be eased by anything less than a *Men in Black* memory eraser.

I look over my shoulder to where my daughter sits a few yards away in the waiting room of Dr. Danver's office, brushing a doll's hair with a gentleness that shouldn't be possible for a child of her age.

She doesn't look like the victim of a kidnapping. She doesn't curl into herself, refusing to play with toys or eat like I heard can happen in the aftermath of a traumatic event. In fact, the only physical sign that something happened to her is the faded three-inch-long cuts on her upper shoulder.

Well, that and the fact that she can't stop her eyes from flitting my way every few seconds.

Dr. Danver crosses her ankles—seeing as the conservative pencil skirt won't allow her legs to move any more than that—and gives me a warm smile. Everything about this woman is warm, from the gray mixing naturally with the light brown hair that's pulled into a simple bun at the base of her head to the laugh lines etched around her kind, hazel eyes.

"How did she seem…when she told you what happened?" I ask, grabbing onto the fabric of my pants to stop from popping my knuckles.

She scans her notes, expression never veering from pleasant. "A bit apprehensive, but I have a feeling that's more her personality than her experiences."

It is, and it makes me feel just a bit better that she seemed to pick up on that.

"I'm going to recommend two months of bi-weekly sessions to start."

"You think that'll be enough?"

She nods. "We don't want to overwhelm her. The goal is coping and moving forward. You'll want to avoid anything that could trigger her trauma. Eventually, we'll ease those things back in doses she can handle so she doesn't grow to view avoidance as a coping mechanism. Still, right now, we just want her comfortable again. We'll start pushing those limits once she's had time to heal. This can be tricky regarding the movies and shows she watches. For instance, she may be susceptible to a movie where the heroine is abducted, even if it's only a seemingly harmless cartoon, so be on the lookout for those."

I nod, scribbling notes on the mini-notebook I keep in my purse. It's usually reserved for when I think of things I may need to do for Mrs. Caster, but it's coming in handy now.

"Now, a three-year-old doesn't understand the idea of coping, so you'll want to be intentional about how she expresses herself. Try choosing activities where she feels safe and is using skills that build confidence."

"And what should we do in the mean time?" I ask. "She barely leaves my side to go to the bathroom, and I'm not sure I have the heart to push her into being independent."

"There doesn't need to be any pushing, but encouraging

independence whenever possible will do wonders. Showing her that she's capable and safe will heal a lot of the fear she's carrying. There's no right answer when it comes to getting back to normal. Just do what feels right for you and Lyla, and know it'll take time to find your new normal."

I go through the motions of writing down her advice as a way to busy my hands. I won't be forgetting her words any time soon.

"Have you considered getting professional help as well?"

The question comes out of left field, and since this is the second time today someone's broached the idea, I'm starting to wonder what kind of energy I'm emanating.

I decide to play off the concern. "I don't think that's necessary."

Dr. Danver smiles, and there's the slightest hint of pity this time. "Lyla isn't the only one who endured a traumatic experience. Coming here was a great first step toward her recovery, but, in my professional opinion, I think you should do the same."

It's not the most absurd idea.

After all, she's right. I went through the exact same thing as my daughter, but there's one difference.

I *deserve* the guilt.

It's all your fault, the cruel voice hisses in my brain, and I don't disagree.

I couldn't protect my daughter when she needed it most. I didn't shield her from the dangerous lifestyle her father lives, and she suffered as a result.

All therapy would accomplish is having a professional tell me what I already know—to keep as much distance between Ryder and me as possible.

And I plan on it.

We each stand, and I reach my hand out to the woman. "Thank you so much for your help and your discretion."

She takes it in a firm shake. "Of course."

I take Lyla's hand, and we walk out of the office, a six-story building full of office spaces for various medical professionals.

The feeling sinks in as soon as we step outside.

I grip Lyla's hand just a bit tighter as a sensation like ants crawling up my back takes hold of me.

It almost feels like someone's watching us, but when I scan every detail of our surroundings, the only people in sight are a group of middle-aged doctors enjoying an early dinner at a park bench on the grassy side of the building.

I can't, for the life of me, pinpoint what inspired the feeling or why it hasn't gone away, but I cling to the charm on my necklace as I speed up toward our car.

The silver Range Rover is still new to me, which is why it takes me a few seconds to locate it. I hadn't wanted to get a new car, but Ryder insisted on it to go along with my cover story. He even had one of his soldiers crash my car so we'd have photographic evidence—as if anyone was going to genuinely question me on the matter.

The watchful sensation doesn't ease, so I let go of my charm to grab my phone, eyes still scanning our surroundings with a near-manic pace as I dial Meredith's number.

"Did you not tell Ryder you'd be late tonight?" she asks as soon as she picks up. Hearing my friend's voice brings a wave of calm, even if the sensation of being watched doesn't fully go away.

I wrinkle my nose. "No, I only sent that text to you."

"Busy day?" I hear fabric rustling in the background, and I already know she ignored my text telling her that she should relax and that I'd unpack my clothes tomorrow.

"Uh, yeah," I say. It's not a lie, but it also isn't the reason I didn't message Ryder, not that she or anyone else needs to know that. "I'm just going to grab dinner, then I'll be on my way."

I get Lyla buckled in while Meredith tells me how Dominic's been bugging her all day about seeing Lyla, and it's only when I'm in my own seat with the car on that the feeling of being watched finally subsides.

I end the call with Meredith and back out of the spot. By the time I leave the parking lot, I've already convinced myself I'm just being paranoid. Talking to Dr. Danver about what happened at the factory just got me riled up. I actually laugh when I realize just how tightly wound I am.

Still, I don't let myself fully relax because there *is* a reason to keep myself guarded and on high alert.

And he's currently waiting for me at home.

CHAPTER SEVEN

Rachel

I pull up next to Ryder's black Ferrari—for someone whose job is staying under the radar, I'm not sure how this vehicle was a practical choice, but whatever—and park the car. When I turn in my seat, Lyla's eyes light up, and a smile spreads across her face.

"Daddy's home?"

"Daddy's home," I confirm.

I reach back to help unbuckle her seatbelt, which hits the window as she throws it off with a force that should've broken it and practically jumps out of the car. After I grab the takeout from the passenger seat, I have to run to catch up with her and make my way inside.

I hear them before I see them.

"Tiger!" Ryder's deep voice booms through the house as I shut the door behind me and walk to the living room.

"Daddy!"

I hear his exhale as he lifts her into his arms, and when I step into the room, I watch Lyla anchor her barely long enough arms around Ryder's neck, tight enough to choke him.

He flicks his eyes to me, but I look away, shifting my attention to taking my shoes off and placing them in the mudroom.

Just the brief moment of eye contact is enough to make me grateful I asked Meredith to stay for dinner tonight.

I'm not used to being alone with Ryder.

Though he's spent countless nights and weekends with Lyla and me over the years, we usually keep a civil distance. It's rare that we have any conversations that don't pertain to Lyla.

47

But this is different.

Ryder isn't just here to spend time with Lyla—he's here to live, to work, to be a regular part of her life, and, consequently, mine.

Until he's called back to Los Angeles.

Meredith being here for Ryder's arrival gives me a sense of control over the situation, a way to enforce that Lyla and I have friends and a life all on our own. His being here isn't going to change that.

"Thanks for getting dinner!" Meredith chirps, taking the large bag from my hands and calling to her son while taking the food to the table.

Dominic, the firecracker of a child, bursts into the room.

"Lyla! You just missed Cars," he says, pointing to the living room where Lightning McQueen is frozen on the screen. "But I paused it so we can watch the end together!"

Lyla untangles her arms from Ryder's neck and beams down at the boy. "Dom, this is my dad!"

Dominic blinks like he just realized that the giant figure holding Lyla is an actual person. His smile grows, and he straightens his back, holding out his hand and sending glances to his mom to make sure she's watching. She gives him an encouraging smile.

"I'm Dominic Ashford," he says in a rush that makes it all sound like one word. "I'm Lyla's best friend."

Ryder chuckles, a low and alluring sound, as he sets Lyla on her feet and accepts Dominic's hand, which is comically small compared to his own. "It's nice to meet you, Dominic Ashford. I'm Ryder Bates."

Dominic blushes but hides it with a scrunched smile, taking Lyla's hand and pulling her to the table. "Sit next to me, Lyla."

Ryder watches Dom lead Lyla away with a blankness that I assume is feigned.

"They're basically siblings," I tell him.

"It better stay that way," he mutters, then sends a look to where Meredith sets the table before looking back to me and lowering his voice. "How was the appointment?"

There's an icy edge to the words, and I'm not surprised.

The decision to keep the appointment from Ryder hadn't been made out of spite, but necessity.

"Good. Elli did an excellent job finding someone. Dr. Danver is great for Lyla," I say, ignoring the underlying frustration in his tone. When I turn my head, I'm a little stunned to find that he's only a foot away from me, close enough that I can smell his cologne. The notes of pineapple, bergamot, and apple bring waves of memories that I repress.

My eyes flicker to my friend, but she doesn't look back at Ryder and me. "I told Meredith the car crash story. She thinks that's what gave Lyla separation anxiety and why she's having a hard time sleeping."

His brows scrunch ever so slightly. "Why tell her anything at all?"

"Meredith and Dominic practically live here. It's easier to give her an excuse for the therapy than it would be to hide it."

"And what exactly did the therapist say?"

"We should avoid any reminders that could trigger a panic attack and work on building her confidence. She suggested we get her into an activity to express herself, so I'll call local dance studios and swimming lessons to see what we can get her involved in."

Ryder's expression doesn't change as he takes in the information, but I don't expect it to. Sometimes talking to Ryder can feel like conversing with a marble statue.

"And why didn't I hear about this appointment until after it happened?"

"Everyone ready to eat?" Meredith calls, mostly to the kids, but she shoots us a smile, too, which I force myself to return.

"I am," I say, leaving Ryder before he can press me for answers.

I know the conversation is inevitable, but that doesn't mean it has to happen right now.

We all take our seats at the table, me at the head with Meredith on my left and both the kids to my right.

Ryder can choose between the seat next to Meredith or the other end of the table.

And, of course, he chooses the latter.

I try not to look at him, knowing the kind of power struggle that we'll engage in if I do. The only time I catch his eye is after I nonchalantly cover my knife with my napkin, but his expression doesn't give away any particular thoughts on the gesture.

"Then I knocked the entire bag over! It's like...." Dominic sizes up Ryder. "Your tallness, and I knocked it all the way over to the ground."

"It's height, Dom, not tallness." Meredith corrects, but Dominic barely looks her way.

Ryder, on the other hand, narrows his eyes, sizing up Dominic right back. "No way. You're too small."

Dominic's eyes widen in horror that someone would actually

accuse him of exaggerating. Meredith chuckles, but I shake my head.

"Ryder," I admonish, but he gives me a shrug.

"It's true!" Dom insists. "I bet I could tackle you to the ground, too."

"Is that right? We might have to test that out."

Now, Dominic's eyes bulge like he's been given the mother of all opportunities.

"Okay!" he practically shouts. "Let's do it right now!"

"Absolutely not," Meredith says. "You're not going to tackle anyone."

Dominic looks at Ryder with pleading eyes. "Will you tell my mom that it's okay if I tackle you?"

Ryder shakes his head, faux disappointment marring his usually stony face. "Can't disobey your mom. Sorry, kiddo, no tackling."

"That's okay. I can show you my karate kicks instead!" Dominic puts both hands on the table as he pushes to stand on his chair, clearly intent on standing on the table.

"Dominic Ashford, you sit down right this instant," Meredith orders in her mom voice, and Dom falls promptly into his seat with a mutter about how he never gets to do anything fun.

"You do martial arts?" Ryder asks.

"Oh, yeah. I'm the best one, too. I even have a green stripe on my belt!"

Meredith sends her son an exasperated look but nods to Ryder. "He's done it for a little less than a year now. We love the place. The owner is a great guy."

Ryder meets my gaze, and I don't miss his squared shoulders, like he's bracing for a challenge.

Instead of saying anything to me, he looks at Lyla. "What do you think about doing martial arts, Tiger?"

He did not just ask her that.

He did not completely bypass me and broach this topic over dinner.

"I'm not sure that's a good idea," I say, my voice far more calm than I'm actually feeling.

"Would I play with Dom?" Lyla asks, and I don't miss the flickering interest in her features.

Ryder looks at Meredith. "Would they be in the same class?"

At least Meredith has the decency to look between Ryder and me uncomfortably before nodding. "The classes are based on age, so they'd train together."

"That would be so fun!" Dominic turns to Lyla. "Take class with me! Mr. Torres is so much fun."

The more he talks, the more she smiles, and I know I have a real problem on my hands.

"Sweetie, Mom and Dad will have to talk about this a little bit more, but we'll see. What if you tried out dance, swimming, or gymnastics?"

Ryder's eyes narrow in irritation, but Lyla only shrugs noncommittally as a response.

The rest of dinner passes with Meredith trying to keep Dominic from doing kicks on the table and me trying to avoid looking at the man directly across from me.

It's not a pleasant meal.

The second Lyla finishes her food, Dominic grabs her hand, and the two of them head for the living room. The sound of cars zooming on a racetrack follows their disappearance.

I'm washing the plates at the sink when I feel Ryder coming up behind me, lowering his voice so that Meredith, who's wiping down the table, can't hear him. "Martial arts is exactly the kind of activity Lyla should be involved in."

I match his volume, not wanting to make Meredith more uncomfortable than we've already made her. "Do you know how many triggers that would have? One mention of stranger danger could send her into a meltdown."

"That could happen anywhere. Besides, we'd be there the entire time if something went wrong. It's exactly the kind of confidence-building activity the doctor suggested. Think about how many skills she could learn."

"Believe it or not, I don't want Lyla to need self-defense skills just because her father has more enemies than he can count."

"Believe it or not, it's a little late for that now."

I want to snap back when Meredith walks in with a dirtied rag. "I swear that boy is a walking mess. This is all from Dom's seat." She lifts the rag, which is covered in pink sauce and rice.

I force a laugh. "Did any of the food go into his mouth?"

"I doubt it, but it doesn't really matter. We made a deal that if he could go a week without being put in time out at martial arts, I'd take him out for ice cream. I really didn't think it would happen, but I underestimated that kid's love for sweets." She rolls her eyes, but her smile is one full of love.

"I'm sure he'll love that."

I watch Meredith go to where Lyla sits on the floor, watching Dominic with pure delight as he does something resembling a kick and a somersault while the Cars credits roll on the TV.

"Dominic, go get your shoes on."

He springs up faster than should be possible. "Ice cream?"

Meredith nods.

"Can Lyla come?" Dominic doesn't wait for an answer before pulling my daughter to her feet. "Come get ice cream with us!"

I take a step forward to offer to go with them, but it's too late.

Lyla's eyes widen with both horror and panic.

"No!" The shriek cuts through the room with the force of a newly sharpened machete. She speeds toward her father, tiny hands fisting Ryder's shirt so hard her knuckles turn white. "I'm not going! You can't make me go!"

Ryder and I exchange looks of absolute shock.

On the rare occasion that the two of us joke, it's usually about how Lyla is better suited for royalty than for us. She's soft-spoken, polite, and abnormally graceful. As a baby, she was never prone to crying fits or tantrums, and she definitely never screamed when she was upset. This kind of reaction is not like my daughter.

Unfortunately, this isn't the first time she's acted this way in the last two weeks.

"Lyla," I gently call.

"No!" Tears spring to her dark eyes, and her bottom lip trembles. "I don't want to!"

"What's wrong with Lyla?" Dominic's voice calls from behind us, and I hear Meredith's hush words ushering him out of the room.

Ryder lifts Lyla in his arms, and she buries her face in his chest as he wraps his arms firmly around her. His eyes don't leave mine, the concern there burning as intensely as my own. When he flicks his gaze down the hall, he doesn't need to use words to tell me what he's thinking.

I head down the hall, hearing Ryder mumbling assurances to Lyla as I go. I find Meredith tying Dominic's tennis shoes, his eyes no longer full of excitement but a heart-melting worry.

"Is Lyla okay?" he whispers.

"Of course," I tell him, then turn my words to his mother. "She had a long day, and I think the appointment was a lot for her. Maybe next time."

Meredith lifts Dominic into her arms, placing one hand on my shoulder. "I completely understand. Please, let me know if there's anything I can do to help."

I nod. "I will."

I walk Meredith and Dominic to the door, waving them goodbye as they go. When I come back down the hallway, I find Ryder pacing the living room, gently bouncing Lyla up and down as she cries into his chest.

Neither of us says anything while Lyla gets the tears out of her system.

The guilt hits with its usual knee-buckling strength, and I barely make it to the table in time to fall into a chair and not flat on my ass.

What kind of mother wouldn't see this coming? That voice asks, and I can't help but think the same thing.

How did I not realize that, after reliving the factory night, Lyla would be fragile? I've been so focused on having Meredith and Dominic around to help mediate things with Ryder that I haven't stopped to consider that Lyla might need time to rest and recharge.

Ryder has been in town for less than two hours, and I've already let him cloud my judgment concerning what's best for Lyla.

He looks over our daughter's shoulder, meeting my eyes with one of his signature unreadable expressions, and I make myself a promise.

No matter what, Lyla will come first.

CHAPTER EIGHT

Rachel

Two hours of hot chocolate, cartoons, and a bath pass before I finally get Lyla to calm down enough to put her to sleep. I had to stay with her for half an hour until she was out before I was able to leave the room without sparking another panic attack.

All I want to do is curl up in my bed and let sleep take over, but I have a feeling Ryder didn't quietly retreat to the pool house for the night.

My suspicion is confirmed when I reach the bottom of the staircase and find Ryder standing beside the table, arms folded over his chest with an *oh yeah, we're doing this,* look on his face.

I sigh and go straight to the kitchen to pour myself a glass of wine. "Ryder, I'm exhausted. Can we do this tomorrow?"

"How many times has that happened?"

I'm tempted to brush him off and head to my room, but I feel that'll only make things worse. It's best to get this over with as soon as possible.

"A few."

"What's a few?"

I shake my head. "Maybe four or five times. Never that bad, though. Usually, it only takes a few minutes to calm her down. I think she was extra sensitive after the appointment."

"Right. The appointment that you hid from me."

My legs ache, but as much as I'd like to take my glass of wine to the couch, I can't. Ryder is fixed in a combative stance that I can't help my need to match.

"I'm not hiding anything. I just don't make a habit of telling you every time she sees a doctor. If you want me to change that, I'll be happy to." I set the glass down and count on my fingers. "She sees the dentist in two weeks, she's due for a check-up at her pediatrician's office in three months, and—"

"That's not what I mean, and you know it," he hisses. "You knew I was coming into town. You could've told me you were going to see Dr. Danver, but you deliberately kept it a secret."

"What do you expect? I'm doing things the same way I always have."

"Things aren't the same as they've always been," he snaps. "And putting me in the *pool house* isn't going to change that fact."

I'd known he wasn't going to like the sleeping arrangements, but it's the way things need to be. Was it cowardly to have Meredith deliver the news instead of doing it myself? Probably. But I couldn't risk falling prey to his smooth-talking as he convinces me that he should stay in the house. I'm smart enough to know that I probably would've given in.

"Things are better this way," I say.

"Please," he says, dramatically sweeping his arm as if to give me center stage. "Enlighten me on how me sleeping in the backyard is better for anyone."

I don't know if it's his snide tone or my own exhaustion, but the voice in the back of my head that usually pleads with me to remain calm goes silent.

"Because the last thing Lyla needs is to get used to you being around," I snap.

"What the hell is that supposed to mean?"

"It means that staying with us for your weekend visits is one thing, but moving in is another. It's not fair for her to get attached to you living with us at a time when she's so emotionally vulnerable. Do you have any idea what that could do to her when you leave? So yes, I have you living in the pool house, which is far nicer than what I wanted to do, which was make you get your own place. The only reason I didn't is that it would only make things worse for her to go between houses when she desperately needs stability. You can get your feelings hurt all you want, but I'm going to do what's best for my daughter."

Ryder's eyes narrow to thin slits, and he takes a slow, daunting step toward me. There are dark clouds swirling in that ominous gaze, but I lift my chin, refusing to cower. He may intimidate the masses, but not me.

"*Our* daughter," he whispers, and the edge in his tone is sharp enough to cut diamonds.

I don't realize that I've been taking one step back for every one of his forwards until my back hits the granite counter .

So much for standing my ground.

One second, I'm watching the storm that spirals around him like an omen of death, and the next, I'm in the center of it.

Dark eyes pin me with unmovable force, daring me to push back when his chest presses firmly to mine. It's like being held down by a boulder, but his muscles are the only part of him that is even remotely rock-like. Gone is the Ryder I compared to a marble statue because, right now, everything about him is so...*alive*.

His brow doesn't set but furrows as he locks and unlocks his jaw with seemingly methodical movements like he's trying to calm himself down, but it isn't working. Big, warm hands that I know all too well brace themselves on either side of me on the counter.

"Lyla is *our* daughter, not just yours," he bites out in the alluring yet venomous tone that Moreno puts to good—or bad, depending on your moral code—use. "You don't get to conveniently forget that fact."

"Fine. *Our* daughter needs support right now, which means—" I shove his chest as hard as I can, and he concedes a step back. "We need ground rules."

"Ground rules," he repeats slowly, near mocking.

"Yes. Things aren't the same as they were the last time we lived together."

"And what exactly do you think 'ground rules' will accomplish?"

"Keeping Lyla our sole priority. Neither of us needs to be distracted from that."

He thinks about that for a moment, and since no snarky comment comes, I go on.

"First, you don't get to order me around. This isn't one of Moreno's bases. It's my home, and I will continue living my life the same way I did before."

"Again, things aren't the same as they were before. You can't ignore the fact that I'm here."

I resist the urge to tell him that I absolutely can ignore him and, in fact, plan on doing just that to survive however long this season of living together lasts.

"I'm not ignoring you, but I'm not flipping the world upside-down for you either."

He gives me a narrowed-eye look that I can't decipher. Whether it's frustration, calculation, or some form of intimidation, I don't know, but I am not a fan.

"Do I make you nervous?" he finally asks, voice dropping several notes and hitting a place inside me that quiets the white noise in my head.

The answer to his question is a resounding and embarrassing *yes*, but, of course, I can't say that, so I take a long drink from my wine before setting it on the counter with a firm clink.

"I'm not nervous, Ryder. I'm just telling you how things are going to be."

"You just defined my being a part of your life as flipping the world upside-down. Seems like the kind of thing that would make a person nervous."

I take a deep breath and remind myself that twisting words is half of his job. "That's how I described what it would be like if I *did* let you boss me around, which is exactly what I was saying I will *not* be doing. So, again, no. I am not nervous."

He looks like he wants to engage in verbal sparring some more, and since I suspect I won't be able to keep up, I go on before he can try anything.

"Next, you'll keep anything and everything work-related out of the house and as far from Lyla as physically possible. She doesn't need anything reminding her about that day."

He doesn't protest, and I'm glad we seem to agree on this, at the very least.

"And?" he prompts when I don't immediately continue.

I eye the space between us warily, then steel my nerves.

"No touching."

"No touching," he repeats slowly, tone void of any emotion that could indicate how he feels about the prospect.

I nod, hoping I come off as nonchalant as he does.

Slowly, in the same taunting manner that Ryder seems to do everything, one side of his lip quirks upward. "You don't have to worry about me touching you."

Ryder takes a measured step toward me, not quite as close as he'd been trapping me against the counter, but close. It's far more tantalizing than if he were to press himself against me. At least then,

I'd have no choice but to face, breathe, and *feel* him. With this sliver of space between us, I'm forced to maintain the minimal distance that taunts me to come closer.

And Ryder knows it.

"Because when I do, it'll be because you asked for it, Rebel."

That nickname. That *damned* nickname.

He hasn't called me that in years, but I still have the same heart-melting, spine-shuddering, palm-sweating reaction I had the first time he said it to me.

Because, deep down, I know the only person who has ever made me feel the least bit rebellious is the man in front of me.

And that ended in a disaster that I barely recovered from.

"Well, it's a good thing we don't have to worry about that then," I say in a brisk voice that I'm proud doesn't reflect any of my conflicting emotions.

I step past Ryder, careful not to make any contact as I move toward my bedroom, clearly indicating my desire to end this conversation.

"Plenty of people co-parent," I say. "I'm sure we can, too."

"And that's what we are? Co-parents?"

"It's all we can be, Ryder."

"There was a time when we were friends," he reminds me and moves toward the back door.

"That didn't work out either."

He huffs a laugh, and his small smile hints that he's remembering just how *friend*-ly we'd been. "Co-parents."

"Co-parents," I confirm as he reaches the door.

"Guess we'll see how this one ends," is all I hear him mutter before the back door closes behind him and the lock clicks into place.

That sound opens the floodgates, and the anxiety that I've been barely keeping at bay over the last two weeks has me wringing my hands and popping my knuckles. I reach for the chunky, half-smooth, half-studded heart-shaped charm on my necklace and cling to it for dear life.

I take one step toward my bedroom before changing my mind, going back into the kitchen to refill my wine glass, then ascending the stairs.

I reach Lyla's room and peek my head in to see my sleeping daughter curled up next to her pink stuffed tiger with a matching pink bonnet over her hair.

I close the door as softly as I can manage so I don't wake her, then go to the room across the hall.

The office.

The door shuts behind me, and I lock it for my own peace of mind before sitting in the rolling chair, ready to dive into the only vice that's *really* been able to ease my anxiety since we got home from Los Angeles.

Then I send up a prayer that Ryder never finds out because if he does, he might *actually* kill me.

CHAPTER NINE

Rachel

16 Weeks Along

I should've known. Like, I *really* should've known that something was going on.

I've never been in the emergency room before, but I'm fairly certain the nurses don't usher patients to private suites or stick their heads in every few minutes to ask if I'd like more ice chips or warm blankets.

Aren't ERs supposed to be wild and chaotic? The waiting room certainly was, so why would I, a pregnant twenty-two-year-old with the lowest level of health insurance available, be treated like I'm some sort of royalty?

That's when the anxious thoughts—which have been relentless between my work schedule and the first trimester of my surprise pregnancy—go silent, and I realize with terrifying clarity just how aware I am of Ryder Bates.

I can't see or hear him, but I swear I can feel him.

My fingertips fiddle with the bandage over my arm where the IV had been before the nurse took it out ten minutes ago. My toes curl, tugging the thin socks down my ankles, and my ears ring like they're desperate for the honey-smooth sound of his voice to reach them.

"Miss Lance?" I barely hear the doctor—whose name I forgot as soon as he told it to me—because that's when I finally hear it.

"Which room?" he barks, and, somehow, the sound is still sweet enough to be considered a lullaby.

The doctor must notice something strange, too, because he doesn't attempt to get my attention again. We both look to the door just in time for it to swing open, hitting the wall with a bang that makes me jump.

Thick beads of sweat slide down his forehead, wetting the black t-shirt that spans over his broad chest. His shoulders rise and fall with concerning speed, and his nostrils flare with each intake of breath.

And his eyes...

Those eyes, which are always so contemplative and thoughtful, are burning with purified rage in a glare solely directed at me.

How the hell did he find me?

I don't get to see the undoubtedly confused nurses bustling in the hall before Ryder slams the door shut behind him. I wonder if he even notices there's a doctor in the room with us because he doesn't spare a glance at anything aside from me.

I'm about to break the tense silence by announcing the doctor's presence when he does it for me.

"Mr. Bates," The doctor exclaims, seeming a lot more star-struck than surprised.

"It's a pleasure to finally meet you. I can assure you we've been caring for Miss Lance with the utmost excellence."

My jaw goes slack.

What the...

With what seems like a great deal of effort, Ryder drags his eyes away from me and manages to hold out a cordial hand to the doctor.

"I'll be sure to inform Mr. Moreno of your dedication, Dr. Rocha." His eyes snap back to me. "Could you give Miss Lance and me a moment of privacy?"

"That's not necessary," I assure him.

"Of course, Sir," Dr. Rocha says, completely ignoring me. He leaves with a respectful nod to Ryder.

Well, damn it.

I make a point of not looking him in the eyes once Dr. Rocha leaves us, but I don't cower either. With my chin held high, I scoot up on the bed and meticulously adjust the covers around me.

"What are you doing here?" I ask and want to pat myself on the back for saying it without letting the words shake.

"What. Am I. Doing. Here?" he repeats, drawling out each word with deadly precision.

One gentle but unyielding hand grips my chin and tilts my head upward.

Rage flashes in his eyes like lightning. Wrath swirls in black clouds that not only block the light but suck any hint of radiance from existence. It's a vicious storm ready to wreak havoc until everything in its path is demolished.

And I am currently on that path.

I've rarely seen any emotion touch Ryder's features, so this unbridled outrage is almost as fascinating as it is scary.

But scary definitely wins.

"What the hell were you thinking by not telling me you were here?" The voice that usually wraps around me like velvet tightens around my throat like it's been a noose all along.

The ease with which he talks to me like I'm a petulant child triggers my anger.

I jerk my head away and push him off me. Then, before he can reach for me again, I scramble to my feet on the opposite side of the bed, glad to have the piece of furniture between us, though I know it won't stop him if he wants to dominate my space again.

"Last I checked, I don't answer to you."

"Last I checked, you're carrying my fucking baby, which means I have a right to know when said baby requires a hospital stay."

"The baby is fine," I tell him. "I didn't want to worry you over nothing."

"Didn't want to worry me over nothing?" His humorless laugh is chilling. "You were rushed to the emergency room after passing out at work! That's not *nothing*. Your blood pressure was at levels that could harm the baby, and you didn't think it was something I needed to know?"

His effortless balance of aggression and concern is almost intriguing enough to distract me from the real meaning of his words.

"How do you know about my blood pressure? Isn't that a private record?" I ask, as another fact processes. "How do you know my doctor? How does he know you? And how did you know I was here in the first place?"

The questions pour out of me, and with them, the realization that I might not know the man whose child I carry half as well as I thought.

It's been a month since Ryder and I confirmed the pregnancy. By that time, I was twelve weeks along. My menstrual cycles have always been unpredictable, so I didn't even notice when my period was absent for so long. Since Ryder and I constantly use protection, I never considered pregnancy as a possibility.

Except we didn't use protection the night we met.

I'd expected to be filled with dread at the news that a man I barely know put a child in me, but—aside from the initial shock—I've felt nothing but excitement.

In fact, I've always wanted to be a mother. Of course, I thought it'd come years from now, once I was settled into a career and married to the father.

But this works, too.

I'm not sure what I expected Ryder's reaction to be, seeing as I made it a point to keep communication to a minimum when we were together, but I was caught off guard by his...optimism. Where the best men in our arrangement would've graciously accepted this responsibility, it was almost like Ryder hoped something like this would happen.

After we confirmed the pregnancy, I thought we'd sit down and figure out what this means for us, for our future.

That didn't happen.

Instead, Ryder moved back to Los Angeles—where he apparently lives—only days after we learned about the baby.

In the weeks we spent our nights together, I was determined to make things as uncomplicated as possible. It seemed simple enough. He calmed my anxiety, and we were physically compatible. We didn't need pillow talk or relationship expectations, only each other's company. Unfortunately, in this attempt to give my mind regular quiet time, I neglected to learn that Ryder never actually lived in Sacramento but was only there for work temporarily.

In the past month, I've seen him once, when he flew in for an appointment that I had last week. He calls me every night, and it's easily the most awkward part of my day. We barely talked when we were in person, so making phone calls feel normal is a chore that neither of us feels particularly passionate about. We've settled for an awkward silence in between him asking how I'm feeling, what I've had to eat, and how much sleep I'm getting.

I should've asked more questions when Ryder said he was moving back to L.A. for work, but I didn't think it mattered.

Now, sitting in a hospital suite across from a man who made my doctor tremble with fear and awe, tracked me down when I was brought to the emergency room, knows my medical records, *and whose baby is inside me right now,* I wish I'd asked more questions.

A hell of a lot more questions.

One moment, Ryder's a ball of tension that's ready to burst with frustration, and the next, he's the picture of perfect neutrality. His hands, which were balled into fists, fall to his sides, and his jaw relaxes from its rigid lock.

"That's not something you need to worry about," he says, with no hint of the poisonous thorn that's been biting into me throughout our entire conversation.

I scan the room, wishing someone else was there to confirm how strange this encounter is. It's like someone is flipping a switch between his moods.

"Let me get this straight. You need to worry when I'm diagnosed with high blood pressure, which I've always had and am fully capable of handling on my own, but I *don't* need to worry about the fact that you could track me down, access my medical records, and influence my doctors?"

"You cannot handle this on your own," he states matter-of-factly.

Of course, that's all he gets from what I said. And as if this isn't already a confusing conversation, Ryder's next words absolutely stun me.

"You're moving to L.A. with me."

We sit in a silence that I can't bring myself to acknowledge is awkward because I'm too busy waiting for the punch line to whatever joke he's trying to tell.

Unless he isn't joking.

"Excuse me," I ask, and the two words are choked and breathless.

Ryder doesn't miss a beat. "I need to stay in Los Angeles for work, and you're coming with me."

The laughter that pours out of me is not amused but a haunted sound that makes me wonder if I'm starting to lose my sanity.

Ryder's stony neutrality is unmoving, despite the boisterous laughter bouncing off the walls.

"I'm sorry," I hiccup between fits of giggles. "I could've sworn you just suggested I move to L.A. with you."

"I'm not suggesting it," he states. "I'm *informing* you that you'll be moving to L.A. with me."

My laughter dies, but the hysteria is very much alive.

"You're serious," I practically breathe the words.

He nods sharply.

"Ryder," I start, shaking my head almost manically. "I can't just pick up and move across the state because you said so! I have work, school, and friends. My parents are here, for heaven's sake! There is absolutely no way that's going to happen."

He scoffs, taking one leisurely step after another around the bed and lifting a hand to tick off items as he talks.

"Work has already been dealt with. You're no longer employed by that dump of a pub. School isn't an issue either. You'll transfer to the online program and finish remotely. Your only two friends just moved away for their respective jobs." He's standing a foot away by the time he ticks his fourth finger. "And your parents are working ten-hour shifts, six days a week, for their landscaping company that's barely making ends meet. They hardly have time to *eat*, let alone see you."

With one last step, we're chest to chest, and I'm backed against the hospital wall, Ryder's muscular arms caging me in on either side.

"Do you really think that staying here will help anything? Working that job could be life-threatening to our child, and finishing your degree in addition to that? Absolutely not. Shay and Rosie won't be around to help you, and neither will your parents."

Tears burn behind my eyes, but I blink them away.

I know I'm not in an ideal situation, but I'm doing my best, and he can hardly belittle me for doing what's necessary to make ends meet. As he's so eloquently stated, it's not like I have a large support system to rely on.

"Come to L.A. with me," he says, and the soothing voice that I've come to find comfort in wraps around me like a blanket. The mask of indifference slips away, and there's a genuine plea in his eyes. "I'll support you and the baby. All you'll have to focus on is school. Your parents and friends won't have to worry about you. You'll be cared for, and, more importantly, the baby will be safe."

"I barely even know you," I whisper, but it's a weak protest, and even I know it.

With the charming quirk of one brow, he holds out one hand in the minimal space between us.

"I'm Ryder Andrew Bates, the father of your child and a man who protects what's important to him." He gently tucks a lock of my hair behind my ear. "And you, Rachel Anne Lance, mother of my child, are *very* important to me."

My hand, which would normally ache with the need to pop my knuckles when put on the spot like this, tingles with the desire to take his outstretched one.

But I can't do it, right?

"Let me take care of you," he says, in the soothing tone I've come to crave. "And our baby."

This is crazy. Certifiably insane, and I want so desperately to blame the fact that I'm going to say yes on his convincing arguments, but that would be a lie.

He's right, of course. I am in a bad place financially, and my support system is nonexistent. What he's offering me is the ticket to solving all of my problems like magic.

So, I'll agree and let him believe that it was his smooth-talking that got me when in reality, the truth is far simpler.

For the first time in a month, my mind is quiet.

I used Ryder's effect on my mind to hush the anxiety before I found out about the baby, and then, when I needed the silence most, he left. The last few weeks, I've been a tightly wound mess. My mind spirals into all sorts of negative scenarios throughout the day, and I can't make it stop.

It's been so bad that when I woke up in the ambulance earlier, I wasn't even surprised that I'd passed out.

I need to go because, whether I like it or not, Ryder is the only one who can give me the peace I need to get through this pregnancy.

"Okay," I tell him, hardly able to believe my own words as they pass my lips. "I'll go with you."

I expect a smug look to settle on his face, but none does. Instead, he looks a little…stunned, like he didn't expect me to actually agree.

That makes two of us.

Ryder nods, but it seems more to himself than me. "There's one thing we need to discuss before we go."

I'm sure there are millions of things we need to discuss before we go, but I humor him anyway.

"And that is?"

"My job."

CHAPTER TEN

Rachel

18 Weeks Along

"Are you ready?" Ryder calls from the living room.

The answer is a resounding *no*, but I realize I need to do this sooner rather than later.

I quickly look in the gold-framed, floor-length mirror and deem my tan pants and loose, white shirt suitable. I'm still getting used to seeing myself in the same reflection as the newly renovated bedroom that's more fitting for a royal than me. The king-sized bed is outlined by a golden frame similar to the mirror, and I'm starting to suspect it is made out of actual gold leaf. From the bed sheets and walk-in closet to the delicate vanity and dark oak desk, this room is the definition of stupid rich.

I've never lived in luxury by any stretch of the imagination, so making this place feel like home will be more challenging than I originally anticipated. The family pictures and minimalistic decor I brought from home aren't as effective as I hoped. Still, I'm sure I'll figure something out.

It's been two weeks since Ryder demanded that I move to Los Angeles, and getting everything in order was embarrassingly easy.

My parents, who were scared half to death by my emergency room visit, were far more comfortable with the idea of me moving with Ryder than I thought they'd be. I'd expected them to refuse on the grounds that he's a complete stranger, but, in reality, they saw him more as a saving grace.

In their eyes, he's the knight in shining armor that can protect and provide for their daughter and grandchild.

"Rachel?" Ryder yells again, and after placing a loving hand over my eighteen-week bump, I slip on sandals and meet him in our shared living space.

"Yeah," I tell him. "I'm ready."

Ryder is clad in a pair of black jeans and a forest green shirt that hugs his muscular build. His eyes roam my outfit, giving me a single, approving nod as he makes his way toward the door.

"We're not driving?" I ask as we reach a gravel path outside our door that leads through the trees surrounding the modest-sized cabin we're calling home.

"It's a nice day, and it isn't a far walk."

He's not wrong. The Los Angeles weather is beautiful, with a cool breeze sifting through the trees of our shaded walk, and beams of sunlight sneaking their way through the leaves to warm my skin. Birds chirp happily as they glide through the air from one tree to the next, and I take a look back to appreciate our small home in the beauty of the woods.

It doesn't look like a home, but like an extra garage, exactly what it had been a week ago. It still has the same industrial look from the outside, but the inside is as cozy as a cabin and decorated like one. He'd had the building completely renovated to meet luxurious living standards within a matter of days.

A quarter mile in the opposite direction that we walk in now had been the entrance security checkpoint to what Ryder has referred to as *the base*.

Our cabin is placed between the entrance gate and the base's main building, which Ryder is taking us to now so I can see it for the first time.

When I asked Ryder why we live so far from the main building he usually lives inside, he only answered that he wants to keep me away from his work.

Ah, yes, his work as a mafia underboss.

Never mind that I didn't know what an *underboss* was until a week ago—the right hand of the family's boss, I've learned—now, it's the job title for the father of my child.

I feel like I should get some sort of award for how calm I remained since hearing this news, considering that the normal—and perhaps even encouraged—reaction would be to run for my life and change my name to never be found again.

Honestly, I don't know how I've been able to keep my cool through learning his job and moving here.

Shock? Probably. But I suspect it's more than that.

I suspect that the several reasons he made for why I should come with him, paired with my need for the calm he brings my mind, means I would've come with him no matter what his job was.

"So, who exactly am I meeting?" I ask, breaking the silence that I would've preferred to keep intact but can't. Now that we're having a kid *and* living together, I figure we don't have much of a choice but to talk now.

"The family boss and capos," he says as if it's that simple.

"The who now?"

"Mr. Moreno is the family boss, I'm his second in command, and everyone else you'll meet is a capo—which essentially ranks them as a captain. Everyone has a job that ensures the base and family runs smoothly. You've technically met the capos, but a formal introduction is in order."

"I have?"

He nods. "The night at the club. The men I was with that night were all the other capos."

I do remember them for the most part, though I can't recall their names for the life of me.

The rest of our walk is quiet. I keep hoping that Ryder will be the one to break the silence, to initiate some sort of conversation to get to know me better, but he doesn't.

And then, the building comes into view.

Building isn't even the right word. *Mansion*, maybe, or even *castle* seem more appropriate to describe it. The white stucco walls practically shine in the sunlight, and the deep red of the roof and accents give off an almost-romantic feel to the architecture.

Though, I'm well aware there's nothing romantic about what lies inside.

"Wow," I say on a breath when we reach the entrance, and though he doesn't say anything, I can feel Ryder's eyes on me.

We make our way inside, and I'm surprised by how normal it all looks. I'm not sure what I was expecting, maybe grimy walls and men walking around with military-grade weapons, but that isn't the case. The halls we walk down are relatively empty. The men we do pass never fail to bow their heads respectfully to Ryder, either before or after the confused gaze they send my way.

We arrive at a set of dark, wooden doors before Ryder stops to face me.

His face is blank, but I can somehow *feel* the urgency in his words.

"I am introducing you to the capos because these are the highest-ranking men within the Moreno family, and they should at least have an introduction to the mother of my child, but you need to be careful. None of them would ever lay a hand on you, but that doesn't mean they aren't dangerous. Do you understand?"

I was already apprehensive about this meeting, but Ryder's warning has my hand tingling with the need to pop my knuckles, and I realize it's the first time I've felt that way when I'm with him. I shove my hands in my pockets to dampen the need, and when Ryder's eyes follow the movement, I know the gesture wasn't lost on him.

I don't trust my words enough to answer him, so I nod, and he opens the door.

Four men stand on either side of the table, but my attention is drawn to the fifth man, who stands at the head.

He's built as large as Ryder, and his stony expression is hard enough to send a physical ache to my chest. Everything about him, from his lightly tanned skin, brown hair, and piercing eyes, to his black jeans and matching tee, screams darkness and dominance.

Sure enough, Ryder gestures to that man first.

"Rachel, this is Joshua Moreno. He's the boss of our family."

I clear my throat and push my shoulders back so I'm standing at my full height.

"It's nice to meet you, Mr. Moreno. I'm Rachel Lance."

His eyes scan me in a way that makes me feel like I'm taking a lie detector test, and I must pass because, eventually, he nods.

"I know. I assume I don't have to remind you to stay out of our business during your stay here."

A ball in the pit of my stomach drops at the comment like I'm a child who was caught snooping where I shouldn't. I have no idea if he notices my discomfort or not, but Ryder takes a small step toward me, so his front covers my back.

I wonder if he knows that the simple act slows my heart back to its normal pace.

"Of course not," I answer, proud of my unwavering voice.

Moreno nods again, and Ryder waves an arm to the other men that, now that I'm really looking at them, I do recognize.

"I'm sure you remember Donovan, Kade, Tripp, and Nicholas from the club?"

Donovan smiles, his long dark hair pulled into a man bun, the same as it was the night we met. Kade nods, his buzz cut trimmed even shorter than the last time I saw him. Tripp wears a disgusted expression that looks permanently glued to his face and doesn't show any sign of caring about my existence at all.

Then there's Nicholas, by far the oldest man in the room, with his slicked-back hair and fitted suit. His smile is wide and kind, but for some reason, it feels...off. His eyes seem to gleam with a calculative glint that steals any warmth his smile might've offered.

Whether Ryder can sense my apprehension or just acts on instinct, I'm not sure, but his firm hand wraps around my hip, and the action is far more soothing than it should be.

"Donovan runs security, Kade runs *cyber* security, Tripp trains recruits, and Nicholas manages the day-to-day base operations," Ryder explains.

"And Ride-her is a glorified P.A.," Donovan says, throwing a taunting smile at Ryder.

"Don," Moreno snaps, and I'm not sure if it was at Ryder's tasteful new nickname or the general outburst. Either way, both Don and Kade suppress grins.

"Thank you for your hospitality," I say, mostly to Mr. Moreno, and my hand holds my stomach protectively. "I appreciate what you're doing for my family."

For the first time since I walked into the room, Moreno shows a hint of a smile, but it's more to Ryder than it is to me. I feel a shift in Ryder's posture, which is only possible because of our current closeness, and I wonder what kind of message just passed between them.

"As you all know," Ryder starts, "Rachel will be staying here during the pregnancy. We'll be staying in the cabin up the road, and I expect everyone to be on their best behavior where she's concerned."

There's a collective "yes, Sir" before we all pause at the knock on the door.

Ryder shifts to open it. "Right on time," he says as a young man enters the room.

And I mean, *young*.

There's no way he's out of his teens, and I can't help but wonder what he's doing here. He has messy dark hair and charming green eyes that crinkle with his excited smile. He's muscular, especially for his age, and he shows off those muscles with a black cut-off t-shirt and dark, ripped jeans. He looks more like a punk than a mafia soldier.

"Rachel, this is Alec. He'll be your personal protection during your time here," Ryder tells me.

I look at Ryder, then the boy, then Ryder again.

He's serious.

Not only am I going to be stuck with security, but he expects me to believe that, in a base full of gangsters, a teenager is the most qualified person to protect me? It's not that I think I'm in any sort of danger, despite being surrounded by the west coast's most notorious criminals, but still, I'd expected a bit more than this.

Alec holds out a hand, face splitting into a wide, boyish grin that automatically makes me like him, despite my wariness.

"It's great to meet you, Rachel."

I'm about to return the greeting when Donovan comes up behind Alec, slapping his hands on either of his shoulders.

"Finally getting a shot with the big boys, huh, kiddo?"

Alec shoves his hands away but smiles nonetheless.

"Fuck off, Don."

"No, I'm serious. It's about time you stop playing around and actually pick up some of the slack around here."

Alec tilts his head with an expression that's equally playful and daring.

"I wonder if you'll be saying that when Moreno gives me your job."

Ryder steps between the boys just as Don steps forward to snap back, and I catch the shared smiles among all the men in the room. The moment brings a sense of peace that I didn't expect, and I wonder if I'll enjoy my time here after all.

CHAPTER ELEVEN

Ryder

Present

I've never considered myself to be high maintenance, but as I drive through the gates of the once-abandoned Air Force base, I realize that Los Angeles might've spoiled me. There were no interior designers hired to make this place feel like it was built for kings.

Also, unlike Los Angeles, this base is made up of several buildings. Armories, bunkers, aircraft hangars, dormitories-turned-offices, and other random buildings that I'm sure have some equally unimportant purpose.

I drive right up to the biggest structure on the property, the old Administrative Facilities building, now called the Hub.

I park my car just as a young man, no doubt still in his teens, descends the steps so fast I think he might fall. When I step out of the car, he smiles with nerves rather than warmth.

"Welcome, Mr. Bates. I can take your—"

I toss him the keys as I pass by and head up the steps.

"Your joyride better not leave this property. If there is a *single* scratch, it's your head."

With a quick look over my shoulder, I find him gawking at my Ferrari like I've just given him the winning lottery ticket, and I chuckle to myself. It wasn't too long ago that I was given the same job as a teenager by the capos in Los Angeles. Of course, they would've killed Moreno and me if they knew we took their cars for a joyride before they were tucked safely in the parking garage. I'm just not as naïve as they were.

My chest constricts at the memory but simultaneously gives me a new burst of determination as I come to the main door of the Hub.

I *will* get my old life back.

The smiling face of John Harris is the first thing I see when I swing the rusty metal door open and step into the mercifully air-conditioned room.

"Bates, long time no see."

John Harris—who is roughly my age—has worked for the Sacramento base since he was thirteen years old.

Adopted from India before he turned one, John lived in luxury until his parents died in an accident. It was revealed after their deaths that his adoptive father had a gambling addiction that left John homeless and penniless. A few of the soldiers caught him stealing from one of the businesses they offered protection to, and instead of sending the kid back to the streets, they took him in. He was fed, clothed, and out of the foster care system in exchange for using his thieving abilities for the family.

His black hair is slicked-back with just enough gel to make him look like he's trying way too hard, and he has a neatly trimmed beard that covers the lower half of his face. He wears a navy blue suit, complete with a tie and a vest that make my army-green pants, loose tee, and sneakers look comically out of place.

I take his outstretched hand for a firm shake. "You know that I prefer going by Ryder."

He weighs his head from side to side. "Not sure it'll take here. I'd get used to Bates if I were you."

Most of the people in this business go by their last names exclusively, but things are different in Los Angeles. It's one of the few bases in any family where we live together. The only one who goes by their last name there is Moreno—for obvious reasons.

Harris glances down at his watch.

"We should get going. Knox and Briggs are in the conference room waiting for us."

I follow his lead, even though I can navigate each of our bases with a blindfold on.

Only seeing Harris at the entrance had me under the impression that the base isn't busy today, but as we walk, we maneuver through groups of men, either deep in conversation, laughing, or walking in silence.

All of them pause when they see me, and the less intelligent of the bunch have the audacity to whisper to each other—and not so quietly.

"Is that Bates? Does that mean Moreno is here, too?"

"You didn't hear? He's been demoted and transferred here permanently."

"No shit? What the hell did he do?"

"I heard he gave a Consoli access to our database."

"I heard he kidnapped Moreno's fiancée."

"No way. Moreno would've killed him for either of those. Had to be something else."

I don't realize I've locked my jaw until we're well out of their earshot, and I force myself to release it. I never considered what people might think about my presence, how they perceive it, and how rumors will spread.

The only people who know the full story of why I'm here are the capos.

Harris pushes a set of glass doors open, and I follow him in, glad to see the walls are opaque and only the doors are glass. I hate being watched during a capo meeting.

The two men waiting inside push their chairs back to stand at our entrance, and I meet their familiar faces with a civil smile.

Which is far more than I get in return.

The man closest to me is one I've only met in passing, Mark Knox. He's in his mid-twenties and one of the newest capos to be appointed. His expression, despite the fact that he's meeting with the family's former underboss, is bored. Nothing like the respect I would've been offered only weeks ago.

But I suppose that's what happens when you betray the boss.

The next man is one I've known since I joined this family.

Warren Briggs.

Briggs is one of the few men that can make me look like it's time to hit the gym. Even entering his mid-fifties, he's built like a tank. You'd never know he was that old, thanks to the lack of smile and laugh lines on his face. His silvery blue eyes resemble steel, and the cropped hair and scruffy beard are more salt than pepper. He looks ready to bite my head off, and if I hadn't known him for years, I might not know that's his happy face.

No one bothers with pleasantries, and though so far this has been a less-than-cordial welcome, Harris's smile is unmoving as we all settle into our seats.

75

Harris is the first to speak. "I've prepared a statement for the soldiers explaining that you're taking a position as a capo here, but I'll let you give the reasoning for it. That should get a handle on the rumors."

"I don't give a shit about the rumors," I tell them. "I'm here to do my job. I don't owe them an explanation."

"A statement would stop them from speculating until they eventually figure out that you're here because you betrayed Moreno and this family," Briggs grunts in his gravelly voice.

I should've figured Briggs would feel this way. He's more traditional than some of the younger capos, having served this family back when Moreno's father, Marcus Marsollo, was the boss. In this world, trust is everything, and since I broke that trust, I don't deserve to be here.

"As I said, I don't care what they think. Moreno made a call concerning my actions, and anyone who has a problem with that can take it up with him, though I wouldn't suggest it."

Briggs' resting face is so lethal that he doesn't have to change it to be glaring at me, though the tension in the room rises noticeably.

"So, no reasoning then," Harris says a little too cheerily, scribbling something on a notepad in front of him. "Next, we're all expected to be at the Mayor's Gala next weekend. It's some environment fundraiser to boost Mayor Franklin's image for the upcoming election. A lot of the local political players will be in attendance, so we need to show our faces; keep up appearances."

Though none of us are particularly excited about attending a gala in our free time, we grumble our acknowledgments.

"Great," Harris says. "Lastly, we need to divide up the capo jobs."

The next twenty minutes are spent putting more and more work on my plate. Most of the jobs are mundane day-to-day tasks like bookkeeping, soldier shift scheduling, and on-base shipment organization. Most of the jobs fall under Knox's jurisdiction since he primarily oversees the base's daily operations, but his list of responsibilities is so long that I doubt he'll even notice the lighter load. I also take over assigning the protection rotation from Harris, who manages the businesses in the areas in and around Sacramento. The only person who doesn't relent any work to me is Briggs, whose primary focus is on sending out and receiving shipments. Since this is the only base that was previously Air Force, it's the perfect place to conduct the majority of the family's shipping needs.

We're about to finish up when I lift a hand. "I'll also be auditing all records that could be connected to Mason Consoli."

Every base has been instructed to begin this process, so I know they've already started, but now that I'm here, I intend to personally investigate. If I were to find the source of the leak myself, it could help my efforts to get back to L.A. as soon as possible.

"That's under my supervision. You're not needed," Briggs snaps.

I lean back in my chair. "More eyes won't hurt."

Harris looks uncomfortable for the first time since the meeting started, leaning forward as if he could get between Briggs and me through the table. "Bates, Briggs is already in the process of working through that information. I don't see the benefit of adding that to your workload."

"The benefit is that I come from the biggest and most successful base in our family and have the knowledge and experience to complete this investigation efficiently." I look to Briggs. "I'll take every report that's been audited already, along with the ones that haven't."

"The hell you will," he grates.

Harris places both hands on the table, pushing to stand in the most un-intimidating warning I've ever seen. Still, it works because both Briggs and I look to him.

"Work together," he suggests.

"No," we answer in unison.

Harris gives us an exasperated look like he's chastising two kids, and not one man who's twice his age and another who's outranked him for nearly eight years.

Knox watches the exchange like we're a movie he's seen dozens of times.

"Briggs, why don't you send Bates the information he wants. He can look it over and see if there's anything helpful."

When Briggs puts in the effort to glare at me, the look is beyond lethal. After a long moment, he unlocks his rigid jaw. "Fine, but this is my jurisdiction. Don't overstep."

Harris's smile grows, and we end the meeting. Knox is out of the room in an instant, no doubt going to complete the endless list of tasks he has. Harris is also quick to leave, taking a call as he walks out. Briggs doesn't move an inch until I stand, and then he does the same.

"I would follow Mr. Moreno to the ends of the earth, and as his former underboss, I respect you." He takes three slow steps around the table, bringing us chest to chest. "But I *do not* respect traitors, and as far as I'm concerned, that's what you are now. Mr. Moreno might be able to give you another chance, but not everyone is so forgiving. If you think you can come here and do whatever the hell you like just because you used to be the underboss, you have another thing coming."

He's about to step past me when I place a rigid hand on his chest. I cut my eyes at him, letting my voice drip with the icy bite that burns in my veins. "This is a temporary arrangement. Before you know it, I'll be at Moreno's right hand again, so I suggest you do your best to stop from becoming my enemy." I want to stop at that since it's all true, but even I have to acknowledge his accusation.

After all, I am guilty.

"I'm not proud of what I did," I whisper, melting the ice in my tone. "Moreno should've killed me for it, but he didn't, and for that, I owe him and Elise my life. He gave me this chance to earn his trust back, and I intend to work my ass off to do just that. As I said before, he made his decision, and if you have a problem, take it up with him. Otherwise, I expect the same level of respect you'd show any other capo."

His eyes narrow even more like he doesn't know what to do with my admission-slash-demand.

After a long moment, he shoves my hand off of his chest, pushing past me to storm through the door.

Welcome to Sacramento, I think to myself bitterly.

By the time I get home, it's exactly five o'clock. It's not uncommon that I'd have to stay late into the evening, but since most of my jobs won't start until tomorrow, I let myself take the evening to spend time with Lyla.

I expect to hear her pattering footsteps as soon as I open the door, but there's nothing. The only sound is the television, which seems to be playing one of the endless princess movies Lyla loves so much, but when I enter the living room, she's not there either.

I take the stairs to go to Lyla's room when a soft, muffled voice stops me.

"As you said yesterday, our office is no place for a small child. I assure you, Mrs. Caster, that my work is getting done just as effectively as it is when I'm in the office." Her voice, though effortlessly alluring as always, is curt, like she's reigning in her emotions to stay composed.

I blame my questionable morals for the fact I feel no guilt as I halt outside the door her voice comes from. It's cracked just enough that I can see the minimalistic design of Rachel's office. I recognize all the same decor from the office of the last house, despite the fact that I specifically gave Rachel money to spend on a new set up so this house would feel different from the last. That money is probably sitting in an account, where it'll stay until Lyla needs it.

Damn Rachel's stubbornness.

From my position in the hall, I can also make out Lyla sitting in her bedroom in front of a dollhouse, too distracted to notice my eavesdropping on her mother.

Rachel sits with her back to me, and even though she's working from home, she wears black slacks and a light blue sweater. Her hair is pulled into a tight ponytail, though it gives her a headache, and she'll be taking it out as soon as she's done working for the day.

Which should be now.

She's clicking through emails as she takes her phone from between a hitched shoulder and her ear, then sets it on the desk so she can grab a nearby notepad. With the tap of her finger, the shrill voice on the other side of the line echoes through the room—and potentially the fucking neighborhood.

"—and I'm sure I don't have to remind you that your work is being watched. It's not going to look good when you aren't here."

"With all due respect, my work should speak for itself."

"But that doesn't mean it will. Rachel, I'm telling you this as a friend—well, and as someone who is personally vouching for you— you need to be back in the office."

Rachel sighs. "I know. I'll do my best."

"Wonderful," the woman says, seemingly pleased with the outcome of the conversation. "I'll see you tomorrow, Miss Lance."

"Have a wonderful evening, Mrs. Caster," Rachel says, lifting her middle finger to the phone as she hangs up.

I crack a smile and step away from the door, intent on going to Lyla.

"For someone whose job requires stealth, you're not very good at sneaking around."

I quickly survey the room and stop when I see a small, circular mirror sitting on a pile of books. It's angled right toward me, so Rachel would've only needed a short glance to notice me. I'm less impressed that she caught me and more impressed that she didn't give away she had until now.

Though I never should've stopped to listen without checking the space, so I suppose that's my fault.

"Is everything all right?" I ask, pushing the door the rest of the way open and stepping inside.

Rachel and I haven't talked since Friday night. I spent Saturday organizing the pool house before spending time with Lyla while Rachel ran errands and Sunday going through emails and unpacking the boxes that had taken up half the dining room—most of which were random cleaning supplies or holiday decorations—while Rachel took Lyla to Meredith's house to play with Dominic.

Anytime we've ended up in the same room, it's been for no longer than five minutes before she thinks of somewhere else to be or something else to do.

"Why wouldn't I be? Obviously, Mrs. Caster and I are great buds," she says dryly.

"Sounds like Caster's a bitch."

Making Rachel smile feels like being handed a coveted award.

"She's not. She's just uptight because our work is being watched."

"Why?"

Rachel leans back in her chair, a mixed look of exhaustion and excitement creasing her features. "I'm up for a promotion, but since I'm technically only a P.A., my work is being examined over the next few weeks to see if I'll be a good fit."

"That's amazing. Congrat—."

She holds up a hand. "Nothing is official yet. Caster wants me in the office full-time to show that I care for office morale, but Lyla isn't ready to be without me."

"I'll work from home," I offer before the words even settle in my brain.

"What?" Rachel blinks like it'll somehow help her hear, and I wonder if she's getting enough sleep because that shit makes no sense.

"I'll work from here, and you can go into the office to get Caster off your ass."

"No. No way."

"Why not?" I ask, crossing my arms over my chest and leaning against the doorframe.

"We literally *just* agreed that Lyla shouldn't be around your work, and now you're suggesting bringing that work into this home?" Rachel shakes her head. "That's the opposite of what she needs right now."

"She won't be around anything dangerous. All I'll be doing is desk work."

"How on earth can you be so sure?"

"Do you really think I'd intentionally put her in harm's way?"

"No, but I think you'd *unintentionally* put her in harm's way," she answers without hesitation.

There's a sinking in her eyes that makes me think she regrets saying the words so blatantly, but she doesn't take them back.

"We need to move forward, right? That's what Dr. Danver suggested. How do you intend to move forward if you won't go back to work?"

She eyes me, no doubt conscious of the fact that she never mentioned the doctor's advice to move forward.

I may have hacked into Dr. Danver's computer to read the files from Lyla's appointment. Sue me—and good luck finding the evidence to do so.

Rachel shakes her head with an exasperated huff. "Don't change the subject. The point is, your work is harmful to Lyla and should be kept from her at all costs."

"And it will be. Nothing even remotely dangerous will take place on this property. I can promise you that, Rachel," I say earnestly. "Are you really willing to give up this chance of a promotion when I'm certain she'll be safe?"

Her face shows every bit of her wary contemplation.

"Besides, I've been away from her too long. I *want* to spend more time with Lyla," I remind her.

With a reluctant sigh, Rachel lifts her hands in surrender. "Fine, but I mean it, Ryder. Any triggers, and I swear I'll kick your ass out."

"Fair enough."

I'm already mentally planning to go to the base in the middle of the night to complete the work I'll have to do in order to justify staying home tomorrow, not that Rachel needs to know that. It's the first time I'm actually glad to be staying in the pool house, where Rachel won't be able to hear me leave for work.

My strategizing is interrupted when I notice that Rachel is popping her knuckles and tugging at the bulky charm on her necklace. If I didn't know better, I'd think it's work that's still bothering her.

But I do.

"What is it?"

"My parents," she mutters, staring at her phone, which lights up with a text from her mother at that moment.

"How are Bill and Lynette?" I ask, and wonder when the last time I saw them was. Christmas maybe? No, Easter. Definitely Easter.

Rachel rolls her eyes. "Annoying since they found out you moved in."

"Didn't they know?"

She shakes her head, staring at nowhere in particular, and I'm willing to bet it's just to get out of making eye contact with me. "Lyla told them yesterday over a video call."

"And why didn't *you* tell them?"

"Because I knew they'd do this."

"Do what, exactly?"

She leans back in the rolling chair and glares at the phone as it lights up again. "They, quite desperately, would like to have all of us over for dinner tomorrow night."

"And that's an issue?"

"I just need a break," she breathes. "The last thing I need is to have my mother talking about her friend's kids who are getting married, then dropping poorly disguised hints about how *we* should get married."

That is a spot-on description of how nights with Lynette and Bill usually go. Sometimes I wonder if Rachel would prefer that her parents view me as a typical, irresponsible prick that knocked up their daughter and left, and not as their dream son-in-law.

I push off the doorway and move to the desk, peering over to read —yet another—message from her mother.

Mom: What time will you be over tomorrow?

Mom: Does Ryder still like Brussel sprouts? Can you ask him?

Mom: Rachel? Are you there?

"Let's just get it over with," I tell her.

"I'm starting to think we don't have much of a choice," she grumbles from her slouched position in the desk chair.

I breathe a laugh and hold out one hand to her.

With a dramatic sigh, Rachel takes it, and I help her to a standing position.

"Fine, but you're the designated driver."

I laugh, shaking the hand I still hold before releasing it.

"Deal."

CHAPTER TWELVE

Rachel

"I'm going to kill him," Elli practically shouts from the other end of the phone, and I turn down the volume so the people shopping around me can't hear her. "I swear he treats me like a child sometimes. He acts like it wasn't *his* idea to make me a capo in the first place, then gets all overprotective and doesn't let me do a damn thing. Ryder never would've let Joshua pull this shit if he was here."

Elise Consoli and I became fast friends, but I guess that's to be expected when we're the only women associated with the Moreno family's boss and—former—underboss. We call each other every few days, and most of those calls, if not all, feature a rant in which Elli relates her latest fight with Moreno.

If I hadn't watched them together myself to see what an undeniably perfect match they are, I'd tell her to drop his ass.

I lived with Moreno for most of my pregnancy, and though seeing him was a rarity, it was more than enough time to grasp that he's not an easy-going person. He's controlling, hard-headed, and ruthless. I never imagined he'd find someone willing to put up with his shit, but it turns out he just needed someone to call him on it.

Enter Elise.

"It's embarrassing as hell, too, especially since Damon moved in with us."

"That's one of your brothers, right?" I don't know the Consoli brothers very well, though I met all three briefly in Los Angeles a few weeks ago.

Elli makes an affirmative sound. "He's the oldest. He just got done with rehab and wanted to take some time away from the business, so I offered to have him stay with Joshua and me."

"I'll bet Moreno just *loved* that."

"Shockingly enough, they actually get along. He'd kill me if he heard me say this, but I think he needs a friend since…well, you know."

Since Ryder was banished.

Right.

I backtrack to avoid that uncomfortable topic.

"Well, you can't blame him for being protective, especially after everything that happened at the factory. Besides, you're only a few weeks into the job, give it some time, and I'm sure he'll loosen up."

"Ugh, you're right. Though…"

There's a thoughtful pause.

"I'll bet I could speed up the *loosening* process."

"Keep it to yourself, Elli," I chastise through my laugh.

"Speaking of loosening up, how are you settling into the new place with Ryder?"

I stroll along an aisle of the grocery store, getting halfway down it before realizing I don't need anything in this section. How the hell did I even get to this side of the store?

I have no idea if the nervous energy comes from the dinner plans with my parents tonight or the fact that said dinner will force me to be in close proximity to Ryder—who I've avoided fairly well since he moved in.

Is avoiding my daughter's father the most mature way of dealing with the current situation?

No. But it's the best I can do to ensure I keep my sanity—and heart—intact.

"Uh, they're going…okay, I guess."

"So, not well?"

"It isn't that, though you were right about his reaction to the pool house. He wasn't happy, but he's not pushing it. I think he realizes it's best for Lyla."

"Are you sure Lyla's the only reason?"

"What do you mean?"

"I don't know," she drawls. "Maybe the fact that you want each other?"

The can of green beans slips from my hands, and I barely catch it before it smashes my foot. "It's not like that," I say, and realize too late how defensive it sounded. "It's complicated."

"How could it be complicated? You want him. He wants you. You're living together indefinitely and have a child together. Am I missing something? I don't see why you haven't jumped each other's bones yet."

Suddenly, I'm hit with memories of when we did just that. It's been years, but I can imagine it as vividly as if it were happening now. His warm, minty breath caresses my skin. His big hands grip my hips with a possessiveness that makes my knees weak. His dark eyes roam my body with enough intensity to make me go up in flames.

No, no, no. I'm not doing this right now.

"You said it yourself. He's here indefinitely, not permanently."

That seems to have stumped her, so she goes for a new tactic. "Well, you could always move to L.A. when he comes back."

"That's not happening. My family is here, my life is here, my daughter's life is here. She needs consistency more than anything. I can't just pick up and move her with the hopes that things work out with her father and me."

"But you admit that you hope things work out?"

She's like a dog with a bone.

"You're incorrigible," I say, scanning the items in my cart to ensure I have everything before heading to checkout.

"I just care about you both and want you to be happy," she defends.

"I am happy. Things are fine as they are. Ryder and I aren't meant for anything more than co-parenting."

"Hmm. We'll just have to agree to disagree."

We hang up after she tells me about how Moreno and Damon ganged up on her in a game called Kemps, and I'm walking out of the store when the same sickening sense of anxiety that I felt after Lyla's appointment hits me again. It doesn't shudder down my spine this time, but rather, it sits like a ball of dread in the very pit of my stomach.

I release the cart that I'm pushing to grab my phone and clutch the heart-shaped charm around my neck.

They're coming for you, that cruel voice hisses, *and they won't let you go this time.*

My heart pounds like it can bust my chest open, and I scan my surroundings with vigilant eyes. I feel only marginally better by the fact that this is a busy parking lot. No one could attack me in broad daylight without a half-dozen people noticing, but that logic doesn't make the feeling go away. If anything, it grows more intense when I find no source for such a strong reaction. I clutch my phone tighter and wonder who I would even call if something went wrong.

I could call my parents or Meredith, but I get the feeling that only one person would really be able to do something if I was attacked.

And that thought gives me pause.

Is Ryder having me followed?

It wouldn't be the craziest thing he's ever done, but doing it without telling me would be infuriating. He knows I'd hate having some shadow following my every move, which could be why he's kept it a secret from me.

With that all-too-likely thought, I slip my phone back into my pocket and load up my groceries.

Bill and Lynette are the most supportive parents on the planet. This was great when I came home pregnant from a man I barely knew at twenty-two years old and when I decided to move to L.A. with that man.

This was less great, however, when they fell in love with Ryder to the point of deciding that I was an idiot for not, in their words, *taking what was being handed to me.*

Any wariness my parents might've harbored for the stranger fathering their grandchild was wiped away when they discovered the level of luxury Ryder lived in and could provide for Lyla and me. It also helped that, for Christmas two years ago, he bought them a house in a neighborhood they could've only dreamed of living in before.

I also suspect—though he's never admitted to it—that Ryder was responsible for the mysterious buyer that bought out their landscaping company. The buyer requested that they still run it and gave them the means to hire enough employees to have a manageable schedule and a hope of developing a relationship with their only grandchild.

They can't understand why I won't marry him, and since I can't tell them the real reason, I figure it's better for them to make me the bad guy than to worry that Lyla's father is.

Because Ryder isn't a bad guy or even a bad father, he's just bad for *me.*

Regardless, my parents love him like he's their own. I realize this is a better alternative to them hating him, but it still gets annoying.

Like now, when Lyla, Ryder, and I walk into their house, they hug the former two before even looking in my direction.

"Ryder! You're looking healthy! What's your diet like these days?" My mother coos after placing a kiss on both of his cheeks.

"Complete garbage compared to one of your home-cooked meals," he answers with a charming grin that makes me want to gag.

Kiss ass.

My father pulls Ryder in for a hug next. "How's the real estate business, son?"

Oh, yes, *real estate*. The cover for Ryder's criminal activity.

"It's going great. Our company recently acquired some land in Texas that has shown a lot of promise."

"That's my boy," my dad says, and I wonder if he'd sound so proud if he knew that land was actually going to be another base for a mafia empire.

"Nice to see you, too," I mutter when my parents finally look my way.

Mom picks Lyla up and places several kisses on her cheek. "Of course, it's great to see you, sweetie," she says to me. "But it's not often that we get to see Ryder. How long has it been since we last saw you?"

"Easter," Ryder answers, a wide, pleasant smile plastered to his face. "You'll have to forgive me for not visiting sooner. Things at work have been particularly crazy the last few months."

Dad claps him on the back. "You know we're always happy to have you."

My parents take Lyla into the living room, and Ryder and I trail behind.

Ryder gestures to my face with a concerned pull between his brows. "You okay? You're looking a little green."

"Fuck off," I mutter and shove him with my shoulder, though it's more like pushing a brick wall.

He laughs as I push my way in front of him to help Mom in the kitchen.

Over dinner, my father asks Lyla questions about what she's been up to lately, but she starts to get shy and quiet, a sign that we all understand means she's getting overwhelmed, so he turns his questions to Ryder.

Dad tries to impress Ryder with whatever recent articles he's read on the real estate business—mixing in his own expertise with landscaping—and Ryder does a fairly good job keeping up with him despite the fact that we both know he had absolutely no knowledge on the topic.

If nothing else, Ryder's presence ensures I'm not the center of attention, so I only have to sit back, relax, and get through this meal.

At least, that's the case before Ryder states, "We're putting Lyla in martial arts."

"Oh? I've heard that's a great sport for kids to get into," Mom notes.

"Very structured and disciplined," Dad agrees.

I doubt they would be this enthusiastic if I'd broached the idea, but that doesn't matter since I made my thoughts on the matter clear the other night.

"We haven't actually decided anything yet," I say, and I know that my frosty tone doesn't go unnoticed.

"Right," Ryder says without missing a beat. "We still need to do a trial class, but as long as it goes well, we'll sign her up."

I stare daggers at him from across the table.

How dare he put me in this position?

Again.

"Like I said," I grate. "Nothing is set in stone. I think Lyla might like another activity more, so we'll explore several options before we pick one."

It's too quick for me to be certain, but I swear Ryder's gaze flicks from me to my untouched knife and back again.

"Oh?" My mother talks like she doesn't notice the tension, and I appreciate the effort. "What other activities are you considering?"

I tick the options off on my fingers. "There's dance, gymnastics, swimming lessons, and even a club that has soccer for toddlers."

"And what do *you* want to do, Lyla?" Dad asks.

We all look to Lyla, whose cheeks redden at the sudden attention. "I want to do what Dominic does," she answers softly.

"Marital arts it is," Ryder declares with an easy grin that makes me want to smack him.

"Just because Dominic does it doesn't mean it'll be best for her," I whisper, but the effect is wasted since everyone—Lyla included—can hear me.

We drop the topic after that, moving on to my parents sharing about a recent project where they redesigned a friend's backyard.

When dinner is finished, Mom and I move to the back patio while Lyla climbs on the playset and the boys clean up from dinner. I tell her about the promotion opportunity and how Ryder is working from home so I can go in.

In return, she tells me that none of her friends has unmarried kids anymore and how she's nervous they won't be interested in coming to my wedding if I wait much longer.

"Sweetie, you know I love you," she starts, and every daughter knows that nothing after that phrase will ever be something they want to hear. "But I just don't understand why you and Ryder aren't making this work. Especially now that he lives here."

Why is this the second time today that I'm having this conversation?

"There's nothing to make work, Mom. We're not a couple, and aside from the making of our child, never have been."

Mom cringes at that, and I'm glad. Serves her right for trying to poke around my love life…or lack thereof.

"Besides," I continue. "He's only here temporarily for work, and then he'll be back in Los Angeles."

"When will that be?"

"There's not a timeline right now. Could be weeks, maybe years."

"You're saying he could be living with you for years, and you're not even willing to try a relationship?" She says it like she's accusing me of a vicious crime and not simply making my own choices.

"Trust me, Mom. Things are better this way. A relationship would only complicate things for Lyla."

Mom shakes her head. "Rachel Anne Lance, you're *allowed* to complicate things sometimes. Being a mother is a wonderful thing, and the fact that you want to protect your child is great, but sometimes it's okay to be selfish."

I nod but don't say anything else. I hope the conversation will pivot, but when my mom starts talking about how beautiful the last wedding she went to was, I excuse myself to refill my glass of wine.

My dad passes me to go outside as I go in, and I round the hallway to the kitchen to find Ryder wiping his hands on a dish towel with the single most priceless expression.

I would argue that Ryder has the best poker face in the world. His composed features are such a huge part of who he is that it throws me off any time he shows emotion so openly.

This is why the look of utter exasperation on his face is nothing short of comical.

"I have had intensive interrogation training that would put any country's military to shame, but if I have to pretend to know about real estate for one more second, I'm going to break and tell your parents *everything."*

The annoyance my mother evokes vanishes, and I laugh so hard my stomach aches. Ryder joins in, the sound soothing and light, like summer rain.

"You should be honored that he likes you enough to read half a million articles on the topic. He just wants to impress you."

"I should've picked a more interesting cover. Real estate is boring as shit."

"And what would you consider interesting?"

He thinks for a few seconds. "Management."

"Management? That's not a job in itself. Managing what?"

"Literally *anything* but real estate. I manage a criminal empire. Wouldn't be that hard to change my product from weapons and substances to—fuck, I don't know, watches."

"Watches?" I repeat with as much composure as I can. "You know what? You're right. You should go into *watch management*."

"You know what—"

He stops when his eyes focus on something through the window. His expression sobers from whatever he sees there.

"What's wrong?" I say, rushing to look, too.

"Absolutely nothing," he breathes, and I follow his line of sight to where my father pushes Lyla on a swing while my mother takes pictures.

Her smile is huge, and now that we're quiet, we can hear her giggles all the way from here.

"It's like she doesn't even notice we're gone," Ryder whispers, and it's only now that I realize, in my haste to look out the window, I've pressed my back against his front, and his breath skates over the shell of my ear.

For a second, I'm thrown back to the night we met. The large presence at my back, his words setting me ablaze, and the warmth of him encasing me so thoroughly that my mind goes so wonderfully silent.

I'm not sure what scares me more, the fact that my muscles relax against his hard body or the fact that, even after everything we've been through, he still has this much control over my body.

It takes physical strength to wrench myself away and take a step back. The cold that replaces him is so brutal that I shudder, and I can't bring myself to look at him for fear that my reaction to him is written all over my face.

I'm sure that it is.

"We should head out there," I say and step toward the back door.

"Wait," Ryder grabs hold of my arm, sending that warmth back through me with an intensity that I'm not at all prepared for. I don't know if it's the way I freeze at his touch or if he feels the same intensity that I did, but he releases my arm almost as fast as he grabs it.

"Let's go on a walk, see how she does with them if we're gone for a while. Being able to stay with anyone aside from us would be a huge win."

He's right, and it probably makes me a shitty parent that I'm deliberating ignoring that fact just to avoid spending more one-on-one time with him.

Of course, my desire for Lyla's independence wins out.

I shoot my mom a text, which she immediately responds to enthusiastically, and Ryder and I walk out the front door.

We don't speak for a while, but we don't need to. The neighborhood is beautiful and lively, thanks to the kids who ride their bikes down the street and the couples who walk their dogs.

I'm careful to keep a solid foot of space between Ryder and me, which isn't easy considering his size and the narrow sidewalk, so I end up walking in the grass most of the time.

Worth it.

"If this goes well, I think we should try having Lyla stay at your parents for an evening," Ryder says, breaking the silence that I would've been fine staying in.

"I'm not sure. It seems a bit too soon for that, don't you think?"

He shrugs. "There's a gala next weekend that I have to attend, and it could be the perfect time to try it out."

"I don't have plans next weekend, so we don't need a sitter."

"Actually, I was hoping you'd join me," he says, with all the chivalry of a gentleman and all the authority of an underboss.

"I'm not sure that's a good idea," I say honestly.

"It's not work-related," he says, and I realize that his work has nothing to do with my apprehension. "Well, it is, but nothing happens out in the open at an event like this. It's just to show my face and intimidate a few big names in the area."

I take a moment to be glad he thinks my apprehension has to do with his work. I wish it was. At least, that would make sense.

"I don't—"

"It's just a night out, Rachel. Don't you think you've earned it?"

"I'm not sure this is the kind of 'night out' I've been waiting for."

Ryder narrows his eyes. "Does it ever get tiring?"

"What?"

"Overthinking everything."

Yes, I think immediately, but glare at him instead of giving him an answer.

"It's one night," he says with an easy smile. "Good food, even better drinks, and live music."

I agree that I deserve this night out, but I'd be lying if I said his dark, hypnotizing eyes, and silky tone have nothing to do with my relenting.

"Fine, I'll go."

His smile grows, and we turn to make our way back to the house.

As we walk, a particularly slow truck passes us, and it reminds me of the watchful eyes I've felt recently. "Are you having me followed?"

"Followed?" he asks, but I don't turn to look at him when I feel his eyes studying me.

"You know, like security." Saying the words out loud, hearing just how ridiculous it sounds, I wish I hadn't said anything at all.

"You think I'd do that without telling you?" he asks, and I'm sure that, once again, my paranoia got the better of me.

Of course, Ryder would never stick protection on me without my knowledge. What had I been thinking?

When we get into the house, I listen for the sound of screaming or crying, but there are only the muffled voices from the TV drifting through the house.

We get to the living room and stop, taking in the scene before us.

Mom sits on her usual spot on the tan leather couch, but my dad sits in his recliner with Lyla cuddled into his side. Her eyes are wide, mesmerized by the screen playing one of her princess movies.

When Ryder locks his awe-strike gaze with mine, I tell myself the heat that courses through my body is only the product of my pride for Lyla.

But that's bullshit.

CHAPTER THIRTEEN

Ryder

"I don't think this is a good idea," Rachel whispers, eyeing Lyla through the rearview mirror as she plays with one of her dolls in the back seat.

"Trust me, you've made your thoughts on the matter crystal clear," I say, shooting her a pointed look that she returns with a glare.

In the end, it was Lyla who settled the matter when she blatantly asked Rachel if she could do martial arts with Dominic. Since Lyla had become so attached to the idea, Rachel had no choice but to relent. She's been giving me the cold shoulder since the appointment was scheduled, but I've been too exhausted to do much about it.

I've worked from home for the last three days, getting as much done as possible while off-site. Then, each night, I've gone to the base until the early hours of the morning to finish the work.

This has left very little time for other activities, namely, sleeping.

"This is going to be good for her," I say. "She's in a class with her best friend, getting energy out and learning to defend herself."

I'm not under the impression that the local martial arts studio is going to teach my daughter world-class ninja skills that'll give her the ability to take down men my size, but knowledge grows confidence, and confidence is what my little girl needs.

We pull into the parking lot, and I help Lyla out of the car before crouching down with my back to her. "Hop on, Tiger," I tell her, and she locks her arms around my neck. Her short legs can't wrap around my body, so I use my arms to hold her there. I smile at Rachel, who's— no doubt intentionally—looking everywhere but at Lyla and me.

"Where's Dom?" Lyla's melodic voice is inches from my ear, and I can smell off her breath that she snuck a few gummy worms from the candy basket before we left.

Guess it'll be our little secret.

"Meredith and Dominic said they'd meet us here," Rachel answers.

We walk inside the lobby just as one of the classes lets out. Dozens of kids race through the lobby, gathering their belongings or finding their parents, and Meredith stands at the front counter talking to the young lady there.

I've taken more punches than I can count and even a bullet on one unfortunate occasion, but I'm almost knocked flat on my ass when Dominic flings himself on my leg out of nowhere. He ignores my existence completely like I'm a ladder he's getting ready to climb to get to Lyla.

"This is going to be the most fun ever!" he shouts.

Lyla squirms on my back, and I gently let her down.

"I'll show you where to put your shoes!" He takes her by the hand, and they race through the lobby and out of our sight.

I look to Rachel, who watches Lyla and Dominic with wide eyes, and I know we're thinking the same thing: Lyla just walked away from both of us in public without so much as looking back.

This is going to be good for her.

The lobby finally starts to clear out, and Rachel and I walk to the front desk.

"There you guys are," Meredith says as if we aren't ten minutes early for the class. She looks to the woman at the counter, who I decide can't be older than twenty-five.

"Elizabeth, these are Lyla's parents."

Elizabeth's smile is warm. "It's nice to meet you guys. Welcome to Torres Martial Arts. In about five minutes, Mr. Torres will call the kids in and do some fun pre-class drills, and then the class will get started. Feel free to take a seat in the waiting area, where you'll be able to watch the whole class."

Elizabeth ties a white belt onto Lyla, and she looks at it like it's made out of those gummy worms she loves so much.

"Dominic! You know you're not supposed to climb on the shoe rack. Get down from there," Meredith calls before chasing after her son.

I steal a glance at where Rachel stands at my side, but she shares none of my optimism. Her brow is furrowed, her eyes unfocused, and her hands repeatedly pop her knuckles.

Rachel has voiced her hesitation about this idea from the beginning, but for the first time, I'm struck with the thought that her reluctance has nothing to do with Lyla after all.

I wrap an arm around Rachel's waist. The action is more instinct than thought, but when her hands relax at her side and her eyes regain their focus, I know it's worth it, even if it technically breaks her *no-touching* rule.

"What are you doing?" she asks, looking around like anyone in this busy lobby would care.

"Why don't you want to be here?"

"I've told you a million times, it could be a trigger—"

"Maybe that's true, too, but it's not why you're practically crawling out of your skin to get out of this place. What's really going on?"

The tension returns, and I tighten my hold on her in response, like I can counteract whatever is driving her to stiffen up. Rachel doesn't answer me and instead shakes her head.

"What is it?" I gently ask again.

She presses her lips together and swallows like something is clogging her throat and blocking her voice. She doesn't protest when I rub my thumb against her waist, so I don't stop, and it reminds me of the day she told me she thought she was pregnant. Back then, she'd held onto me like I could shield her from anything, and I wonder what exactly stops her from doing that now.

Likely the fact that we're in the crowded lobby of a martial arts studio, but that's beside the point.

"I don't know what it is," Rachel finally whispers. "The idea of being around people who are training in self-defense, it just…it brings it all back."

"Brings what back?"

"The helplessness," she admits, meeting my gaze for the first time. Those mesmerizing eyes carry exhaustion that I can practically feel radiating off of her.

Fuck, why hadn't I thought of that?

Lyla isn't the only one who was traumatized by the factory night. Rachel's been able to use Lyla's needs to disguise her own.

"Is that why you asked about security the other night? Rachel, I'd be happy to—"

"No," she shakes her head adamantly. "I don't want security. I just hated that, when it mattered most, I wasn't able to protect Lyla, or even myself for that matter."

"Let me train you."

"What?"

"I can train you, same as I did with Elli."

"You trained Elli?" she asks, raising a skeptical brow. "Why?"

"She was tired of feeling helpless. Well, that and because Moreno told me to," I admit, and my chest feels significantly lighter when she cracks a smile.

"I don't know, Ryder. I'm not sure I'm ready to face that yet."

"Dr. Danver wants Lyla to build confidence. Why shouldn't you?"

Her voice drops to a barely audible volume. "There were so many of them when we were taken from the house. I'm not sure any level of training would've helped."

I shift closer to her so no one overhears our conversation, but also because seeing her like this and *not* being close to her feels wrong.

"Maybe, maybe not. I can't speak for back then. What I can do, is promise that learning to protect yourself now will give you, and me, a hell of a lot more confidence if you should ever need it."

She doesn't say anything for a long moment, and I wonder if she, too, is prolonging this rare moment of intimacy. If it were up to me, we'd stay like this for as long as possible.

Of course, it isn't up to me, and Rachel steps back, putting enough space between us to send the message that the moment is over.

"Okay," she says, with a nod. "One session, and if I don't like it, we stop. Deal?"

I nod. They're not the best terms, but I'll work with them.

Just as Elizabeth said, a tall man with cropped dark hair in a black uniform with the name, Jacob Torres, embroidered on it, stands at the door and calls in the class. The kids, about ten of them, rush into the room, but the teacher stays behind, greeting Lyla with a warm smile and a high five. He gently coaxes her into class with the help of Dominic, who refuses to leave her side.

Rachel and Meredith find seats, and I trail behind them, opting to stand against the back wall, giving me a good view of the classroom and the lobby.

There's another class for an older age group on a separate floor across the lobby, being run by a young woman with long blonde hair and a curly-haired brunette. The parents from both classes prove a comfortable lull of voices indulging in small talk.

Unfortunately for me, Rachel and Meredith participate in this small talk.

Two moms sit near the girls, leaning in to introduce themselves to Rachel as Carol and Amy.

"I'm Rachel." She points to where Lyla stands with her arms folded. "Lyla's mom. She's trying class today for the first time."

"Well, welcome!" Carol says. "I think you and your husband will be very pleased with the program. It's really great."

I pretend I can't hear them.

"Oh, uh." Rachel blanches, then cringes before settling on. "He's actually just Lyla's father. We aren't together."

Carol and Amy look at each other, then to Meredith. "You didn't tell us you finally found someone to take your place."

"What place?" Rachel asks.

The eye roll is evident in Meredith's tone. "As the single mother, everyone tries to set up with Mr. Torres."

Rachel takes a moment to assess the man, who's explaining a roundhouse kick on a miniature punching bag to the kids, and I find myself wishing I was at an angle that allowed me to read her face. Since I'm not, I follow her gaze, trying to see what it is these women seem to find interesting about the instructor.

He has a muscular build and sharp features that make him look like the kind of guy I'd want to recruit for the family. Though his dark features would objectively be considered traditionally appealing, even I can see that his appearance isn't what has these moms fascinated. It's the way he treats their kids. Everything about his tone and countenance is dedicated to making the class fun, having the kids repeats after him in silly voices or having them walk like animals as he lines them up for drills.

"I'm not sure he's my type," Rachel says.

Amy shakes her head. "That man is everyone's type. I mean, come on, just look at him! And think about what a great stepdad he'd make."

"I'm not looking for something right now. Lyla is in a tough spot, and she's my focus."

"Just don't forget to focus on yourself, too," Carol coos. "I mean, you have needs."

Fuck, is this how all women talk to people they've just met?

Besides, they're having this conversation within my earshot as if I'm not her...her what? I'm not Rachel's anything. I have no claim over her that would warrant avoiding the topic of relationships.

The realization is about as easy to swallow as battery acid.

I push off the wall, heading to the front counter without another look in their direction. I fold my hands at the front desk, smiling— what I hope is—politely to Elizabeth.

"How can I help you?"

"Can I get some more information on the program?"

"Of course!" She nods, clicking through some screens on her computer, then nodding in Rachel's direction. "Would you like your wife to join us?"

The correction is on the tip of my tongue. It's an easy mistake to make, a simple, understandable mishap, but when I look over my shoulder to where Rachel sits among the desperate housewives of Sacramento, the urge to correct Elizabeth's assumption is nonexistent. In fact, it sends a feeling of satisfaction through my chest, and I can feel my smile warming to a genuine one.

"It's all right," I tell her, sending one last, admittedly hopeful look to Rachel before turning to the counter again. "I'll catch her up later."

"Ready?" I ask, standing at the back door with Lyla in one arm and two water bottles in my other.

"Define *ready*," Rachel mutters, walking into view wearing shorts and a loose shirt. Her hair is braided back on either side of her shoulders, and she's wearing a pair of tennis shoes that are so old I remember them from before I even knew she was pregnant.

"Willing to give this a try even though you don't want to," I say in a way of definition.

She rolls her eyes. "Let's just get this over with."

I lower my body so Lyla can open the back door for us, which she does with a giggle. Rachel murmurs something at my back but follows us outside nonetheless.

We spend the first fifteen minutes stretching, and Lyla enthusiastically joins us. She performs her own version of each stretch, which is the only thing easing the tension between her mother and me.

I realize, with a pang of bitterness, that this is the first the three of us have spent any real time together since I moved in. Most of the time, Rachel is all too happy to pretend I still live hundreds of miles away.

By the time we've finished stretching, Lyla has lost interest and gone to the playhouse with a few of her dolls.

We start the workout from there with a series of push-ups, sit-ups, and squats, which increase in repetition with each round. When we finish that, I grab my equipment bag from the pool house and return to where Rachel is lying on her mat, staring up at the sky as she catches her breath.

I'd be lying if I said I didn't let my eyes linger on her chest, which is only visible because her shirt has shifted in her reclined position. As she lays there—black bra on full display from my vantage point—I recall the dozens of times I had her panting on her back just like that.

This isn't exactly the same, but I'll take what I can get.

For now.

"I haven't had a good workout in weeks," she huffs when I stride toward her.

"And we've only just started." I take two jump ropes from the bag and toss one to her.

She looks between me and the rope with open distaste. "Aren't these for kids?"

I hold out my hand, which she takes with a groan as she stands.

"No, they're not for kids," I say as I set a timer on my smartwatch for our reps. "We're going for endurance, not speed, so pace yourself."

The next hour consists of jumping rope, planks, and sprints. We're both dripping with sweat and chasing our breath when Rachel narrows her eyes at me.

"I thought we were going to learn self-defense. I could've gone to the gym if we were just going to work out." She takes a long gulp of water, tossing the bottle aside when it's empty.

"If your endurance wasn't so impressive, we would've started by now."

"What do you mean?" she asks, taking *my* water bottle and finishing it off, too.

"Now that you're finally tired, we can actually start training."

She pushes her head forward, like she needs to be closer to hear me better, and blinks with dramatized timing. "I'm sorry, I could've sworn you just implied that we're just now *starting* your self-defense lesson."

"We are."

"You must be out of your damn mind. I am exhausted. There's no way I can do anything else."

"Trust me, you can," I tell her, taking the water bottles to the pool house to fill them.

When I return, Rachel is glaring at me, and I'm starting to wonder if that expression is just a habit every time she sees me.

"I'm going to pull a muscle or something. Isn't it dangerous to over-exert yourself when working out?"

I hand Rachel her water bottle and grab two shield-shaped pads from the equipment bag.

"We're not working out anymore. Besides, you're in shape and can handle pushing your limits."

"Oh, right, because you know my limits *so* well," she says with an eye roll that might as well have been audible.

"As a matter of fact—"

She lifts her hand. "Make a comment, and I swear I'll punch you."

I suppress my smile and secure one pad over each hand. "As it happens, that's up next."

"Getting to punch you?" Rachel asks with a bit too much excitement.

"The pads."

I don't miss how her shoulders sag in disappointment.

I hold up the pads, instructing her on a simple jab and cross combo to start. Once she's done that a few times, I add hook punches, then uppercuts. We do the combination over and over again, and finally, I add a knee strike to the end.

We try out a few more combinations, mixing in some ducks and blocks when I swing the pad at her head and body. Her movements are smooth, graceful even, and there's a part of me that's proud to see her doing so well. If her concentrated squint and curled lips are any indication, she seems to be enjoying the drills, too, despite her initial hesitation.

When she leans over her knees to catch her breath, I throw the pads aside.

"Finally done?"

"Not quite," I tell her, and she groans again, looking over to where Lyla is half-asleep, watching a movie on her tablet while lying in the playhouse.

"We're going to go over a few scenarios. We won't drill them like everything else, but I want to go over them briefly at the very least."

"Scenarios?"

""The most statistically likely self-defense-related situations you could end up in."

If she'd warmed up to the idea of self-defense training at all in the last hour, it vanished at that moment. The wariness snaps back into her posture like a rubber band, and her body language becomes closed and guarded.

We've officially reached the end of her comfort zone, but unfortunately for her, the capability and confidence she needs lie well beyond the limits of comfort.

"I think we've done enough for today."

"You can handle it," I tell her, knowing it's true even if she doesn't believe it. "We'll start with a simple wrist grab, then move to a shoulder grab." She doesn't react beyond her cautious expression, so I press on. "After that, we'll try a hook punch attack, then a grab from behind."

The last suggestion makes her stiffen, and I know I've hit a nerve.

Her head shakes absently, and an almost-lost look begins to gloss over her eyes. She's going back there to the memories that are tying her down and preventing her from moving on.

Sorry, Rebel. I can't let you go there alone.

She's gazing more *through* me than *at* me, which is why she doesn't react to what I pull out of the equipment bag until I'm standing directly in front of her, holding the plastic knife at my side.

From any distance, the shiny silver could make the blade look real, but even though she's close enough to see the scuffed-up plastic that proves it fake, Rachel still holds her breath like she's staring into certain death.

She takes a small step back. "No."

"No?"

"No," she repeats, firmer this time.

"Why?"

Her eyes never leave the weapon, and it doesn't take a genius to guess where her apprehension stems from. After all, I've watched her avoid the utensil at every meal we've had together. "They had knives when they took you?"

She doesn't say anything or even look up, but the sinking in her brow is confirmation enough.

"How did it feel?"

Rachel finally looks up at me, and though her eyes narrow in surprise, they're still covered by that lost glossy haze.

"How did it feel?" I ask, slower this time. "When they came into your home and held you at knife-point?

Rachel's mouth tightens as she tries to step past me to get to the house, but I block her path.

"How did it feel when you saw them hold a knife to our child?"

I barely hear the strangled whimper that she tries to suppress, which is in contrast to her distant, frosty expression, and tells me that I'm getting closer.

"How did it feel when you watched as they sliced her arm open?"

"Shut up, Ryder! Just shut up," she grates, shoving at my chest, but I don't relent.

She's still being held in that grip of fear.

"How did it feel, Rachel? When they took you and Lyla, then locked you up?"

"It was hell." She practically spits the words, and I watch the exact moment her eyes spark with a fiery passion that brings her fully back to the present. "It felt like the purest, most *absolute* form of hell to be unable to help the *one* person who I have dedicated my life to protecting. I felt hopeless and worthless and like nothing could ever make up for what a horrible mother I am."

She shoves me again and is scooping up a sleeping Lyla from the playhouse, and walking inside before I can stop her.

I'll let her come to me once she's had time to cool off. I'll explain that I'd rather she be mad at me than lost in the memories that hold her hostage. She'll be too busy fuming with anger to remember how the memories from that day stormed into her consciousness and tried to drag her into reliving them.

The same blazing passion that had her yelling at me is exactly what she needs to fight through those moments, even if pushing her to that point makes me the world's biggest asshole.

I'll gladly be Rachel's villain if it means saving her.

CHAPTER FOURTEEN

Ryder

20 Weeks Along

"All in favor of the M.A.C. Project?" Moreno asks, and I clench my teeth as we wait for the results.

Moreno, Donovan, and Kade all raise their hands. I expected that, but when the man beside me raises a hand, too, I'm completely blindsided.

"What the fuck do you think you're doing?" I hiss under my breath, but Tripp remains unbothered.

I'd walked into this meeting with the numbers to postpone this vote. I'd known I wasn't going to win, but half would've forced at least another week of deliberation.

Nicholas sits across from me with both hands firmly on the table, just as he said he would.

The traitor next to me shrugs. "I never liked this in the first place. If I could vote against the idea as a whole, I would, but since it's going to happen either way, better now than later."

"All right then," Moreno says as he pushes to his feet. "It's done with, and there's no changing it now. Nicholas, start making the arrangements."

"Yes, Sir," he replies, courteous as always despite being on the losing end of this particular vote.

"Meeting adjourned. Ryder, stay," Moreno demands, and the other capos scatter within seconds.

The door slams shut after them, and I waste no time.

"This is bullshit, and you know it," I bite.

Moreno folds his arms over his chest. "I know this isn't what you wanted, but the timing is too optimal to pass on."

"The timing is exactly the issue!"

"Watch it," he says with a glance at the door. I know he cares more about other people eavesdropping than my actual disrespect. "We knew this day would come."

"But now? When the mother of my unborn child is here? Come on, Joshua. This isn't safe for her, and you know it."

"It's perfectly safe as long as she continues to stay away from the base. You're free to send her home when the project starts, or anytime, for that matter."

"You know I can't do that," I say through tightly clenched teeth.

That would mean spending the end of the pregnancy apart, and there's no way I'm doing that. She's staying here where I can make sure she and the baby are healthy.

Moreno clasps a hand on my shoulder. "I know this isn't ideal, but even you have to admit that this is the best opportunity we're going to get. We can't miss out on the off-chance something goes wrong."

He's not wrong, which only pisses me off more.

I shrug his hand off and storm out the door. My frustration doesn't ease in the slightest as I walk the short distance between the base and the cabin. Usually, I'd feel some sense of peace at coming home to Rachel, but right now, nothing short of a re-vote is going to ease my black mood.

Things have been...strange since Rachel moved in two weeks ago.

Our interactions aren't as effortless as they used to be. Before finding out about the baby, we had a good thing going. Sure, we didn't do much talking, but we had realistic expectations of each other, and we were okay with that.

Then the baby came along, and her health problems, and my work. All of a sudden, what was a simple, steady hook-up, is now a tangled mess of a relationship that neither of us knows how to navigate.

Eventually, we'll need to sit and talk through the future, but I'm trying to give Rachel more time. In the span of two months, she's learned she's pregnant with a stranger's child, then moved to a new city with said stranger, who turned out to be a mafia underboss. Safe to say, she's had her fair share of surprises for a lifetime.

But, in the two weeks she's been here, she hasn't shown any signs of wanting to talk, and since I don't want to push her, I've just waited.

Since I'm working long hours at the base each day, all I know is that Rachel focuses on her schoolwork during the day and is normally tucked away in her room by the time I get back each night.

Alec assures me she eats three times a day, so I don't have a good excuse to go in and see how she is.

So, I haven't.

But tonight, I'm home earlier than normal, so I hold out hope that her soft, still-nervous smile will drag me into better spirits.

That hope is crushed into a million pieces when I walk in to find Alec and Rachel hunched over a document at the table. They're so engrossed in whatever it is they're looking at that neither of them even notices my arrival.

I take slow steps toward them and see Rachel's shoulders stiffen. At the same time, I recognize what they're looking at.

Rachel twists in her chair to look up at me with wide eyes, but I barely notice as I close the distance and snatch the paper off the table.

Alec, who'd been in the middle of saying something prior to my walking in, goes pale when he notices me. "Ryder, I—"

"You must be out of your *fucking* mind, Alec," I shout, a rare occurrence, though it feels more than appropriate now.

Rachel, who looks both cautious and annoyed, reaches out for the paper. "It's not a big deal, Ryder. Calm down."

I pull it out of her reach before she's even close to taking it. "You have no idea what is and isn't a big deal. You know you're not supposed to involve yourself in what we do."

"It's only a food organization spreadsheet for next month," Alec explains, far calmer than I would've expected of him. "There's nothing incriminating there. I swear. I never would've—"

I take three slow steps toward the boy, who matches each of them backward but doesn't avoid my gaze.

"Is the spreadsheet used at this base?"

"Well, yes, but—"

"Then you have gone against a *direct order* to keep her away from any and all business. I'll be taking this to Moreno."

His bravado cracks at that. "Wait, you don't have to—"

"Go."

I bite the order, and he doesn't hesitate before running out of the cabin, taking the spreadsheet with him as he does.

When I turn, I do so slowly, expecting to see Rachel curled into herself, but that's not how I find her. She sits up tall in her chair, eyes narrowed into slits as she glares at me with more force than I knew she possessed.

"What were you thinking?" I ask when she says nothing.

She breathes out a laugh devoid of humor. "You should be more concerned with what I *am* thinking, which is that you're a complete asshole."

"You both know the rules and blatantly went against them."

"It was a spreadsheet to order food for next month! He had no idea how to interpret it, so I helped because I look at spreadsheets all day. If you're mad, be mad at Nicholas for giving Alec a job he wasn't prepared to do!"

"It wasn't your place."

"And what is *my place*, Ryder? Besides being stuck inside this stifling fucking cabin with nothing but my schoolwork to keep me company. You know, I thought when you brought me here that we'd be working together to figure out this whole 'having a kid' thing, but no. You leave at the crack of dawn and come back well into the night most days. You *never* try to talk about the future, our child, or even just how our fucking days are! I know absolutely nothing about you, and what I do know doesn't make me like you very much!"

For a minute, all I can do is stare at her. I knew she was likely starting to get bored, but I didn't think she felt like this.

Why didn't she tell me?

When would she have had the chance, asshole?

For fuck's sake.

She points after Alec. "And if that is how you act when you're mad, then I'm not sure I want you anywhere near this child."

Rachel's gaze wanders like she's lost and trying to figure out how she got here. She breathes deeply, one hand over her heart and the other holding her stomach.

It's only now that I remember I'm supposed to be keeping her calm, not riling her up and adding to her stress.

For fuck's sake.

I step toward her, and when her eyes widen as she steps back, I freeze in place. That small ounce of fear in her eyes feels like a wrecking ball ramming into my stomach and stealing my breath.

"I shouldn't have come here," she whispers before disappearing into her room.

CHAPTER FIFTEEN

Rachel

"So, what did he say?" Meredith asks, literally on the edge of her chair.

"According to Mrs. Caster, he said my work is nothing short of outstanding," I tell her, relaying the conversation I had with my boss only a few hours ago.

Meredith smiles wide. "That promotion is yours. I already know it!"

Her enthusiasm is contagious, and I can't help but share her smile. It's been great to work in the office like normal over the last week, and all signs are pointing to this promotion being handed to me on a silver platter at the management dinner in a few weeks.

Meredith leans back in her chair, scooting it with a screech that draws attention from the other parents in the lobby, but she barely seems to notice since we're all watching our kids go through an obstacle course.

Being in the martial arts studio doesn't feel as nerve-racking as it had last week, and I have no idea if that's due to how much Lyla loved it or Ryder's lesson over the weekend.

If I expected an apology after he threw trauma in my face like a festival pie, I was sorely mistaken. In fact, we've barely even seen each other in the few days it's been since we trained.

The day after our fight, he was gone from the early morning hours until almost midnight, which might not be so strange if it weren't for the fact that it was a Sunday. Though, I suppose his line of work wouldn't conform to traditional working hours.

Yesterday he left as soon as I was home from work, and I didn't see his car in the driveway until I woke up this morning. He even seemed to be in a hurry when he met me earlier in the parking lot to bring Lyla to me after my workday.

Encounters like that are the only ones we've shared, and we rarely make eye contact, let alone speak. It seems that my plan to avoid Ryder is working better than ever.

"How is she liking it?" Meredith asks, angling her head toward our kids, who are helping pick up equipment from around the floor.

"She says she loves it, but I'm not sure if it's the martial arts or being with Dominic that she actually enjoys."

"And how are things since her father moved in?"

I shrug, showing none of the complicated emotions that I feel about this particular topic. "Fine. Kind of boring, actually."

Meredith nods. "Well, that's good."

"What do you mean?"

"Just that it's better to be boring than complicated or combative. I don't know many co-parents who could live together and not kill each other."

I force a smile. "I guess you have a point."

The kids pour out of the classroom, and Lyla runs toward me. Dominic grabs his mother by the hand and practically drags her to where he put his shoes. She shoots me an exasperated look as she goes.

"How was class?" I ask Lyla, picking up her shoes from where I kept them beneath my chair. She sits to put them on, smiling up at me with a grin that melts my heart and any remaining apprehension I've reserved for her taking these classes.

"It was fun!" Her eyes focus on something over me, and somehow, her smile widens. "Hi, Mr. Torres!"

"Hey, little ninja," comes a friendly voice from above me, and when I look up, Mr. Torres is looking down at me with a charming smile. "Hi, Mrs. Lance. I'm Mr. Torres. I just thought I'd come and introduce myself."

He doesn't hover for long and takes the newly vacated seat at my side.

"Actually, it's just, Miss," I tell him, flashing my ring-less finger. "And please, call me Rachel."

"Oh, my apologies, Rachel," he says. "Feel free to call me Jacob."

He holds out his hand, and I take it, surprised by how calloused, yet warm, it is.

"Lyla is doing great in class so far. I think she's going to thrive in this program."

I look down at Lyla who looks ready to burst from the compliment. "That's so nice of you to say. Thank you, Jacob."

"Of course. She's a great kid," he says.

We share another smile before he goes to talk to a few other parents, and I help Lyla get her shoes on.

"Ah, what was that all about?" Meredith whispers when she and Dominic come up to our side. Her eyes are playful and far too suggestive.

"Nothing at all. He was just being polite," I insist as we walk outside, but I know she won't believe that.

When the feeling hits me, my heart sinks as my awareness rises. Ryder said he wasn't having me followed, and I believe him, which means that this is just paranoia, right?

Would I feel this paranoid three times in one week?

I work to pinpoint the particular spot I feel watchful eyes coming from, but I can't calm my breathing enough to actually process where that could be. The nausea that roils inside me would make me throw up if I wasn't so focused on holding Lyla's hand and searching my surroundings.

It only makes me feel marginally better that Meredith walks by my side, seeming to feel none of the anxiety that must be radiating off me. It's actually starting to scare me, and I realize that it might be time to talk to Ryder about this.

Maybe someone is following me.

They're going to take your daughter, the voice hisses. *They're going to hurt you.*

"I think he likes you. He didn't have a talk with me when Dominic joined…." Meredith continues her musing, but I can't hear what she says over the pounding in my ears. I scan the busy parking lot, but once again, nothing stands out.

Okay, I tell myself, with all the calm I can muster, *the feeling always goes away once you're in the car. You just need to get to the car.*

This piece of information gives me the strength to give Meredith a normal farewell as Lyla and I go another row up to our car.

I'm scanning the area like a crazy person as I get Lyla in her car seat and slide into mine. I reverse out of the parking spot on autopilot, still searching for anything that could be the reason for my spiking anxiety. When I pull onto the main road, I wait for the feeling to subside.

It doesn't.

If anything, the alarms in my head blare even louder as I cruise down the busy street. I search my surroundings, looking in the rearview mirror for anything out of place, and, for a reason I can't explain, I keep focusing on a black truck with tinted windows.

It's a few cars behind me, driving along like every other car, and there's no logical reason I should be wary of it, but I am, and I trust my instincts.

The hiss is loud and clear like it's trying to hush any hint of logic left in my brain. *They're coming for you, for Lyla. This time, no one is going to save you.*

For the next few miles, I cast shaky glances at the truck every few seconds, but it stays at a distance. When I'm coming up on the highway ramp, I decide to put my theory to the test.

I stay in the far left lane until the absolute last possible second, then make a sharp right to make it onto the ramp. It's a risky as hell maneuver that sends me across two lanes, and I hate that I have Lyla in the car with me for something so dangerous.

And I hate even more that I'm right.

The black truck makes the same drastic turn, though it gets blocked by another car and has to slow to get around. At first, I think I've gotten away, but the truck cuts through traffic and makes it to the ramp.

And now it's speeding toward me.

Like black claws dragging me into murky water to drown, I realize that Lyla and I are in very real danger.

You don't stand a chance. You might as well give up now, the hiss taunts and every muscle in my body threatens to freeze up, but I can't. My life and Lyla's depend on how I handle this situation.

"Lyla, sweetie, do you have your headphones?" I ask in a calm, collected tone.

"Uh, huh."

"Why don't you watch a movie?" I ask, and she nods enthusiastically, grabbing the tablet and headphones to do just that. She's normally not allowed to watch movies in the car, and I'm hoping she'll see my diversion tactic as a treat.

You can't protect her. You can't even protect yourself! What kind of mother keeps putting her own child in danger?

I bite my lip so hard I taste blood, but the pain is easier to focus on than the thoughts that grab me in a vice-like grip by the throat.

The truck is gaining speed, and I know that I have to do the same if I want to put distance between us. As I merge onto the highway, I get to the left-most lane as quickly as I can and match the traffic there. The truck is several cars behind me, and I use this moment to grab my phone from my pocket and dial the number of the only person who can help me.

"Hey, what's up?" Ryder's voice is pleasant, albeit surprised, since I only call to have him talk to Lyla.

My words are rushed in a voice low enough that Lyla can't hear them.

"I'm being followed. It's a black truck, and they've been watching me since I was at the martial arts studio."

"Where are you?" he asks, snapping into a tone that's all business.

"Highway eighty, heading west toward the house."

"Do not go home," he says, and I hear rustling in the background like he's running, and then all sound from his end goes quiet.

"Ryder?" My voice breaks on his name as the black truck gains speed, weaving through cars at an alarming rate.

"I'm here, I'm here," he says. "I just ordered soldiers in the area to head your way."

"What am I supposed to do?" The hysteria is making its way into my voice, and I send looks to Lyla constantly, making sure she's blissfully unaware of the current situation.

"Keep driving. I'm tracking your car now, and I'll give you directions. For now, stay on the highway and keep as much distance as possible between you and the truck. Is Lyla okay?"

"Yes. She's watching a movie, so she's not paying attention." I send another look to the truck, which is only a few cars away now. I'm already going ninety and still gaining speed. "Ryder, they're getting closer."

"Stay calm, Rachel. I'm right here, and I promise you're going to be okay," he says with such certainty that I have no choice but to believe him, even as I watch the car get closer.

"Okay," I whisper.

"You're going to get off the next exit, but I want you to wait to get on the ramp until the last minute."

I can do that. I mean, I just did that. I tell myself that over and over again, reaching for any confidence I can muster, but my reservoir is empty.

My eyes flit to the mirror as the exit comes into view, and the truck is only one car away at this point.

"They're close, Ryder." My words sound strangled.

"I know, baby, but you're almost to the ramp, okay? You can do this, Rebel."

Somewhere in the back of my mind, I don't miss how he calls me "baby" and "Rebel" with the kind of ease that suggests it's a habit, but I don't have the time or energy to process that right now.

"As you're swerving to the exit, I want you to see if you can catch any part of their plate information."

"Okay."

The exit comes, and it's a miracle that I'm able to jerk the steering wheel and send my car across three lanes without another car getting close to hitting us.

"Mom!" Lyla squeals from the backseat, and my eyes catch her panicked gaze and enough of the truck's position to know they're locked in by a semi, unable to make the same maneuver as me.

"You got this, Rebel," Ryder says in my ear as the left tires graze the grass and make it onto the ramp.

"I-I didn't get the plates. I couldn't—"

"That's okay." His voice is soft, gentle, and exactly what I need to hear right now. "Take a left, then go straight for a few miles."

"Okay," I confirm and look to Lyla, who still regards me with wild eyes. "Sorry, sweetie. I didn't mean to scare you. Everything is okay."

Lyla stares for another second before putting her headphones back on, refocusing on her movie.

Ryder stays on the phone with me, though he doesn't talk unless he's giving me directions. I'm so flustered that I don't even ask him where we're going. I just focus on pulling air into my lungs and driving safely.

"You're going to ruin your joints," Ryder says after a moment.

"Huh?"

"That's the third time I've heard you crack your knuckles."

"I'm not sure there's evidence proving that," I say, and Ryder's breathless chuckle does a hell of a lot more to relax my tense muscles than it should.

"Take the next right."

"It's gated off," I say, and at that moment, the gates slide open. I don't question him again and turn down the gravel path.

When I pull into what seems to be some sort of aircraft storage, I realize Ryder's brought me to the Sacramento base.

He's standing at the end of the road, and I waste no time parking and flinging my seatbelt off. By the time he rounds the car to my door, I've thrown it open and fallen into his arms.

I have no idea what comes over me, but I start shaking and barely recognize the feeling of being in my own body as it trembles. Ryder doesn't start an interrogation like I expect him to. Instead, he places both arms firmly around my body and crushes me to him.

I hear Lyla's voice from the car, and Ryder shifts forward to reach the driver's door and lower the window so he can see her. He begins to talk to Lyla as if all is well with the world. Asking how martial arts was, what she learned, and how much fun she had.

The entire time he doesn't ease his hold on me and even rubs his thumb across my skin. It's the same gesture he repeated in the martial arts studio when we went for Lyla's trial, and, like then, I force myself to focus on the feeling of his skin touching mine as I take deep, steadying breaths. When Lyla starts her movie again, Ryder moves his mouth so it's right next to my ear.

"Are you okay?"

I'm not, but I can't bring myself to admit that weakness out loud, as if he hasn't guessed it from how I'm still shuddering in his hold.

"I'm sorry," he whispers, surprising me enough that I pull away just enough to look at him. I'm grateful that he doesn't ease his hold on me. "I thought—if I pushed you to confront your fears about what happened—you'd be too angry with me to dwell over what happened at that factory. I could *see* how you started to fall back into those memories. All I wanted to do was get you out of them."

That's why he was such a dick?

It's a ridiculous notion based on twisted, manipulative logic.

But it worked.

I went inside, called Elli to rant, and busied myself with extra work that Mrs. Caster didn't need to be done for another week. I didn't waste an hour staring into space, playing that day on a loop. I didn't drown in my own helplessness. I didn't obsess over Lyla like she could disappear any second.

And most importantly, I didn't lock myself in the office with my toxic vice.

But the fear that he saved me from then is now dragging me into the abyss of hopelessness with a ferocity I can't overpower in my current state.

"How did it feel?" Ryder had asked me.

It feels worse than I can put into words, and I'm done with it.

Ryder must take my silence to mean I'm still mad at him because he goes on. "Not everyone knows what it's like to have everything they live for threatened right before their eyes. Those of us who do, are never the same. We don't live the same, see the same, or even *breathe* the same. So, I can't train you the same either. You know what it's like to *need* to survive, and as horrible as that place in the back of your mind is, there's a power there that gives you strength and determination that could save your life. But I shouldn't have pushed you—"

"You're right," I breathe the two simple words, and he stares down at me with an unreadable expression. "I do have a need to survive, and I can't stand how helpless I felt just now." I take a deep breath, knowing this isn't something that I want to do but something I need to do. "I want to train with you. I want to know how to protect myself and Lyla. I want my confidence back."

His brows pull together, and I know this isn't what he'd expected. I didn't expect it either, but it feels like I don't have a choice anymore. My life is intertwined with Ryder's, and whether he's the reason I was followed today doesn't change the fact that I can't guarantee I'll live a life without needing to protect myself.

"Okay," he says with a nod. "We'll start tomorrow."

CHAPTER SIXTEEN

Rachel

"Why can't we just get to the self-defense part?" I groan, rolling to my back on the yoga mat in the grass after completing my last set of push-ups.

Ryder sits on his mat a few feet away, watching me catch my breath in only my sports bra and leggings. A hint of a knavish gleam in that gaze makes me wonder if his thoughts are purely training-based.

"You're not tired enough," he answers.

"Not tired enough?"

He nods, pushing to his feet to grab the shield-shaped pads. "Chances are, when you need these skills most, it'll be when you're already at your limit. So if we train at that limit and push it, it'll better prepare you should you ever need to defend yourself."

I don't have an answer, so I stand and get in my guard stance, ready to find and push those very limits.

We go over the same combinations of jabs, punches, hook punches, and uppercuts that he showed me a few days ago, but my attitude has done a one-eighty. I'm not doing this to prove a point or placate Ryder. I'm doing this because *I* want to.

Because I need to.

I hit faster, strike harder, and duck, dodge, and block like my life depends on it. I can imagine the target isn't a pad, but whatever creep was following me yesterday.

Once I'd calmed down at the base, Ryder drove Lyla and me home. I waited for the inevitable questioning, but it didn't come. It still hasn't. I have no idea why Ryder didn't want any more of the

115

information I had—admittedly, not a lot—but I figure he has the situation under control. Besides, it's not like I want to talk about what happened, anyway.

His attitude toward our training has shifted, too. He took the training seriously before, but there's a level of urgency that wasn't there before.

I'm not under the impression that I'd be able to protect myself from a car chase with what Ryder is teaching me, but I need to build up my confidence. When I needed it yesterday, it was like drawing from a drained well, and I'd barely been able to hold on to my sanity when I needed it most.

So, if this is what it takes to build my confidence, I'll do it.

I shoot periodic looks at Lyla, who is playing with building blocks on the other side of the window just inside the house. She's in a world of her own, and I couldn't be more grateful that she was oblivious to the car following us yesterday.

"Ready to move into self-defense?" Ryder asks, sliding the pads off his hands and regarding me carefully like he's bracing for me to close off.

I nod. None of the nerves and anxiety that riddled me during our last session rear their ugly heads. It's almost like the fear from yesterday has silenced any remaining hesitation I had about all of this.

The first drill is—as Ryder calls it—a wrist escape. He grabs my wrist, and I shoot my hand downward, aiming a palm strike at his nose. Next he grabs my shoulder, and I swing my arm out of his hold then practice hammering my fist into his elbow. There's an attack from a hook punch and another where he grabs me from behind.

And then we move into ground defense.

"If you're not comfortable, I won't push you," Ryder says when I hesitate to lay down, leaving out the implied *again*.

"No," I tell him, shaking my head as I lower myself to the ground and lay on my back. "I want to do this."

"Okay," he says with a nod, then lowers onto me.

There's something about the way he traps me between his legs, looming over me like it's the most natural position.

If someone asks me on my deathbed, I'll admit with my dying breath that maybe—*maybe*—I don't mind being in this position with Ryder.

I wonder if his thoughts mirror mine, but his eyes are stony and his face is equally expressionless, which is when I remember that he's trained like this before.

"Did you do this with Elli?" I want to slap myself in the face as soon as the words leave my lips.

Not only have I blurted an insecurity, but I didn't disguise the distaste I have for the idea in the least.

Unsurprisingly, Ryder's lips pull into a teasing smile, and now I want to slap *him* in the face. "Jealous, Rebel?"

There he goes using that damned nickname again, and when we're already in such a…compromising position, too.

Bastard.

I roll my eyes, trying my best to play off my embarrassment and—yes—jealousy.

"Don't be ridiculous," I scoff. "I'm curious, that's all."

He doesn't look like he believes me for a single second, and I don't even blame him.

"Sure you are, but to answer your question, no, I didn't do this with Elli. Moreno would've put a bullet in me if I'd come close."

"What does that say about Moreno? That he'd give you another chance after betraying him but would kill you for teaching Elli ground defense."

Ryder's lips twist in an expression I don't recognize. Half smirk, half…taunt? But there's something else in there, too, like an understanding of sorts.

"It says that he knows exactly what he wants," Ryder says.

I'm suddenly overly aware of our closeness and the searing heat his gaze carries as he takes me in beneath him. I clear my throat and flick my eyes to the window, relieved Lyla is still occupied with her blocks and not looking toward her father and me. "So, now what?"

The next several minutes are spent learning to trap his leg with mine, then buck my hips to roll us so I'm on top of him. We add a few strikes meant to stun, and he goes over small variations to the technique.

As hard as I try to focus on the drill, I can't quite shake the part of my brain that's constantly mindful of how close Ryder and I are to each other. I keep thinking I'll get used to it—get used to *him*—but it hasn't happened yet.

I'm about to tell Ryder that I think I have this one down as he lowers on top of me once again, but before I get the chance, his gaze locks on mine, solemn and sincere. "Close your eyes."

"What? Why?" I ask but close them, anyway.

With my eyes closed, my attention zeroes in on each place Ryder touches. Feeling him is all I *can* do, and it's damn overwhelming.

He shifts overtop of me, and as much as I want to find out what he's doing, there's a part of me that relishes the unknown.

That same dangerous part of me wonders if he'll touch me like he used to…

His breath brushes my neck as he says, "You know I would never hurt you, right?"

The question, combined with our current position, should have me opening my eyes and shoving him away with every ounce of my strength. Call it bravery, curiosity, or just plain stupidity, but I nod instead.

"I need to hear you say it," he says in a throaty voice that shakes the rusty gates where I keep the memories of us locked away.

My mouth goes dry and it has nothing to do with the heat.

"I know you'd never hurt me," I whisper, but as I say the words, I realize they aren't fully true. He'd never hurt me physically, but I have scars that run soul-deep with his name on them.

I don't take the words back since doing so will force me to confront that particular scar. I'd rather take my chances and just trust him right now.

The cool sensation of metal skims across the heated skin of my throat. The contrast of my hot skin to the cold metal makes me shudder, even from the minimal contact, as it slides from one side of my jaw to the other.

What on earth is—

I go rigid with the realization of what he's holding.

"Don't," Ryder says, lips still only inches from my ear. "Don't open your eyes. Don't push me away."

But the urge to do those very things is nearly overpowering.

"Ryder," I say his name in a broken whisper that would embarrass me if I wasn't overwhelmed with a sense of betrayal.

How could he?

Only the flat side of the blade meets my skin, but he may as well be driving it into my chest.

"Focus on the cold."

It's an order, spoken as a lullaby—a dangerous use of Ryder's effortlessly compelling voice. I feel like the sailors that jump into the ocean after the siren's call, only to be drowned beneath the waves.

I might have fought against the order if I wasn't already frozen in place. There's not much else I can do but trust him.

I focus on the blade, how it chases the heat away, then replaces it with the sting of its cold. He moves it back and forth over my throat in an easy rhythm, like a deadly waltz over my skin.

The knife leaves my body, and with it, I feel a shuddering breath of relief. I'm not sure why I don't open my eyes yet like somehow I know I'm not supposed to.

And I'm right.

The blade gently brushes my collarbone, and I gasp at its iciness. Beads of water and sweat roll down my chest, creating a burning and freezing trail. I know without asking that he's dipped the blade in his water.

He mimics the same rhythm as before, only over my collar instead of my throat, and I have no idea when my lips part to let in a steady flow of air to my lungs. I'm so lost in the intensity of the conflicting sensations that I don't remember when my heart returns to its normal rate, but it beats strongly.

When the knife lifts again, I'm shocked to my core when I find myself waiting patiently for its return. Sure enough, the newly chilled blade meets my chest, and when parts of me tense in anticipation, I know it isn't because of the fear that is waning with every second.

Ryder doesn't follow the same rhythm as before and instead trails the blade from my chest, over my bra, and down my stomach.

I have no idea how long he trails that blade across my skin, but when it loses its chill again, I feel his breath at my ear.

"You don't need to be afraid of a blade. It may have the power to hurt—to kill—but I find that the most dangerous things have the ability to bring just as much pleasure as they do destruction."

I open my eyes to find myself trapped, not only by his body covering mine but by the raw honesty in those hypnotizing eyes.

For a heart-wrenching second, I can't help but wonder if that's what Ryder is to me—a blade meant to bring me earth-shattering pleasure and soul-crushing destruction.

CHAPTER SEVENTEEN

Rachel

It's harder than I'd like to admit to leave Lyla with my parents, but when she's swept inside by my mother, who promises her ice cream for dinner, I know she'll be just fine.

I considered backing out of this gala at least a million times, but in the end, I didn't decline the invitation. Instead, I put on my forest-green, floor-length gown with a flattering slit that goes to my mid-thigh and pull my hair into a slick ponytail that falls to my shoulder blades.

I deserve the night out, right?

We pull up to the Sacramento Art Museum, where the Mayor's Green Initiative Gala is being held, and Ryder helps me out of the car before giving the keys to the valet.

I expect us to walk with the usual foot of distance between us, but when he holds out his arm, I take it without fighting, using the excuse that I'm not used to wearing heels to rationalize my lack of argument.

The men at the door don't stop to take our names as they do the rest of the guests, and I feel silly for letting that surprise me in the least. This is Ryder, after all. Wherever he goes, doors open for him.

I've been to this museum before and know it's breathtaking without a hint of decoration. It has high ceilings and meticulously painted clouds surrounding the cathedral-style windows that let sunlight pour in during the day.

But now?

Now, it's like stepping inside a garden straight out of a fairytale.

Whatever event coordinator was hired for this event will no doubt be given a generous bonus for the decor alone. Red and pink lights cast a romantic hue over the spacious room, complementing the hundreds of roses that line every wall. Dark green vines drape across the ceiling, and the chandeliers have pink light bulbs just for tonight's event. Each table has a floral arrangement that would put any bride's bouquet to shame, and even from here, I can see the porcelain plates with dark leaves painted on them.

Several candelabras taller than me are placed on either side of the main walkway as we pass, and each one is lit with a live flame. The pathway leads to the wide dance floor, where couples sway with a band that plays a contemporary tune I don't recognize.

I'm so busy taking it all in that I don't realize Ryder is leading us through the crowd until I hear someone call his name.

I recognize the men as the Sacramento capos, but only from meeting them in passing over the years.

Harris, who called out to Ryder, has a woman tucked under one of his arms. She wears a black gown and a small smile on her plain face.

Knox stands to his left, seemingly deep in conversation with—who I assume is—his date. She's a tall, slim girl with petite features that seem fitting for a model.

Then there's the man who stands on Harris's right. Briggs. His unpleasant grimace—which I quickly note becomes even more so when directed at Ryder—is balanced by the beaming smile of the woman on his arm. She looks to be around Briggs's age, but unlike him, she has laugh lines that ameliorate her grin.

"Gentleman," Ryder greets, and they all nod in response.

Harris steps up and claps Ryder on the shoulder. "Bates, good to see you." His eyes fall on me, and I appreciate that they don't linger. "Rachel, it's lovely to see you again. How are you?"

I offer a polite smile. "I'm well, thank you for asking. And yourself?"

"Doing great," he says and gestures to his date. "This is my girlfriend, Ava. Ava, this is Bates and Rachel, his..."

Harris' eyes widen as he realizes that he has absolutely no idea what I am to Ryder.

Join the club.

I save us all from the awkward mishap by widening my smile and holding my hand out to Ava. "It's nice to meet you."

Harris looks relieved, then takes the opportunity to introduce Ryder and me to the other women. The one with Knox is Emily, who is just his date for the evening, but the woman with Briggs is Donna, his wife of almost a decade.

The women are nice enough, and we find ourselves gravitating toward one another and end up in a conversation about our jobs. Ava is a secretary for a law firm in the area, Emily is actually a model (which I was proud to have guessed), and Donna is a teacher. I explain what I do, which takes a while since it's such a hodgepodge of tasks at the moment, and I find myself smiling as I do. It's a good reminder that I don't just work to have a job. I actually enjoy what I do.

It's then that I feel Ryder's gaze on me. I don't even have to look to know the level of intensity that I'd find there. I can *feel* it.

My back straightens on instinct, and only a moment later, his warm hand settles on my waist.

The women continue their conversation, which has shifted to how bad the local construction has become on populated roads, but it's Ryder who has my attention.

"Excuse me," he says to the group as he pulls me from them without ever breaking eye contact. When we're a few steps away, he leans in to ask, "May I have this dance?"

The well-mannered side of me wants to accept this invitation graciously, but the logical side wonders why on earth Ryder would want to *dance*, of all things. It's much safer to politely decline the offer and continue socializing with the other women. Lord knows I don't need to be tangled up in Ryder Bates more than I already am.

But when he softens his gaze, letting go of the rough exterior he wears like a badge, I feel my resolve slipping.

"One dance," he whispers.

Apparently, that's all it takes.

I don't wait this time. I only nod, take his hand, and let him lead me to the dance floor.

As if someone is playing a cruel joke on me, the band plays the opening notes of "Yesterday" by The Beatles.

I hadn't noticed until now that we garner significant attention from those around us. I have no doubt their fascination is for the man whose hand leads me through the crowd. The air that surrounds Ryder is thick with an authority that they can't figure out.

While their attention stirs the nerves I thought I had a handle on, Ryder is the picture of perfect confidence. It's as if he can't feel the hundreds of eyes that seem to follow our every move.

When we reach the center of the floor, one of his hands splays across my lower back, pulling me into him as I wrap an arm over his neck. Our other hands meet, and we interlace our fingers with ease.

I clear my throat of the nerves that clog it. "So, what's all this about?"

"I'm not sure I know what you're referring to."

I begin to roll my eyes but stop when I remember that we continue to draw a lot of attention.

"I didn't take you for a dancer," I say as nonchalantly as possible.

He deliberates for a moment before answering, "We're keeping up appearances."

I huff at that but don't say anything.

We dance in perfect time to the music, and I admire Ryder's ability to lead, though I'm sure he's never done it before. That's just how Ryder is. He can step into any role, and even if he has no idea what he's doing, he'll make it seem like he was born to do it.

As we dance, I begin to relax, the same way I always do when I'm held in Ryder's arms. There's nothing careful or thoughtful about how my body moves as I let the music and Ryder guide me. I don't have to worry about stepping on his toes or how we're perceived by the crowd, and I relish in this moment of blissful silence.

I hadn't noticed how closely he leaned in until his words are spoken directly into my ear.

"You look absolutely stunning tonight," he whispers, and I tighten my hold on him.

"So you've mentioned."

It's the first thing he said when I walked down the stairs earlier this evening.

"Not enough."

"Well, thank you," I say, and drop my eyes to our feet, focusing on how we move together and not on how my stomach is nearly bursting with butterflies.

Butterflies? Really?

Still, I can't look up and risk him seeing how much those words affect me. How much *he* affects me.

"Why am I here?" I ask, still unable to meet his gaze.

"What do you mean?"

"Why did you ask me to come with you tonight?"

"I told you—"

"It's not because of Lyla. We could've done different things tonight and still let her go to my parents."

He pauses for only a moment. "I wouldn't want to be the only one without a date, now would I?"

"Your ego can handle it. Or you could've found another date," I say, ashamed of how much I dislike that idea.

A long moment passes, and I think he won't answer me at all, but his forehead touches mine, shooting a wave of excitement and nerves straight to my core. He pushes until I have no choice but to roll my head up and meet his gaze head-on.

In this position, we're so close that our noses are almost touching, and our lips are a breath away.

"Is it so hard to believe I want to spend time with you?"

"Ryder, be serious—"

"I am serious, Rebel. I wouldn't want to be here—or anywhere for that matter—with anyone else."

It feels like my heart beats louder than the music, and I get so lost in his eyes that I feel like I could just fall right into them.

Our bodies slow but don't stop when the song fades out. We're chest to chest, holding onto each other with a grip like the other is our only hope of survival. Like if we let go, we'll never recover from the damage.

Right now, I can believe that things went differently three years ago. I can imagine that Ryder is my safety net, source of comfort, and steady anchor. I can imagine that being this close to him is a luxury I have every day and not every few years.

I can imagine that he's mine.

But he isn't, and that realization brings me back to earth. The tingles that jolt through my fingertips go still, the heat of his skin on mine burns with shame, and the excitement of our closeness thickens to guilt with the gravity of the reality check.

I believed that he was mine once, and I barely recovered.

With that thought, I release my hold on him and step back, hating the emptiness I'm left with. I expect to see surprise or maybe even hurt when I look up, but Ryder's face is set in its usual neutral expression.

Well, if he can turn off his emotions so easily, then I can, too.

I force a smile and nod in the direction of the bar.

"If you'll excuse me," I say, leaving before he can object. I'm halfway to the bar when I feel his presence coming from behind me, but when I turn, the stress eases when a large man steps in Ryder's path, stealing his attention. Before I turn back to the bar, I catch Ryder's gaze, which clearly says we need to talk.

This whole night was a huge mistake.

I should've known Ryder would pull something like this. He wants me, but not enough to put me first. I can't act like this is some surprise. I've always known where his priorities lay, but I refuse to settle for second place.

Third, when including Lyla.

I'm walking—vodka martini in hand—back to where the capos' dates are chatting when I'm struck with that sickening feeling of being watched.

My skin crawls, and I can't help my need to cross my arms over my body like I can somehow protect it from this invisible scrutiny. Like every other time this feeling has hit, I scan my surroundings for anything that could be the source.

Unlike every other time, I find an answer.

Harris talks animatedly to Knox, who doesn't appear to be listening, but the man who stands with them turns his attention to me.

Briggs.

He's glaring daggers, and I can't, for the life of me, understand his reason for sending such hostility my way.

He looks away as soon as our eyes meet, and it's then that I realize I've stopped walking. I glance around to ensure Ryder is still occupied, then continue my walk to the other women when I confirm that he is.

Ava goes on about some antique shop she frequents, but I can barely hear her. I find myself sneaking glances at Briggs, who doesn't appear to notice or doesn't let on if he does.

I'm about to force myself to stop after just one last glance, but he isn't there when my eyes flash to the capos.

I find him only a moment later, moving through the crowd and sending quick glances around as if ensuring he's going unnoticed. Even the other capos seem oblivious to Briggs's disappearance, and the feeling that settles in the pit of my stomach demands that I do something about it.

My fingers unconsciously grip the charm around my neck.

I am not helpless. I am not weak.

These are the words I repeat to myself on a loop as I navigate through the crowd, careful to keep sight of Briggs as he presses on in front of me. He walks through a set of old double doors, turning left toward what's labeled *The Mirror Hall.*

There's hardly anyone in this area, and they all seem to be interested in the bathrooms located nearby, so none of them bother looking my way as I wander down the deserted hall in the direction Briggs had to have taken.

The floors are white marble, with gold-crested pillars on either side of the walkway. The further I walk, the louder the clicking of my heels becomes, so I pause to pull them off my feet. With my heels in one hand, clutch in the other, I tiptoe down the hall.

I reach the end of the hall, where it breaks in either direction, but when I hear voices murmuring, I quickly duck into a room with its door cracked open. I almost close it but decide I don't want to make any noise if I can help it.

When I turn to see what room I've ended up in, my muscles freeze, my blood runs cold, and my lungs refuse to pull in air.

The room is small, but one wall is entirely made of glass, giving a clear view into the large, mirror-filled room with half a dozen men lining the walls, all holding a large gun I couldn't name. Two more men stand in the center of the room.

One of them is big, maybe seven feet tall, and has a scruffy beard, bald head, and nasty scowl. The other man is Briggs, who, though he's shorter, shows no sign of being intimidated.

"You better start talking because I won't stand for my time to be wasted," Briggs spits.

I wait, frozen in fear for one of them to notice my unwanted presence, but no one so much as glances my way. When none of them —even the soldiers who have a clear line of sight to me—do, I take a closer look at the room I'm in.

My view into the mirrored room is only that of a large pane, and the tinted glass, paired with the fact that no one seems to be able to see me, finally makes it click.

It's a one-way mirror.

I can see them, but they can't see me.

My relief is minimal and lessens even more so when Tall Guy puffs his chest at Briggs. "Sheriff's department is cracking down on the substance control in my crew's territory. You're going to have to up our profit to make it worth the risk we're taking to sell your products."

Briggs' laugh is nothing short of bone-chilling. "You knew the risks when you agreed to take this job in the first place. You'll get paid the exact amount we agreed on."

"That's not going to be enough for my guys."

"That's not my problem."

Tall Guy cracks a taunting smile. "I didn't want it to come to this,

126

but if you're not going to raise our profit, my guys may be inclined to work *with* the Sheriff's department for immunity if they feel they're in danger of being made."

With that, he walks to the door right next to the one I went through, just on the other side, meaning he's walking in my direction.

Briggs doesn't move after him, but as Tall Guy nears one of the soldiers by the exit, one wave of Briggs' hand is all they need to spring into action. Two of the soldiers move in sync, each grabbing one of Tall Guy's shoulders and slamming his head into the pane of glass less than a foot away from me.

It happens so fast that I jump back with a screeching yelp.

Only the sound never passes my lips, thanks to the hand that covers my mouth.

My eyes bulge, and my stomach sinks with horror at what I've gotten myself into when a certain scent creeps into my nostrils.

Pineapple and bergamot.

Ryder.

His arms trap me, and I'm too shocked by the slam against the mirror to fight against him. I watch in stunned silence as Briggs slowly trudges toward Tall Guy, dazed by the blow to his head. As Briggs walks, he takes out his handgun from a holster, his blazer concealed, and I realize that each of the capos likely came here armed.

"Did you really think you could just come in here and wave your threats around?" Briggs asks, cruel amusement dripping from the words.

With a jerk of his head, the soldiers kick Tall Guy's legs from behind, so he falls to his knees. They take one of his hands and spread it flat on the ground.

"You know, I'm feeling generous today, so I'm going to show a bit of mercy. If you start groveling now, I might *consider* letting you live."

"You—you can't kill me!" Tall Guy insists, but his voice is void of all confidence.

In one fast motion, Briggs lowers himself to the ground and slams the butt of his gun on one of the man's fingers.

"Close your eyes," Ryder whispers in my ear at the same time the man's wail pierces the otherwise silent room.

I don't think twice. I just do as Ryder says and squeeze my eyes closed like my life depends on it.

The next ten minutes are straight out of a horror film.

Briggs takes his time crushing each one of Tall Guy's fingers, then moves on to breaking his nose before pummeling his face until the groaning becomes sobbing pleads. He only lets the man go once he's begged for his life and agrees to cut their current rate in half.

"We're Morenos, and you're nothing. Remember that," Briggs clips, then I hear the shuffling of footsteps grow faint as the room clears.

I don't open my eyes when everything goes silent. I don't open my eyes when Ryder releases me. I don't even open my eyes when I hear the door of the small room click shut.

It's only when I feel Ryder's hands pushing me against the wall, trapping me between it and his body, that I finally open my eyes.

And wish I hadn't.

Any relief I felt from not being discovered by Briggs vanishes the moment my eyes meet Ryder's.

Storm clouds.

No, storm clouds are nothing compared to the fury I'm staring into.

This is a hurricane right before the apocalypse and the end of the freaking world.

It doesn't help that we're even closer now than we'd been on the dance floor. He's no longer dominating my space. He is my space. Everything around me fades, and there is nothing but Ryder.

"What the *actual fuck* were you thinking?" he grinds out each word slowly, letting the brutal bite sink in with every syllable. "Do you have any idea what could've happened if they'd heard you? Do you want our daughter to grow up without her mother?"

How dare he throw Lyla in my face as if *I'm* the reckless one between us.

"Don't act like any of the danger I've been in is the result of my own choices. If it's so dangerous for me to be here, why the hell would you bring me?"

He props his elbows against the wall on either side of me, biceps flexing as he invades my space even more somehow. "It wouldn't have been dangerous if you'd stayed with the women like you were supposed to. You almost compromised a mission that's been in the works for weeks now."

"Mission?"

He shoves off the wall so suddenly that I gasp at the loss of closeness. He turns his back to me, rubbing his temple with his thumb and taking long, deep breaths.

I can't help how my gaze flits between him and the door as I mentally calculate how far I can get before he catches me. My heels are already off, so I don't have to worry about that.

"Don't even think about it," Ryder snaps.

I swear I didn't say anything out loud. How the hell did he know?

I roll back my shoulders, trying to summon as much bravery as possible. "What's going on, Ryder?"

He only shakes his head.

"You know, I wouldn't be able to ruin a mission if you didn't keep me in the dark all the damn time," I scoff and go to the door.

A hand slams against it the second I touch the knob, and I don't attempt to pull it open. We stand like that for a moment, Ryder's front pressing into my back.

"A particularly violent gang under our family has been demanding higher pay. As you saw, they went so far as to threaten us. They needed to be put in their place."

I replay what I heard, and it fits what Ryder's telling me now.

"Briggs was charged with handling it while Harris and Knox ran security outside. I was supposed to be keeping an eye on the party to make sure no one went to the Sheriff or his team before we got to the gang, which I couldn't do because I saw you wander after Briggs. Why the hell would you follow him in the first place?"

"I just, I had this feeling—"

"You put your life on the line for a *feeling*?"

The pure mockery flushes my cheeks bright red, and I shove at Ryder's chest. "My life was perfectly safe, thank you very much," I bite and quickly distinguish the best way to describe the instincts that landed me here. "And yes, I had a feeling that Briggs was harboring—I don't know...hostility toward me. Toward you."

To my amazement, Ryder actually laughs. It's far from his genuine laughter, but it's the nicest sound I've heard since coming in here.

"Briggs despises me, but he's too loyal to do anything against the family."

"How the hell was I supposed to know—"

One second, there are several feet between us. The next, Ryder's body traps mine against the walls, and his hand clamps over my mouth. My eyes flash, and I'm about to struggle to hell and back when I hear faint footsteps in the hall.

"No, Sir," a muffled voice grunts. "I'm positive. He's been quite distracted tonight." With each word, he gets closer until I'm sure

129

Briggs is the voice's source.

"Yes, Sir," he says, and since no one responds, I decide he must be on a phone call.

The next words come from directly outside the door Ryder has me pressed against. "The mother of his kid. He brought her along as his date."

Ryder goes rigid, and his confusion mirrors my own for only a fraction of a second before the realization settles in.

Briggs is talking about Ryder. About us.

"They might've left," he says, voice growing more distant as he continues to walk, but we hear the next statement clear as day. "The other capos don't have eyes on them, but my men have secured the back. It'll be a safe meeting place as soon as you get here to take the package."

There's a last muffled, "Yes, Sir," before we can no longer hear his footsteps or words.

CHAPTER EIGHTEEN

Ryder

What the actual fuck did I just hear?

Maybe I can rationalize it as a drop-off Briggs never told me about, but if that were the case, he wouldn't be talking about me. So what the hell is this *package*?

I slowly ease off of Rachel and take a few steps back. My mind is racing with possibilities, but they all center around one possibility...

"What was that about?" Rachel whispers.

"It doesn't matter. I'll handle it."

"Handle what exactly? It sounds like Briggs is out to get you."

"And if he is, it's none of your business. I will handle it."

When I turn, I'm not prepared for the level of ferocity Rachel's glare directs at me. "None of my business? Ryder, I heard him myself. He was talking about you!"

I place one hand on either of her shoulders and level her with a glare of my own. "I. Will. Handle. It."

She shoves me away with one hand while the other fiddles with the bulky charm on her necklace.

"You have no idea how infuriating it is to always be in the dark with you. I'm just trying to move on from all the shit I've already gone through because of you, but you barge into my life and make moving on impossible! Then I see Briggs glaring at me before slipping away, and I follow him because I can't help but wonder if he's the leak finishing what Mason started! These aren't things I want to think about, Ryder! I want a *normal* life with *normal* issues! I didn't ask for any of this. The least you can do is give me some peace of mind and not keep me in the dark all the time!"

She's heaving by the time she's finished her monologue, and though she said a lot that likely needs to be unpacked, I ignore all but one part.

"How do you know about that?" I ask, my voice controlled but loaded with authority.

She freezes, the realization of what she's revealed hitting her full force. She tries to meet my gaze, but my eyes are firmly locked on her hand, which still clings to the heart-shaped charm.

"Know what?" she asks, but I don't believe her act for a second.

"You said, *leak*. How do you know we're looking for a leak associated with Mason Consoli?"

"I didn't—I don't—" She drops her hands to her side and straightens her back with a pathetic show of bravery.

Without her hand in the way, I have a clear view of the charm, or rather, the barely noticeable line that runs diagonally across it.

"Is that your final answer?"

She says nothing in her defense, and her features lose all bravado.

My hand snakes forward before she has the chance to piece together my objective, and I rip the chain from her neck with a firm snap. With the flick of my thumb, the charm splits in two, revealing the thumb drive hidden inside.

"I can explain," Rachel breathes, but it's barely audible.

I shove the charm into my pocket. "And you sure as hell will, but first..."

The speed with which I grip Rachel's hips and haul her into me gives her no time to react, let alone resist, as I crush my lips to hers, and when I say "crush," I mean it. This isn't one of the sweet, tender kisses we've shared in the past. This is rough, animalistic, with the passion of the anger she's inspired by keeping who-knows-what from me.

With one hand on her hip, I keep her firmly pressed to me and use my other hand to tug her neat ponytail, so she's forced to angle her head up, giving me more leverage over her.

As I take out my frustration on those beautiful lips, Rachel's reaction isn't lost on me. Not one bit.

Her hands, which were pressing to my chest to hold me back, now clutch my jacket like her life depends on it. She kisses me like she has just as much anger harbored as I do, and I wonder if that is the case.

Just as suddenly as I take her lips, I pull away.

She opens her mouth, no doubt to question me, but I've already grabbed her hand and begun pulling her from the room. She barely has time to grab her shoes and bag from the floor before we're in the hall.

"What the hell was that?" she asks, pulling me to stop as she slides her heels back on her feet.

"Our alibi," I answer in a voice void of emotion, and for the first time in years, I have to work to achieve that tone because I am most certainly *not* void of emotion.

Not one damn bit.

The combination of my rage toward her and my need *for* her is a violent torrent that demands a release that I cannot give. So instead, I keep a cool mask over my features and remind myself that punching a hole through the wall of the city's art museum will only make things worse.

We're about to enter the main room when I tug her to my side, wrapping a possessive arm around her waist.

"Let me do the talking."

"What are you going to say?"

"It'll be more alluding than saying."

She ponders that for only a moment before tensing with realization. "You're going to make them think we—but we didn't."

"Trust me, I fucking know," I grunt, discreetly adjusting my pants to hide the evidence of my dissatisfaction.

"Why do we need an alibi?"

"Because we can't let Briggs know we heard anything. Just stay quiet, and look dazed." I look down, noting her smudged lipstick, disheveled ponytail, and wide, glossed-over eyes. "Yeah, just like that."

Those eyes narrow but keep their addled fog.

Rachel clings to my arm, and I'm not sure if it's part of the act or if the last hour's events have taken a toll on her. Either way, I tuck her protectively into my side as we approach the capos and their dates in the same place they'd been when we'd arrived.

"Rachel! There you are," Ava calls enthusiastically. "Where have you been?"

The others take in the messy hair and wrinkled blazer with skeptical eyes. If our appearance isn't enough to convince them, Rachel's clouded eyes and hand gripping my arm for dear life certainly do the trick.

"We were having a look around. You know, the bathrooms are

incredibly spacious," I say casually, dropping my hand dangerously low on Rachel's hip. "Unfortunately, we must be getting home to our daughter. It was nice seeing you all."

The knowing eyes that scan our appearance as each capo and their date bid us farewell only add to Rachel's embarrassment and—thankfully—the validity of our excuse.

We sit in thick, restless silence the entire drive home.

I want to push Rachel to talk as soon as we get in the car, but I don't trust my ability to control my temper—an issue I have never had before—so I don't.

We pick up Lyla from Rachel's parents, and she falls asleep in the back seat, giving Rachel an excuse to keep quiet.

I still can't believe I didn't notice that the bulky, charm that's been a permanent fixture around Rachel's neck the last two weeks was a thumb drive. I assumed it was a tacky gift from her mother.

I can guess without confirmation what I'll find on the drive. After all, the information she knows isn't public, even to soldiers within the family. The leak is a secret that only the capos of the Moreno and Consoli family are privy to.

What else does she know? And how the hell does she know it?

I swear, if Elli has been telling her things, I'll rat her out to Moreno, who will take her out of her capo position as fast as he put her in it.

We pull into the driveway, and Rachel is out of the car before it's parked. She pulls Lyla from her seat and carries her inside without sparing me a glance.

I turn the car off and make my way around the house, straight to my pool house. After a speedy shower, I throw on a pair of sweats and a tee before making my way inside, thumb drive clasped in my tight fist.

I settle in the desk chair of the office and wait.

Only a few minutes later, she walks in, hair falling loose over her shoulders. She's traded her gown for a sweatshirt and a pair of black shorts, all traces of makeup wiped away from her naturally flawless face.

She doesn't say anything as she closes the door and settles on the chaise against the wall. We sit in thick silence, and it isn't long before she gives in to it.

"It started the day we got home from L.A.," she starts, elbows resting on her knees and eyes downcast. "I took the week off work, but had to answer a few urgent emails, so I set up the desktop at the hotel. When I logged on, it was open to a program I didn't recognize. I wasn't trying to snoop. I really wasn't."

When her eyes meet mine, shining with honesty, I realize my mistake.

For fuck's sake.

I bury my face in my hands. "I didn't log out of the database."

I came to visit Lyla a few weeks ago when Moreno was working from his house in Redding. The trip had been brief, but he sent over files I had to look through during my stay here, and I didn't log off when I was done.

Rachel nods.

"I rarely use that computer, but since I was working from home, I had to. I was going to exit out of everything, but then you got a message with all the notes from the capo meeting you had about the factory night." She shakes her head like she's trying to rid herself of memories. "I wasn't sleeping, and I was barely eating. My anxiety was so bad. When I saw that message come in, I didn't think twice before opening it, and Ryder...." She levels me with an earnest gaze. "I don't regret it. There was so much information there that you never told me, like how the Consoli family is working to uncover how Mason communicated with his followers and that the Moreno family is working to find the leak in resources that Mason was taking advantage of.

"I had more peace after reading that message than I'd had in days...but then it became, well, an addiction." She gestures to the thumb drive. "I started compiling everything I found onto the thumb drive, so any time I got anxious, I'd just go through it and add anything from the database that could've related."

"Do you have *any* idea how dangerous this is?" I shake the charm for emphasis. "This information could put a huge target on your back. If Moreno found out about this, he could have you *killed*, Rachel."

She opens her mouth, but I cut her off.

"And this doesn't just affect you. What about Lyla? Or me? I'm already walking on thin ice. I'd lose my place in the family and maybe my life, too."

Rachel pushes to her feet. "I didn't do it to get anyone in trouble. I did it because when I feel helpless, like someone is watching me, or like I'm unable to protect my daughter, it's the only thing that can calm me down! You have no idea what it was like seeing those men hurt

Lyla. Wouldn't you be searching for some sort of comfort that it won't happen again? That's what this thumb drive is for me."

"What do you mean by feeling like you're being watched?"

Rachel closes her eyes with a resigned sigh as she falls back into the chaise.

"Is this about the black truck?"

She nods but refuses to open her eyes or answer.

"Was that day the first time you'd seen the truck?"

She nods again, and I think I'm on the wrong track until she adds, "But it was the third time I felt someone watching me."

If I thought I couldn't get angrier, I was wrong. The riot of violent urges is jarring enough that I almost crush the charm in the palm of my hand. I have never been so furious with someone, with myself, with *the fucking world.*

"Why is this the first time I'm hearing about this?" I ask through gritted teeth.

"Why is this the first time you've asked?" she snaps, eyes sparking with her own fiery indignation. "I was in a car chase last week, and you never asked a damn question about it."

I clench and unclench my jaw, and I'm not sure what it is that gives me away, but she sucks in a sharp breath.

"You didn't believe me," she whispers.

"I did believe you," I correct, and raise a placating hand. "But I thought it might've inspired some paranoia after I pushed you during our training session."

The look of dejection on Rachel's face finally breaks through the flames of my wrath, cooling them to a simmering dread.

"I looked into it, but when I didn't find any evidence that someone was chasing you, I figured it was some punk kid. How long have you felt like you were being watched?"

She doesn't look at me. "Will you believe me if I tell you?"

I'm across the room in two strides, lowering to her eye level and covering her hands—which try to repeatedly pop her knuckles—with my own.

"Of course, I'll believe you. I'm sorry I didn't press for answers before."

She must hear the sincerity in the words because she finally looks at me. She looks so beautiful that I have to force myself to return to the desk chair. If I don't put space between us, I'll take her lips as savagely as I had at the gala.

Only this time, I won't stop.

"The first time was after Lyla's appointment with Dr. Danver. Then it happened at the grocery store, and taking Lyla home from martial arts, which was when we were followed. I never noticed the truck itself until it was following us. Before that, I just had this really…disturbing feeling of being watched. I thought I felt it again tonight when Briggs was looking at me, which is why I followed him."

I take long breaths to suppress why frustration with the situation and focus on analyzing the potential implications of what she's said.

"Do you think it has anything to do with what we heard from Briggs tonight? I mean, if he was talking about you, is it possible he could be watching me?"

"I don't have enough information to make assumptions, but the timing is strange," I say with a shake of my head. "I'm going to handle this. I don't want you worrying about any of it."

The look of utter absurdity she gives me would be comical under different circumstances.

"You're about four years too late for that," she says flatly. "You're not just kicking me out of this."

"I am, actually. This is family business, and you don't need to be involved."

"Trust me when I say *I wish* that were true, but it isn't. I'm tied to this family whether you like it or not."

For fuck's sake.

If I keep Rachel involved, I'm risking my position in this family, not to mention her safety. But if I say no, I can't guarantee she won't go behind my back and continue her research unchecked. Not to mention I'd be depriving her of the only source of peace she's clung to since the factory night.

Cutting her out is better in the long run. It may be hard at first, but she'll find comfort in other things. We'll keep training, and I can have a security team assigned to her and Lyla. Anything to help her feel safe again. Then she won't have incriminating information that could get her in trouble with Moreno or other families if they think she'll be a valuable source of information.

Even as my brain comes to its conclusion, another—certainly dumber—organ has other ideas.

Maybe it's the mesmerizing eyes that are pleading with me. Maybe it's the way she's curling into herself as if preparing for the blow of my impending rejection. Or maybe it's the fact that my lips still taste of *her*.

"We do this. We do it my way. Whatever I say goes, and if you deviate from my instruction, I will cut you out. Understand?"

My words bring her physical relief. She sags her shoulders, and for a moment, I wonder if I see a glisten of wetness in her eyes. Of course, she doesn't let a single tear fall.

"I mean it, Rachel. There will be no going behind my back and no going rogue."

"Fine, but you can't hide things from me, either. When it comes to anything Mason-related, I have a right to know."

I press my lips into a hard line, deliberating this request. I understand why she'll want this, but I can't agree to unrestricted, unlimited access. I need to reserve the right to withhold whatever information I deem necessary.

I lower my head in a gesture that could be received as a nod. "I'll tell you anything you need to know."

She doesn't catch my careful wording, or perhaps she realizes that's more than I would normally allow. Either way, she accepts it.

We each stand, an arm outstretched for the handshake that will seal our deal. I walk until I'm invading her space, just like I have so many times tonight, and I wonder if it'll ever feel close enough.

I doubt it.

CHAPTER NINETEEN

Rachel

22 Weeks Along

"I'm really trying to understand the point of these shows, but I can't. I've seen some fucked up shit, but this is just *disturbing*," Alec says.

"Got to say." Donovan shares Alec's distasteful expression. "I agree. What do you even like about this stuff?"

I laugh because the irony is just too much to ignore. "It's interesting. I mean, the actual acts are gruesome, yeah, but the thought process behind it all is interesting. You guys are just being babies. Kade isn't complaining."

We all look to Kade, who occupies the chair while the rest of us share the couch. His face remains stoic as he answers, "I'm with the guys on this one. True crime as entertainment is twisted."

"I'm sorry, remind me again what it is you all do for a living?"

All of them open their mouths, no doubt, to list the differences between their jobs and these shows, but none of them gets the chance. The cabin door opens, and Ryder steps inside, slicing through the comfortable atmosphere and replacing it with stuffy tension.

Donovan clears his throat. "We better get going. We'll see you tomorrow, Rachel." He stands, and Alec and Kade do the same.

I wave goodbye but don't look away from Ryder.

The boys make their way to the door, mumbling, "See you later, Ride-her," as they go.

Usually, the nickname would amuse me, but not now.

"I'll be back after the appointment," Alec says, but Ryder shakes his head.

"Don't bother. I'm staying in tonight," he answers, and I almost huff.

Guess I'll be spending the evening in my room.

The door shuts behind them, leaving me alone with Ryder.

Alec has spent every day with me since I moved here, but Donovan and Kade only started joining him regularly last week. He says it's because they have nothing else to do, but I know better. These are mafia capos, after all. There's no way they're short on work to do. Alec started bringing them because he noticed that Ryder and I hadn't talked in two weeks.

Aside from asking about the baby, our communication is nonexistent.

A few days ago, when Kade and Donovan didn't realize I could hear them from the kitchenette, I heard them mention something about the *M.A.C. Project.* They didn't say anything about the project itself, only that Ryder had been in the minority by voting against it. They'd speculated that it could be the reason he was in such a dark mood two weeks ago, but I don't let myself accept that as an excuse for his behavior. I don't care what projects do or don't happen at the base. I deserve a level of attention and respect that Ryder has refused me.

I'd considered leaving that night, but to go where?

So, I started putting a plan together.

Finishing my degree virtually is still the best option, so the real concern is finding a place to stay and a job I can balance with my school at a reasonable stress level. Crashing on my parent's couch is only a temporary solution, so I've kept an eye on available apartments back home. The hardest part is finding a job that fits my needs. I haven't nailed down anything yet, but so far, my options seem to be delivering for an on-demand food app or stretching the truth on my resume to get a job as a receptionist.

I've even looked up plane tickets home, and the cheapest one leaves in three days.

The night of our fight, leaving had seemed like the only option, but now that so much time has passed, it feels more like a bitter obligation to go. I mean, how can I spend the next several months living under the same roof as a man who will barely look at me, let alone talk to me?

It's not like he's fighting very hard to keep me here.

"How are you feeling today?" he asks, with a formality that fits the stifling air.

I give him a small, forced smile. "Fine."

He nods once, angling toward the door. "Are you ready to go?"

My hands automatically go to my stomach, which flips in excitement. I may not be the biggest fan of my present company, but I won't let that ruin today. As a matter of fact, I'm not sure anything *can* ruin this day.

Today, we'll be learning the gender of our child.

Ryder opens the passenger door for me and helps me inside before driving us the short distance between our cabin and the base.

When it came time to find a doctor in this area, I wanted to *go* to a doctor's office, like any other person would, but Ryder didn't like that idea. He wants an on-call private doctor to work out of the base's infirmary.

The compromise was that I'd choose my doctor, and Ryder would buy them out. It's a complete waste of money, in my opinion, but since it's not my money, I didn't fight him on it.

We don't speak for the entire ride, and I don't wait for him to open my door once we're parked, which earns me a narrow-eyed look that I ignore. I don't know the base's layout well, but I do know where the infirmary is, so I don't wait for Ryder to lead me as we make our way there.

We get to Dr. Cane's office, and I change into the gown provided to me while Ryder waits outside the room.

When I'm ready, I unlock the door, and Ryder takes that as an invitation to join me. We don't say anything as we take our seats, his on the wooden chair by the door, mine on the examination table.

Right on time, Dr. Cane steps into the room, his graying hair and soft smile firmly in place.

I'd tried to find a female doctor, if for no other reason than to give the middle finger to the male-dominated organization, but in the end, I chose Dr. Cane. He was one of my favorite candidates—with an excellent record and even more impressive bedside manner—and in the end, I didn't want to force any woman into this environment.

"Miss Lance, how are you feeling?" he asks, wrinkles creasing his fifty-six-year-old face in a welcoming smile.

I return the warmth with my own grin, and it's the first time the expression has come naturally since Alec, Donovan, and Kade left. "I'm a little more sore than normal, and my heartburn has been getting worse, but other than that, I'm feeling good."

He nods, turning the monitor on and preparing his equipment. I try not to look at Ryder, though I can feel his gaze on me, no doubt frustrated that I hadn't answered his same question as thoroughly as I answered the doctor.

Dr. Cane washes his hands and slides on a pair of gloves. "You ready?"

"Very," I tell him.

"Then let's get started."

He squirts the jelly onto my stomach, and my heart leaps when the static-filled screen comes alive as the transducer meets my swollen belly.

I'm mesmerized as the screen moves with the remote, though I can't make out a damn thing on the black-and-white screen.

Maybe that concentration is why I don't notice Ryder coming closer until the heat of him covers my side, bringing with it a comfort I didn't realize I needed.

When I turn to look at him, my breath catches at the sight of him on his knees at my side. Lowered this way, our eyes are leveled, and his are softer than I ever remember seeing them. He doesn't say anything, but when he lifts one hand, he says more with the gesture than he ever has with words.

His palm hovers next to mine, a question dancing behind the deep, brown eyes that I'm content to lose myself in. I can't explain why, but it feels so natural to lift my hand and place it in his. It's the first time we've touched—*really* touched—in weeks, and I think back to how we'd touched far more than this before we found out about the baby.

Back then, we hadn't known anything about each other but moved together so naturally, like it was all we ever knew, and I wonder if the physical intimacy is what's missing now. Maybe we're having a hard time getting to know each other because we took away the one part of our relationship that was truly effortless.

It's a dangerous way to think, but it makes me squeeze his hand just a little bit tighter as if I can commit this feeling of safety to memory so I never forget what it feels like to be touched by him.

"Mr. Bates, Miss Lance, are you ready to learn the sex of your child?" Dr. Cane asks.

Neither Ryder nor I bother to move our gazes from each other like we're unwilling to risk losing the understanding we seem to have formed.

"Yes," we say in unison.

"Congratulations. You're having a baby girl."

I close my eyes with a face-splitting smile, and warm lips gently kiss my forehead. It's a moment of complete and utter joy that eases itself into my memory and soul. I truly would've been happy with either gender, but knowing I have a little baby girl growing inside me now fills me with so much happiness.

"Thank you, Dr. Cane. Would you mind giving us some privacy?" Ryder's low voice asks, and I hear the doctor's murmured agreement before the door closes.

When I open my eyes, I'm faced with Ryder's brilliant smile, and the sight of it, mixed with the news of our having a girl, brings one word to mind.

Perfect.

We don't say anything, just bask in the light atmosphere after so many days of tense interactions. Slowly, like he doesn't know it's happening, Ryder's smile fades as he stands. He takes a rag from the counter and begins to wipe the gel from my stomach with a gentleness that would suggest I'm made of glass.

His eyes never waver from my stomach, but mine are trained on his every movement. The pure joy we shared just seconds ago wanes as his expression turns neutral, and I hate it.

And I hate that I hate it.

"I never meant to isolate you," he finally says, setting the rag down and picking up a new one. He wets it and wipes my stomach clear of any remnant of gel, and there's something so intimate about the level of care he's taking.

"Bringing you here wasn't a way to trap you, and the last thing I want is for you to regret coming with me. I want you to enjoy staying here." Once it's clean and dry, Ryder rests a tender hand over my stomach. "You were right. I haven't taken the time for us to get to know each other, but it was never because I don't want to."

"Then, why?" I ask on a breath.

There's a long pause, so long that I wonder if he's going to answer me at all, but when I study him—*really* gaze into that seemingly natural face—I see it for the mask that it is. I see the war raging behind guarded eyes, the tension ticking in supposedly resting lips, and I understand.

Ryder never meant to cut me out.

He just never knew how to let me in.

He's never had to make himself vulnerable for someone.

"My dad left before I was born," he says quietly, confirming my theory. "It was always just Mom and me. She struggled financially, which is why I joined this family. For the first time in my life, we were provided for, but it was so much more than that. I found purpose, a place where I belonged. A *family*." He sets the rag on the counter then stands at my side, returning his hand to my stomach.

"My mom passed away a few years ago, and I had this family to fall back on, but now…now, I can't stop thinking about how you'll take the baby back to Sacramento once she's born. I'll have a daughter, and she'll be raised four hundred miles away from me. I've had a difficult time coming to terms with that, which is part of the reason I've kept a distance."

"And the other part?"

His eyes catch mine with no hint of the neutrality I've come to hate. Instead, that gaze narrows like I'm missing something painfully obvious to him.

"Rachel, you're pregnant from a man you barely know, who moved you to a new city and turned out to be a mafia underboss. Is it so surprising that I gave you space to adjust to your circumstances?"

Space to adjust.

He'd given me space to adjust.

All this time, I thought he wanted nothing to do with me when, in reality, he didn't want to overwhelm me. When I'd waited for him to show some sign of interest, he'd waited for me to show some sign of comfort, of readiness.

"I didn't think about it like that," I admit. "I just—I thought you didn't want anything to do with me. That you only brought me here out of obligation."

He breathes out a sound that would imply my logic is anything but. "I've already taken so much from you. The least I could do was allow you to set the terms of our relationship."

I wonder what it is he thinks he's taken from me. If he thinks I mourn the loss of my youth, cut short with impending motherhood. If he thinks I miss my friends who are off living their dreams. If he thinks I long for the city I've called home my whole life. And though some of those could be true—to an extent—I wonder if he realizes just how much he's given me.

A daughter whose arrival I can hardly wait for. A safe home without the burden of financial strain. The opportunity to focus on my degree and health with minimal distractions.

The only thing he has truly taken from me is himself, and I didn't realize just how much that meant to me until recently.

So, I decide I'll take him up on the offer to set the terms of this relationship. "Friends."

"You want to be friends?" he asks with a faint but genuine smile.

I nod. "We skipped that part, and it seems like the best place to start if we want to get to know each other."

"Then friends it is," he confirms, then clears his throat. "But, there is one more thing. I need to ask you a favor."

"What kind of favor?"

His smile falters, and for the first time, I see nervousness, and hesitance, in the man who always seems so much larger than life itself. "I need you to consider staying after she's born. Maybe not forever, but long enough for me to form a relationship with her, too."

Just last night I was looking up plane tickets to fly home. I'd been preparing to figure out this whole *parenting* thing on my own.

Now, only hours later, I find myself considering a completely different future, one where L.A. becomes my home for more than the duration of this pregnancy.

"I'll think about it," I tell him.

And it should scare me that a part of me already wants to agree.

CHAPTER TWENTY

Rachel

Present

"We're getting nowhere," I grumble, taking another still-warm paper from the printer and setting it out on the floor.

Ryder doesn't even glance up from his laptop as he continues printing record after record. "These things aren't always a quick find."

"But we don't even know what 'these things' are."

"Or if 'these things' exist," he agrees.

I shoot him an annoyed look that makes him chuckle.

Glad someone's amused.

It's only been three days since the gala, so I suppose I shouldn't be surprised that we haven't figured anything out yet, but it's still discouraging. I guess I thought whatever it is we were looking for would have become obvious by now, but it hasn't.

Ryder only spent a few hours going through my thumb drive before he moved on since it's all information he already knew. Now we're going through the Sacramento database, printing damn near every file submitted over the last two months, and laying them out around the room, which is a horrific mess.

When I asked how the hell this is supposed to show us anything, Ryder just shrugged and said that spreading it all out would be better than scrolling on a screen over and over again.

We only work a few hours at a time, between when I get off work and when Ryder leaves to go…well, I actually don't know where it is that he goes at night. I suspect the base or maybe one of the clubs in the area that the family owns, but he's never told me as much, and I haven't asked. As it is, the lines between us have blurred to an almost non-distinguishable point, especially after the gala.

We never talked about the kiss or the fact that he let the capos and their dates assume we'd slipped from the party to hook up. I'm not sure why I expected him to bring it up so we could clear the air and re-establish boundaries, but he hasn't, and neither have I.

If he wants to pretend it never happened, that's fine by me.

Aside from an hour-long training session yesterday, all our interactions since the gala have either been about taking care of Lyla or going through the files.

I look around the room that's covered in records. There are so many of them that we'll run out of space soon, and the fact that Ryder hasn't looked up once to inspect what we have so far isn't reassuring.

You're just wasting your time. You're never going to find anything useful in here, that ever-present, callous voice hisses.

"Stop that," Ryder says, looking up for the first time just to glare at me while I pop my knuckles.

"Stop what?"

"Convincing yourself this is all for nothing. It'll take time, but we'll figure it out."

How the hell did he know what I was thinking? Then again, this is Ryder. Perceptive to a fault and just as calculating.

I drop my hands at my side. "I need a break." I set the tape down and walk out of the office without waiting for a response, but instead of turning to the steps, I go down the hall to Lyla's room.

Her door is cracked open just enough that I can see her curled between her favorite pink blanket and the stuffed tiger that Ryder gave her a year ago. Seeing her so peacefully asleep slows my spiral of dark thoughts, and I focus on the fact that she is here and safe.

At the end of the day, that's all that matters.

I wish I could capture this moment and bottle it up for when those fears take over. I'd give anything to go back to this second, when her peaceful sleep calms me and reminds me that everything is okay.

Everything can change at a moment's notice, and I won't take these moments for granted, especially after what Lyla and I went through a few weeks ago. I'll relish in them and use them to ground me when anxiety creeps into my mind.

The idea hits me with a force that makes me gasp, and I cover my mouth to stop waking Lyla as I rush back to the office. Ryder's on his feet when I walk in, either hearing my gasp or sensing my urgency.

"What's wrong?" he asks as I shut the door behind me.

"Anyone could've changed them, right?"

"Changed what?"

"The records," I tell him. "If you were tampering with records, wouldn't you go back and cover up the evidence?"

Ryder eyes me. "Yes, but we can't trace any changes made without having that software in place prior to the change."

"Exactly. We need a reference point that *hasn't* changed."

I see the second recognition hits him, and Ryder turns to lift my thumb drive off the desk.

"Every file on that drive was saved offline as soon as they were submitted," I say.

"So, if someone went back and changed it, this drive would have the original," he finishes, eyes sparking with something both surprised and impressed. It's one of the rare moments he lets emotion openly touch his face, and it makes him so undeniably handsome that I have to force myself to look away.

I gesture to the drive. "It'll only help if the original file was tampered with, not if it was false to begin with, but comparing what's on the drive with what's currently in the base is a starting point."

He nods. "Let's get started."

An hour later, the mess of printed records starts to come together, and putting each file in chronological order takes up most of that time. The information covers so many topics that arranging it in an understandable way hasn't been easy, but we've done a decent job.

We start by taping up the records from the live database, then we'll go back through and cross-reference them with the thumb drive's files.

So far, we have brief biographies of all Mason's known followers placed on the timeline when their betrayal was discovered. Then, there's the description of the resources found at the factory Mason used as a base. The rest of the records are inventory and financial summaries from every base ordered by Moreno to be submitted for this specific investigation. Each one is placed on the timeline according to its timestamp.

I finish taping the last few files on the wall while Ryder takes everything in.

When I turn to him, he's focused on the pictures of Mason's followers. I don't recognize any of the soldiers that betrayed the Moreno family, but Ryder clearly does.

"I worked with some of them for years," he mutters, stepping forward to get a closer look. "Hard to believe they just turned on the family like that."

Something in the way his brow creases, his jaw grinds, and his shoulders lock up with tension prompts me to do something I probably shouldn't.

Breaking the very rules I set myself, I close the space between us and brush one hand along Ryder's back in a show of comfort. The second my hand makes contact, his tense muscles relax, and though I'm sure it's only his surprise, I let myself believe—for just a moment—that I relax Ryder as much as he relaxes me.

I feel his eyes drop to watch me but don't have the guts to face whatever calculative gaze I'll find if I look up. So, instead, I lower my hand and clear my throat. "Ready?"

Time passes in a blur of checking and double-checking every detail of the most mundane financial records in the Moreno database—and that's coming from someone who majored in finance. We each pick a file from the thumb drive, and assess every line of it next to the ones on the timeline.

The printer spits out another document, and I pick it up, holding it to the wall to start checking it.

But they aren't the same file.

"Did you skip a record on purpose?" I ask, blinking out of the fog the mindless work has put me in.

Ryder looks up from where he's printing the next few documents. "I haven't skipped anything."

I look at the record in my hand that details the Rohypnol shipments for June, then to where the matching document on the wall hangs; an entire row—a week according to our timeline—below where we're at now.

We lock eyes with the realization. He's out of his chair in a flash, and we're holding the two papers up to one another.

Our lungs seem to sync as we pull in a sharp breath at the exact same time.

Because the dates aren't the only thing that don't match.

The amounts don't, either.

"This is a *forty thousand* dollar difference, Ryder. That's not a small amount. How the hell was this not noticed by anyone?"

He doesn't answer, but I can practically see his mind racing as he studies the evidence. I don't know how long passes before he rips the copy from the wall and takes them back to the computer."What are you doing?"

"This was fucking genius," he mutters, more to himself than me.

"Genius? More like *insane* that no one found this before us."

"We only found it because we had an earlier copy to compare it to." Ryder doesn't look up as he types away on the computer.

"You're telling me that no one would've noticed that kind of money missing?"

His fingers suddenly stop typing, and Ryder's lips part with a heavy sigh as he leans back in the chair. "For fuck's sake…"

"Are you going to explain what's going on?"

"Okay," he says, turning to face me with an enthusiastic bounce that's more fitting for our daughter than him. "Rohypnol isn't a regular street drug. It doesn't provide a high as much as help someone disassociate. Because of that, it's often used for the purposes of sexual assault. Another name for it is the 'date rape' drug."

My blood freezes in my veins, and my stomach rolls.

I've always known Ryder's job required him to actively work against the law and that he was capable of doing things I never want to know about. I've never liked that particular aspect of his job, but I accepted it because, in my head, he only hurt other, equally bad people.

But sexual assault?

"You-you sell Rohypnol for sexual assaults?" I practically choke out the words, taking a step away from him as I do.

Ryder lifts a hand. "No—well, technically, not anymore."

That doesn't ease my stomach-churning nausea one bit.

"Before Moreno took over, his father had a prostitution ring in place. It's the first thing Moreno got rid of when he came into power."

"So, you have no part in it?"

"None. It's a nasty business and not worth the hassle." I shoot him a horrified look, and he adds, "And even people like us have boundaries. Sex trafficking isn't something the Moreno family takes part in."

I crack my knuckles, but it brings no comfort. "What does this have to do with the records?"

"Right," Ryder says with a nod. "We still sell Rohypnol, but only to a few medical facilities that do shady work. It's one of the least profitable products we sell, which is why it was able to go under the radar, especially at this base, which is the main location for shipment imports and exports."

He points to something on his laptop, and I inspect the receipts. "These are the records for Rohypnol over the last few years, and they're all roughly the same." He scrolls down. "Until you look back to two years ago."

The profit lowers as he scrolls back, and according to these receipts, the cost has slowly tripled over the last two years.

"Someone's been raising the price of Rohypnol?"

"If that number stays in the budget, it can be pocketed," he confirms.

"Wait a minute." I gesture to the screen. "If this has been going on that long, why was it altered last month? Even if it's been raised over the last two years, the forty thousand dollar jump doesn't follow the pattern, and it should've been submitted incorrectly, not edited."

"Impossible to say for sure, but it could have to do with the aftermath of the factory night. Maybe Mason's followers needed to pay off anyone who could incriminate them, or it was used for some of them to go on the run."

"So, just to summarize, the original record—which was still higher than it should be—was submitted at Moreno's request and downloaded onto my flash drive. Then, a week later, someone went back and jacked up the price to clean up Mason's mess?"

Ryder nods. "And that's assuming it's related to Mason at all, and not just someone exploiting a crack in the system."

Even I know that's unlikely. After all, the Morenos are looking for a leak, and this is a full on flood. It can't be a coincidence.

Ryder's eyes suddenly go distant, lost in thought.

"What is it?" I ask.

"Anyone can submit a report, but not everyone can edit one."

"Which means?"

"Someone with capo-level access had to have done it."

"Briggs."

He gives me a pointed look. "It's too early to make assumptions."

"Too early? We're literally staring at the proof! You need to tell Moreno about this."

"Absolutely not," he says without half a second of hesitation. "All we have is speculation. I still need to look into the Rohypnol supply at the base and make sure we're right about this. Besides, someone could've used one of the capo's accounts to do it. Still, if we can find out which account was used, it would narrow the search."

"Is there a way to track that?"

Ryder goes quiet once again, slowly nodding as he seems to come to a decision. "There might be."

"How?"

He lifts his gaze to mine, the resolve there hitting a place inside me that makes my chest swell with something I can't name. "We're going to throw a party."

CHAPTER TWENTY-ONE
Rachel

If I'm being completely honest, I could get used to this whole "co-parenting" thing.

Since Ryder moved in, I haven't missed a single day of work. David has told me several times that my work is of excellent quality, and Mrs. Caster thinks this promotion is as good as mine. At this point, it's just a matter of waiting for the management dinner for everything to be officially announced, but that's still two weeks away.

Lyla's been doing great, too. Yesterday, she spent a few hours at Meredith's house in the evening without me there, and had a blast. It's been nothing short of thrilling to watch her come out of her fear, and I'd be lying if I said it had nothing to do with Ryder's presence.

Lyla has never had her father around for more than a few days at a time, and before Ryder moved in, I would've argued that she was perfectly fine with that arrangement, but now, I'm not so sure. After watching how she interacts with him, how she subconsciously lets her guard down when he's around, and how she clings to him like nothing can touch her when he's there, I wonder if we deprived her of the father-daughter experience. They've always had a special, unbreakable bond, but there's no denying that it's different now that they live together. Their relationship is stronger, and I think Lyla is, too.

As if the thought of him has the power to conjure, Ryder's Ferrari glides into the parking lot of Lyla's martial arts school. He pulls into the spot next to mine, and I climb out to greet them.

When Ryder steps out of his car, the black slacks and white button-up are so different from his usual casual wear that I can't help how my eyes rake over his entire body.

"You're dressed up," I note.

I can't see his face while he helps Lyla from her car seat, but I can imagine the knowing grin that's plastered there.

"I have to run some errands before tonight, so I got ready early."

And here I almost let myself forget what tonight is. I've been so nervous about the prospect of hosting the capos and their partners that my knuckles are sore from how many times I've cracked them.

"Right. Is there anything I need to do to get the house ready?"

"Nope," he answers, handing me Lyla's book bag. "The cleaning crew left an hour before we came here, and the catering staff won't get there until I'm back."

I've never had a cleaning crew or catering staff in my life, and though I'm uncomfortable with the idea of strangers being in my home, I do appreciate that cooking and cleaning isn't something I have to worry about in preparation for tonight.

Ryder hugs and kisses Lyla goodbye, then offers me a warm smile as he climbs into his car.

When Ryder drives off, Lyla and I walk inside the studio. She's quiet as we go, but she's never been a particularly talkative child. It's what I love most about her friendship with Dominic. He's lively, whereas Lyla is reserved. They balance each other well.

Speaking of the wild child, he's on top of Lyla the second we step inside, taking her by the hand and leading her to take their shoes off.

I find Meredith watching them and go to where she sits in front of the windows of the classroom.

She stands to hug me, and I accept it, noticing that she still wears her scrubs. "Delayed at work again?"

She shrugs and takes her seat. "Dennis wanted to finish our chess game. It's hard to say no to that charming smile of his."

Meredith is about as saintly as a person can be. She lost her parents at a young age, and got knocked up by her abusive boyfriend, who left when he found out about the pregnancy. We don't talk about the past often, so I don't know all the details that lead to her getting a job at the daycare I sent Lyla to, but it seemed like fate that we'd become friends.

We met in passing several times at the daycare, then found ourselves talking more frequently. The friendship grew naturally from there, and I'm not sure either of us knew how badly we needed the other. By helping each other, I was able to work my job full-time, and Meredith was able to finish her degree and get a job working at a local nursing home.

Dennis is her favorite resident. He's an old man whose three adult children work demanding jobs in San Francisco, meaning he doesn't see them often. Meredith, in her abundant kindness, takes Dennis to them once a month for a weekend.

I'm about to ask how the sweet old man is, when I hear Dominic's consoling voice from across the room. "It's okay, Lyla. You're okay!"

My stomach drops, and I scan the room for my daughter. She's sitting on the floor by the shoe cubbies, knees pulled to her chest and face buried in her arms. Dominic kneels at her side, rubbing a hand against her back as he shoots a worried look at his mother and me.

I'm across the room and pulling her into my arms within seconds, and Dominic reluctantly goes to his mother.

"What's wrong?" I ask in a hushed tone, not wanting other kids or parents to listen in.

She shakes her head but doesn't say a word.

"Your class is going to start soon. Why don't we take your shoes off so you're ready?"

Her tiny hands fist my shirt, anchoring her to me in silent objection.

The flashback hits suddenly and far too realistically.

We're not in a martial arts school but in the back of a crowded van surrounded by men who want to hurt us. My arms are wrapped tightly around my daughter, who cries into me with every ounce of fear we're feeling. My hands are wet with blood as I keep a firm hold on the cuts that the monster of a man left on my child's arms.

What kind of mother can't protect her own child?

I blink back my own tears as I'm too slowly brought back to reality. Am I shaking?

"What do we have here?" A low, enthusiastic voice asks.

Jacob Torres is crouching down beside us, and I force a smile, violently pushing the trauma aside, but it's Lyla that he's looking at.

She tilts her head ever so slightly to see him, and I wait for her to return to her hiding, but she doesn't.

"She's just nervous, is all," I say, stroking her hair in a soothing motion, though I don't know which one of us I'm trying to comfort.

"That's okay. Sometimes I get nervous, too," Jacob tells her, and I feel the curious tilt of her head. Jacob reads the question there like she's said it out loud. "Oh yeah, all the time. In fact, I'm a little nervous about teaching today," he says in a stage whisper like it's their little secret. "But, I think I can do it if you come with me. What if we face our fears together?" he asks with a small smile.

After a long moment of no response from Lyla, I'm about to tell him that she'll just watch today, but slowly, she lifts her head from my body. I watch in fascination as my daughter gives Jacob a small, barely noticeable nod.

Lyla lets me help her remove her shoes and follows Mr. Torres into the classroom with the hoard of toddlers ready for class. Dominic stands dutifully by her side, glaring down at any kid trying to partner with her.

I settle in beside Meredith, watching in amazement as Lyla does an entire drill without looking at me for comfort. She just watches Mr. Torres with curiosity.

"If Lyla has any issues tonight, please feel free to call, and I'll come get her," I tell Meredith.

"Of course, but I'm sure she'll do great. She's spent plenty of time at my house."

"I know, I know. This is just her first full night without Ryder and me, and we're a bit nervous about it."

She eyes me quizzically.

"What?"

"You two have been pretty cozy lately."

"Oh, please," I say with a roll of my eyes. "You know it isn't like that."

"Isn't it, though?"

"No. We're co-parents, that's all."

"Huh," she says, pressing her lips together like she's physically stopping herself from saying anything more.

Meredith really is a saint, but she's also honest. She's the kind of friend who would never let you buy a dress that didn't flatter you. I have a feeling I'm about to be stung by that honesty.

"What?" I reluctantly ask.

"Rachel, we're not talking about some random hook-up that you see on occasion. We're talking about the father of your child and the only man you've ever been in love with."

My chest constricts at the casual mention of the four-letter word I avoid at all costs.

"And now you're living together and acting like you didn't spend the last three years picking up the pieces of your heart." She gives me a small, sad smile. "I just don't want to go back to that time when you barely slept or ate. You're finally in a healthy place, and I don't want to see you lose all that progress."

Another fact about my friendship with Meredith, we met when my heart was freshly shattered. Sometimes, I forget that she saw the after-effects of my relationship with Ryder when things completely fell apart.

When *I* completely fell apart.

She's not saying anything I don't already know, but it's easier to ignore when it's kept inside me. Now that it's out in the open, it's much harder to pretend I have everything under control.

"I mean, it hasn't been the easiest past few weeks, but we're doing okay," I defend when she gives me a look like she doesn't believe a word I say. "We set clear boundaries as soon as he moved in and haven't overstepped."

Each of those rules come to mind now.

No ordering me around.

No business in the house.

No touching.

Three memories accompany those rules.

Agreeing to follow his lead with our investigation.

Spending hours going through the Moreno database.

Ryder's lips savagely taking mine at the gala…

Okay, so maybe *some* overstepping has occurred, but Meredith doesn't need to know that.

"Just be careful," she tells me. "I want what's best for you. You know I'd support you no matter what, right?"

"I know," I say, and I do. Meredith was there when I was at my lowest, and I can understand her apprehension at the possibility that it can all happen again. But I won't let it.

This time, *I'm* in control of the situation.

We spend the rest of the class watching the kids. Jacob does a great job keeping an eye on Lyla without pulling attention away from the other students. If they're doing a drill in groups, he makes sure to put Lyla in his, and I even catch the reassuring glances he sends my way as if he can feel the waves of anxiety that roll off me from the lobby.

Despite the persistence from the lobby moms about how perfect Jacob is, I've never seen him that way.

He's a handsome man, with dark hair that's cut short and very sharp features. When those hazel, oval eyes and square jaw are arranged in a smile, it's undeniably contagious, but when one of the students hits another in class, and those features arrange into a deep set frown, not a single kid steps out of line again. The sleeves of his black uniform are rolled up to his elbow, showing off tanned skin and impressive muscles that make him the total package.

He's handsome, good with kids, and a successful business owner.

Maybe I do see what those moms are getting at...

When the class ends, Lyla is the last one to leave, and by the time she gets to me, a lot of the parents are already leaving. Dominic stays with her, of course, and Mr. Torres follows them out.

Jacob lowers himself to Lyla's level and holds out his hand for a high five. "I couldn't have done it without you."

Her smile is wide when she claps her tiny hand against his, and he shakes it like it hurts.

"Are you trying to break my hand with a high five like that?" he asks, earning him a hardy giggle.

Dominic also gives Jacob a high five, working to make sure his high five is even harder than Lyla's, and I swear I catch Jacob suppressing a wince.

"Shoes?" Dominic asks, and Lyla nods before they head in that direction, followed by Meredith.

I face Jacob. "Thank you so much for taking time with her. She can be shy, and this is doing wonders for her."

His smile stretches, revealing perfectly straight teeth. "I'm glad to hear that. Lyla's a great kid."

I look over to my little girl, who's biting her lip in concentration as she puts Velcro on her left foot before moving to her right shoe. "I'm not sure it's any thanks to me, but she is incredible."

"I doubt that's true," he says, then lowers his voice just a little. "Miss Lance—"

"Please, call me Rachel," I interrupt, and his smile grows.

"Right, *Rachel*, I really don't want to overstep any boundaries, and I can assure you that I've never done something like this before, but I was wondering if you'd be interested in going out with me sometime."

The question comes from left field, and I'm momentarily speechless.

"I know we've only met a few times, but I'm really interested in getting to know you."

He's asking me out? On a date?

It's my immediate reaction to politely decline, but I give it a moment of thought. What possible reason do I have to say no? He's everything I should want and everything that's good for my daughter. Don't I owe it to myself to at least give it a try?

"I didn't mean to make you uncomfortable. It's just—"

"I'd love to," I tell him.

After exchanging phone numbers, Jacob and I part ways, and Meredith shows up with the kids in tow at my side. Her eyes are wide as saucers when she whispers, "What was that about?"

I press my lips in a firm line until we're out the door and walking into the parking lot.

I scan the lot for any suspicious cars, but I haven't felt those watchful eyes since I was followed by that black truck. Still, I walk with my guard up and study my surroundings intently.

"Uh, he asked me out on a date," I say, still stunned by the whole thing.

Meredith's jaw goes slack. "Are you serious? I *literally* called this. You said yes, right?"

"Yeah, yeah, I did."

Meredith goes on listing all the ways Jacob is perfect as we walk to our cars, but I can't help the part of me that wonders if my definition of perfect is just a bit different from everyone else's.

We're not even halfway through this dinner party, and my face already aches from smiling so much. If I ever thought becoming a mother at twenty-two would make me feel like I missed out on party years, I was wrong. As lovely as the gourmet catering service and lavish decor Ryder organizes to be brought into our dining room are, I'd rather curl up on the couch in pajamas and fuzzy socks with my daughter.

Instead, I'm wearing my nicest black dress pants and a white blouse that flatters my willowy frame. I hadn't intended to match Ryder, but when I walked out of my room and remember he was in black slacks and a white button-up, it hadn't felt worth it to change. So, not only do we look like a functional couple, we look domesticated as hell.

The capos all come dressed similarly to Ryder, and their dates—all the same women who came to the gala—look just as fashionable.

We socialize and engage in small talk about absolutely nothing in particular until the catering service has our first course ready. The waiters—because having a meal catered wasn't enough, we also needed to be served—fill the glasses with wine and the plates with food.

The conversation flows naturally, though it's mostly driven by Harris and his girlfriend, Ava, who seem to have never-ending stories about their travels and adventures. Emily engages with them since she's done a fair amount of traveling herself, but Knox remains silent at her side. Briggs is just as quiet, and his wife, Donna, doesn't do much talking either but wears an unwavering warm smile.

It's the last couple, as reserved as they are, that I watch like a hawk throughout the meal. I hadn't paid much attention to them at the gala, but I'm far more aware of Briggs since I suspect him of being the thief and my stalker. I hope to catch some nervous tick or anything that could aid our investigation. Instead, I find myself watching how he interacts with his wife.

They have a closed-off air surrounding them, and I expect that to translate to cool interactions, but if anything, they move as a unit. When we first sit down, he pulls out her chair in a practiced move, like it's been done a million times before. I lose track of how many subtle glances he's sent her way as if periodically checking to make sure she's okay. He even breaks proper dining etiquette to rest his arm over her chair and rub his thumb over her shoulder.

It's fascinating to watch such a brood-ish man act so chivalrously.

When dinner is over, I offer to take the women for a tour of the house while Ryder takes the capos outside for a game of poker.

We stop in the upstairs hall, where a series of four paintings hang.

"What are all of these?" Ava asks, looking from one picture to the next.

"They were a Christmas gift from Ryder last year," I explain.

I've never been a gift person, but this particular present might be the best I've ever received. The first is of a woman who holds the hand of a small child as they walk down a snow-covered street. The second shows the same woman and child, only they walk down a beach. The other two are similar, depicting the woman and child walking down a wilderness path with the warm colors of autumn, and also a field of brightly painted flowers.

It's a series called *Mother and Me*, and I fell in love with it as soon as it was given to me.

When Ava and Emily debate what country they think each painting is meant to take place in, I feel Donna step up to my side.

She's a short woman with light blonde hair cut just above her shoulders. She has such a soft, feminine look that it makes me wonder how she could be the wife to such a hard, jaded man like Briggs.

"What a lovely gift idea. Ryder seems like a wonderful boyfriend."

"Oh, no, we aren't—" I stop myself since I really have no idea what to say. Ryder and I really aren't anything more than co-parents, but as far as everyone here knows, we hooked up at the gala just last weekend. "It's complicated."

She doesn't look surprised by this answer and nods. "Things with these men usually are."

"Were they for you and Briggs?" I don't realize how intrusive the question is until it's too late. "I'm sorry. That was out of line. You don't have to answer that."

She waves a dismissive hand and smiles. "As a matter of fact, yes. I'm a second-grade teacher, so I'm sure you can imagine I never imagined marrying a mafia capo. I didn't know what he did until we'd seen each other for several months."

"What did you do when you found out?"

"Left him," she answers, and I have absolutely no words. She laughs at my bewilderment. "But he didn't let me go that easily. He pursued me for six months, sending me gifts, leaving me romantic messages, and even going so far as to get in good with my folks."

"And you took him back?"

She nods. "Eventually. I thought knowing what he did, meant I knew *him*, but that wasn't the case."

That, I can understand. I never felt like Ryder's job defined who he was.

His priorities did.

"Can I ask you something?"

"Of course," she says, a warm smile on her soft features.

"Forgive me if this is overstepping, but do you ever feel like you're second place?"

"Second place to what?"

"The family. Their duty *to* the family."

Donna's laugh is a light, comforting sound. "These boys don't see the world the same way we do. To you, there's the Moreno family and the family that you and Ryder created, but to Ryder, there's just *family*. There's no first place or second place. Family is everything to them, and though we may not take part in their business, we're still part of that family."

We go downstairs a few minutes later, but I don't hear a single word the women say. I spend the rest of the evening replaying Donna's words on a loop, considering what exactly *family*, means to me.

CHAPTER TWENTY-TWO

Ryder

I wish I could focus on the game of poker that I'm losing like a rookie, but I can't. My thoughts are reserved for the woman inside, entertaining the capo's dates, so I have the chance to pick their brains now that they've been loosened up with food and alcohol.

Her hair falls down her shoulders in loose, natural curls that I know she spent a lot of time arranging. Her outfit is the perfect mix of professional and elegant—now lacking the bulky charm that I locked away in a safe—and I can't bring myself to care for the money I'm losing as I let my focus take her in.

Beautiful is such an inadequate word to describe my Rachel. She's not only beautiful in the sense of her physical features but in her genuine kindness, her pure intentions, and her unwavering strength. It's no wonder the other women gravitate toward her, though she minimally contributes to their conversation. She hosts like she was born to do it, even if she's likely counting down the minutes until she can throw on her pajamas and a pair of her favorite fuzzy socks.

The women pass around a bottle of wine to top off their glasses, and after Rachel politely declines, she glances in my direction.

For fuck's sake.

One—not particularly expressive—look from her is enough to make me want to kick every one of these bastards out and have this woman all to myself. I don't care if all we do is talk, hell, I'll even take her yelling at me if it means I get to spend time with her.

I'm not under any illusions. I know how Rachel feels. I know that three years ago, she walked away from me—from us—and hasn't looked back.

But I have.

I'm not sure there's a single thing she could do that will ever change how I feel about her.

And right now, in a moment where absolutely nothing significant is happening, those feelings are damn-near overwhelming, leaving a physical ache that reverberates just behind my ribcage.

Rachel—oblivious to the torrent of need tearing me apart from the inside out—lifts a curious brow. I subtly shake my head in answer and scratch my chin to play it off like I'm assessing the cards in my hand.

Before the women came back from their tour and stole my focus, I genuinely enjoyed playing poker with the capos. It's a surprisingly pleasant combination of cards, whiskey, cigars, and exchanging war stories. Harris does most of the talking, but I jump in from time to time, and even Briggs—as reluctantly as he seems to do everything— shares a few stories from the days of his prime. Knox is quiet, and I'm still trying to figure out if it's his personality type or if he's still not used to the dynamic of being a capo instead of a soldier.

When I catch Rachel checking her watch for the fourth time in a minute, I decide to put the plan in motion.

"I finished auditing the records that could be related to Mason Consoli's efforts," I state nonchalantly, and I pour two fingers of whiskey into my glass.

Harris drops his head back. "And here I thought we were doing so well avoiding work talk."

But Brings regards me with a mix of interest and ire that blend effortlessly. "Is that so?"

"Didn't find a single thing," I say with a shrug. "I have a flash drive for each of you, so everyone can take a look before we call it, but I'd say it's safe to assume our base isn't where Mason was taking from."

"And what did Moreno say about this?"

The mention of Moreno is salt in the wound, and Briggs knows it.

"I figured you'd appreciate looking through the files before we send him the verdict."

Briggs nods, a sly haughtiness icing his features. "I'll take a look and personally give Mr. Moreno my thoughts when I see him in a few weeks."

I know he's baiting me, but I can't help giving in and raising a single brow to ask the question for me. Briggs is all too smug when he leans back in his chair. "The capo conference is coming up, and Moreno has already extended my invitation."

Of course, Briggs would be invited to the capo conference. One capo from every base comes to L.A. once a year to meet with Moreno for a week of meetings and training. I hadn't expected an invitation, but it's the first time since Moreno came into power that I'll miss it.

I know better than to give Briggs the satisfaction of getting a reaction out of me, so I only nod and return to our game.

We play a few more rounds, and I shoot Rachel a text, letting her know it won't be much longer.

Harris leans back in his chair. "Got to say, Bates, this was pretty nice."

"This is a typical night in Los Angeles. We should do it more often."

"Not sure Harris's wallet could handle this as a routine," Knox jabs.

It's one of the few things he's said all night, and I take it as a victory.

"One night of bad luck doesn't mean shit. I rarely lose," Harris retorts.

Even Knox chuckles at that.

There's something peaceful in the fact that tonight brought out a more relaxed side in the capos. Nights like this really are typical back in L.A., and it's strange that none of the capos here are close the way everyone back home is.

Home.

The usual longing that accompanies that word doesn't have the same sobering effect as it has since I left, and though I'm sure it's only time that's eased the pain of my exile, I can't stop my eyes from wandering to the woman inside for the thousandth time.

Two hours later, Rachel opens the door to the office I've been waiting in since everyone left an hour ago. Just like I predicted, she's wearing a matching set of silk pajamas, and bright pink fuzzy socks that Lyla gave her for Mother's Day. She also carries two cups—one a mug with a tea bag hanging from the side, and the other is my newly refilled whiskey glass.

I thank her as I take it. "Anything from the women?"

"As far as I can tell, they don't know anything," she says as she settles into the chaise. "At least, I'm sure that Ava and Emily don't.

They haven't been around long enough that they'd be trusted with anything. Donna's been with Briggs for over a decade, so she's the only one who might be involved, but I doubt it."

"Why?"

She weighs her head from side to side. "I don't know, I just—I like her."

I point to one of the pictures hanging on the timeline that still decorates the wall. "And I liked Nate until I had to put a bullet in his head. Liking someone isn't an indication of whether they're a traitor."

She rolls her eyes and pulls her legs beneath her.

"I only spent a few hours with her. Most of it was listening to Ava, and Emily relay the most recent season of The Bachelor. So, excuse me if the brief conversations we had didn't give me the impression she was a thief."

It was a long shot, but we had to be thorough. The real test is for the capos, starting with how they reacted to the news that I didn't find anything in my search. Unfortunately—but unsurprisingly—the reactions weren't telling. For instance, Briggs hates that I took this project in the first place, so his indignation was expected. Harris looked pleased, but that could easily be because Briggs and I weren't at each other's throats, and Knox didn't show a reaction at all—no big surprise there.

The second part of the test is starting any second now.

Like I've manifested it myself, the chime I've been waiting to hear finally sounds from the computer.

"Is that it?" Rachel asks, coming to stand at my side.

"One of them," I say, and we look to where the screen confirms that one of the flash drives has been inserted and opened.

"What if they don't look through it tonight?"

"They will," I assure her. One thing all capos have in common is that we're workaholics. Combine that with the urgency of finding where Mason got his funding from, and it's guaranteed that each capo will go through the files as soon as they can.

"Can you see who opened it?"

"Knox," I answer.

The next chime comes in, and we lean in closer to look.

"Harris."

One more chime, that's all we need.

"How do the flash drives show you this?"

"They have a virus on them. It's minimally invasive, nothing they

165

should be able to trace, but it'll tell us when they're accessing the files. The only aspect of the virus that'll actually affect their personal accounts is that I've tailored it to specifically alert us when any report that's been submitted is being altered."

"That's a thing?"

I shrug. "Kade's made all sorts of viruses like it. They can be customized, so—"

I'm cut off by the sound of the last chime.

"Briggs," I confirm. "That's all of them. Once they look through the files, they'll agree that nothing is out of place. Then, it's just a matter of waiting for our culprit to feel safe enough to alter files again. Then, we'll know exactly where it's coming from."

Now that the virus is in place on each capo's account, I can submit this month's Rohypnol record in a few days. I've set the rate lower than it's been for months, hoping it will force the traitor to take action. It won't be low enough to raise suspicion, but enough that whoever is doing this will probably edit it.

"We have to celebrate. You know what? I think I have a bottle of champagne downstairs. I'll go get it." Rachel practically skips out of the room, and her enthusiasm is one of the few things I can count on to force a smile out of me.

The same overwhelming desire that had me emptying my wallet to the capos sucks me in again, this time with the force of the realization that we're actually alone. It's the first time we've been together without the threat of Lyla or anyone else interrupting us.

Within five seconds, I've come up with hundreds of reasons to convince her to give what we had another chance. Within ten seconds, I stood from my chair to do just that.

At the twelve-second mark, a buzz from the floor stops me from where I stand, and I reach to pick up Rachel's phone. It must have fallen when she darted from the room. I turn it over to check for any cracks on the screen from hitting the floor—there aren't any—but there is a message.

Unknown number: Hey, Rachel! It's Jacob Torres. If you're up for it, I'd love to take you out tomorrow night. Let me know!

Torres? As in, Lyla's martial arts instructor? When the hell did he get Rachel's number?

Senseless outrage surges through my veins like pure adrenaline as I spend who-knows-how-long staring at that message. I have half a mind to delete it before she sees, and I might've if she didn't walk in at that exact moment.

"What's wrong?" she asks, her smile still firmly in place as she holds two empty glasses and a bottle of champagne.

Maybe her good mood is only partially because of the progress we made tonight. Maybe she was already happy from *Jacob fucking Torres*.

I wear my impeccable poker face as I hold out her phone. "I didn't know you and Mr. Torres were well aquatinted."

"Did you look through my messages?" she demands, dropping her smile and snatching the phone from my grasp. She barely gets the glasses on the desk before they shatter on the ground.

"You dropped it, and I was checking for cracks when it came through," I say, tone far calmer than what I'm feeling. "It's extremely inappropriate of him to use the number you gave him on Lyla's paperwork to ask you on a date. I'll go to the studio tomorrow and deal with this."

"It's not like that," she says, and...fuck, is that a nervous smile? "He asked for my number earlier today, and I gave it to him."

"Are you serious?"

Whether by my clipped tone or hostile words, I've got her full attention now. She lowers her phone, scanning me as if to assess my mood before narrowing her eyes to meet my challenge. "And what if I am?"

"You would go out with a guy like that?"

Her eyes flare like I've dropped a match on a gallon of gasoline. "A guy like what? Who loves kids? Owns a *legal* business? Has a steady, *normal* life? You're right, Ryder. I'm out of my damn mind for considering going on a date with such a man."

"And I'm what? Some thug?"

"I never said that. Besides, who even said you were in the running?"

"I used to be."

"That was *four years ago*, Ryder."

"And you still have no idea what you want."

"Or maybe I just have the good sense to know it isn't you."

I stare into the eyes I dream about every single night and search for an ounce of regret—of anything that would indicate she spoke out of anger and not truth.

But all I find is unwavering conviction.

I gesture to the phone she clutches with white knuckles. "And what are your *senses* telling you now?"

"That I should give Jacob a chance," she says without a second of hesitation.

I spent the entire night wondering how to win back the only woman who has ever owned every part of who I am.

She spent the entire night waiting for another man to ask her out.

The resentment—and yes, fucking embarrassment—that accompanies the realization makes me think it would've been more merciful for her to fire two bullets into my chest. I'll admit it sounds preferable to this shit.

I don't trust myself to do or say something I'll regret, so I give her one sharp nod and storm out the door.

CHAPTER TWENTY-THREE

Ryder

30 Weeks Along

"Your girl was in the garden again this morning," Nicholas huffs, not looking up from his phone. "*Without* Alec."

The familiar irritation that comes every time one of the capos talks about Rachel cuts through my good mood.

Jealousy?

Damn fucking straight.

"I know," I answer coolly. "She thinks she's sneaking out, and I've been letting her get away with it since she's not hurting anyone."

Moreno chuckles from across the conference table. "Didn't realize that's how things work around here."

"When you're trying to keep the woman bringing your child into the world happy, you'll bend your rules, too."

"Doubt that," he mutters, going back to answering emails while we wait for Tripp and Kade to get here so we can get this meeting over with.

I use the time to shoot Rachel a text.

Ryder: I'll be back soon, and I have a surprise for you.

She responds only seconds later.

Rachel: I have a surprise for you too. See you soon.

It's been two months since I asked Rachel to stay with me, and though she hasn't given me an answer to the particular question, our attempt at friendship has created a healthier environment for both of us. I come home early enough to have dinner with her, and we've started watching a post-apocalyptic drama just to have something to do together. Our conversations come more naturally, and we've started to talk about what things will be like once the baby comes.

Since where they'll live is still undecided, we've only nailed down the things that won't change based on location—the first being finances. It hasn't seemed like something even worth discussing to me since I have more than enough to provide a perfectly comfortable life for her and our daughter, but Rachel doesn't see it quite so simply. Though I try to convince her otherwise, our compromise is more of a child support situation. I'll provide money, and Rachel will use it at her discretion, either to buy whatever the baby needs or to set it aside in a separate account for her future.

We discuss things like schooling—a private education neither of her parents had access to growing up—and the activities we want her to participate in when she gets older. As far as my job goes, we'll slowly introduce her to what I do as she grows up rather than hide it from her completely.

The only thing we can't seem to decide on is a name.

Between open communication and intentional quality time, things are better than ever. So much so that coming home to Rachel is the best part of any day.

When I'm at work, she's doing endless school assignments or studying for quizzes and tests, so nights are a time for us to relax.

Though she hasn't said it outright, she seems to be more comfortable around the base, too. She no longer pops her knuckles and lowers her head when we walk the halls and pass soldiers. Instead, she walks the halls with the same ease that she does the cabin, and I'm making every effort to increase that comfort.

Last week, I took her to the base's shooting range and taught her how to use a gun. We used silencers so we wouldn't hurt the baby's eardrums, but halfway through the session, we were stopped by the flutter of kicks against Rachel's stomach. We spent the rest of that hour waiting for her to do it again.

Donovan and Kade make a habit of joining Alec and Rachel a few days a week to watch her favorite shows. When I voiced my displeasure at the frequency of her spending time with other men, she simply told me that getting to know the other capos makes her feel more comfortable. I didn't argue after that since my goal is to convince her to stay with me.

Which is the only thing we haven't talked about.

I've done my best not to pry since pushing Rachel won't gain me any points, but it's damn hard, especially when I'm getting more and more used to having her around every day.

"All right," Moreno says, pulling my attention from my messages and thoughts of Rachel. Hell, I hadn't even noticed the other capos came in.

"The M.A.C. project is less than two months away. What are we still waiting on?"

"Travel details, but that can't come from our end. We haven't pushed communication, as you asked," Donovan answers.

Kade lifts a hand. "I emailed you the document that'll need to be filled out before I can complete the security clearance."

"I'll work on getting both," Moreno confirms, shooting me a look so I know to jot down the note.

The next hour is spent detailing the LAPD's new substance abuse and gang activity protocols that'll be going into effect at the end of the month and our plan to work with our contacts on the inside to get around them.

Once the meeting's agenda is complete, Moreno waves a dismissive hand. "All right, everyone out."

The other capos don't waste a second getting out of the room, but the look Moreno shoots me keeps me in my seat.

When the door shuts behind them, Moreno leans forward in his chair. "I sent those travel details to you four days ago. Why didn't Donovan have them?"

"Must have slipped through the cracks," I say in no particular tone. "I'll send it to Donovan by the end of the day."

Joshua's nostrils flare. "That was a direct order that you disobeyed. I have every right to kick your ass out of here and half a mind to do it. What the hell is your problem?"

I jab my finger into one of the thick files on the desk that contains everything about the M.A.C. project. "*This* is my problem. It wouldn't kill us to push the project by one month."

He pushes to his feet. "You know we don't have that option. We have a small window of opportunity to act, so that's what we will do. If this was any other capo, you'd tell them to get their head out of their ass and do their fucking job."

I stand to match his stance. "This isn't any other capo. It's me. The woman about to give birth to *my daughter* will be in danger if we go through with this project."

"As long as she doesn't overstep, she'll be perfectly safe."

"That's bullshit, and you know it, Joshua."

Not only does he let the remark slide, but his glare shifts to a tired exasperation as he braces his hands on the table. "I get that you're worried, but you don't need to be. Nothing will happen to her or the baby," he says, and I can feel the conviction in each word. "I can't do this if you're not completely on board. I need to know that you'll still back me even if you don't agree with this."

Maybe there's a world where I give in to the temptation to tell him to shove this project up his ass, but in this world, I only have one real option. I swore allegiance to this family, and I will honor that oath until my last breath, and Joshua damn well knows it.

"I'll back you," I tell him. "If anything, and I mean *anything*, happens to Rachel or the baby, I'll deliver the consequences personally."

"And I'll be right behind you," he says with a small, openly relieved grin.

By the time I finally get back to the cabin, I'm feeling marginally better about everything at the base. Moreno didn't cancel the project, but it's good to know he'll protect Rachel at all costs.

As soon as I open the door, the unmistakable smell of fresh paint gives me pause.

What the hell?

"Rachel?" I call, setting my bag down on the counter as I search the small living space. She comes out of her bedroom with light pink paint streaked across her cheek.

Her hair is pulled back in a bumpy ponytail, and she's wearing… are those *my* sweatpants? And that is definitely my shirt. Both articles of my clothing have paint smeared across them.

She has a paintbrush in one hand, a bottle of water in the other, and a smile so wide it creases every inch of her face.

Despite my confusion, I decide that—mess and all—this girl is who I want to come home to every night for the rest of my life.

"Come on," she says, nodding to her room.

When I follow her inside, the smell of paint increases tenfold, but that's not why my jaw goes rigid. Every item of furniture is moved to the center of the room and covered in plastic wrap, and the walls are bare, aside from their newest coat of paint.

I point to the ladder that's set up along the wall. "Did you climb up there to reach the top of the wall?"

She presses her lips together to tamper down a smile but I'm not amused. "Rachel, do you have any idea what could've happened if you'd fallen?"

She waves me off. "Alec has been here all day until a few minutes ago."

"And he *let* you do that?" I ask, pulling out my phone. "I'm going to fucking kill him."

Rachel is at my side in an instant, lowering my phone with a gentle hand and catching my attention with her heart-stopping smile. "You think I would've listened to him?"

"He should've told me."

"You think I would've listened to you?"

"Damn straight you would've." I rest my hand on her stomach. "That's *my* daughter in there, and if you think I'll let you do anything that could hurt her, then you don't know me very well."

I wait for her snap response, but it doesn't come. Instead, her smile grows. "Ryder, why do you think I painted this room?"

I pause to look around again, realizing I hadn't thought past the danger she put herself in. If she's painting the room a light pink, that means she's making...a nursery? But what's the point if she's just going to—

When I look at Rachel, my heart constricts with utter joy at the realization.

"Does this mean you're—"

"Staying. Not forever, but I figure a year or two in L.A. wouldn't be the worst—"

Her words are cut short when I scoop her into my arms and spin her around.

"Ryder!" she squeals, but I don't let go even when I stop spinning her.

Her heated cheeks, which still have paint across them, and bright eyes shine with affection, and I forget that we're supposed to be friends and do the only thing that feels natural.

I kiss her.

If I could sell the high I feel from kissing Rachel, I'd be the richest fucking man on the planet. There's nothing so addictive as her lips molding to mine like we can be permanently sealed together. Her arms wrap around my neck so tight I feel light-headed, though I'm not convinced the loss of blood flow is responsible for my dizziness.

The push and pull of our bodies moving against each other is euphoric, unlike anything I have ever known. It doesn't matter how long my lips dance with hers. It will never be enough. I could kiss Rachel until the day I die and still not have my fill of her.

And she's staying with me.

If someone asked me how long it's been since I started kissing her, I wouldn't have an answer. All I'd say is that when the knock on the door came, I nearly murdered the person on the other side.

Only, that's my surprise for Rachel, and it'd be a damn shame to taint this moment with homicide.

"Who's that?" Rachel asks when our lips part, and I love the sound of her breathy, dazed voice.

"*That* is your surprise," I tell her, and though the last thing I want to do is remove my arms from around her waist, I force myself to take her hand and pull her through the cabin.

I pull open the front door, watching Rachel's face as her features morph from curiosity, to shock, to disbelief and, finally, pure joy.

"Mom? Dad? What are you doing here?" She crashes into the couple with a force that should knock them over, and they receive her with open arms.

"Sweetie! It's so great to see you," her mother says in a tight, emotional voice.

"Ryder flew us out here. Can you believe it?" her father asks, pulling away from her to hold his hand out to me. "It's an honor to meet the man taking care of our little girl."

I take his hand and give it a firm shake. "The honor is all mine. I'm thrilled you took me up on the invitation. I trust the travel accommodations were suitable?"

Lynette nods enthusiastically. "A private jet, Rachel. Can you believe it!"

Rachel pulls away from her parents, eyes shining with moisture that never falls, and the look she gives me is the first unreadable one since we've met. Or, perhaps it's full of so many emotions that I can't pinpoint each of them.

"Come inside. I'll make some tea," Rachel insists as she ushers her parents through the door.

They move to the living room, and Rachel is about to follow, but she stops herself, turning to me with a look I can decipher. Whole-hearted gratitude.

"Thank you for this," she says, placing a kiss on my cheek. "It means so much to me."

I'm overcome with a sense of awe as I watch her walk away to make tea, and the realization hits me with a certainty I couldn't fight even if I wanted to.

I am falling in love with this girl.

And I have absolutely no intentions of letting her go.

CHAPTER TWENTY-FOUR

Rachel

Present

"I'm sorry, go back. A date?"

I tuck the phone between my shoulder and ear as I fold the laundry. Lyla and Dominic are playing with a mix of action figures and dolls, so lost in their own world that I'm not in danger of being overheard.

"You heard correctly," I tell Elli.

"And what does Ryder think about that?"

"Does it matter?"

"So, he's pissed."

"Again, does it matter?" I ask, and I hate that it's a question I've been asking myself on repeat since last night.

"Seems like it should. You're so well suited for each other, but you seem so intent on fighting that."

"Because we tried once, and...it didn't end well."

There's a thoughtful pause before she finally asks, "What happened?"

It's not that my history with Ryder is a secret, but for some reason, the idea of digging through the past isn't something I can bring myself to do right now. Not after last night. Not after Ryder spent all night sending me awe-filled looks that had me second-guessing every rule I'd put in place for us, only for him to remind me that he's an egotistical ass.

Who even said you were in the running?

I used to be.

What right does he have to throw that in my face?

"It's a long story that I'll tell you another time, I promise." I set down the clothes and fall into a chair. "Jacob is *good*, Elli. He's good and uncomplicated, and those are the things I need right now."

"I know, I know. And, of course, I want you to be happy. Let me know how it goes tonight?"

"I will." I look to Lyla and Dominic, who have ditched their toys in favor of wrestling. "I need to let you go. The kids are rough-housing, and I already know someone's going to get hurt."

Once I have the kids distracted with action figures and Barbie dolls again, it's time to talk to Ryder.

When I accepted Jacob's invitation last night, he didn't waste any time, and we have reservations tonight. Since my parents have a dinner party and Meredith is working the night shift, Ryder will have to watch the kids.

I don't like the idea of pushing the date in his face any more than I already have, but I can't get around this.

With a deep breath, I step onto the back porch and pull out my phone. I'm not sure how long I stare at his contact, but my knuckles are sore by the time I finally press the call button.

I've decided he won't answer by the third ring, but then the pool house door opens. When I turn toward it, Ryder is leaning against the door frame, his phone in one hand and a bored expression on his face.

"Can I help you?" he asks, with a tone that matches his expression and grates on my nerves.

Ryder is a gentleman and rarely anything but perfectly cordial toward me. He must still be angry about last night if he's being frosty now.

I hang up the call and roll my shoulders back. "I was wondering if you're staying home tonight or have other plans."

"I won't be leaving."

Here goes nothing.

"I need you to watch the kids."

I'm careful to refrain from phrasing it as a question. After all, he's Lyla's father and has every bit of the responsibility to her that I do, so it's not like watching her, and Dominic is too much to ask. He was probably already planning on spending time with them.

He doesn't ask where I'm going or what I have planned.

He knows.

The temptation to give excuses is strong, but I remind myself that I don't owe him anything.

We're co-parents.

That's it.

I lift my chin and brace for a fight. After all, that's what happens when Ryder doesn't get his way. He pushes me up against some wall, and demands what he wants from me.

"I'll watch them. Enjoy your night," he says instead, shutting the pool house door behind him.

Did he just...walk away?

No demands. No questions. No arguments.

Nothing.

That's good, right?

So, why does it feel like I just lost something?

Jacob and I follow the hostess to our table, and I'm glad I'm wearing my nude flats and not a pair of heels. My ability to walk without complications allows me to take in my surroundings.

The restaurant that Jacob has brought me is one of the nicest I've ever been to. He told me to dress up, but even my light pink cocktail dress pales in comparison to the floor-length gowns that some women wear. The color scheme of the restaurant is primarily tan and black, with lit candles and a small vase of chocolate orchids adorning pearl-white tablecloths.

We're led to a table in the middle of the restaurant, and I'm both surprised and flustered when Jacob pulls out my chair for me as I sit. I accept the gesture with a shy smile, admiring his appearance as I do.

Jacob is handsome in his martial arts uniform, but now he is downright gorgeous. He wears black slacks and a matching button-up that's left open on the top three buttons. The sleeves are rolled up just below his elbow, and each time he flexes, I get a damn good view of those muscular, veiny forearms.

He takes the seat across from me and flashes a Hollywood-worthy smile. "What do you think?"

"This is beautiful," I say as I appreciate the lavish scenery once again.

The waiter comes over with two menus and a basket of bread that he sets in the center of the table.

"Mr. Torres," the waiter greets. "Can I get you the usual?"

The usual? Does Jacob come here a lot? Does he bring dates here a lot?

"Please," he answers, then gestures to me. "Do you have a wine preference?"

"Surprise me."

Jacob's grin widens. "The usual for us both, please."

The waiter leaves us, and I busy myself looking at the menu. "Do you come here often?"

Jacob laughs, and it's so carefree. I'm actually caught off guard by how genuine it is. I like that sound. I like that sound a lot.

"They book out weeks in advance, but the manager is a childhood friend, so he gets me in when there are cancelations." His cheeks flush even in the darkened room. "I usually come with my mother."

That would explain why he wanted to go out so soon if he knew there was a cancelation.

"So, you know what I do for a living," he says. "What about you?"

"I work at an accounting firm," I tell him and wave off his widened eyes. "I know, really boring, right?"

He laughs again. "Not at all. I've always been horrible with numbers. My manager, Elizabeth, has to help me with anything book-keeping-related. Did Lyla get her mother's genius?"

I repress my growing smile at the compliment. "She's smart, but I'm not sure I had anything to do with it. I'm afraid she got more of her father's stoicism than anything."

"She's always been a quiet kid?" he half-states, half-asks.

I nod. "More so lately. Martial arts has been really good for her. She's been through a lot."

"I didn't know that," he says with perfect sincerity. "Can I ask what happened?"

I consider my words and decide to go as close to the truth as I can.

"A few weeks ago, Lyla and I were involved in an accident in L.A. when we went to visit her father. She's been jittery and afraid to be alone since then. Martial arts is helping bring her confidence back."

"Well, I'm glad to hear it's helping."

The waiter comes back with our drinks, and we order our food. The steak for him and the ravioli for me.

When Jacob asks if I have any hobbies, I tell him. "True crime shows and shooting."

"Shooting? Like guns?" he asks, and I realize that probably wasn't the best topic for a first date, but his expression seems more impressed than appalled.

"Yeah, Lyla's father taught me how when I was pregnant, and it's been a soothing habit ever since."

As I tell him, I realize it's been far too long since I've gone. I make a mental note to rectify that.

"I'm not sure I've ever heard someone refer to shooting as *soothing*, but I admire the interest."

Jacob tells me about his shooting experience and the other martial arts styles he trains in. I smile and laugh when expected but can't help noticing the lack of anything resembling a spark.

But that's okay, right?

Jacob is a great guy. We share interests and ambitions, he's an extremely attractive man, and he's great with kids. By all logic and reason, I should be head over heels for a man like him.

Our food comes, and we eat in content silence before moving to the topic of our childhood. Jacob tells me how he moved eight times during his twelve years of grade school due to his father's work in the military. Then I share that I'm Sacramento born and raised, only having left for a few months during my pregnancy.

The conversation continues, and before I know it, the restaurant has begun to clear out. Jacob takes the check and leads us to his car.

The radio plays nineties hits while we discuss how good the food was, and I can't help but feel like I'm hanging out with Alec, Elli, or Meredith. The easy conversation and light-hearted atmosphere bring comfort, but still no hint of flame.

And maybe that's not such a bad thing.

Sparks and flames may warm the heart, but they're also unpredictable, flickering one moment, then burning everything in their wake the next.

Jacob can give me stability, affection, and a normal life.

We pull up to my house, and Jacob comes to open my door for me, ever the gentleman. He places a hand on my lower back and leads me to the front porch. When we get there, I don't search my purse for my key, only look at Jacob with a coy smile.

"I had a great time tonight," I tell him. "I'd love to do this again."

He returns my smile, but there's an edge of sadness to it.

"I would, too," he says, then sighs, dropping the smile altogether. "But I'm not sure we should."

My mouth falls in an O-shape, and I honestly have no idea what I'm supposed to say to that.

"You're an amazing woman, Rachel. I really enjoyed spending time with you, but I'm not sure if the timing is right."

"What do you mean?"

"You brought up Lyla's father in every conversation we had, and I don't even think you realized it. I don't know the situation, but whatever it is, I don't think it's over."

I shake my head and breathe a faint, disbelieving laugh. "There is nothing going on between Lyla's father and me. We just have a complicated history. We're way over it."

"I'm not sure someone who let Elizabeth refer to you as his wife is *way over it*."

Ryder did what? Why wouldn't he have cleared that up? I'm sure it was just an oversight, or that Ryder didn't hear her correctly.

"Like I said, I really like you, Rachel, but I'm looking for someone who can be all in. If you feel like that's something you're ready for, then I'd be honored to take you out again."

It's right there.

He's offering me the life Ryder never could. All I need to do is open my mouth and tell him yes, that I can be all in with him.

So, why am I picturing Ryder right inside that door? Why is it him that I want standing here with this offer? I can practically feel how the warmth of him would radiate onto me, how my body would subconsciously lean toward him, how we'd be wrapped up in each other's embrace before we even knew what was happening.

And I know that Jacob's right.

My silence is enough of an answer for us both.

"Thank you for a lovely night, Rachel," he says, leaning forward to place a chaste kiss on my cheek. When he leans back, his smile is polite. "I hope you know there's no ill will here, so I do hope you'll keep bringing Lyla to class. She's a great kid."

I murmur a thank you and watch as Jacob walks to his car in long confident strides.

Once he's in the car, I fish for my key, unlock the door, and wait to hear any sign of life from Ryder or the kids, but there's nothing. I don't hear the TV, Ryder's low voice, or Dominic's wild antics.

I reach for my phone to call Ryder when I hear a high-pitched squeal from outside. My feet carry me as my mind paints all the horrific images a mother never wants to think of. When I get to the back door and pull it open, I'm frozen in place at what I see in the backyard.

The pool area is a complete disaster. Way more than three towels are laid around the patio, some looking like they were actually thrown into the pool. Water guns, pool noodles, and blow-up floats are scattered everywhere. Two open pizza boxes, several paper plates, red solo cups, and a two-liter of pop litter the table on the deck, but that's not what I can't look away from.

It's almost ten o'clock, long past Lyla and Dominic's bedtime, but here they are, swimming in the pool in their swim vests and matching goggles.

"My turn! My turn!" Dominic shouts.

Ryder stands in the middle of the pool, bare from the waist up, and picks up the boy with ease, before throwing him across the pool. Dominic squeals in delight before splashing into the water.

Lyla paddles toward her father. "Me again! Please, Daddy!"

He does the same to her while Dominic swims over for his next turn.

Though I haven't made a sound, Ryder turns to face me, flicking water from his face. As soon as his eyes are on me, my stomach flips, my lungs compress, and my skin tingles with the sparks I spent all night searching for.

I'm not a stranger to Ryder's body, but it's been years since I've seen the meticulously sculpted muscles he still works diligently to maintain. Ryder's white swim trunks hang low on his waist, and the V leading downward is deeply defined. The contrast of the white fabric against his black skin makes him look angelic, but there's nothing pure about the hungry gaze that ravishes my body like it's a treasure to be cherished.

That flame burns from somewhere deep inside me. A place I swore I wouldn't fall into with Ryder.

Not again.

So, instead of yelling about how late it is or how impossible it seems for only three people to have made the disastrous mess on the patio, I simply descend the deck stairs and grab two dry towels.

"Come on, kids. Let's dry off and get ready for bed."

CHAPTER TWENTY-FIVE

Rachel

The kids don't protest when I bring them in to get ready for bed. They even spare me the usual arguments as to why they should stay up longer, and they each fall asleep as soon as their heads hit the pillow. Unsurprising since it's nearly three hours past their bedtime.

I make my way to the back deck. I don't particularly want to clean the mess tonight, but I know I definitely won't want to deal with it in the morning, so I may as well get it over with.

When I get outside, the first thing I notice is that the mess is gone. The second is that Ryder sits on the edge of the pool, feet dangling in the water. He doesn't turn at my entrance, but I know he can sense me.

The same way I can always sense him.

I slide off my heels and go to him, not caring that my dress meets the wet concrete as I sit and dip my feet in the warm water.

"If you're coming to lecture me about bedtimes, you should know they both promised not to be assholes tomorrow."

"One late night won't kill them," I say, and Ryder looks at me with a raised brow. I shrug. "As long as late pool nights don't become a habit, I don't mind. They seemed to have a lot of fun."

What I don't tell Ryder is that it's difficult to be angry after seeing how happy the three of them were all playing together in the pool. It's a memory the kids, and I, won't soon forget.

"How was your date?" Ryder asks, and that last word has a bite of ice.

I think very carefully before answering him. It didn't end well since Jacob called me out on still having feelings for Ryder, but technically, the date *itself* went great.

"It was nice," I say, with as little expression as possible.

I hope he won't push it and will leave my love life alone for once, but I should've known better.

"Just nice?"

"Mm-hm."

"Interesting," he says, and I can hear the knowing smile.

I look to scowl at him, but my eyes don't go to his face. They go to the uncovered chest that I've done an excellent job of ignoring so far, but not anymore. It's been years since I've been this close to Ryder when he's shirtless. Once upon a time, it was an everyday luxury—one that I took for granted.

His eyes on me are a flame, heating my skin, and the growing smile on his lips is a taunt that I pretend to ignore.

"What's that supposed to mean?" I ask, looking away to ignore that damn smile.

"I'm not sure any great love story ever started with *just nice.*"

"And what would you know about great love stories?"

His chuckle hits places inside me that it shouldn't. "I know that there should be more passion than *just nice.*"

"Maybe there was," I say with a slight tilt to my head. I didn't come out here to antagonize him, but if he's going to be a jerk, I won't sit here and take it. "Maybe it was the most passionate I've ever felt."

"It wasn't," he says with no hesitation and all the confidence in the world.

I ignore him. "Maybe we talked and laughed all night. Maybe he had one hand just a little too low on my back. Maybe he pressed me up against his car and kissed me. Maybe we barely made it into his back seat before he—"

One second, I'm sitting on the edge of the pool, and the next, every nerve in my body is on hyper-drive as I plunge into the water. It soaks through my dress in an instant and the fabric clings to me like a second skin. My makeup has to be running down my face, and my hair must be a mess as I splash to the surface.

"What the hell, Ryder!" I shout once I break the waterline. When I wipe the water from my eyes, I only see his devilish smile before the splash of him jumping in blinds me again.

I may not be able to see him, but I *feel* him.

It's like everything is moving in slow motion when Ryder's hand reaches for me under the water, brushing the skin of my inner arm as a hand settles on my lower back, pulling me into him like we're magnets. The movement is smooth, done with so much ease that not even *I* can doubt how natural it feels to be pressed together.

I can't touch the floor of the pool, but it doesn't matter because Ryder's hold on me is as strong as steel chains and just as binding. His other hand cups my cheek, keeping a possessive hold while ensuring I don't look away like he knows I'm tempted to.

Ryder towers over me like certain doom, and it scares me how much it *doesn't* scare me. The intensity boring into me has the power to bring kings to their knees, and I'm furious that I want to rest in the arms capable of bringing such destruction to the world.

"He couldn't bring out one bit of the passion inside you. The way your eyes light up like a fucking fire, the way your heart races twice its normal speed, the way your fingers dig into my chest, and your toes curl without you even realizing it's happening. *That's* how I know there wasn't passion between you and *fucking Jacob*. Because I know *you.*"

Like trying to break free of whatever hold he has over me, I force myself to relax my fingers and uncurl my toes.

"You're right," I practically spit. "Jacob didn't do such a fantastic job pissing me off, but you seem to do it so flawlessly."

"Anger is passion, too, Rebel."

"Not the kind I'm looking for."

"You want to know why you've never found *what you're looking for*?" His lips barely brush against mine, eliciting goosebumps that cover my body, though the pool is warm. "Because you've been looking in the wrong fucking place."

"And you're the right place?"

He pulls back just enough to look at me with an honesty I can't deny. "I always have been."

I'm not sure which of us leans in first, only that when our lips finally meet, I lose all control. It's like he's flipped a switch, turning any reason or sanity off, leaving only a primal need.

I don't push him away, tell myself this is wrong, or even think.

I just *feel*.

His hand wraps around my neck to pull me to him like he can't get close enough. The hand that holds my ass runs up and down my waist like he's trying to commit the curves to memory.

I can't keep my hands still, either. I let them roam his body just like I've been dying to since I got home. They trail down his muscles with every ounce of the possessiveness that bubbles in my veins.

It feels like my *right* to touch him, to have him all to myself.

"You taste even better than I remember," he grits out between furious kisses, and I wrap my legs around his waist in answer.

"Needing more, Rebel?"

"Ryder," I plead, but it's interrupted by our kiss and my barely coherent thoughts.

He slows, taking my bottom lip between his teeth with a tug before letting it go. "Say it."

Whether it's the sheer need to keep kissing him, or the wall of pride that towers higher than any other defense I've built, I don't know, but something keeps me from answering.

My hands trail down his back, and his skate over my skin beneath the water. The sensation of his gentle yet firm fingertips brushing against me is wholly intoxicating. I close my eyes to take it in until I realize where those fingers are going.

The hem of my dress is pulled up in one smooth motion, and my gasp comes at the same time that Ryder's fingers graze the outside of my underwear. He doesn't pull the fabric down or push them aside. Instead, he slides his fingers up and down the thin material in agonizingly slow movements.

"Ryder," I say, so breathy that it sounds more like a moan than a warning.

"It's been a while, but you remember how this works," he says, eliciting that familiar heat that shoots straight to my core.

I don't remember moving in the water, but suddenly my back hits the edge of the pool. As if to make it even harder for me to think straight, the hand around my neck wraps around my throat in a greedy hold that never fails to make me weak in the knees. He doesn't squeeze but holds firmly enough to keep my attention on him as he applies pressure to my most sensitive part.

"You won't get what you want unless you ask for it, Rebel."

As if to prove his point, he removes the pressure again.

"No," I breathe without my brain's permission.

His chuckle echoes against the water, and I don't even have the decency to regret my shamelessness.

"Say it," he grates, biting the shell of my ear before licking at the spot with his tongue in a maddening movement.

"Touch me," I relent, in the lusty voice that only he can bring out of me.

He presses his fingers to my core, and I suck in a breath. "You'll have to be a bit more specific."

My need for him outweighs my pride, and I finally give in. "Finger me, Ryder."

"That's a good girl," he says, and I don't have the chance to respond because he plunges two fingers inside me. I cry out, but the sound is swallowed by Ryder's lips, capturing mine.

The sensation of his fingers thrusting into me, his hand squeezing my throat, and his lips owning mine has parts of my brain shut down altogether—more specifically, the logical part that knows I'll regret this in the morning.

I press my chest into him, reveling in how his hand flexes around my throat before moving to grope my breasts. He doesn't bother being gentle as he kneads them through the fabric of my dress.

My moans echo against the water when his mouth leaves mine to glide down the collar of my dress. With his teeth and one hand, he tears the fabric, giving himself full access to my chest. I gasp at the motion, and as if I'm not already so stimulated, he chooses that moment to shove a third finger into me.

"Fuck," I groan and arch my back, molding every part of my body to his.

"I'm tempted to give you that, too," he mutters against my skin.

"Yes," I say without thinking, but I don't dare to take it back.

"Ask, Rebel, and I might." He sucks in a breath, no doubt at the way I clench around his fingers at his order.

"Fuck me, Ryder."

He removes his fingers, and I watch, utterly mesmerized, as he pulls his swimming trunks down and lines himself up with my entrance.

When he looks down at me, all teasing and taunting are gone, leaving only unbridled desire and a single question. "Are you sure about this?"

If I gave the logical part of my brain a chance, it would probably remind me of the millions of reasons that my answer should be *hell no*, but I don't. I let my body speak for itself and finally give in to the temptation that's been driving me crazy since Ryder moved in.

"Yes."

Then his hands are gripping my hips, pulling me with the need of a madman as he slides inside me. As ready as I was, the sting of taking all of him burns like fire and mixes so beautifully with the feel of his lips adoring my throat and his fingertips digging into my skin.

His rhythm is unrestrained, urgent like he can't control himself, and it's a sentiment I share. I wrap my arms around his neck and hold on like my life depends on it, relishing this moment.

Because I feel so full, not just physically but emotionally and mentally. At this moment, I feel like I'm grounded in something that will steady and protect me. At this moment, I feel like everything might actually work out.

With the arching of my back against the concrete of the pool's edge, and the rolling of my hips, Ryder hits the perfect spot, and I feel myself getting closer and closer to that blissful peak.

"I've missed this," Ryder grunts, so low I almost miss it in the water splashing against the pool's edge. But his next words are said clearly. "I've missed *you*, Rachel."

There's no denying that I echo his feelings because just hearing him say the words have me coming apart in his hold. I bite his shoulder to muffle my cry when my release hits full force. My vision goes black, and the feel of Ryder moving ruthlessly inside of me is all I can focus on as I ride the waves of pleasure.

As if my fall triggers him, Ryder's grip on my hips tightens to a deliciously painful point.

"Fuck, Rebel," he grates, and his thrusts turn spasmodic as he fills me with his release.

We stay like that for long moments, my legs wrapped around his waist and his arms holding me to him like I'm precious. Our foreheads rest against each other, his breath skating over my skin, and I savor every inhale of him.

After who-knows-how-long, Ryder pushes my forehead with his, so I'm forced to look into his eyes. "Tell me that isn't the passion you're looking for."

I don't say anything because we both know it is.

CHAPTER TWENTY-SIX

Rachel

30 Weeks Along

I didn't realize how badly I needed to see my parents until they were sitting across from me in the living room. I have a great relationship with my mom and dad, but since we all work demanding jobs, we don't spend much time together, even when we live in the same city. Having this chance to truly relax, hear about their work, and share how my classes are going, is something I cherish more than I can express.

Ryder gave us privacy with an excuse about having to get some work done for the real estate company he works for, then drove off—to the base, I'm sure.

We spend hours talking, but when my father steps outside to take a call, my mom slides to the edge of her chair. "So, what's the situation with Ryder?"

I take a sip from my water, using it as a moment to gather my thoughts on that particularly confusing topic.

"We're just figuring out how we'd like to parent, that's all. Not much of a *situation*."

She gives me the kind of knowing look that only a mother can. "Don't you lie to me. I know you two were making out before your father and I arrived."

I cringe, partly because she hit the nail on the head and partly because no one should ever hear their parents talk about *making out*.

"What would make you think that?" I ask, popping the knuckles of my left hand, then right.

"Your messy hair and the fact that you looked on the brink of passing out. Are you going to deny it?"

I sag my shoulders, giving up the act altogether.

"To be honest, I have absolutely no idea what we are," I admit.

"What do you want to be?"

His, I think wistfully.

"Good parents," I say instead.

She nods, then stands from her chair to come to sit beside me on the couch. She lays a hand over mine. "Being a good parent isn't just about taking care of your child. It's also about taking care of yourself."

"What if things don't work out and then I'm—" I stop myself before the word *alone* leaves my lips. "I'm just trying to figure all of this out."

"If it helps, your father and I think Ryder is a good man, and I'm not just saying that because he seems to be able to care for you financially. He cares about you deeply."

"How do you know?"

She raises her brows with a slight head tilt. "Rachel, he sends us updates on you all the time. He lets us know whenever there's an appointment or a particularly good or bad day. At first, I thought he was just kissing up to us, but today I saw how he looked at you, and I'm sure it's more than that."

I don't say anything to that because I have a very real, very scary feeling that she's right.

Saying goodbye to my parents is bittersweet. I wish, more than anything, that they could stay longer, but they're starting a project tomorrow and can't delay it.

Spending time with them has filled me with a sense of peace that I didn't realize I was missing. Not to mention it eased the homesickness that's been increasingly more difficult to ignore since I moved here.

Overall, it was perfect. The only part I can't quite shake is my conversation with Mom. I'm not sure if I wanted her to tell me to take the chance with Ryder or not, but her insistence that I should take care of myself has only confused me more.

How am I supposed to balance what I want for myself with what's best for my daughter? What if the two conflict?

The thoughts war in my head as I trudge to my room.

"Where do you think you're going?"

I almost jump out of my skin at Ryder's low voice coming from the direction of his bedroom. I almost forgot that he came back from the base before my parents left.

He leans against his bedroom door frame, arms crossed over his chest. The tight T-shirt hugs his muscles, and his sweatpants are slung low on his hips. Those thick lips that took mine just hours ago are pressed in a firm line, and the scruff surrounding it is neatly trimmed.

Those dark eyes regard me, and I can't decide if what I see there is the absence of emotion, or if there are so many, that he doesn't know where to begin expressing them.

He looks gorgeous.

Or is that my hormones just getting the better of me?

I scan him up and down twice more.

No, he's definitely gorgeous.

I point to my room. "Bed."

"Using the plastic wrap as a duvet?"

I'd completely forgotten about the painting project that took up most of my day.

"I'll just grab my clothes and sleep on the couch," I say and move to the door.

"Oh, no, you don't." He wraps a firm hand around my upper arm.

"What are you doing?" I ask, more taken off guard by his touch than the actual gesture of stopping me.

With a small tug, I'm being pulled in the direction of his room. "Taking you to bed."

"W-what?"

Ryder's lip tugs up in a wicked smile. "Get your head out of the gutter, Rebel. I'll sleep on the couch, and you can sleep in my bed."

I have no explanation for why that answer causes a dip of disappointment to settle in my gut, but it does. I've never considered what it might be like to sleep next to Ryder. The only time we even got close was that first night we met, but there wasn't much sleeping...

Now, I can't help but imagine how my small body would fit so nicely tucked into his. How he'd wrap those broad arms around me and rest his angular chin gently on my head. I wonder if I'd fall swiftly to sleep or be too enamored by his scent and the sound of his soothing heartbeats to give in to unconsciousness.

"That really isn't necessary," I tell him, in no particular tone, as we go to his room.

In the months since I've moved here, I've never been in Ryder's room. It feels like crossing a boundary since we are only just getting to know each other.

The king-sized bed has a glass table on either side of it and a dresser across from it with a small television. There's a door to the bathroom on my right, but absolutely nothing personalizing the room. There are no pictures, decorations, or signs of the man living here besides the smell of pineapple and bergamot.

"Really," I say with a small step back, "I still need my clothes—"

I'm cut off when he releases my arm to reach behind his back and pull his shirt over his head. I'm stunned into silence as I take in the wonder that is Ryder's body. His chest is sculpted to perfection, from the sharp lines defining each and every muscle to the black hairs dusting his pecks and trailing from his belly button down past the hem of his pants...

Ryder clears his throat, which is when I realize he's been holding out his shirt to me since he took it off. I wonder for all of one second if he noticed my less-than-subtle gawking, but the knowing smile on those damn lips answers that question for me.

"Might as well change into more of mine," he muses, and I'm about to ask what he means when I remember what I'm wearing.

I only put on his t-shirt and ridiculously large sweatpants because all of my clothes felt too tight against my stomach. They were folded in a neat pile on the dryer in our small laundry room, so I'd taken them, figuring he wouldn't mind.

Now that his eyes rake over the outfit as if it's fine lingerie and not sweats, I know I was right. He doesn't mind one bit. If anything, the possessiveness in his eyes makes me wonder if he *likes* having me in his clothes.

But that only confuses my jumbled thoughts more, so I can't bring myself to take his shirt.

"I can go get my own clothes."

"I don't want you around the paint fumes."

"That's ridiculous. I've been around them all day long."

"And if I'd known that, I would've put a stop to it sooner."

"Paint fumes have an extremely low chance of harming an unborn baby. Pregnant women paint nurseries all the—"

"A low chance is still a chance. Therefore, you won't be going in there. I'll have someone finish the job tomorrow. Until then, you'll stay in here."

"This is insane, Ryder." I step toward the door, but two strong arms stop me before I can reach for the handle. Before I know what's happening, my back is pressed against the wall, both of Ryder's arms caging me in as he towers over me.

"As I said earlier, this is *my* baby inside of you. If you're going to be reckless, I'll have no choice but to handcuff you to me for the remainder of this pregnancy."

I have no idea what scares me more, the deadly seriousness of his warning or the fact that it *doesn't* scare me.

"You don't get to play caveman with me," I say, in a tone far softer than I intend.

One of his hands cups my stomach. "Until this baby is born, I sure as hell do." His eyes skate down my body with awe that makes me feel like the most beautiful woman in the world. "And maybe even after."

It's on the tip of my tongue to question him, to challenge his so-called claim over me, but I don't. It would be a lie, and we both know it. So, instead of fighting a losing battle, I yield to the burning temptation that I have resisted too damn long.

I kiss him.

I have to stand on tiptoes to reach, but it doesn't matter. Our lips meet with all the fervor they had earlier today, and his arms pull me closer to him.

I pull him down and let my tongue explore his mouth with the same passion he does. My hands arduously trace his bare chest like I could memorize every ripple of his abs. When my hands travel downward, I tug at his pants until his hand wraps around mine to stop me.

"What is it that you want, Rebel?"

"You," I answer because it really is that simple.

He chuckles against my lips, and I wish I could bottle the sound. "Then say the words."

I'd almost forgotten this request, which he's made every time we've been together. The night we met, he told me he liked that I'd know I asked for the pleasure he gave me, but now that I know him, I wonder if there's more to it.

"You always ask me to *say the words*. Why?"

He pulls back just enough to study me as his thumb gently strokes my chin and finally answers. "Most people find silence uncomfortable. They'd rather fill it with idle conversation than face potential discomfort. I happen to be quite fond of silence, and I think that how a person reacts to it says a lot about them and what they're looking for.

Usually, it's validation, praise, or just someone to listen to them, but that night, at the club, you never bothered to fill the silence."

His thumb trails up to brush my bottom lip. "For the first time, I *wanted* someone's words—needed them. It drove me crazy that I couldn't read you like everyone else. Your words were all I had to go off of, so I kept asking for them."

"You're telling me that after two months of hooking up, you still needed my words to determine that I wanted you?

I feel, rather than see, his growing smile. "Oh, I knew by then, but I'd also learned another vital piece of information."

"And that is?"

One hand trails down my body in a slow, taunting caress.

"It turns you on to ask for your pleasure, Rebel. Asking me to fuck you, take you, own you."

His fingers dip beneath the fabric of my sweatpants and one slides along my aching core, slick with the wetness there.

"Makes you soaking wet."

As if to prove the point, he dips two fingers inside me for all of a single moment before he pulls them away, then brings those very fingers to his lips. The sight of him licking his fingers—licking *me* off his fingers—is one I never would've expected to make me weak in the knees, but if he wasn't pressing me to the wall, I'm sure I'd fall on my ass.

I could try to deny his claims or retreat in embarrassment from their accuracy, but there'd be no point.

So, I reach up on my tiptoes, sweep my tongue across his cheek until my lips are just below his, and say the words both of us are waiting for.

"Fuck me, Ryder. Take me. *Own* me."

And he does.

CHAPTER TWENTY-SEVEN

Ryder

Present

I reach out in my half-asleep state and jolt to a sitting position when I find the spot beside me empty and cold.

My plans to bring to life the vivid and downright-deviant dreams that filled my sleep are squashed to bits. I wish that was an exaggeration, but it isn't. Every time I close my eyes, I see Rachel coming apart around me in the pool.

It was fucking fantastic.

It wasn't even that I got to fuck her again—though, again, because I cannot stress this enough, it was *fucking incredible*—but everything that happened afterward, too.

Instead of shutting down or closing off like I feared, Rachel didn't voice a single protest when I carried her bridal style out of the pool and to her room. I knelt before her, pulled the wet dress from her body, then switched between drying her with a towel and kissing every inch of her perfect body. She didn't even argue when I handed her my shirt to sleep in. Her own clothing would've made more sense—considering that we spent the night in *her* room—but the idea of seeing her in my clothes again was too good to pass on.

I laid her in bed and climbed in behind her. Maybe she was asleep, unaware of what she was doing, but I like to think that her curling into me and holding my arm with both hands was more than just a subconscious reaction to my being there.

After all, that's exactly how she used to sleep by my side in Los

Angeles.

I go through my morning routine, unable to do anything but replay last night on a loop, a fact that has me rock hard and ready for round two.

Then three.

Then four.

Then *fucking forever*.

If I thought I over-exaggerated how good Rachel felt over the years, I was only kidding myself. If anything, she feels better than I imagined.

And I imagined a lot.

Then to sleep beside her again? Fucking heaven.

Now that I've had a taste of her, I'm addicted all over again, and there is no chance of rehabilitation. Rachel might think she has a choice in how things will play out between us, but she doesn't.

Her brain will try to tell her we're not a good match, but her body knows better.

I swear if her over-active mind is trying to spin itself into believing last night was wrong, then I'll have no choice but to drag her back to bed caveman-style and show her how *right* this is.

How right *we* are.

I rush through the bare minimum tasks of getting ready, and go to hunt Rachel down.

When I open the door, there's a sizzle and popping coming from the kitchen, and the scent of bacon fills the entire house. I don't hear the kids, but it's still early, and they had a late night, so that doesn't surprise me.

When I round the kitchen, Rachel stands beside the stove, which is alive with bacon and eggs cooking, but she's staring absently at the ground, fingers wrapped around a mug of coffee like it's the only thing keeping her alive right now.

"Morning," I greet, and I can't help my smile when she jumps, splashing her coffee onto the floor.

"Fuck, you scared me," she says, reaching for a rag, but I'm faster.

I grab it before she can and kneel to wipe up the mess as she stares down at me with a wide range of emotions.

Excitement. Fear. Nervousness. Lust.

It doesn't tell me where exactly her head is, but it's a start.

I wipe up the coffee with a few strokes of the rag and toss it into the sink from my kneeled position. Once my hands are free, I skate gentle fingers up Rachel's legs.

"What are you doing?" she asks in that breathy voice that drives me fucking crazy.

I lean forward, pressing my lips to her toned legs like they're things to be adored, and to me, they are. Everything about Rachel deserves to be cherished.

"You're making breakfast," I murmur against her skin and feel the goosebumps form beneath my lips.

"Uh, y-yeah."

My lips travel upward, climbing from her knee, closing in around her thighs, and, finally, that spot right between her legs. "I'm ready to eat."

I press a firm kiss to her apex, and she gasps. "Ryder, the kids could come down here any second."

My hand slowly trails up her leg, dipping beneath her shorts to pull her underwear aside, only to find, *thank fuck*, that she isn't wearing any. My fingers graze her core, which is already wet with arousal.

"Right now, I'm only worried about you coming, Rebel."

Her soft moan is all I need to hear before pulling the fabric aside to slide my tongue across her, and *fuck* does she taste delicious.

"Ryder," she pants, "I don't think—"

"Hmm," I hum against her most sensitive spot and revel in her body shudder, "I was worried you'd start thinking too much about all of this."

Her eyes blaze with that flame I'm desperate to burn in. I flick my tongue against her, savoring the sight of her eyes closing with the sensation before she glares again.

"It's a red flag when a man tells you you're thinking too much."

"And is it a red flag if you come all over my face within seconds of being finger fucked?"

I emphasize my point by sliding another finger inside her and sucking her core into my mouth. She arches against the counter, face contorting with the most beautiful moan.

She grabs my head, holding me with a grip that begs me to stay put. "Want me to keep going, Rebel?"

She groans but doesn't answer, aside from pushing my head harder. I won't let her move me an inch.

I halt the movement of my fingers, which are curled deep inside her.

"Wait," she gasps.

"If you want me to keep going, you'll have to ask for it like a good girl."

"Fuck you, Ryder."

"There will be plenty of time for that later. Now, say it."

She doesn't say anything and, instead, rolls her hips against my lips, and when my eyes travel up her delectable body, I swallow hard.

She only has one hand on my head now, slowly caressing me in the most mesmerizing pattern. Her other hand has slipped beneath her t-shirt, roughly squeezing her breasts. Her eyes are hung low, and those big, beautiful lips are parted, letting loose gasps with every roll of her hips against my face, even though I'm not giving her the stimulation she's after.

Fuck me, my little rebel wants to play games.

I narrow my eyes in acceptance of her challenge and shove three fingers deep inside her. My tongue moves against her center like I'm a starved man eating my first meal in weeks, and honestly, that's what it feels like.

Having Rachel again is throwing away years of sobriety to fall back into the most lethal kind of addiction. Tasting her sweetness, feeling her spasms of pleasure, and hearing her delectable moans make me wonder how I ever survived without her.

How did I go on with my life when she was hundreds of miles away?

I suck her into my mouth at the same time that I repeatedly hit the most sensitive spot inside her, and she jolts against me. Her walls tighten, and she closes her thighs around my head to hold me in place.

I pull out of her hold with ease. "We both know I'm not letting you come until you say the words."

"Don't you dare fucking stop."

"Not those. I know you like being my rebel, but if you want to come, you'll be my good girl and *say the words*."

I squeeze her ass in one hand while my fingers curl fast and hard inside her, and my tongue circles her again and again. "Oh my—Ryder, I—*fuck*—"

"Come on, baby," I say, gently biting the sensitive skin of her swollen folds as she arches her back with a gasp.

I feel her resolve melt away as I pump my fingers in and out of her. My tongue flicks and sucks as she says the beautiful words. "Please don't stop eating me, Ryder. Make me come. *Please*, make me come," she pants.

"That's my girl," I mutter before going into hyper-drive.

It only takes a few more pumps before she's biting down on her fist to stifle her cries as she comes apart on my face. I lick up every last drop of her, even when she jerks as I lap against her overstimulated core.

I place one last kiss on her center before pushing to my feet and taking Rachel's lips, making her taste herself on me. She doesn't resist and kisses me back just as passionately.

"That wasn't a mistake, neither was last night, and neither was any other time we've ever been together."

She tries to avoid my gaze, but I grip the back of her neck and gently force her eyes to lock with mine.

"This isn't good for Lyla," she whispers.

"How so?"

"She'll be able to sense that things are weird between us."

"Then things won't be weird between us."

"Little late for that."

"Says who?"

Her expression, a mix of wariness and defeat, hits me in the chest and settles there uncomfortably. "Then what are we, Ryder? What is this?"

I shrug, wrapping my arms around her and pulling her into me with another kiss.

"Two people who don't want to stop being together. Can't it be that simple?"

Her body molds to mine, seeming to agree wholeheartedly, but that reeling mind seems so intent on fighting this.

"Things with us have never been simple."

"Then let's make them simple," I insist. "We'll be together however we'd like to be until I move out. No titles, no rules, no drama. Just being together."

"Just being together," she repeats, not sounding too convinced by the prospect.

Then, the padding of footsteps comes down the stairs, and I turn just in time to see two sleepy toddlers walk into the room.

Dominic looks the grumpiest I've ever seen, with a frown that pairs comically with his wicked case of bedhead. On the other hand, Lyla looks perfectly rested and happy to be up for the day.

I'd be willing to bet she dragged him out of bed before coming down here.

Lyla's tiny face scrunches in disgust as she points to the stove, which has bacon and eggs burning on it.

"Do we have to eat that?" she asks, looking horrified at the idea.

"Ew, that smells gross," Dominic agrees.

I reach over to turn the stove off and step away from Rachel to scoop Lyla into my arms. "No, Tiger. We're all going out for breakfast."

When I look at Rachel, she's staring at us with a mix of affection and concern. I know the latter is for herself, but there's no need for it.

For now, I'll let her cling to the notion of a simple hook-up until I'm gone since the truth would send her running.

Because when I do move out, there's no way in hell I won't be taking her with me.

It's mid-afternoon when Rachel and I finally convince Lyla to go down for a nap, and even then, she only agrees once Meredith comes to get Dominic, and she no longer has a playmate.

Once she's down, Rachel and I go outside to train despite the merciless late-August sun beating down on us. The heat drains both our energy levels, so the workout portion goes faster than normal, and we get into the strikes and defense drills we've been reviewing with each session.

Rachel's progress is nothing short of admirable. She's visibly more comfortable with each drill, and it shows in how naturally she moves with them. It's hard to believe that just a few short weeks ago, she'd been adamantly against the idea of training with me.

And today, I'll be taking it a step further.

Since easing her fear of knives in our second training session, we've only worked on learning how to defend against them, but now that the drills come easily to her, she's ready for the next level.

After we go through the usual defenses with the fake knife, I place a real—though mostly dull—one in her hand.

"What are you doing?" she asks, looking at the object warily.

"Today, you're going to learn how to use a knife."

"What? Why?"

I reach out to close her hand around the handle. "Because defense is only half the fight."

She weighs the weapon in her hand, looking at me with wide eyes that make my head go to dark, devious places. "But this is a *real* knife. Shouldn't we start with the fake one?"

"You can handle it," I assure her.

"You're not afraid I'll cut you?"

"*I* can handle it." My smile widens with her narrowing eyes, and that flicker of defiance gives me all sorts of ideas on how to tame her...

As if she can read my thoughts, she lowers her head and clears her throat. "So, what do I do first?"

"Same as defense, it's important to accept the possibility of getting cut. If you let it surprise you, your opponent will take advantage of the distraction," I tell her as she inspects the weapon in her hand like it wields her and not the other way around. "The key is making sure you're not cut anywhere that could cause significant damage. The more control you have, the better."

"Try not to get stabbed," she says with a nod. "Got it."

An hour later, I'd never know Rachel was repulsed by the blade she swings. She hasn't mastered the weapon by any means, but she no longer looks at the knife like it came from the pits of hell. In fact, I'm starting to think that if she hadn't had trauma associated with the weapon, she'd be fond of it.

We get into our fighting stances, and she moves first, slashing the knife upward, but I only have to lean to the side to avoid it. Her frustrated groan would make me laugh if I wasn't so focused on how her body twists, sending her free hand toward my stomach. I catch the punch right before it makes contact and twist her arm so her back is to me.

I begin to release my hold as she slackens since that usually means we're going to start over, but she surprises me when her elbow swings back to connect with my ribs. I breathe out a hiss, which she uses to wrench out of my hold.

Next time, I'm making her tap out.

She swings downward, knife in line with my shoulder, and I wait until the last second to block it, but it doesn't get that far. Rachel pauses before the blade is even a foot away from my body.

I strike my hand against her wrist in a motion that knocks the knife from her grasp, then swing my leg behind hers, using her shoulders as leverage so I can take her down with ease. The second her back hits the ground, I use one hand to pin her wrists above her head and use the other to gently stroke her face.

"That was nicely done, Rebel."

"Oh, shut up. I haven't even managed to take you down once."

"I happen to like getting you on your back."

Her breaths heave from the exertion, and her skin glows against the sun, drawing my eyes to her chest, which is only covered by a poor excuse for a sports bra. My free hand kneads one of her breasts, and her breath hitches, letting the slightest moan escape those delectable lips.

"Ryder," she whispers. "Will you fuck me?"

I pull back at the question, but only because it's the only time she's ever asked me without being prompted to do so. A wicked smile pulls at my lips, and I decide it's much better when she asks of her own volition.

"How can I say no?" I ask, releasing her wrists and dragging my hands down her precious body.

My thumbs hook beneath the fabric of her bra to peel it off when I feel the tip of the dull blade just below my belly button. When my eyes find Rachel's wild ones, I realize the ploy she's used to finally get the upper hand on me.

The look of pure pride on her flawless features is breathtaking, and all I can do is stare in awe.

"For fuck's sake, Rebel."

The widest smile spreads across her face, and she goes to drop the blade, but I wrap my hand around hers and lift the tip of the knife over my heart.

"Aim higher next time. Heart, stomach, lungs, even the throat makes a great target." I bring the point back to where she'd had it below my belly button. "This won't do as much damage."

Rachel nods, still wearing that sultry gaze that drives me insane, but her narrowed eyes and curled lips assure me that she's taking all of my notes seriously.

She gives the knife a light toss to the grass beside us, then uses her newly free hand to cup the bulge that's been rock-hard since I climbed on top of her. "So, are you going to do it or not?"

I lower to my elbows so I'm hovering over her full lips. "Do what?"

She gives me a knowing look.

I dip down, taking her bottom lip between my teeth. "You'll have to remind me. What was it you wanted again?"

Her eyes flare with the rebellious nature that seems to be reserved for me, and I'm painfully hard by the time she dramatically sighs. The sultry voice that could bring armies to their knees is the only sound I care to hear for the rest of my life. "Fuck me, Ryder."

I take her lips, swallowing her gasp of delight as I do. It's the first gentle kiss we've shared since I moved here, and it's just as breathtaking as the furious, frenzied ones. Though, this one has a certain...intimacy. It's like we're no longer two people but a single entity created to be together.

I'm about to make good on her polite request, but a beeping from my left stops me. I wouldn't bother moving from my current position for just any tone, but this particular one is important.

I move off Rachel and grab the phone, reading the notification.

"Is that what I think it is?" Rachel asks, climbing to her feet to stand beside me.

I nod. "Someone just edited a submitted record, and we can track it."

CHAPTER TWENTY-EIGHT

Ryder

We're up the stairs and in the office as fast as possible without waking Lyla from her nap.

I settle into the chair, and my fingers fly across the keyboard.

"Anything?" Rachel asks, hovering just over my shoulder.

I grab hold of her hips and pull her onto my lap. "What the hell are you doing?" she demands, struggling to get to her feet.

I keep a firm hold on her and press my lips to the shell of her ear. "Keep squirming like that, and you'll have to take care of this." I roll my hips, and she stills.

I kiss her temple with a laugh as I log onto the computer and search for the edited file.

When I find it, I scan it over, and over, and over.

"What the hell…?"

"What's wrong?"

I shake my head, running through the numbers again for any sort of mistake on my end. "We caught someone embezzling, but it's not on the Rohypnol records."

"What?" Her eyes scan the computer, and I point to the receipt.

"It's in the office supplies. Not only those but *all* the base's supplies. The most mundane purchases. Fuck, I never would've thought to look here."

"Wait, so someone is taking from the supplies *and* Rohypnol?"

"Hopefully," I answer.

"Why, *hopefully*?"

"Because otherwise, we have two unrelated cases, and if that's true, then this just got a hell of a lot more complicated."

The possibility seems incomprehensible. If we're right, and there really are two separate sources embezzled from the Sacramento base, the fact that no one has caught onto it yet is suspicious as hell.

"Can't we trace this edit? Knowing where it came from is a good starting place."

I nod, going to do just that.

"What are you going to do if it shows up at the base?"

"I'll have to include Kade. He should be able to track any activity within the base better than I can, but I don't think it's being messed with there."

"Why not?"

"Anything entered into the database on-site leaves a sort of footprint. When I looked for one attached to the Rohypnol records, I found nothing. This person could be doing a damn good job hiding their tracks, but it's more likely they did it off site. There's more wiggle room that way."

Rachel's leg swings around, so she's straddling me in the desk chair. She braces her hands above my head, putting her chest at my eye level.

"You know, all this tech talk is kind of sexy."

"You're not allowed to talk to Kade anymore."

She laughs, breasts bouncing directly in front of my face. "It's only sexy when you do it."

"Is that right?" I ask and nip at her bottom lip to get that delectable moan out of her. The sound is downright addictive.

I'm about to take another hit when the IP address loads behind her, and I'm staring at the answer to what Rachel and I have been searching for.

What the fuck…This can't be right.

Whatever Rachel sees in my expression is enough to suck the playful mood from the room.

"What's wrong?" she asks, turning to look between me and the computer. "What does it say?"

I pull the chair closer, reaching past Rachel to rerun the test. I'm so anxious about the results that I barely notice how she wraps her arms and legs around me, gluing us together as she awaits my response.

"Ryder, what's going on?"

The numbers come up again—exactly the same as before.

"This is our IP address," I tell her. "According to this, the embezzling is coming from here."

"What? How is that possible?"

"I have no idea," I tell her honestly. "It has to be some hack or maybe a flaw in the virus I gave the capos. Someone must be disguising their IP address as ours to hide what they're doing."

This is bad.

If this gets out, it'll ruin any remaining trust between Moreno and me. I'll be declared a traitor of the family, and that's if he lets me live long enough to explain—judging by the fact that he hasn't looked me in the eye or even talked to me in weeks, I doubt he will.

Why me? If someone's trying to hide what they're doing, why not use a random IP address? Why not pick any other capo?

Because no other capo betrayed the family, I realize with bitter regret.

Could this be someone getting revenge?

Or, more likely, someone setting me up to take the fall if they're suspected of being found out.

"What are we going to do?" Rachel's low voice brings me back to the present, and when I look into her gaze, shining with worry and affection, I know I'll do whatever it takes to protect her and Lyla.

Whatever's happening, I need to handle it quickly and quietly.

"I need to make a call," I tell her, placing another kiss on her head before gently easing her off of me.

"No way in hell," she says, clinging to me tighter as I stand. "You're not shutting down on me. Whatever is going on, we're handling it together."

"That's not how this works."

I grip her hips, pushing her to put space between us.

Rachel's arms tighten to a deadly grip around my neck, and her legs wind themselves around me like ivy.

"It is now," she declares.

My fingers dig into her waist, but she only meets my challenging stare with the same iron-strong will I've always admired.

"Don't you dare shut me out of this. We got this far together. We'll finish this together."

It's on the tip of my tongue to tell her no. After all, she's already far more involved than I was ever comfortable with, and I need to get her out before it gets any worse. The more distance I can put between her and my work, the better.

"Don't shut me out," she whispers, and that simple, softly spoken request sinks beneath my skin and etches itself into my bones with the realization that I *cannot* deny her.

I can, however, protect her from getting caught in the middle of my mess.

"I need you to promise me that you will never tell anyone what you've learned about the family," I tell her, infusing an urgency in my tone to convey the importance of this demand. "No matter what happens, you cannot tell *anyone*."

"I won't," she says with a sincerity that can be felt. "I promise."

Hearing her say the words gives me only a small sense of peace. It's not even about how I'd be killed as a traitor if anyone found out how much I let her know. It's about the danger *she'd* be in—by my family and our enemies.

"I don't have the software I need on this computer to track whatever type of hack this is. I'll need to acquire and download the software without being traced."

"Why not go straight to Kade?"

"Because whoever did this has the ability to frame me for everything, and if they decide to do that before I can prove my innocence...."

Rachel's eyes go wide. "Moreno would know it wasn't you."

"Maybe, or maybe he'll see me as a threat that needs to be eliminated."

It's a black-and-white way of seeing the situation, but I've seen men killed for far less than what I'm facing now. I press a kiss to Rachel's cheek in an attempt to ease her rigid posture and furrowed brow. "Besides, I don't want this touching you or Lyla. The sooner it's handled, the better."

The absent look covering Rachel's features bothers me to my core. She starts to untangle herself from me to go, but I hold her face between my hands. "We'll figure this out, Rebel. I promise."

I'm not sure if it's my promise or touch that eases the wariness in her gaze, but I'm relieved to watch it melt away. I take her lips in a long kiss before she stands to go.

My phone is in my hand as soon as the door closes behind Rachel.

There's only one person who can get me what I need *and* keep it from Moreno.

"Hey Rachel, what's up?" Elli asks a little too cheerily.

I figure she's with Moreno and has to disguise the call.

"I need a favor. Can you get alone?"

"Yes! Of course, I want to hear about work. Give me just a few seconds."

She covers the microphone, but I hear her mumbling to Moreno and his grumble of a response.

"Hey, what's up?" she asks in her normal voice.

"Where did you go? If you're nearby, Moreno's just going to listen in."

"Um, he's not exactly in a position to follow me right now," she admits after a beat.

I try my best to wipe that image from my memory.

"I need some software sent over to me, but I need it done off the books."

There's a long pause. "What exactly are you up to?"

"It's a long story."

"I have time."

"Good. You'll need a lot of it to get what I'm asking for."

"Ryder," her voice lowers to a whisper. "I need to know I'm not doing something that'll betray Joshua. As much as I want to help you, I can't do that."

"I'm not asking you to. I think someone is trying to frame me for embezzlement. I need this software to help track them down."

"And if Joshua got word, he'd trust you even less," she fills in.

"Exactly."

Elli sighs. "Okay, but if he asks me about this directly, I won't lie to him."

"Deal."

"So, what do you need me to do?"

"You'll need to get into Kade's office. He has everything I'll need and the means to send it without being traced. Any idea if you can get in there without being noticed?"

"As a matter of fact, Joshua and Donovan are about to head to a few of the local businesses, and Kade is at the San Diego base fixing the security breach they had there. Now is as good a time as we'll get."

It's good that Moreno and Donovan are out for the evening because, even with my help, it takes Elli two hours to comb everything to find what I need. Having her send the software to me through an offshore email that can't be traced takes even longer, but it's worth it when my laptop chimes with the incoming email.

"Did it go through?"

"It's here." I lean back in my chair, relaxing for the first time in hours. "Thank you so much, Elli. This is a huge help."

"Of course. I'm happy to help."

"Well, I'll talk to you later. Enjoy your first capo conference," I tell her and ignore the bitter sting of what has to be jealousy.

"Oh shit! I can't believe I forgot to tell you. I overheard Joshua and Donovan talking about the capo conference a few days ago. They mentioned inviting you instead of Briggs to represent the Sacramento base."

My limbs go frozen. "Really?"

"Joshua said he needed more time to think about it, but I think there's a good chance he'll agree."

The idea of going back to L.A., even just for the capo conference, feels like a weight being lifted off my chest. Being back home, seeing my family, and getting a brief glimpse at what life used to be like for me.

It's everything.

"I've also been dropping hints about wanting to see you, so I'm sure that'll help your case, too."

I laugh at the thought of her likely poorly veiled hints and how Moreno would fight tooth and nail against them before inevitably giving in.

"Thanks for the heads up," I tell her. "And for the software."

"Keep me updated on everything, okay?"

"I will," I promise her, and we end the call.

I stare at the computer screen, which now has everything I need to track down whoever wants to frame me.

I'd been ready to dive into this project only a minute ago, even if it meant not getting to the base until the late hours of the night for my routine work.

But now?

If whoever this is realizes that I'm coming for them, they won't hesitate to use this information against me. I suspect Moreno would believe me eventually, but anything could happen during whatever investigation would take place.

I wouldn't get the invite to the capo conference, and I sure as hell wouldn't get my title back.

Two weeks.

That's not a long time to push this off.

Besides, as far as Rachel and I can tell, this embezzling has been going on for years. Two more weeks aren't going to matter.

With a long sigh, I close the software, lock the computer, and leave the office.

CHAPTER TWENTY-NINE

Rachel

"I got one last box for you!"

I hold out the cardboard box to Dominic when he races into my room. He snatches it from me with a mumbled thanks before dragging it into the living room to add it to the makeshift castle he and Lyla have made.

"I was starting to think I'd never get everything unpacked."

"Well, we aren't done yet," Meredith says and gestures to the stacks of clothes on the table that still need to be gone through. "But we're close."

I toss the clothes in piles, mostly to donate or throw away. "I can't thank you enough for helping me with this. I owe you big time."

"You don't owe me a thing. You know I'm happy to help out," she says with a genuine smile that reminds me how lucky I am to have a friend like her.

Since Ryder and I discovered he's being framed, nothing new has come to light. Ryder says the software he obtained would take time to fully deliver, download, and run, so we shouldn't expect answers for at least another few days.

So, we've spent the last two weeks living as the happy little family I never dared to dream we could be.

Ryder still watches Lyla while I go to work, and then when I get home, we either train or the three of us spend time together, going on walks, to the park, or swimming. Once we put Lyla to bed, we barely make it to the bedroom before we pull each other's clothes off.

The only part of our routine that I hate is that Ryder doesn't stay with me through the night.

As soon as he's thoroughly exhausted my body, he cleans us up, plants a breathless kiss on my lips, and then leaves. Though he's never said it outright, I know it's to go to work at the base. Between watching Lyla, spending time with me, and working, I'm not sure when Ryder has time to sleep, but when I asked him about it, he assured me I had nothing to worry about.

I'd wanted to push the topic, but when his hands trailed down my body and his teeth skated over my skin, I forgot my own name, let alone my worries. Besides, he doesn't seem over-tired or frustrated by the arrangement. In fact, he seems as blissful as I am, and it makes me wonder if he, too, wishes this was a permanent arrangement.

"So, are we going to talk about it?" Meredith asks, eyes never straying from the clothes.

"Talk about what?"

When she does look up, it's to give me a *don't bullshit me* look and a wave toward my bedroom. "I've been here almost every day this week, and Ryder's clothes have been on the floor of your room every time."

My cheeks flame in equal parts embarrassment and frustration. Embarrassment since I was planning to keep things between Ryder and me a secret, and frustration because I've repeatedly told him to pick up his shit.

"It's complicated."

"Is it? Because last I checked, you're either sleeping with someone or you aren't."

"Keep your voice down," I hiss, looking to the kids who are, thankfully, too wrapped up in their own world to hear us.

"I just mean that there isn't a label on it. We're enjoying each other's company."

"*Enjoying each other's company*'? What happened to being careful? What happened to remembering that he's the one who shattered your heart?"

"I haven't forgotten," I tell her because it's true.

The morning after we had sex in the pool, I planned to tell him it was a mistake. That it was a fluke and we shouldn't let it happen again, but when he came into the kitchen that morning, he seemed to know exactly where my mind had gone, and then he sunk to his knees and made me see stars.

True to his words that morning, we haven't let things be weird or complicated. We don't talk about labels or the future.

On the one hand, I'm relieved to be free of the weight of expectations, but on the other, I know my feelings are not so black and white. It's not as simple as enjoying Ryder now, only to lose him at any given moment. I'm not sure if I can handle that.

And I plan to tell him as much tonight before I leave.

He's staying with Lyla and Dominic for the weekend while Meredith takes Dennis to see his children, and I go to my work retreat. I figure it'll give us both a few days of clarity to think through how we want to proceed with our relationship.

But until Ryder and I talk, I decide it's best to play things off for Meredith. "There's no harm in enjoying things the way they are right now."

"Even though he'll eventually leave again?"

The words sting, which I'm sure is exactly what she wanted them to do.

Meredith sighs, putting a hand over mine. "I'm not trying to be unsupportive. You know that if this is what you want, I'll have your back, but I want to make sure you've really thought this through."

I know she's only trying to protect me, so I'm not upset with her. I just hate that the past Ryder and I share warrants this level of concern, so I offer her a kernel of the truth. "I think it might be real this time."

She says nothing, and I lift my head to see her watching me with sympathetic eyes.

"Don't look at me like that."

She blinks like she's snapping out of some daze. "Like what?"

"Like you pity me."

"I don't pity you. I just want what's best for you, that's all. If you say that's Ryder, then I believe you."

I nod because, honestly, I have no idea if this is best for me.

Can't it be enough that I want this? Want him?

We don't talk as we finish sorting through the clothes, putting what's to be donated in a stack by the door, and throwing out what we've deemed trash.

While Meredith hands me Dominic's Cars-themed book bag, the kids are still occupied with their castle, which will probably be their focus all weekend. "He should have everything he needs, but honestly, I let him help me pack, so it might be a complete mismatch set of clothes."

"Not a problem. I'll let Ryder know," I assure her.

"And how does he feel about being Mr. Mom this weekend?"

"He's a father. It's his job whether he likes it or not," I laugh. "But I'm sure he'll do great."

Meredith says her goodbyes to her son, then comes to give me a hug. She pulls back with a hesitant pause. "I'll support you no matter what," she tells me.

My smile is wide and real. "Thank you. I don't know what I'd do without you."

She shrugs, her short hair bouncing atop her head with the motion. "You'd probably still be living out of boxes."

She's probably right.

"Again, Mama!" Lyla shouts, and I go in to tickle her stomach as she squeals in delight.

"Shh!" Dominic hisses, getting so close to the TV screen it's a wonder he can even see the images on it.

"Okay, okay. You kids watch your movie. I need to pack," I say and move to stand.

Lyla clings to me. "I don't want you to go," she whispers, burying her face in the crook of my neck.

"I know, baby girl." I ease her away so I can look into her eyes. "But Daddy will stay with you, and you'll have a blast."

She contemplates that. "Will Daddy make us cookies?"

I try to imagine Ryder baking in the kitchen, and the picture is laughable. What's even funnier is that he'll do it if she asks.

He'd do anything for this little girl.

"I'm sure he will," I tell her. "I'll be in my room, okay?"

She nods, settling in and smiling forward, whether it's at the movie or Dominic, I'm not sure.

I go to my room and grab a suitcase, sit it on the bed, and grab my favorite work outfits. I'm going all out this weekend. With this being my first time being invited to the management dinner, I need to put my best foot forward.

I can't help but smile as I think about the promotion that's so close I can taste it.

"Having a good day?" His low voice seeps into my bones and settles comfortably there.

My smile grows at Ryder's mere presence. Strong arms wrap around my body, encasing me in a warmth I would live in forever if given a chance.

"Don't go," he murmurs into my neck. The rumble of his chest and the brush of his breath over my throat twists something in my stomach. My chest clenches, and I have half a mind to simply agree.

It's only a few days."

"Too long," he says, planting a long, sensual kiss right behind my ear, and I shudder.

I turn in his arms, "Don't worry, I won't be alone."

His eyes lose any playfulness, narrowing to thin slits of promised destruction.

"Excuse me," he says slowly, annunciating each word with an icy edge.

Surprised that he lets me, I gently ease out of his hold and saunter over to my bedside table. I open the top drawer and pull out the black silicone toy I keep inside.

When I turn to Ryder, his rigid stance eases slightly. Those cloudy eyes turn greedy with lust. He licks his bottom lip, and the sight makes me want to throw myself into his arms.

I don't, yet.

Ryder takes slow, menacing steps toward me, and my core tightens with each one. When he's within reach, one hand plucks the toy from my fingers, and the other wraps itself around my throat, thumb pressing my chin up until I lock my eyes with his.

"No more toys for you unless I'm the one using them," he rasps. "Besides, I want you lonely this weekend."

"That's not very gentlemanly of you."

His smile is wolfish. "Never claimed to be a gentleman. I want you wet and wanting when you get back here. Then I'll show you just how *un-gentlemanly* I can be."

I melt into him as our lips meet, and I forget all about my half-packed suitcase.

Our kiss is interrupted by the buzzing of his phone, but since he doesn't acknowledge it, I don't either, and we let it go to voicemail.

Ryder scoops me into his arms, lifting the toy with a mischievous smile. "Ready to play, Rebel?"

I open my mouth to say exactly what he wants to hear, but I'm interrupted by his phone buzzing again. "Should you check that?"

His lips press together in a hard line. "Right now, I don't give a fuck who it is."

I bite down my growing smile.

The buzzing stops but is immediately followed by a ringtone that makes Ryder go rigid. The lust in his gaze dies as his eyes dart to his phone, which is out of his pocket and in his hand in an instant.

"It's Moreno," he whispers. "This must be important."

The disappointment that sinks my stomach is so sickening I almost make a break for the bathroom, and maybe I would if I wasn't so caught up in Ryder's expression, which is equal parts expectant and nervous.

Ryder never looks nervous.

"What is it?" I ask.

At the same time, he answers the call and brings it to his ear.

"Sir," he says, and the stony, all-business voice sucks any light from the room.

The words on the other side of the call are muffled, but I can make them out.

"It's been decided that you'll be attending the capo conference in Briggs's place to represent the Sacramento base," Moreno says, each word cold and aloof, like making this call is the last thing he wants to be doing.

"I'll be there, sir. Thank you."

"Leave immediately. I expect you to be here before it starts. Don't make me regret this," he grunts before the beeps indicate the call has ended.

For a second, neither of us moves. Ryder doesn't pull the phone from his ear or his eyes from whatever spot on the floor they're fixated on.

The implication of Moreno's invitation tries to settle in, but my heart fights it off because Ryder wouldn't do this to me.

"Ryder," I whisper, my voice barely audible.

His slow-spreading smile is one of disbelief, and unmistakable joy.

"I can't believe this," he says, shaking his head like he's talking to himself more than me. "I figured he would've asked by now."

The words, said so softly, slice me open with the mercy of a dull blade.

He knew this was a possibility? The *one* weekend he's supposed to stay with the kids, he knew there was a chance he'd be invited to this conference, and he didn't say anything about it?

"I have to pack. I need to leave within the hour to make it in time." He moves to the door.

"Leave? You—you can't leave." Disbelief drips from every word, but Ryder doesn't hesitate in his stride.

"What the fuck?" I grit as he reaches the door, and my chest squeezes to the point of pain.

When Ryder turns around, there's genuine confusion on his face, and it's worse than if he were being malicious. At least then, he'd acknowledge how this affects more than just his own life.

He really doesn't give a fuck about mine.

"What's wrong?"

"*What's wrong?*" I laugh—*really* laugh. "*What's wrong* is that you can't leave. You're watching the kids this weekend."

He looks taken aback like the thought of staying never even occurred to him.

"This conference is a big deal, and Moreno personally invited me. Saying no isn't an option."

"Then make it an option," I snap. "This weekend is huge for me, too. You know I'm up for a promotion and won't get it if I'm not there."

He gestures to my phone. "Your parents can watch the kids."

"Lyla won't be comfortable without one of us for that long," I say, hating how much it sounds like a plea. "You can't do this."

"I have to," is all he says, and I can't, for the life of me, see past my anger to decipher whether there's even a hint of regret in his expression.

But I'm willing to bet there isn't.

"What about me? What about my job? Doesn't that matter?"

"Of course it does, but there will be other promotions, Rachel. This is my *only* chance to get back everything I lost."

Everything he lost.

His old life, his underboss position, and the glory it gave him.

That's what Ryder cares about. That's all he's ever cared about.

Why did you think, for even one second, that he would choose you? He never did. He never will.

For once, I wholeheartedly agree with the serpentine hiss.

I expect the realization to hit me with the weight of sadness, but all I feel creeping over me is a simmering rage.

I can't believe I let him do this to me *again*.

"You are such a bastard," I say through a humorless laugh that burns my throat. "You've only ever cared about your fucking job, never Lyla and me. Our family means nothing to you."

"*Nothing*? I lost *everything* choosing you and Lyla over my boss. You can't fault me for trying to get it back!"

217

"*We* are supposed to be your everything. But you're right. You did put us first when the other option was letting us die. You know... maybe I should be glad that it wasn't just my life on the line because if it had been, you never would've betrayed Moreno."

"That's not true," he practically spits.

"No? Then how do you explain leaving me three years ago?"

He finally—*finally*—shows some sliver of emotion, but it isn't hurt or regret like I expect. It's confusion. "Everything I did was to protect you."

"Is that what you tell yourself? That you were a *hero* that day?"

"I don't know what you want me to say, Rachel. This is too important to walk away from."

Something inside me breaks, and the words come heartbreakingly easy. "I want you to say that *I'm* too important to walk away from. That you want your job, but you want me *more*."

That break in his expression widens, and the vulnerability, the desire to give in to my request, is clear as day. His eyes soften as he regards me, his shoulders tense like he's ready to take me in his arms, and his mouth parts as if prepared to let them roll off his tongue.

He *wants* to say it.

But he doesn't.

And just like that, the silence that was once sacred to me has ruined any chance of a future with Ryder.

I feel so fucking stupid.

I put my trust—*my heart*—in the hands of the one man proven unworthy of it.

Against my better judgment and Meredith's advice, I ran into his arms like a lamb to the slaughterhouse. I knew nothing good could possibly come from being with him, but I did it anyway.

When my eyes find his, I'm sure they look as dead as I feel inside. "All I ever needed was for you to stay, but you never could."

"You want to talk about staying?" he scoffs. "*You* ran from me, Rachel, not the other way around."

"You think I *ran away*?" I laugh, but the sound is bitter. "Ryder, I left because a life without you was better than a life where I would never come first, and this." I gesture to his phone. "Just proves that I was right to leave when I did. My only regret is believing that you ever actually loved me."

"I do—"

"Don't," I cut in, unable to stand hearing the words. "Don't you dare mock me by saying it now. You made your choice, so go." I point to the door. "Get out, Ryder."

His brow furrows and it's the first time tonight that he actually looks conflicted. "Rachel, I—"

"Go."

We stare at each other for a long moment, and I can tell he's on the brink of fighting me, of pinning me against the wall and demanding to have his way, but he doesn't.

I wish I knew what was going through his head when he slowly nods, accepting this broken relationship as the price for his title, and walks out of the house.

CHAPTER THIRTY

Ryder

I barely make it to the couch of the pool house before my knees go out, and I bury my face in my hands.

I've been waiting for that call for two weeks, hoping—*praying*—for the invitation to go back to Los Angeles. Now I have it, and all I can think about is the woman I left inside.

She thinks I never loved her?

Everything I've ever done was *because* I love her.

Even walking out of that house—despite it being the very last fucking thing I wanted to do—was only forcing myself to respect the boundaries that she was putting in place. She wanted me to go, ordered me to, so how could I deny her?

But for her to think that I *never loved her*?

What have I done that was so wrong for her to have come to that conclusion?

I did everything she asked, gave everything I had, and when she decided to walk away, I respected that choice even though it tore me apart from the inside out.

I thought I could do it, be an underboss, a father, and Rachel's, but sitting here, in this fucking pool house with no title, a daughter I barely see, and a woman that thinks I never loved her, I wonder what I've actually accomplished.

Maybe Rachel and Lyla would be better off without me—safer, for sure. My daughter would never have been kidnapped. She wouldn't live in a shadow darker than night itself. She wouldn't have to learn self-defense to build her confidence. She wouldn't be in therapy before she could even read.

Maybe it'd be better if I just left and never came back, giving them a quiet life away from the danger of my world.

But I can't.

I won't.

And I'm smart enough to know it isn't just Lyla I can't stay away from.

Whether she likes it or not, Rachel is a part of me that I can't bear to part with. I did once, and I haven't been whole since. Maybe I could've fooled myself into believing I'd moved on, but after these weeks spent together, I know I never did.

Rachel may be mad at me now, but it doesn't matter.

I'll win her trust back—I'll win *her* back.

It's not even a choice at this point but a fact that both of us have to accept because there is simply no other way.

I know I'm supposed to push to my feet, pack, and drive to the life I've been working to earn back since I got here, but I can't bring myself to move. The weight of what I left in that house is too heavy.

I left because a life without you was better than a life where I would never come first.

That's not how I remember things.

That's not what she told me all those years ago when I begged to know why she was leaving.

I *did* choose her.

Right?

But the more I think about that day, the less sure I am.

When my phone buzzes, I have half a mind to ignore the message, but the slight chance that it's Rachel is the only reason I pull it out.

Elli: Congratulations! I am so excited to see you! When will you be here?

My hands work on autopilot, but I go to my contacts instead of typing my answer.

He answers on the first ring.

"Moreno," he answers, voice clipped as it's been with me for weeks.

"Thank you for the invite, but I have to decline," I say, my voice sounding not at all like my own, but when the guilt crushing me eases, I know I'm making the right choice.

"Excuse me?" The question is more confused than frustrated—though the frustration is certainly evident.

"I can't come to L.A., not this week anyway."

"Do you have any idea what you're doing right now? You don't deserve this chance, but the capos pleaded your case, so I allowed it. Now, you have the audacity to decline a direct invitation from your Boss?"

I know the weight this choice carries.

I know I am admitting to giving up the job that has defined me for the better half of my life. I'm telling my boss, the man I still consider my best friend, that I have more important things to do than take my title back.

And with that comes a freedom I've never felt before, not because I'm walking away from the job—that part actually feels like shit—but because choosing Rachel is a euphoria I've never fully given into.

"Yes, sir."

"Why?" he asks, and it's the first time his tone toward me is anything more than icy. "What could be more important than this?"

"Rachel," I answer without hesitation like I should've inside.

It's a long moment of silence, and I know he's waiting for me to go on, but the answer really is that simple.

"You're sure about this?"

"Weren't you?" I ask.

When he laughs, it's a relief to hear genuine amusement there. "I was willing to do whatever it took."

"I think I'm starting to understand that myself," I admit.

"This won't look good to the others."

"I know."

There's a long silence that I let myself believe is companionable before he finally says, "Goodbye, Ryder."

Moreno ends the call.

I stand from the couch, debating the dozens of ways I could apologize to Rachel—starting with words and ending with some very generous actions—but stop the second I'm on my feet.

I lock eyes with the window on the far left side of the pool house. Normally, I wouldn't pay it any attention, but normally it would be closed.

Right now, it isn't.

I take a step closer, suddenly feeling the presence of eyes on me. I reach for my gun, but it isn't strapped to my side.

Fuck, I took it off in the car and didn't put it back on since I was too eager to get inside to Rachel.

Movement flashes behind me, and I feel the prick of a needle at the same time I whirl around, but it doesn't matter. I can't see anything.

My vision goes black, my knees buckle, and I'm out before I even hit the floor.

CHAPTER THIRTY-ONE

Rachel

"Lyla! It's time for a bath!" I call, turning the water off now that it fills half the tub.

I wait for her response and call out again when it doesn't come. When there's still no answer, my heart drops as I race to her room.

She's probably hurt or worse.

No, no, no. I shove these thoughts away and nearly collapse with relief when I see her curled on the floor of her room.

That is, until I notice the tears streaming down her face.

"What's wrong, baby girl?" I ask, lowering myself to the floor and pulling her into my arms.

She buries her face in my shirt, pointing at the floor, where I find a framed picture of Ryder holding her as an infant. For a second, the lump in my throat is so thick I can't say a word.

"You miss Daddy?" I ask, but the words are strangled.

She nods.

I shake my head, but it does nothing to ease the fury burning me from the inside out.

What kind of father would go an entire week without contacting his daughter?

Being mad at me is one thing, but taking it out on Lyla by neglecting their daily calls is a level of low that I never thought Ryder would stoop to. Ryder rarely misses a call with Lyla. He always makes it up to her in one way or another—often with extra long calls or deliveries of flowers or stuffed animals—but he hasn't bothered reaching out since he left seven days ago.

Maybe this is what I needed.

The fact that Ryder is normally an amazing dad makes it so much harder to hate him.

This week, it's been easy.

And right now, holding our daughter who's crying because she misses him so bad, hating him is a fucking breeze.

Not only has Ryder's neglect made Lyla more emotional, but she's had major regression since he went to Los Angeles. She's refused to go to her martial arts classes (no matter how much Mr. Torres and Dominic tried to coax her), she's barely talking, and she's wet the bed twice.

I called Dr. Danver, who said the lack of stability Lyla is experiencing from Ryder leaving will take time to adjust. I need to give her all the support that I can so she doesn't feel like she's been abandoned.

I don't care how hurt Ryder's fragile ego is. There is absolutely no excuse for this.

And though the impact it's had on Lyla is my greatest grievance, I can hardly ignore how this has affected my job. Since Meredith was already in San Francisco when Ryder left, I was forced to miss the work retreat, and the promotion was given to another candidate. Then, with Lyla's regression, I'd had to take another full week of—unpaid— leave. Mrs. Caster is so furious that not even David's words on my behalf have helped. She'll be interviewing candidates for my position by mid-week if I'm not back.

I'm embarrassed to admit that I really thought Ryder would do the right thing. I waited for him—rather pathetically—to come back inside that night and tell me that he was choosing me, but he never did. I watched from my bedroom window as he pulled his car around to the pool house, loaded his stuff, and drove away.

You weren't worth it to him. You never will be. That hiss repeats the words it's chanted since Ryder left, and it's getting more and more difficult to push them away.

Once Lyla is bathed and dressed, I settle her on the couch with a princess movie and head to the kitchen. I'm far enough away that Lyla shouldn't overhear anything, but I still have her in my line of sight.

I stare at the black screen of my phone, thinking through the dozens of things I want to say to Ryder, all while fiddling with the heart-shaped charm around my neck.

The morning after Ryder left, I'd been bleary-eyed and so anxious my knuckles ached, so when I saw the necklace sitting on the desk in the office, I'd barely thought twice before looking through it the same way I used to, then securing it around my neck.

My phone chimes with an incoming call, and I actually wonder if it's Ryder for a moment. It isn't, of course. Elli's name lights up the screen, and the relief accompanying that realization tells me I can use a few more minutes before I call Ryder to chew him out.

"Hey, Elli," I answer in a voice far lighter than I feel.

"I swear I'm being choked by all the testosterone in this fucking base."

"That bad?" I ask and fight the urge to ask about Ryder.

"Bad isn't the word I'd use. I mean, considering that I'm the country's first female capo, I was well respected. But damn, these capos are such...*men*. I mean, everything is a competition, which I don't get since we're all the same family. They might as well have just pulled down their pants to measure their—" A grumpy mumbling interrupts her.

"Oh, relax, it's an expression," she replies, and I assume the voice was Moreno's. "Anyway," she says to me, "how are things there?"

"All right," I tell her, omitting the part about how I haven't slept, have barely eaten, and held my sobbing daughter because she misses her father so much.

"I'm planning a trip to come visit soon. I've never been to Sacramento, and I need some girl time. These calls can only help for so long before I'm afraid I'll start to go crazy."

"Feel free to visit anytime," I tell her, and I wonder if she can hear how hollow the words sound.

"Good! It'll be strictly for fun, too. Gosh, I cannot work with Briggs for another moment. Every conversation with him feels like talking to a brick wall. I thought Joshua and Ryder were hard-headed, but he's like an *actual* statue."

That makes me laugh, and for the first time in a week, I don't feel like I'm being suffocated to death by my pathetic heartbreak.

"Yeah, he's intimidating," I agree, then process the implications of her statement. "Wait, why was he even there? I thought only one capo from each base came."

"Yeah, it was Briggs."

My mind and heart don't seem to process this information the same way. My brain is full of questions, like why two Sacramento capos went if only one was needed or why Elli hasn't mentioned anything about seeing Ryder even though she's been missing him for weeks.

On the other hand, my heart has sunken to the pit of my stomach in a mix of terror and dread because somehow—*somehow*—it knows that something is very wrong.

"What do you mean?" I say in a tight whisper. "Ryder left last week."

My brain slowly begins to process what my heart already knows.

"Rachel," Elli says my name slowly, or maybe she doesn't, and it only sounds that way because I'm on the verge of passing out. "Ryder never came to the capo conference."

If he never went to the conference...

I hear Moreno's voice in the background asking questions that I can't make out.

"What's going on? Where's Ryder?" Elli asks, but I can barely breathe.

"He left a week ago," I choke out. "I-I haven't seen or heard from him since. If he didn't go to L.A.—"

Moreno's voice is now coming through the phone, urgent and authoritative. "Rachel, stay where you are. We're on our way."

I barely hear him. I sink to the floor as the realization hits me with the full force of its horror.

Ryder is missing, and wherever he is, he's in trouble.

CHAPTER THIRTY-TWO

Rachel

38 Weeks Along

I peer around the corner, triple checking that no one is here as I walk the path to the garden.

The weather is absolutely beautiful, and I refuse to stay inside— even though I've been explicitly instructed to. I imagine Ryder won't be please when he learns I faked acid reflux to convince Alec to get me medicine from the base so I could sneak out to come here.

I happen to think it was a stroke of genius on my part.

Getting out of the cabin to spend time among the warmth and liveliness of the garden will be worth whatever anger Ryder directs my way. His rules—or *suggestions* as I fondly call them—have become stricter in the last week. He hasn't told me why, but from the bits and pieces I've managed to overhear from Kade and Donovan when they think I'm not paying attention, I've deduced that the M.A.C. project— whatever it is—starts this week.

Since Ryder voted against it initially, I can only assume his protective nature is the reason he's become overbearing when it comes to my security this week. He won't take this little trick lightly, but I can't be expected to sit inside all day and wait for him to come home every night to finally give me attention.

Though, I do love our nights together.

Ryder and I spent a lot of time together in my apartment before we knew about the pregnancy, but back then, we didn't really know anything about each other. It's different now, sharing a home and a bed with someone who I know so intimately, and not just in a physical sense.

Ryder has gone from a man I barely know to my best friend.

The man who was a big, bad underboss is now the man I wake up to every morning. The man who likes his eggs scrambled and his burgers rare. The man who wakes me up with a kiss on the forehead and a mug of herbal tea. The man who takes me out to fancy dinners some nights and cuddles me in sweatpants other nights.

The man who I am madly in love with.

I can't even pinpoint the moment it happened. What was once only infatuation grew slowly until it weaved itself into the very core of my being. I had the realization only yesterday when he knelt beside the bed to plant kisses on every inch of my swollen stomach.

The chest-clenching, toe-curling sensation of his lips pressing to my skin was something far stronger than physical attraction, and when I tried to figure out what exactly that was, only one word came to mind.

Love.

I expected the thought to scare me, but, on the contrary, putting a name to my growing feelings feels so *right*.

Naming the emotion is one thing, but confessing it is another entirely. I was up all night going back and forth on whether to tell him or leave things as they were. The last thing I want to do is complicate things between us. Still, when I think about the way his eyes follow my every move, like he can't bear to look away, I can't imagine he doesn't feel the same way.

More than just telling him how I feel, I also plan to tell him I want to stay here permanently.

I've come to love Los Angeles, and it isn't just because of Ryder. Every Tuesday and Thursday, Alec and I watch new episodes of true crime shows (since Don and Kade declared them "a show for psychopaths"). Donovan is teaching me to play poker, and Kade brings his gaming console over so I can play racing games—though he beats me every time. Even my parents have come to visit two more times since Ryder surprised me several weeks ago.

Tripp and Nicholas are the only capos who completely ignore me, but I don't mind. The only one I haven't gotten to know well is Mr. Moreno himself, but Ryder tells me not to worry about it.

"It's nothing personal," he had told me one day when I mentioned it a few weeks ago. "Moreno doesn't involve himself with people outside the family."

"And what exactly am I?" I had asked.

Ryder only thought for a moment before pulling me to him and answering, "Mine."

I dropped the subject after that, letting him sweep me off to our room.

I pull in a deep breath of fresh air, proud of my plan to come here. I figure everything will be fine as long as I get to Ryder before he has the chance to rip Alec's head off. There's no way I could survive being cooped up in the cabin for another second when I have so much on my mind. I've been popping my knuckles all day, and I can't sit still for longer than a few minutes at a time.

I round a corner, the stone gazebo coming into view, the small fountain, and a bench I sit on. Even if Ryder finds me here, the peace this place brings is well worth facing his wrath.

"I thought I was alone out here," comes a voice to my left.

I nearly jump out of my own skin at the sudden sound. It's a damn good thing I peed before I came here because otherwise, my overly-compressed bladder would've failed me.

I look over my shoulder to where a man is striding down the path from the opposite direction that I had come. Though I haven't made an effort—or been allowed by Ryder—to get to know anyone aside from Alec and the capos, I feel I recognize most of the men around the base.

But I have never seen this man before in my life.

His dark hair is long and styled to be swept back, but a particularly rebellious lock hangs over his eyes in an oddly charming way. He wears a suit, unlike most of the men here, who usually wear jeans and tees. The suit clings to his tall frame, and while it's flattering, it's also somehow off-putting. It fits him like a glove, yet it still seems like he's playing dress-up.

Then, there are his eyes. They're the most mesmerizing honey brown I've ever seen and have this alluring effect that I don't at all understand.

"Do I know you?" I ask though I'm almost sure I don't.

One side of his mouth quirks up. "No, I'm not from around here."

There's nothing threatening about the words or even how he says them, but for some reason, the instinct to cover my stomach with my hands is irresistible.

The man notices the gesture and holds up a placating hand. "I work for Moreno, I assure you. I just don't frequent this base. As a matter of fact, it's my first time here."

I scan him, but his smile is easy, and his eyes are warm, giving the impression I'm safe. So, why is there an underlying current in the back of my mind that questions that very fact?

"Well, welcome." I gesture to the garden around us. "You seem to have found the best part about this place."

He points to the other side of the bench. "May I?"

I nod, and he takes a seat, allowing a few feet of space between us that I appreciate.

"You must be Rachel," he says as he leans forward on his elbows.

When I turn questioning eyes his way, he holds out his hands again. "Kind of hard to not hear about you. You're the only woman who's ever lived on the base."

That's fair enough.

"How many weeks along are you?"

"Thirty-eight," I answer. "My doctor says the baby could be here any day now, but I doubt that."

"Why?"

"My mother, grandmother, and great-grandmother all gave birth on their exact due dates. I imagine I'll be the same."

He smiles, but I swear there's an edge of sadness there. "Boy or girl? Or did you not want to know?"

"Girl."

"Have any names picked out?"

"Not quite," I admit, with a shake of my head. It's the one thing Ryder, and I haven't been able to agree on since becoming a functional couple. Both of us like the idea of naming her in honor of our mothers, Lynette and Delilah, but we haven't settled on anything.

The man wears a ghost of a smile. "That's such an exciting part."

"Do you have kids?"

He looks to be around my age, younger maybe, but I know that doesn't necessarily mean anything.

When his smile falls, I wish I hadn't asked. He looks at me with a somber expression. "My girlfriend was pregnant but passed away a few months into the pregnancy."

My chest aches at the very thought, and though I don't know this man, my heart hurts for the pain that must've caused him. "I am so sorry for your loss. No one deserves to go through something like that."

When his eyes scan me, I get the strangest sensation crawling up my spine, like I've said something wrong.

"Uh, what was she like?" I ask to break the strange tension.

The question works like a charm. He's no longer giving me that weird look, and instead, his eyes fill with an awe that I can almost *feel*.

"Perfect," he says, with a smile and a distant look in his eyes. "Her name was Mary Anderson. She was the strongest, smartest, and most incredible person I'd ever met."

My chest squeezes, and I find myself wondering how Ryder would describe me if someone asked. Would he have this same level of admiration? Would he speak of me so highly? Would love shine in his gaze at the simple mention of my name?

I want to ask him more about the woman since it seems to raise his spirits, but a familiar voice breaks our conversation.

"Rachel!" the voice calls, coming around the corner. Alec huffs, bending at the waist and propping himself up on his knees with his hands. "Are you *trying* to get me killed? Because that's what'll happen when Ryder hears—"

It's at that moment that Alec notices the man sitting at my side. He straightens like a board, eyes flying wider than I've ever seen them before, and his face drains of all color.

"Fuck," he breathes. "Come on, Rachel, we're leaving now."

"Nice seeing you too, kiddo," the man beside me remarks in a dry tone, all signs of his grief tucked away.

What the hell would cause Alec to have such a reaction?

It's then that I realize I have no idea who the man beside me even is.

I stand, using Alec's extended hand to support me as I do, and look into the man's honey eyes.

"What's your name, anyway?"

His smile is wide, despite the grim topic we've been discussing.

"Mason Consoli. It was nice meeting you, Rachel. I hope to see you again soon."

CHAPTER THIRTY-THREE

Ryder

Present

Nothingness.

That's all there is.

No images, no memories, no time, no *anything*.

For fuck's sake. Why do I have to be conscious again?

There's nothing worse than being conscious in this state when my mind won't process anything about where I am or what's going on. All I know is that I *don't* know what's happening, how I got here, or how to get free. My mind can work enough to process present thoughts but not enough to come up with anything useful.

It's like nothing truly exists.

My skin—at least what I think is my skin—buzzes with the need to move or do anything at all.

But I have no control over my body.

The faint click of a doorknob is the only sound able to break through the nothingness, and I cling to it. I use the measured footsteps to ground myself to reality, and force my way through the haze.

I'm struck with the sense of déjà vu.

I've done this before, multiple times. I've heard the click, focused on it with all my might, and tried to fight through the cloud encasing my mind.

It's never worked, but that doesn't stop me from trying.

I'm desperate for any sign of where I am. If only I could find my eyes...

"Open," a muffled voice orders.

That voice.

That damned fucking *voice*.

Thanks to the lack of control over my body, I don't react, or at least, I don't think I do.

There's an irritated huff before pressure squeezes my chin, tugging it down. Liquid flows down my throat, and my natural reaction to swallowing takes control, greedily accepting the offering.

If I could sort my thoughts, I might've realized how dehydrated I am.

Water continues going down my throat, and that same déjà vu strikes again when the liquid turns warm and thick. Maybe soup? I can't say for sure, and even if I could, it wouldn't make a difference.

There's a sound like metal clinking before the pressure around my wrists and ankles releases. "Come on. Don't make this more difficult than it needs to be," the voice says, and something cool—likely a knife —presses somewhere against my skin.

Maybe my throat?

As if I wasn't already disoriented, the world spins when hands pull me to stand. I follow, unable to even consider resisting.

I'm a puppet, moving how and when this puppet master orders, unable to so much as think for myself.

Somewhere in the back of my mind, I seem to know where we're going, like the steps we take are familiar to me. A door squeaks open, and the echo reverberates around us.

A bathroom.

That familiar part of me knows to sit as the hands guide me down.

There's another, softer squeak, and this one is followed by the beating of water against the linoleum.

Still, as the thoughts process, there's nothing outside of what's physically happening. It's like I'm trapped inside a bubble, and there's so much I need to know just outside of it, but it's too far out of my reach to obtain.

Then, there's that voice.

Like a halo shining in the otherwise blackness, there she is.

I just wish her words didn't hurt so damn bad.

I left because a life without you was better than a life where I was never first for you.

"*I did put you first!*" I want to scream to her, my angel of torment.

As I'm pulled like a marionette to my feet, stripped of clothing, and pushed into the water, I relish in the loss of consciousness when memories of that day steal me from this nothingness.

38 Weeks Along

I burst into Moreno's office with the force of a hurricane. The door slams against the wall, sticking there when the doorknob breaks through it, but I don't give a fuck.

In a flash, I have Mason by the collar, shoved against the bookshelf. Books rain down around us, one falling on my head, but I don't even blink.

"Ryder!" Moreno barks. "What the fuck are you doing?"

My voice is a feral growl. "I gave you one fucking rule, Consoli. Stay the fuck away from Rachel, and what did you do?"

He doesn't answer, and I slam him into the shelf again, more books falling as I do.

"Ryder!" Moreno calls, but I ignore him.

Mason lifts his hands as much as he can in his position. "I was just in the garden, and she happened to be there. I don't see how that's my fault."

"You fucking—"

A firm hand wrenches me back, and I let it. Mason gasps for a full breath, looking at Moreno with wide eyes. "The hospitality here is shit."

Moreno, whose hand still holds my shoulder, gives him a warning glare. "You were ordered to stay away from the girl."

"Her name is Rachel," I snap. My eyes shoot back to Mason, who sports an unbothered expression that fuels my murderous rage. "And if I see you near her again, I will personally deliver a different part of your dismembered body to every member of the Consoli fucking family. You got that?"

A wild, unrestrained spark of sadism flashes in his eyes. It's brief, but I catch it. Mason might have others fooled by his designer suit and Cheshire Cat grin, but I see the act that hides a fucking psychopath.

"I have no intentions of even looking in your girl's direction. It was an unfortunate coincidence to run into her. I'll be more vigilant."

"You better fucking be," I spit, chest heaving with each draw of breath.

"Mason, give us a moment," Moreno orders.

"Of course, Boss."

The door clicks behind him, and Moreno looks at me like I just asked him if we should abandon the mafia life to settle into a career of social media influencing.

"What the actual *fuck* is your problem?" he asks, and I'm just sane enough to appreciate the lack of belittling in his tone.

I point to the door. "I never wanted that motherfucker here in the first place! I voted against it every single fucking time it came up, but I was outnumbered. Then the one and *only* fucking condition I have for him is broken within the first day of him fucking being here!"

"Watch your fucking tone," Moreno says, with a stare that's cold enough to bring some of my sanity back. "I understand you were against this, but no harm was done. The girl—"

"Rachel," I grate.

"Rachel," he amends, not particularly chivalrously, "is perfectly fine, correct?"

I give one tight nod.

"Then it seems the real issue is that she was somewhere she shouldn't have been, correct?"

I narrow my eyes to thin slits, scowling at him in a way I never would if anyone else was present. When his only reaction is a lifted brow, I take the elephant statue from the bookshelf beside me and throw it into the wall. Not even the crumbling drywall helps my simmering anger.

Moreno looks at me with a blank expression. "Feel better?"

"No."

He sighs, taking leisurely steps to pick up the statue, which is somehow still perfectly intact. "I suppose I've been meaning to do some redecorating," he says in an infuriatingly nonchalant tone. He lifts the statue. "This would look nice in the guest room overlooking the garden, no?"

"Fuck you, Joshua," I say with a barely visible grin.

He smiles like I'm sure he's been dying to since I slammed Mason against the wall.

"Here to help."

My anger with Mason settles to a comfortable loathing, but my anger toward Rachel is still buzzing under my skin.

I ditch my car, hoping the walk to the cabin will cool me off. Instead, it gives me more time to recall all the reasons she shouldn't have been in the fucking garden today.

First, I told her to stay in because of Mason's arrival. Second, she's never supposed to go anywhere without Alec or me. Third, *because I told her to stay in.*

Yeah, it's worth restating.

I throw the door open, earning me a startled gasp from the kitchen. When I burst inside, Rachel jumps, clutching her heaving chest. When she registers it's me, relief eases every crease of her face, despite the clear fury on mine.

I have no idea if she doesn't see my anger, or simply ignores it, but regardless, she gestures to the stove with a shy smile. "I made us dinner."

My lack of reaction is what finally coaxes her into understanding. Her smile fades, and for the briefest moment, I'm sober enough to hate how I made it go away.

But then my conversation with Alec comes back to me.

"Sir, I have something to report," he says, nerves shaking his voice.

"I'm a busy man, Alec. Instead of telling me you have something to report, just fucking report it."

"Right." He swallows. "Rachel wasn't at the cabin when I got there, and —"

I shoot to my feet, my chair screeching back from the force. "Where the fuck is she?"

"I have her now!" he assures me, but that only somewhat eases my anxiety. "We're back at the cabin, but I wanted you to hear it from me. She was in the garden for a walk on her own."

I slowly lower back into my chair. I'll be talking to Rachel about this later, but I suppose that isn't the worst thing that could've happened today. "If that's all —"

"It's not," Alec says slowly. "She wasn't alone when I found her."

Somehow I know. I just know what he's about to say.

"She was talking to Mason Consoli."

It's not even about her exposure to the family business. It's the simple fact that this man has the ability to betray his own flesh and blood. Though it works out in our favor now, a man capable of that is capable of far worse. He may be pledging his loyalty to our family now, but he's done it once before and stabbed that promise in the back.

No man in his right mind will allow that kind of danger to exist near the mother of their unborn child, but seeing as I am outnumbered on votes, my only choice is to protect her the best I can.

But I can't fucking do that if she insists on rebelling against every order I give.

"What the fuck were you thinking?" I ask, voice low enough to hint at the level of fury just beneath my calm façade.

"Excuse me?" She plants a hand on her hip and regards me with an expression like *I'm* the one at fault here.

"You know that you're not supposed to go anywhere alone."

"I was perfectly safe."

"Perfectly safe?" I laugh. "This place is anything but *perfectly safe*. The man you met is bad fucking news."

"He seemed nice to me. I thought you just wanted me away from whatever project you have going on right now."

I clench my fists over and over again to stop myself from damaging *another* wall. "How the hell do you know about that?"

"Because I'm not an idiot. I've heard about the M.A.C. Project for weeks now, and I don't intend to get involved with it, so you can calm down."

I take slow steps toward her and she has the good sense to look wary.

"Mason Anthony Consoli," I bite out. *"That's* the M.A.C. Project. He's a traitor to his own family and a dangerous, fucking person. You will *not* disobey me again."

She abandons the stove and whatever she's cooking there. "You think I *obey* you, Ryder? You think you have any say in the things I do? You don't. If I follow your rules, it's because I've deemed them justified, not because you say so. You don't control me."

In one long stride, I'm crowding her space. "As long as that child is inside you, I absolutely do control you."

A look of horror strikes her features so suddenly I almost reach for my gun.

Rachel blinks rapidly. "Well, judging by the fact that my water just broke, I don't think that'll be too long."

CHAPTER THIRTY-FOUR
Rachel

Present

Seven days.

It's been seven days since anyone has seen or heard from Ryder.

Seven days since the fight that left me heartbroken and so angry that I was too blind to notice that something was very wrong.

It's three in the morning, and I'm sitting at a conference table surrounded by the Sacramento capos, Moreno, Elli, Donovan, Kade, and Alec.

I half-expected Elli's oldest brother, Damon, to come since he still lives in Los Angeles and seems to be close with Moreno, but Elli explained that he went back home to Chicago during the capo conference and will stay until we figure things out.

I took Lyla to my parent's house immediately after hanging up with Elli. Whatever storm is about to hit, I want to keep my daughter as far away from it as possible.

The L.A. capos stopped by the house as soon as they got in town an hour ago, and after a quick inspection of the pool house, we all came to this base for an emergency meeting.

I'm still surprised I'm here at all, that Moreno didn't just take a statement from me and shoo me off, but I'm damned glad he didn't. I can't just sit at home and wonder if Ryder is dead or alive. I need to *do* something.

Elli had one of the soldiers fetch coffee for everyone, and though I cradle mine between my shaking hands, I don't need the caffeine's help to stay awake. I was barely sleeping when I thought Ryder was an asshole who was ignoring me. Now that I know he's missing and could very well be hurt, or worse, just the idea of sleep sounds like torture.

"Rachel, tell us absolutely everything that happened the last time you saw Ryder," Moreno orders in a detached tone that makes me wonder if he feels any emotion at all toward his oldest friend's disappearance.

I tell them about my fight with Ryder, how I had my work retreat scheduled, how Ryder got the call to go to L.A., and how I watched him pack his car and drive away.

No one says anything for a long moment. The only sounds in the room are Kade's fingers against the keys of his laptop and Donovan and Harris each taking notes off what I've said. Alec lays a supportive hand on my shoulder from where he sits beside me, and Elli takes one of my hands in hers from my other side.

Moreno's brows pinch together. "You saw him leave?"

I work to not flinch when that voice hisses.

You watched him leave so easily when you were pathetically waiting on him to come back to you.

I fiddle with the charm around my neck and nod to Moreno.

"What time was your fight?" he asks.

"I'm not exactly sure. Just after eight, maybe?"

He pulls out his phone, turning to show everyone a call log timed at eight-thirty. "Ryder called me after that fight and declined the invitation."

He did what?

"Why would he leave if he already declined the invitation?" Elli asks, and everyone seems to consider that.

But I can't stop wondering why he would have declined the invitation. He was dead-set on going to that conference when he walked out on me.

What changed his mind?

"Are you sure he wasn't already driving when he called you?" The question comes from Harris.

"Positive. I would've heard it."

Kade looks up at me from his screen. "And you watched him pack up the car to leave?"

I nod. "The car was pulled right up to the pool house while he packed it."

"That doesn't make any sense," Moreno says, and we all look at him. "Ryder packs light when he travels. Why would he have needed to pull the car up?"

No one says anything, and the silence—the utter lack of answers—makes me so sick I'm sure I'd throw up if there was anything in my stomach.

Donovan perks up first. "You said you saw the car in front of the pool house, but did you ever actually *see* Ryder?"

I open my mouth to tell him I did but freeze.

Did I?

I flash through the memories from a week ago. I'd had puffy eyes and a sore throat from my crying fit and had stared out the window at his car in front of the pool house. I'd seen movement, someone lifting things into the trunk, but the full figure never came into view.

It could've been anyone.

"Oh my gosh." I say on a shaky breath. "No, I didn't."

He nods. "So, someone else could've been doing the driving."

"But how would they have got to my house? I didn't see any other cars."

It's Alec who answers with a shrug. "There are a million different possibilities. Someone could've used a ride-share app for all we know."

"Have we tracked his car?" Elli asks.

Kade nods. "Traced it as soon as we found out he was missing. It's abandoned in a grocery store parking lot which, coincidentally, doesn't have working security cameras. We'll head over there to check for clues soon, but whoever did this was careful to stay hidden."

Donovan looks up from his notes to the Sacramento capos with cold cruelty. "I want to know how the hell none of you noticed that Ryder hadn't been to the base in a fucking week?"

Everyone looks at the three capos.

"We never see Ryder," Harris answers with a wince. "He never comes to the base during the day. He comes exclusively through the night."

"Why?" Moreno asks.

"Lyla," I answer, realizing the weight of what Ryder sacrificed for me. "He watched her during the day so I could work, then went to the base every night."

Harris nods in confirmation.

I meet Briggs' eye for a moment, and my stomach roils at the brief flicker of smugness there. It's gone before I can even be sure I saw it, and he's back to his usual scowl.

Could *he* be behind this?

He could be the one stealing from the base and did something to Ryder when he realized we were onto him. I've always felt off around him like he was out to get Ryder, and maybe he is. Maybe I was right all along.

I don't realize I've tensed until Elli squeezes my hand reassuringly—at least, I think it's reassurance until I look at her. When our gazes lock, she doesn't look at me like she feels sorry for me, she looks at me like she's searching for something, and I have no idea what that is.

I lift a brow in silent question, but her face goes neutral in the blink of an eye. Before I can figure out what the heck just happened, she stands, lifting our cups of coffee. "Rachel and I are going to get refills," she declares as if my cup isn't still completely full. "We'll be back."

Moreno sends her a look that she doesn't acknowledge because she's too busy gesturing for me to follow her. I don't argue. I only stand from my chair and follow her out.

There's a soldier outside the door standing guard, and she smiles at him. "Show us to the kitchen, please."

We walk in silence until we reach an empty industrial kitchen. Elli sets the coffees down, thanks the soldier, and waits until he's gone before finally turning to me.

"What's going on?" she asks in a hushed voice.

"What do you mean?"

She studies me for a long moment like I'm a puzzle she can't solve. "There's more, isn't there? There's something else going on that you didn't tell everyone."

My heartbeats are suddenly so much louder than they were a second ago, pounding in my ears like they'll tell the truth for me, but I can't do that.

Ryder made me promise I wouldn't tell them what I knew, no matter what. It would put his standing with the family on shaky ground, and could even put Lyla in danger.

What if I tell them what I know, and they think he stole from the base? What if they think he ran off because he was worried about being discovered? What if they declare him a traitor and stop looking for him?

I can't risk that.

"I have no idea what you're—"

Elli places a hand on both of my shoulders, leveling me with a look that screams the urgency of our situation. "Ryder called me two weeks ago asking for tracking software because he thought he was being framed for embezzling." Her stare bores into mine. "But you already knew that, didn't you?"

I press my lips in a hard line. I can't expose this investigation when it could make the situation so much worse. I can't find Ryder without their help.

"Rachel, please," Elli's voice is pleading now. "You need to tell me what you know. If I know what's going on, I can help, but keeping this a secret isn't helping anyone, especially Ryder."

I'm damned if I do, and I'm damned if I don't.

If I keep this secret, I keep Ryder in good standing with the Morenos and guarantee their help to find him, but I could also deprive everyone of key information that could lead right to him. On the other hand, if I tell them, they might not believe Ryder is worth saving if he might be a traitor.

Can I risk that?

And, more importantly, do I even have a choice anymore?

I take a deep breath and steady my voice. "It wasn't him, Elli. I swear it wasn't, but what if they think it was?"

She shakes her head, visibly relieved by my minimal confession. "No one is going to think—"

"Moreno already doesn't trust Ryder. What if he thinks Ryder took the money and left?"

"Joshua might be working through his anger toward Ryder, but deep down, he knows Ryder wouldn't hurt this family. We need to tell him."

"Tell me what?" The stern voice snaps from behind us, and we both tense at the sound. My body goes rigid, and I close my eyes, briefly catching Elli's apologetic stare before I do.

"I suggest one of you starts talking," he says, and I slowly turn to find his cold eyes darting between Elli and me.

I swallow hard, thinking through any possible way to get out of this, but there isn't one. I glance down the long hallway, where anyone can just walk in.

"Not here," I whisper, dropping my head in defeat.

Elli takes my hand, and we follow Moreno to a private room across the hall. I know as soon as we walk into the room whose office it is. His bergamot scent hits my nostrils like a drug I can't get enough of, and it makes me almost physically ill to know the man who this scent clings

243

might not be alive right now.

Moreno takes a seat in Ryder's chair, and Elli and I sit on the couch against the wall.

"Start talking," he orders. All the ice in his tone is directed at me and me alone.

I don't. Not right away. I take a few deep breaths and think very carefully about how I should handle this situation.

If I mess this up, Moreno will believe all of this is Ryder's fault, and he'll give up on the search. I need to get this right.

"We don't have all day, or did you forget your daughter's father is missing?"

"Joshua!" Elli admonishes, but his hardened features don't ease.

"Ryder never wanted me involved in any of this," I finally start. "He had no idea what I was doing."

Moreno's eyes narrow, and he leans forward, elbows resting on the desk. "And what exactly were you doing?"

Instead of answering, I reach behind my neck and unclasp the necklace. I open the charm to reveal the thumb drive and gesture to the computer. Moreno doesn't protest and simply trades spots with me.

I plug the thumb drive into the computer, open the files, and tell them everything.

I start with how I tracked information on Mason Consoli, like my life depended on it. I tell them how I was watched and eventually followed. I tell them about the gala—what I watched Briggs do to the man in the mirror room, and then what Ryder and I overheard about a meet-up. I tell them how Ryder learned about my snooping that night and tried to stop me, but I wouldn't let him. I tell them how Ryder and I decided to work together to figure out what was going on with Briggs and how we found evidence of embezzling in the Rohypnol records. I even tell them about the dinner party we had with the capos and how afterward, records were changed that traced back to our IP address.

"He didn't do it," I tell him. "I know you still hate Ryder, but he didn't betray you."

"Fucking hell," he mutters.

Elli eyes him, seeming to find something in his expression that I don't. "What?"

He shakes his head. "You're not supposed to know any of this. I can't believe Ryder fucking allowed this."

"He didn't," I snap. "I kept tabs on Mason's case behind his back and followed Briggs at the gala. You should be more concerned about what *he's* been doing this entire time."

"What do you know?" Elli asks, but it's directed at her fiancé.

He shakes his head again, eyes flashing in my direction.

Elli gives him a knowing look. "It's too late to keep her out of this, Joshua."

He heaves a resigned sigh.

"I was at the gala," Moreno admits. "The package from Briggs was for me."

"What?" Elli and I ask in unison.

For the first time in the four years that I've known him, I catch a hint of guilt on Joshua Moreno's face.

"I moved Ryder here because I don't trust him anymore. I assigned Briggs to keep an eye on him while he was here. He's been watching Ryder to ensure he's still loyal to this family. The night of the gala, I came to personally collect the information he'd gathered."

I am not—nor have I ever been—a violent person, but the fury that bursts to the surface demands a release, and before I know what I'm doing, I've taken three steps forward and slapped Moreno across the face.

His head snaps to the side, and Elli's shocked gasp rings in the otherwise silent room, but I can't find it in myself to regret it.

"Fuck you, Moreno. Fuck you and this entire family!"

"Rachel…" Elli takes hold of my shoulders, trying to pull me back, but I don't let her. "You need to calm down."

"Do you have any idea how much he's given to you? He chose you over *everything*. He only wavered when our child's life was at stake. He might've gone behind your back then, but he never stopped fighting for this family, and you damn well know it. He dedicated his entire life to standing by your side, and this is how you treat him? I know you're his boss, but I thought you were his friend."

I'm heaving when I'm done with my outburst, and I relish in the freedom that's come with my honesty. Elli looks horrified, and I await Moreno's retaliation for my physical and verbal attack.

His face is stoic, like I didn't say a single word, but the energy around him is thick, pooling around us like a looming threat.

When he speaks, his voice is not only composed but gentle. "Princess, can you give Rachel and me a moment?"

Elli doesn't move, and when I process her cautious expression, I wonder if she's worried he'll hurt me. I'm so angry right now and high on the liberation of screaming the feelings I've bottled up for so long that it's really *his* safety she should be worried about.

After a long minute, she releases my shoulders, presses a kiss to Moreno's cheek—the same one that's still bright red from my palm—and walks out the door.

"If you're going to threaten me, you should know that I'm not afraid of you, Moreno," I tell him, voice unwavering.

I wait for the threats to spill and ready myself to brave each one.

But they never come. Instead, Moreno fights a smile.

What the...

"I used to hate you."

The statement comes out of left field, snapping me out of my grief and anger, even if momentarily.

"I'm not your biggest fan either," I mutter.

"I don't hate you anymore. But I did, back when you lived at the base."

Again, the confession is so unexpected that it takes me a moment to form a response. "And what possible reason would you have to hate me?"

"For the same reason, you hate me."

"I never said I hate you."

"Didn't have to," he says with a shrug. "When Ryder first met you, I didn't think anything of his fascination, but two months later, when he saw you practically every day, his focus started slipping. So, I told him we were moving back to L.A. in the hopes it would clear his mind, but then you were pregnant, and the next thing I know, he's renovating a cabin on site to bring you with us." He shakes his head. "I was so fucking pissed, but not even I could talk him out of the whole *dad* thing."

I narrow my eyes at his lack of empathy, but he waves me off.

"The entire duration of your stay, I only had half of Ryder. Having Mason come to the base for the first time was vital for our long-term goals, and before you came along, Ryder would've been completely on board, but instead, he fought me the entire process because he didn't want Mason anywhere near you. I thought it would get better once Lyla was born, but..." he shakes his head. "Things got a lot worse after you left."

My chest aches as I recall what the days following my return to Sacramento had been like for me. Sleepless nights, not because of an infant, but because I'd grown so used to strong arms holding me. Tasteless food because I had no one to share my meals with, and the hissing of anxious thoughts tormenting me at every turn.

He could never love you.

He abandoned you.

You're not worth it to him.

Moreno goes on. "Ryder was a fucking train wreck. He messed up the simplest shipment orders and was late to every meeting—when he bothered to show up at all. I'd never seen him like that before, and I haven't since. He got his act together when I threatened his position, then he did a complete one-eighty. He threw himself into his job, more so than ever before. At first, I thought I got through to him, but that wasn't it. He was distracting himself from the fact that you were gone. I don't think he's been the same since."

The idea that Ryder felt the same pain I did during that time comforts me in a twisted way, but it shouldn't. After all, we weren't grieving the same things.

"He missed Lyla. It had nothing to do with me."

I'm answered by yet another emotion I didn't know Moreno possessed: pity. "He didn't move into the cabin to stay with Lyla. He didn't rush back after every shift to have dinner with Lyla. He didn't come in late because he made breakfast and watched shows with Lyla. Ryder loves his daughter, yes, but he is *in* love with you."

"Why are you telling me this?" I ask in a voice on the verge of cracking.

"Because I didn't get it then." He looks to the door. "But I get it now."

I nod, doing my best to ignore the stab of jealousy that taints this otherwise surprisingly pleasant moment. Elli loves a man that would burn down the world just to see her smile.

I love a man who wouldn't choose me.

"Why did Ryder call you?" I ask. It's been bothering me since Moreno mentioned it in the meeting. "Why did he decline the invitation?"

"He said you were more important."

I can't move for a long moment as those words run over and over in my head. My chest squeezes hopefully, but the idea of believing Ryder said that feels like agreeing to have my heart broken all over again. He couldn't have told Moreno that, not right after he left me.

But there's this rebellious part of my mind, the one that Ryder always seemed to be able to reach, that believes it wholeheartedly. That part can picture all too clearly how Ryder would put me first because it's what I've always hoped would happen.

When I look up, I stare right into Moreno's reddened cheek, and I'm struck by a wave of guilt. "I'm sorry. I shouldn't have hit you. It was way out of line."

He actually cracks a smile. "Can't say many people would be walking out of this room alive after laying a hand on me, so count yourself lucky. As for the information you're privy to, I don't need to remind you of the consequences of revealing that to anyone, correct?"

My stomach drops at the threat laced in his lively words. "Of course not."

"Good, and I expect *all* snooping to cease from here on out," he orders, then ejects the thumb drive from the computer. "I'll have Kade look through everything that's in here to see if it can help us find Ryder."

I nod, throat thick with the emotion of my renewed sense of determination. "We need to find him."

"We will," he says with a sharp nod, and it's said with such certainty that I have no choice but to believe him.

CHAPTER THIRTY-FIVE

Ryder

Fuck.

Everything hurts.

Or maybe it doesn't.

Fuck if I know at this point.

I hate being conscious.

Not that sleep is much better, but wakefulness in a zombified state is a fate worse than death, which somehow is a thought my slow-ass brain *can* process.

Another fun thought my brain has held onto is that this can't be the worst of what's coming for me. I'm trapped, I know that much, but despite it feeling like my days are timeless and endless, I know it's only transitional.

Whatever fate awaits me will be worse still.

There's the déjà vu that comes every time I process the same thoughts repeatedly on a loop, but what else can I do?

Oh yeah, wish for death.

It's not a pastime I'm proud of, but, you know, limited options and such.

There's something so morbid in being trapped inside your head, wishing you'd die already so the torment can be over. The real kicker is when my brain entertains the idea that this *is* death.

Wouldn't that be a stupendous revelation?

A faint click of the doorknob has become my personal form of heroin, and I await the measured footsteps that always follow. I've finally reached a mental capacity to know this routine, which I'm counting as a win just because I fucking can.

First, the voice will say…

"Open," I hear, right on time.

This time I'm able to find my mouth and do it. Sometimes I can do that, others I can't. Maybe one day I'll know why that is, but right now, I'm just proud to identify the liquid flowing down my throat as water.

And right about now…

Like clockwork, the liquid goes from cool and thin, to warm and thick.

Soup, I've decided, though I can't pinpoint what kind.

Then…

The pressure around my wrists and ankles loosens, and I wish I could find the will to stretch them. I can't. So, I just follow as the hands pull me up. An arm wraps around my waist, and I know exactly where we're going.

The bathroom.

I sit on the toilet, then move to the shower, just like all the other times.

Surprisingly, I keep my small dose of consciousness through the whole shower. I even think the dipshit doing this to me brushed my teeth while I was in there.

Weird.

I'm seated, dried, and clothed before the hands guide me back to wherever I'm being kept.

A chair?

Fuck, my ass is sore from this bullshit.

I hear a light clink of glass and am filled with unease. With all my strength, I locate my mouth and force the words out.

"Don'd," I slur, barely audible, let alone distinguishable. I try again. "Don'd do hit."

"I wish I didn't have to," is all I hear before I feel the cool liquid going into my veins.

Come on, brain, at least give me something to think about.

My brain, the cruel fucker it is, does.

38 Weeks Along

The anger from Rachel's solo trip to the garden is long gone, replaced by the most abundant sense of joy and excitement.

"It's too soon!" Rachel says for the hundredth time in the thirty-second car ride to the base.

"Dr. Cane said a perfectly healthy baby could be delivered two weeks early. There's nothing to worry about," I answer, also for the hundredth time.

"My mom, grandma, and great-grandma all went into labor on their due dates."

"And my dad left before I was born. We're making new family traditions."

"Ha ha. Very funny," she says dryly.

I park the car at the same time Alec bursts through the doors with a wheelchair. "I got it! I got it!"

"Over here," I say, gesturing to Rachel's door, and he brings it over immediately.

We get her in the chair and set off down the long corridors of the base. I'm not sure if Rachel notices the soldiers' wide eyes that are glued to her, or maybe she's become used to them. Either way, she doesn't pay them any mind, and I love how unbothered she is.

"Ugh," she groans.

"What's wrong?" I ask, leaning down to be closer to her.

I'm not sure I've smelled anything as intoxicating as her vanilla shampoo.

"I just remembered how she's about to come out of me, and I'm not particularly looking forward to the process."

I laugh and take note of how her shoulders loosen at the sound. "You're going to make childbirth your bitch, Rebel."

She laughs, unable to hide the nerves that shake it, but that's to be expected.

I'm fucking nervous, too.

After what feels like an eternity, we get to Dr. Cane's office, who's already set up and ready for our arrival.

"Miss Lance, how are you feeling?" he asks, and even in the state of panicked joy that we're in, his voice is laced with calm.

I knew I liked this guy.

"Nervous," she admits.

His smile is warm. "There's no need to be." He gestures to the machinery around him. "Everything here is state-of-the-art. I have no doubt this will be an exceptionally smooth birth. Can we help Miss Lance up?"

I help pull her to a standing position, and the doctor hands her a hospital gown.

"We'll step out so you can change," Dr. Cane says, and he and Alec step out of the room. They both give me a brief, expectant look and if I didn't have both hands on Rachel, I would've flipped them off.

"I can change on my own, you know," she says once we're alone, but there's no real conviction in the words.

I slide to my knees, pulling her pants down gently.

"Why let you, when I can do it so much better?" I ask, and decide then, as her face pulls into a wide smile, that I will spend the rest of my life making this woman laugh.

The rest of my life...funny how that doesn't sound long enough.

I help her change, opening the door for Alec and the doctor once she's covered.

This time I brush Alec off and lift her up onto the bed myself, planting a kiss on her forehead. "Still light as a feather."

She scrunches her nose and stifles a laugh. "Oh, hush."

"Now what?" I ask.

"I'll do an exam to see how far along she is, but then it's just a waiting game."

I point to the door. "Out," I tell Alec.

"Be nice," Rachel mumbles from beside me.

Alec holds his hands up. "Not offended. I'll be right outside," he says as the door shuts behind him.

"Ah, ah," Rachel's gasps have me rushing to take her hands in mine.

"What's wrong, Rebel?"

"Just doesn't feel the best," she strains, face contorting.

"Just keep breathing," Dr. Cane says, lifting his head from the other side of the table. "Miss Lance, you're already five centimeters dilated. I have a feeling this is going to go by very quickly."

"Is that a good thing?" I demand.

"For her, it is," he says.

Rachel squeezes my hand, and when I look down, a light sheen of sweat is already covering her face.

"Do you need ice chips? An ice pack? A fan?"

She lets out a laugh that turns to deep breathing as another wave hits her.

"I'm okay," she says, breathing through the pain.

The sense of pride swells in my chest as her strength is overwhelming, and she hasn't even started pushing yet.

"You've got this, Rebel. Little Delilah is going to be a breeze."

"Little Lynette," she corrects, then pauses before shaking her head with a faint smile. "What about Lyla? A mix of their names."

"Lyla," I whisper, and something in my chest warms. "I love it."

Rachel's lips press together as she tries to control her emotions. "Lyla Bates."

I bring Rachel's knuckles to my lips, pressing gentle kisses there. "You're giving her my last name?"

She nods, and I wonder if my heart could feel more full.

That's when the lights go out.

Rachel's grip on my hand turns bruising. "Ryder? What's going on?"

Every killer instinct in me is screaming, and I pull my phone from my pocket to cast light in the room, and Dr. Cane does the same.

"I have no idea," I tell her honestly.

A power outage isn't something that just happens to a place like the base. We have a military-grade system and backup generators.

The fact that they haven't kicked in yet is a bad sign.

"Mr. Bates, is there any way to find out what's going on?" Dr. Cane asks, voice tight but still very much collected.

My phone rings, and I bring it to my ear at the same time the base's alarm system goes off. The ear-piercing blare slices through the room with blade-like brutality, and Rachel winces in protest, bringing her hands to cover her ears.

"Moreno?" I shout into my phone.

"The base is under attack," he shouts back.

The base is under attack.

Now of all fucking times?

When the woman I love is giving birth to our daughter?

My mind races through the facts.

Rachel is in labor.

This baby is coming fast.

Dr. Cane needs his equipment to deliver my child safely.

The power is out.

The base is under attack.

Fuck. Fuck. *Fuck!*

Every meeting where I protested Mason's arrival at the base flashes through my head. Every time I insisted he wasn't safe for Rachel to be around, I was ignored.

What are the odds that the base would be attacked at the exact same time Rachel goes into labor?

On the exact day, Mason Consoli comes to town?

I have to protect her. I have to eradicate this threat and ensure no one touches Rachel or our child.

I will do whatever it takes to protect them, even if that means doing the last thing on earth that I want to do right now.

The words feel like acid in my mouth, but I say them anyway. "I'm on my way." And I hang up the phone.

"What?" Rachel shrieks, somehow louder than the alarms.

"The base is under attack. I need to go handle this so you and the baby are safe."

I place a kiss on her forehead, and Rachel grips my arm so hard her fingernails draw blood. "Ryder," she says, voice rough as a gravel road and just as dry. "Please don't leave me right now. I can't do this by myself."

"I'll be right back," I insist, tugging out of her hold.

"Please!" she shouts.

"Miss Lance, I need you to remain calm," Dr. Cane tries, but she ignores him.

Tears stream freely down Rachel's face, mixing with the sweat that mats her hair to her forehead.

"Ryder, I am begging you. Please, don't leave me," she pleads, voice breaking on the last word.

It takes everything in me to go to the door.

"I promise I'll be back once it's safe," I say, open the door, and race down the hall to find and end Mason Consoli.

CHAPTER THIRTY-SIX

Rachel

Present

"I've printed out phone records, bank statements, and the base activity log for you to look through. If anything looks out of the ordinary, you call right away, okay?" Kade drops the box of documents on my kitchen table with a loud thud.

"Okay," Elli confirms with a nod.

"Where is everyone else going?" I ask since I went to pick up Lyla from my parents when the plan was put together. It's a good thing I did because otherwise, I might not have remembered that it was my day to watch Dominic, so I stopped to pick him up when I got Lyla.

Luckily, Meredith isn't privy to the chaos going on. I'd told her about my fight with Ryder, but all she knows is that he suddenly went on a business trip and cost me my promotion. I can tell she wanted to say something along the lines of, *I told you so,* but luckily for me, she held her tongue. We haven't talked about it since he left, and I'm glad since I'm not sure I could get through that kind of conversation right now.

Harris steps forward, gesturing between himself and Knox. "We're heading to San Francisco. The base there has the most advanced security system with eyes all over the state, so we're going to see if they have anything that can help us or if they've heard anything."

Moreno points to himself, Donovan, and Kade. "We're going to Redding to meet with some capos from the Marsollo family. If there's talk of Ryder's whereabouts within criminal family circles, they'll know about it."

"The kid and I are going back to our respective bases. Someone needs to be running the place in case things get out of hand," Briggs grunts.

The "kid" in question is Alec, who's currently ignoring the capos in favor of talking to Lyla, who eagerly tells him about the martial arts teacher who looks just like him.

I don't see much of a resemblance between Jacob and Alec, but in Lyla's three-year-old mind, I'm not surprised she made the connection with their somewhat-similar features. I'm only surprised it took me this long to realize that's why she felt so comfortable going into the classroom with Mr. Torres after just meeting him.

Elli walks the boys to the door, locking it behind them and turning on the fancy new security system Kade just installed.

She stops in the kitchen, grabbing two mugs of tea before coming to sit next to me at the table.

"I thought you were a capo, too. Why aren't you going with them?" I ask as she settles in and hands me a mug.

She takes a long sip from hers. "I am, but Joshua doesn't want me in the field unless it's absolutely necessary."

"Does that bother you?"

"I thought it might, but no. My being there won't do any good if it's distracting Joshua from doing his job. Besides, I'm still pretty new to all of this."

I nod and take the stack of files from the box, plopping them down in front of each of us.

Elli picks up a paper and shakes her head. "I'm not sure how this is going to do much good. I have no idea what *normal* is."

I don't either, but looking through these papers is better than nothing at all, which is the only reason I agreed to do it.

"You take the phone records, and I'll take the bank statements," I say, switching our stacks. "Just make sure we recognize all the numbers coming through."

When she doesn't say anything, I turn my gaze to Elli and follow her line of sight to where Dominic is slowly scooting closer and closer to Lyla, who doesn't seem to notice.

"Watch," I whisper. "He'll get close enough to lay his head on her shoulder. She'll pretend to be annoyed by it, then she'll rest her head on his."

We watch the kids in fascination as my exact words come true, as I knew they would since I've seen them do this a million times.

Elli laughs softly. "They're absolutely adorable. That's your friend's son?"

I nod. "She's a single mom, too, so we take turns watching the kids. They spend most of their time together."

She nods, processing the information with a focused eye. I have no idea what she sees there, but after a moment, she shakes her head, picking up a paper with a smile.

"Shall we?"

Two hours later, the job I hope will give me a sense of purpose leaves me more powerless.

"Would you consider ordering chipotle three times in one day *suspicious?*" Elli asks.

"The worst part is that each time, he got the same exact meal," I mutter, and despite the heaviness of our situation, we laugh at that. "He could eat a burrito bowl for every meal for the rest of his life and be perfectly fine with that."

I expect her to laugh again, but when I look up, she's studying me with an expression I know all too well. It's the same one Meredith, and my mother give me when I talk about Ryder. She's worried about me, or rather, my heart.

"You seem to know Ryder really well," she says, and I know she's only pretending to read over the invoice in her hands.

"Well, he is Lyla's father."

It's a long moment before she finally asks, "Is that all he is?"

It would be so easy to deny it the same way I always do. It would be so easy to tell her we're only co-parents, nothing more, nothing less. It would be so easy to brush off the relationship like it's nothing.

But it isn't nothing.

He isn't just Lyla's father, an ex-fling, a former underboss, and a Mafia capo.

He's Ryder—*my* Ryder.

I set the paper down, dropping any remaining defenses that I have because I'm so damn drained that I can't keep up the facade.

"I love him," I admit, relishing the words but hating the emptiness that comes from the fact that it's him I want to express this to. "I have loved him for years."

"I knew it," Elli says, but there's not a hint of smugness on her face. "Why haven't you told him?"

"I was going to," I tell her, thinking back to the single best and worst day of my life. "The day Lyla was born, I planned to tell him I loved him. I actually met your brother that day, Mason, when he came to the L.A. base for the first time."

"Wait, you knew Mason?"

I shrug. "We met briefly. Anyway, Ryder was mad that I talked to Mason, and we fought. I went into labor mid-argument, and he took me to my delivery room within the base."

I think back to how we'd picked Lyla's name just before everything went to hell.

"I was in labor when the base was attacked. The power went out, and alarms started blaring from everywhere."

Elli's eyes widen, but I don't stop my explanation, knowing that if I stop now, I might not be able to get through it.

"I begged him to stay with me, but in the end, he left. He thought he could protect me by eliminating the threat, but all he really did was show me that when it comes down to it, he's not going to pick me."

Elli opens her mouth like she wants to find the bright side, but no words come out. After a moment, she simply rests her hand over mine. "I'm sorry, Rachel. I can't imagine how that must have felt."

I place my hand over hers in thanks. "You were right," I tell her, and she lifts a questioning brow. "After my date with Jacob, Ryder and I started...well, we got back together, I guess."

"You did? Why didn't you tell me?"

"Because of exactly what happened last week. When it came down to it, Ryder chose his work over me again."

"Except he didn't," she counters. "He did choose you. He just never got the chance to tell you that."

Those words sink in, and though I know in all logic they're true, the idea of Ryder putting me before his work is too dream-like for me to simply believe.

Elli's phone buzzes with an incoming call, stealing our attention when we read Kade's name flashing on the screen.

"Hey, Kade. Have an update for us?"

I can't hear his answer, but Elli responds, "Yeah, she's right here. Give me a second."

She holds out the phone, and I take it, hoping I'll be able to hear him over the nervous pulse pounding in my ears as a million different scenarios come to mind of what he could have to tell me.

"Hey," I say, breathless in my worry.

"I just ran over a dozen different tests to figure out who was trying to frame Ryder for embezzling," he says, voice void of emotion as usual.

Excitement, real excitement, buzzes through me for the first time in days.

"And?" I prompt.

"Rachel, this wasn't a hack," he says slowly like I should understand the significance of that statement.

I don't.

"What do you mean?"

"I mean, someone wasn't using your IP address as a cover-up. The embezzling *was* done from your home."

"That's impossible."

"I thought so, too, but I keep getting the same results."

"Then something is wrong with your software," I snap, stomach curling in on itself in my panic.

"That's not all," he says hesitantly.

I think I'm going to be sick.

"According to these records, it started around the time Lyla was born. A few months after you moved home from the base."

I feel like the world is spinning around me and if I wasn't sitting, I'd probably collapse on the spot.

"You're not actually suggesting this was *me*, are you?" I never considered that I could be framed for this, too, but if Kade is right, the evidence isn't looking good. I would've had the means to access the database from my time in L.A. and motive with how things ended with Ryder and me.

"No one is suggesting anything, but I need you to think very carefully. Is there anyone who has access to your home? Anyone who could've possibly done this?"

"No. No one. Absolutely—"

No. No. *No.*

Pulling air into my lungs is a torturous feat, and I have to grip the table to keep myself grounded.

"Rachel? What's going on?"

This can't be possible. There has to be some other explanation. *Any* other explanation.

"Rachel?" Elli asks from behind me, but I can't focus on anything.

Anything except the brown-haired boy currently curled up next to my daughter.

A hand holds my shoulder, pulling me back to reality. I turn to Elli and judging by the terror in her expression, my face must be as ashen as it feels.

"What's wrong?" she asks, taking the phone from my death grip and holding it high enough that Kade can hear us.

"I think I know where Ryder is," I tell her, not wanting to believe the words to be real but knowing, somehow, that they are.

Her eyes go wide. "Where?"

But I'm already walking past her to get my shoes on. I hear her scrambling behind me, saying something to Kade, or maybe it's Moreno now, judging by the growling that I can hear from here, but I block them out.

"Rachel!" she shouts, grabbing my upper arm as I step out the front door. "Where the hell are you going?"

"Promise me you'll stay with the kids?" I ask, ignoring her questions completely. "I need you to swear to me that you'll stay with them and protect them no matter what."

The fear shining back at me shoots down to my core, but there's so much pain and dread there that it's barely a drop in the bucket.

"I would never let something happen to these kids," she promises me. "But you need to tell me what's going on. You're scaring me."

"Do you trust me?"

"Of course I do, but—"

"I promise to call as soon as I know something for sure," I tell her, pulling my arm out of her grasp.

"Rachel!"

I stop halfway to my car and find her face as grave as mine.

"Don't you dare leave this child orphaned, do you understand?"

"Next time I come home, she'll have both her parents."

And with that, I climb into the car and drive away.

CHAPTER THIRTY-SEVEN

Rachel

38 Weeks Along

There are moments in our lives that define us. Moments that change the very essence of who we are, altering our DNA until we barely recognize ourselves when we look in the mirror.

I've experienced a few of these moments.

Holding my grandma's hand as she passed away when I was ten years old and developing a habit of popping my knuckles when I felt anxious like I did that day.

Not being able to afford a school field trip in the fifth grade, and realizing, for the first time, the level of true poverty my family lived in.

Standing in my apartment in the arms of a man I barely knew, realizing I was pregnant with his child.

But somehow, none of those feel so important now. Like they were only child's play.

I know, even in the midst of this moment, that my life is never going to be the same.

If I thought I knew what true pain was, I was only kidding myself. This heart-wrenching, soul-crushing pain is unlike anything I have ever felt before.

It hasn't wounded my ego, hurt my feelings, or bruised my skin, and fuck, I wish it would. That will be so much easier to bear.

Instead, it feels like Ryder tore my chest open, dug his fist into my chest, and slowly ripped through everything in the path of my heart, which he wrenched from my helpless body. The weight of his abrupt rejection in my time of need is so heavy that it feels like I'm drowning.

I stare at the door that's barely illuminated by Dr. Cane's phone flashlight and swallow the realization that Ryder left me here after I begged him to stay.

He left like it was nothing to him.

Like *I'm* nothing to him.

"What do you need?" Alec asks, pulling me from my useless longing to where he's speaking to the doctor.

Alec wears a fiercely determined expression that I've never seen before, and, damn, it's scary. He doesn't look like a kid anymore. Not one bit.

Dr. Cane is breathing deeply, mouthing words to himself, and ticking off things on his fingers. "Okay," he mutters. "Okay, I can deliver the child in these conditions, but I'm going to need a few things from the main infirmary.

He lists the things off to Alec, and I wonder how he'll remember all of them, but judging by the look of pure focus on his features, I know without a doubt that he will.

When Dr. Cane is finished with the list, Alec bolts from the room, and I once again stare at the door as it shuts behind someone I thought wouldn't leave my side.

Maybe they'll both come back.

Or maybe they'll get hurt, and I'll never see them again.

"You need to breathe, Rachel," Dr. Cane says, and somehow his voice remains calm, despite the blaring alarm still echoing throughout the room. "I know that's asking a lot right now, and it might feel impossible, but for the baby's sake, you need to relax."

I strain to take deep breaths, but thoughts of my baby girl push me to get through.

"Do you think you can get that to stop?" I grit, pointing to the alarm.

He nods, and I watch as the old man climbs a chair and uses a reflex hammer to beat the hell out of the alarm until it finally stops.

"Thank you," I manage, and a wave of pain hits as another contraction rocks through me.

"Don't worry, I have the epidural right here, Miss Lance."

Oh, thank goodness.

Dr. Cane grabs what he needs and moves behind me, but I barely notice what he's doing. It's like there's a gravitational pull to the door, stealing my ability to look away even if I wanted to.

Walk through that door, Ryder, I silently plead and immediately feel stupid.

He wouldn't stay even when I begged him. My thoughts can't do shit.

"I'm going to administer the epidural now. Are you ready?"

"Yes," I say breathlessly as another wave of pain hits.

Then, like a dream come true, the door swings open.

But the man who steps inside isn't Ryder.

It isn't even Alec.

Nicholas Belford.

"What—what are you doing here?" I ask, unable to do anything about the complete vulnerability of my position and situation.

It's then that I notice the look of complete ease that he wears. No worry for the base's safety. No concern for the lost power. No qualms about my state of labor.

"Sir, you shouldn't be—" Dr. Cane's words are interrupted by the bullet that Nicholas lodges in his brain without so much as a blink.

An ear-piercing shriek comes from my lips, and a fear so potent I can taste it fuses with the blood in my veins, becoming a part of me that it feels like I'll never be rid of.

I wrap my hands over my stomach, tears streaming down my face as I try not to hurl, but Dr. Cane's blood is splattered across the wall, and I have no doubt mine will follow.

But Nicholas doesn't raise the gun at me. He takes slow, *painfully* slow steps forward. I wish I could move away, but I'm frozen in fear and pain. I can't do anything as he closes the distance between us.

"G-get a-away from me," I sputter.

He clicks his tongue in disapproval. "You should know I take no pleasure in taking your life."

Another sob, but I can't help it. It's not even myself that I'm worried about, but the child that I so desperately want to live through her first night in the world.

"Then don't," I choke. "Please, I'm begging you. Don't do this."

But what has begging got me so far?

"Really, I have no choice," he huffs, eyeing me with disgust that I can't even begin to process. "I'd hoped Mr. Moreno and Ryder would put a stop to this before it got to this point, but since they didn't, I have to."

"A stop to what?" The words heave out of me as another contraction takes over, and I let loose a scream that Nicholas doesn't even seem to notice.

"It was bad enough that they're working with another family's traitor—as if it isn't a disgusting dishonor—but then they bring you here?" He gestures to my body with his gun, and I cringe away. "You're a nobody—irrelevant to this entire family, yet our underboss moves you in like a guest of honor and not his whore."

He taps the barrel of the gun against my stomach and I'm so afraid he'll shoot if I move, so I don't.

"Bringing Mason here was the last straw. This family spits in the face of tradition, and it's a mockery of what Moreno's father stood for when I led under him. I hoped Moreno would make a good boss, but if this is how he intends to run his empire, it will burn. This push from me will help him more than he knows. The best part is that Mason's arrival ensures I can pin the entire thing on him," he laughs like the idea is genuinely amusing. "It all worked out quite well, really."

"Please," I beg. "Please, don't do this."

He shrugs like this is all so mundane and not the brutal end of my and my daughter's lives.

"Like I said, I won't take any pleasure from this," he says and cocks his gun before lining it up with my stomach.

I never really understood the whole *inhuman strength* thing that people always talk about mothers having, but my first burst of it comes with a fury I don't quench. I grip the barrel of the gun and twist at the same time the trigger is pulled. Gas from the shot burns my hand, but I barely notice as I furiously jerk the weapon back. I use all the strength I have to ensure the barrel doesn't turn toward me, but in the struggle for the weapon, it's not easy.

Nicholas has strength and training on his side, but I have something just as powerful. An angle that breaks his trigger finger when I snap the gun to the side.

His wail rivals the still-blaring alarms in the hall, and I use the brief moment of surprise to toss the gun across the room.

I regret the choice for two reasons.

The first is that the gun fires for a third time as it slams into the wall, and I have just enough mental capacity to appreciate that no bullets hit me, even as another contraction does.

The second comes with the realization that Nicholas is now crossing the room to grab the abandoned weapon.

The pain—emotional, mental, and physical—is too much.

He won't get close enough for me to grab the gun again, and I'm in too much pain to get off the table, let alone try to get away.

I watch the last moments of my life in slow motion.

Nicholas lowers, takes the gun in his uninjured hand, and begins to rise to his full height. His expression is one of exasperation and fury, and I despise that it's the last face I'll ever see.

So, I close my eyes as the fourth shot rings through the air.

"Rachel!" Alec's voice is what wrenches my eyes back open, and I wipe at my tears to see him standing in the doorway with his raised weapon. Only when I pull my hand away do I realize the wetness coating my cheeks isn't tears but blood.

Nicholas's blood.

Nicholas—who lays limp on the floor with a hole through his head.

The realization that Alec got here in time—that he saved my life, my daughter's life—is enough to make me openly weep.

He charges toward me, and I cling to him with each sob, even as the cries morph from relief to horrific pain.

"It's okay, Rachel. You're safe now," he mutters on repeat.

"Alec," I cry as another contraction hits. "The baby. She's coming."

I watch as he visibly shuts his fear and worries down, a mask of perfect determination coming over his features.

"I'm not going to lie to you, I have no fucking idea what I'm doing, but I swear to you that I will do whatever it takes to ensure you and this baby are safe."

I nod. The ball in my throat is so thick that words aren't even an option.

"Okay," he says with a firm nod. "Let's have a baby."

CHAPTER THIRTY-EIGHT

Ryder

Present

For fuck's sake.

Again? Why do I have to be conscious *again*?

I never imagined I'd wish to be subjected to active torture, but at this point, at least it'd be *something*.

Anything.

I'm so fucking tired of *nothing*.

And there's the doorknob. Cue the padding footsteps...and there they are.

As per my minimal habits, I open my mouth and wait for the cool water to come.

When it does, I gulp it down eagerly. It's pulled away, and I open my mouth again, ready for the heat of the soup.

"Not today," the voice says.

I know I'm not in a good situation, but the simple fact that something is different about today gives me a surge of hope. Different is better than nothing.

The pressure of restraints leaves my wrists, just to be replaced a moment later by something cold. Handcuffs?

I let them guide me to stand—not like I have much of a fucking choice—but we don't walk the path to the bathroom. We take a turn, and when I stumble, I'm just glad to have finally located my feet. If only I could control them and get the hell out of here.

The pressure of a hand under both of my arms is all I have to rely on as I'm carted up a set of stairs, which I only know because of the grumbling of the asshole leading me.

For fuck's sake, this is humiliating.

When I get out of this, I'm planning the most elaborate death for this son of a bitch.

The doorknob clicks, but this time it's right in front of me, and bright light hits my eyelids, though nothing is actually visible since they're still closed.

I try to open them, but I'm fighting the darkness. Still, light seems to seep through something when I attempt to pry them open. I concentrate as best I can, waiting for something, *anything*, to hint at where I am and who has me.

Come on, eyes, I mentally chant.

With another turn, my feet falter, but the light hits my eyes again, but I can't see a damn thing.

What the...? A blindfold, I realize. My eyes haven't been closed this entire time. They've just been covered.

I'm relieved to have this bit of information but furious that I'm unable to glimpse at anything that could help me out of this.

Another door opens, slamming shut with an echo that suggests the room is hard-surfaced.

A garage, I'm sure.

This is confirmed when a beep is followed by a click, and I'm shoved into the back of a vehicle. The shove is careless, and my head hits a hard surface, but it's worth it because the blindfold shifts.

It's not much, but it's enough that I can finally blink my eyes clear of blurriness and get a good look at my captor.

What I see gives me a sense of complete and utter hopelessness.

Fuck, I really thought this was real life, but it isn't. This must be a dream. At least, that's the only logical solution for what I see because I can't, for the life of me, imagine what possible reason *she* has for being here.

I blink my eyes again, but her side profile is clear as day. She catches my eye, giving me a remorseful look that I don't believe for a second.

For fuck's sake.

"You, of all people, know what lengths a parent will go to protect their child," Meredith says as she slams the truck shut.

Postpartum

* * *

I burst through the doors of the hospital, storming over to the front desk, where I already have the attention of every nurse.

"Rachel Lance," I bark.

"Right this way," one says without hesitation, leading me quickly down the hallways, though it still feels like way too fucking long before we get to the door of the nicest room the hospital has to offer.

I don't thank the nurse, I just throw the door open and freeze in place the second I step inside.

She's beautiful.

So fucking beautiful.

Wrapped in light pink cloth, held to the chest of the woman I love.

My daughter.

I barely notice that Alec sits on the bed beside Rachel, cooing over the infant. In fact, I can't pull my eyes from the precious life.

"I need to make a call," Alec states, and I don't bother addressing him as he exits the room, leaving the three of us alone.

My family.

My family.

I force myself to look away from the little girl to her mother, the woman who has given me the most precious thing I could ever possess.

Her eyes have dark circles beneath them, and they're red and puffy like she's done a lot of crying since I last saw her, which isn't surprising.

While the entire Moreno family was running around like headless chickens looking for Mason, who was assumed to be behind the power outage and security system failure, the real culprit was after my girls.

We didn't know what was going on until Alec called from the ambulance he'd summoned for Rachel after delivering my daughter himself. Eventually, we located Mason, who was restrained in Nicholas Belford's suite, and his plan to frame Mason for killing Rachel and our child fell into place from there.

I rest a hand on Rachel's cheek, stroking the soft skin there.

"I'm sorry I wasn't there," I tell her.

Not only was I unable to protect her, but I also missed the birth of our daughter.

She doesn't say anything, but she's had a long twenty-four hours, so I'm sure she's just tired.

With one finger, I brush my daughter's cheek, feeling the most profound sense of belonging as I do.

"May I?" I hold out my hands to take her, and without much of a reaction, Rachel gently hands her over.

"Support the head, and cradle her to your chest," she says, voice cracking with exhaustion.

I nod because I've read every article and book on the market in my free time since learning about this pregnancy. I know exactly what I'm doing.

I take my daughter in my arms, and, for the first time in my life, I feel like my purpose is so much bigger than myself.

"She's so beautiful," I whisper. My smile feels like a permanent fixture, and I look up to share it with Rachel, but her face is blank, and her eyes are hollow. "Are you okay, Rebel? I know that must have been a nightmare. I'm so sorry you had to face that alone."

"I wasn't alone," she states, eyes trained on the perfection in my arms. "Alec was there for me. He saved her life."

"We owe him quite a bit," I murmur, and I already know how he'll be repaid for his quick thinking and bravery.

When Rachel doesn't answer again, I let the silence settle and relish in the pure perfection of holding our daughter.

"Lyla Bates," I say, needing to hear her name, to say it myself.

My daughter. This is my daughter.

Lyla—

"Lance." Rachel breathes the words out.

"Huh?"

She nods to our daughter. "It's Lyla Lance."

The joy I'm feeling can't be diminished, but there's a deep betrayal that slices through my core. "What? I thought you said—"

"I know what I said," Rachel says, reaching out and taking Lyla from my arms. "But this makes the most sense."

"The most sense, how?"

"Doctors visits, school paperwork, it'll just be a lot easier when our names match," she states like it's a plain fact.

I open my mouth to tell her their last names will match—if the ring in my pocket has any say on the matter—but she speaks first.

"Being a single parent is hard enough without the name complicating it."

"What are you talking about? You aren't a single parent, but it's not a big deal. We can talk about it at home and make the change later."

Rachel's had a long day, and I don't want to stress her out when what she needs is rest.

"Ryder."

Her features harden, and the way she says my name, like a declaration, twists my stomach into knots before the rest of her words are even spoken.

"I'm not changing Lyla's name, and I'm not going home with you."

I wait for her to explain. She doesn't, and I'm hit with knee-buckling nausea.

"What are you talking about?" I hear myself ask, but I don't want to hear the answer.

"The doctor wants me to stay through the night because of the nature of the birth, but as soon as I get the all-clear, Lyla and I are moving back to Sacramento."

"The hell you are," I grate. "You said you'd stay."

She drops her eyes, but I get the feeling it isn't out of shame.

"I shouldn't have," she finally says. "It was a rash decision on my part, and now that Lyla is here, I just can't imagine staying."

"*Rash decision*, my ass. You've been imagining this just fine for weeks."

"And now I'm seeing clearly. I mean, come on, Ryder, you can't really expect me and our infant to live in a mafia base that was just attacked, right? This isn't right for her. She needs something safer than that, something more stable."

"We'll move off the base. We'll get a house nearby," I offer, but it sounds more like a plea.

"It's still too close to what you do. You can't look me in the eye and tell me that this is the safest place for her."

"The safest place for you and Lyla is with me."

"It wasn't last night," she says. "Ryder, I'm not changing my mind on this, so you can save your energy. I'll be her primary caregiver, and you can visit anytime you want."

She's going to leave.

The woman I love, the woman I was going to ask to be my wife, the woman who I saw forever with, is walking away from me and taking our child with her.

For fuck's sake.

I do something that I've never done in my entire life.

I beg.

"Rachel, please, don't do this."

When her eyes finally meet mine, a single tear slides down her cheek. The sight breaks my heart even more if that's possible.

"I'm sorry," she says. "We tried. Things didn't work out, but that doesn't mean we can't co-parent. This is what's best for us, for Lyla."

I wholeheartedly disagree, but I keep that fact to myself. Pushing Rachel, snapping at her right now, won't do us any good. I could find dozens of excuses and reasons to coax her into changing her mind, but quite frankly, I don't want to.

I want her to stay because *she* wants to, not because I force her.

"I'll do anything, Rachel, anything to keep you with me."

She regards me carefully, with a hope buried deep under the sadness glossing over her gaze.

"Come with me," she asks. "Come with me to Sacramento. There's a base there, right? Come with Lyla and me and work from there."

She knows I can't just up and leave. That's not how this works. I swore my life to Moreno, and as long as he needs me here, I can't leave.

"Are you giving me an ultimatum?" I ask, and I can feel my defenses rise into place.

She must see it, too, because that small flicker of hope burns out like a candle in a hurricane.

Rachel shakes her head. "Just putting things into perspective. We live in different worlds, Ryder, and this one wasn't made for Lyla and me."

"Rachel, I'm in love with you," I tell her, needing her to at least know this much.

"I know," she says in a strangled whisper. "I wish that was enough."

And that's how the best day of my life became the worst.

The days—okay, weeks—following weren't any better.

I withdraw from Moreno, and the capos, and the quality of my work is laughable. I stop going to poker nights and the bar when the others go out. I even throw a punch when Donovan suggests I try getting over Rachel by getting someone else under me.

Because, even now, I know there is no getting over Rachel, and, as cruel as it sounds, I'd rather live in this pain than attempt to.

I don't move back into the base but live in the cabin that still holds the smell of her vanilla shampoo—which both soothes and tortures me. We video chat every day so she can show me how Lyla is doing, but we don't talk about anything real.

Every few weeks, I travel to Sacramento to visit, but they're quiet trips. Rachel avoids me at all costs, and when she can't avoid me, she's silent.

The words I wanted from her so badly are gone.

Now and then, I get the urge to steal them from her because I know, deep down, she'd give in with the right persuasion. But, as much as I want her body, it's her heart that's shut me out and that isn't so easily manipulated.

It's just like the days before the pregnancy when we avoided all real conversations. At least then, we still spent time together and had physical intimacy.

Now, we have nothing, and I feel the weight of that loss every second of every day.

Several weeks after Rachel is gone, Moreno sits me in his office and tells me that if I can't get my shit together, I'll lose my position. Without Rachel or Lyla, my title is all I have left.

So, I throw myself into my work.

I take on more responsibility, work longer hours, and fix hiccups in the system that have been long overlooked just because I have the time to.

I elect Alec to step into Nicholas' position, and the others agree after how he handled everything the night of the attack. He thanks me as if he didn't earn this himself. If anything, I'm the one who needs to be thanking him.

I fall into a routine.

Work becomes my life. I visit the girls when I can and call every day. Eventually, I learn to expect Rachel's silence, and though it's painful as hell, after several months, the sharp sting dulls to an ache.

Sometimes, I wonder if the pain will ever go away, but after all these years, it never has.

And there's a twisted part of me that hopes it never will.

CHAPTER THIRTY-NINE

Rachel

Present

I pull into Meredith's driveway in record time, having broken every roadway law on the ride here. My phone is blowing up with calls from Elli, Kade, Alec, and even Moreno, but I ignore them all.

I race from my car to her front door, taking the spare key from under the potted plant to the left of the porch stairs. I don't even consider knocking. Instead, I unlock the door and throw it open in one motion.

"Meredith!" I scream, not holding out hope that this is all in my head.

It isn't.

Though I have no idea what her motives are, I know she's the one who's been embezzling from the base, likely for years now. Did she know who I was when we met? Was our meeting even a coincidence? Was any of our friendship real?

But none of that matters right now. I can't feel the sting of our lost friendship over my fear for Ryder's safety. Nothing matters aside from him.

"Meredith!" I scream, but there's no answer again.

I search the house, going through the kitchen, living room, and dining room, then making my way upstairs. I check Meredith and Dominic's room with no luck, and I'm starting to wonder if I was wrong about everything.

But then I get to the basement door.

I forget Meredith has a basement since it's unfinished and only used for storage, but now, I can't tear my eyes from the door that seems to be taunting me.

It's the first time I slow since I've stepped foot in the house, but I can't help it. The chill creeping upward goes bone deep, and I'm genuinely afraid of what I'm about to find.

I open the door, and the click of the knob echoes off the narrow walls.

Flipping on the light switch, I force my feet to descend the stairs even when nausea slams into me as the room comes into full view. I've been in this basement only a few times, but this isn't what it looked like before.

The stained-fabric armchair with restraints on the arms and legs sits beside a metal table littered with discarded needles. There's an empty glass on the other side, but other than that, the concrete room is bare.

My hands clutch my chest with the crushing realization that Ryder —*my* Ryder—was kept in these conditions. He was strapped to this chair and injected with who-knows-what for an entire week.

And now he's gone.

Am I too late?

This is all your fault. The voice comes with its usual hiss and a rush of guilt that nearly knocks me on my ass.

I'm about to turn on my heels and get out of this nightmare of a room when the half-full glass on the table catches my eye.

Or rather, the condensation on the glass.

I force my legs forward, brushing my fingers against the cool moisture.

They must have just left.

I run up the steps, phone in hand, and dial Moreno's number. I know he's going to be furious with me for taking off without explanation, but I couldn't reveal Meredith's potential involvement until I confirmed it. If I'd been wrong, it could've meant dire consequences for her and Dominic.

But I'm not wrong, and the consequences have long surpassed dire.

"I swear, I'll put a hit on your ass if you don't tell me what the hell is going on," Moreno practically growls the words.

"Meredith Ashford," I tell him, ignoring his less-than-gentlemanly greeting. "My friend—Dominic's mother—she's the one who took

Ryder."

"And why the fuck didn't you just say that?" he asks before murmuring her name to someone, likely Kade.

"I had to be sure, and I am now. I'm at her house, but it's empty," I tell him, and steady my voice so it doesn't break as I tell him the rest. "I-I found a chair in the basement...it has restraints attached to it, and there's a bunch of needles on a table...I think he's been drugged this whole time."

"He isn't there now?"

"No, but they couldn't have left long ago," I tell him about the condensation on the glass.

"Is there anything else you can tell us? What she drives, license plate number, anything?"

I know the make and model of her car but nothing else, so I give him that information, and Kade has the license plate number in a matter of seconds.

Damn impressive.

"Do you have any idea why she'd do something like this?"

"She has to be the one who's been embezzling from the base. Maybe she thought he was onto her? But that wouldn't explain why she kept him alive."

There's a long pause before he asks, "In that basement, did you see any evidence that he'd been tortured?"

Stomach acid crawls up my throat, and I strain to speak. "No. Just the needles."

"That's good," he mutters. "If money is what she's after, she's likely planning to sell him to an enemy family."

"What would happen to him then?"

Moreno doesn't answer that.

"I'll call Elise's brothers to get the Consolis on this. If other families are involved, we'll need all the help we can get."

"Hey!" I hear Kade's muffled shout from somewhere behind Moreno. "A traffic camera just caught the car on Kilkenny Street. The GPS is taking her to a parking garage off Six and Sycamore. Do we have soldiers in the area?"

"No soldiers," Moreno grunts. "If this gets out, other families might take advantage of our crisis. And we still have no idea who is aligned with Mason. We can't risk it."

I type the address into my phone. "I'm only twenty minutes from there. I can—"

"Don't even think about it," Moreno clips. "Get in your car and go home to your daughter."

"How far away are you?"

He hesitates. "An hour."

"That's too late."

"I'm not fucking around, Rachel. You will get in your car and go home *now*. This is family business, and you have no right getting involved."

"Ryder is my family, too, and I could be our *only* chance of reaching him in time. I'm sorry, Moreno, but I have to go."

I end the call before his protests come through. My phone is ringing again within seconds, and I put it on silent, not wanting it to be off in case I need them to track me.

I turn to leave, but for some reason, a white envelope gives me pause.

It sits on the table, a normal place for mail to go, but not for Meredith. She has a basket in her office where she meticulously organizes all her mail. Besides, this doesn't look like any regular letter. There's no address or stamp, just one word written in fine script across the front.

Dominic.

I don't feel the slightest hint of guilt as I take it with me when I run to my car.

CHAPTER FORTY
Rachel

I spent the drive to the parking garage in a state of numbness. I don't remember a single part of the ride, only that I speed the whole way.

I pull in, realizing with a mix of shame and dread that I have absolutely no idea how I'm supposed to find Meredith's car. She could be on any of the eight levels, and even if I find her, what exactly am I supposed to do that will help Ryder?

There's an open spot a few spaces from the entrance, and I swing into it, deciding I'm better off on foot.

When I go to pull the key from the ignition, my hands shake, and I pop my knuckles over and over again. I feel that slithering hiss before the words echo in my head.

How are you supposed to do anything useful?

You're only going to make things worse.

You have no plan and no idea what you're doing.

Maybe Moreno was right. I should've gone home. I barely know self-defense and didn't think about grabbing any sort of weapon when I left the house in a hurry.

I grab the door handle, but I can't bring my hand to pull it open.

You couldn't save your own daughter. How are you supposed to save Ryder?

When you fail, who will be there for Lyla?

You might as well just give—

No.

It's only a deep breath, forcing air into my lungs and clarity into my brain, but it's enough. Enough to make me recognize the fatal flaw

I've clung to my entire life.

Ignore. Repress. Distract.

I thought I was coping.

I thought people like Ryder—who calmed my mind—and projects like keeping tabs on Mason, which busied it, were healthy ways to deal with the thoughts that plague me, but it isn't. It never has been. It's a way to divert my attention, but it solves nothing.

And right now, I can't afford to get in my own way.

I don't need a distraction or someone to silence my thoughts.

I need to fight them.

"I can do this," I whisper, needing to hear the words. "I am strong. I am capable. I am not a victim."

I wish I was strong enough that this mantra would seize my shaking and replace my fear with sure confidence, but I'm not.

I am strong enough, however, to open the door despite my near-crippling panic and climb out of the car.

I whisper the words again. "I can do this. I am strong. I am capable. I am not a victim."

I grab a hoodie from the back of my car and slide it on. It's not a fool-proof disguise, but it'll give me a little more anonymity.

As casually as I can, I do a lap around the floor. I'm trying to come off as confused like I don't know where I parked, but I'm sure any onlooker just thinks I'm a creep.

When there's no trace of Meredith's gray van, I go up a floor and repeat the process. By floor four, I'm feeling frustrated. By floor five, discouraged. Floor six, angry. Floor seven, hopeless.

Still, I trudge up to floor eight, all the while whispering those words on a loop.

"I can do this. I am strong. I am capable. I am not a victim."

With each step, I see flashes of Ryder. His larger-than-life aura that sucked me into his orbit from the second I turned to face him in that club. His strong arms that pulled me to him as we watched movies together over the months I stayed in the cabin while pregnant. His complete and utter awe that melted my broken heart the first time he laid eyes on our daughter in the hospital. His striking features that were arranged in a fiery determination that could've set a whole factory on fire when he burst into the cell Lyla and I were held in by Mason Consoli. His playful nature that had him throwing Lyla and Dominic across the pool.

With each memory, I feel my determination harden to steel. I might not have a brilliant plan or extensive training, but the sheer will to hold both Ryder and our daughter in my arms tonight eats away at the fear.

"I can do this. I am strong. I am capable. I am not a victim."

As soon as my head is above the concrete ground of the eighth floor, I see the familiar gray van and freeze before going any further.

Meredith's car is right in front of me, giving me a direct view of the driver's side of the car. Luckily for me, she faces forward, overlooking the city.

Though I'm not in her direct line of sight now, she'll see me in her peripheral vision if I attempt to get any closer. I'm running through my options when the slam of a car door makes me jump.

The sound comes from the car parked across from Meredith, and one look is all I need to recognize it.

The black truck.

As in, the black truck that followed me.

There's a heavy set of footsteps, and I wait for what feels like an eternity for the man to finally step into view and cross toward Meredith's car.

He's big, well over six feet, and with a thick build to match. His clothes are a ripped gray tee and stained jeans. They don't match his frame but do match his patchy beard, receding hairline, and need for a shower. He has to be well into his forties, and I wonder what Meredith is doing getting herself involved with a man like him.

As he approaches the passenger side of her car, she turns her back to me as she looks at him, and I barely think before I make a break toward them.

Thankfully, my tennis shoes carry me soundlessly through the garage, and I make it to Meredith's blind spot just in time to hear the man's door slam shut. I have no idea what I'm going to do if they drive away right now since that would immediately give away my position, but I don't worry for long. Their conversation carries out of the car with perfect clarity.

"If this comes back on me, I swear I'll have every family hunting your ass," the man huffs.

"It won't," Meredith assures him. "I did exactly what you asked. No one has suspected a thing in the week I've had him. They only just realized he was even gone a day ago. If they were going to trace it to me, they would've by now."

I know Meredith is responsible for this—the scene in her basement confirmed that—but there's something about hearing her admit that she's been holding Ryder hostage for a week that feels like taking a physical blow to the chest.

"You better be right about that."

"I am. Now, you can take him from here."

His laugh is a deep, bellowing sound. "And give you a chance to double-cross me? I don't think so. You're staying with me until the trade-off."

"That's not what we agreed on."

"It's what's going to happen."

"But—"

"My arms dealer is a floor down. I'm going to grab a few items from him before the meet-up. Don't do anything stupid while I'm gone."

His door opens, and I cower on Meredith's side, praying that he doesn't come in this direction because, if he does, I am royally fucked.

By some miracle, he goes to the stairwell on the opposite side of the garage, and his footsteps echo further and further away.

My chest expands with a relieved breath.

I have half a mind to barge into the car and demand she releases Ryder, but with the man coming back—with weapons, no less—that isn't my best option. At a momentary loss, I pull out my phone.

If nothing else, updating Moreno could help.

Rachel: Found them. 8ᵗʰ floor of the garage. She's with a man, and they mentioned going to another location for a trade-off. His license plate number is MRA711.

Moreno: I'll handle it from here. Go home. Now.

Rachel: How far out are you?

Moreno: Go home.

Rachel: How far?

Moreno: Half hour. We'll make it. Leave now before it's too late.

A half hour? Meredith and this guy are minutes from taking Ryder to who-knows-where. They won't make it in time.

The idea hits me like one shot too many, with a wave of nauseating hope.

Rachel: I can stall.

I already know messages of protest are going to be flooding my phone, and there's a solid chance he'll make good on his threat to put a hit out on me for disregarding his orders, but I tuck my phone away and crawl to the passenger side's front tire.

Lowering myself even further, I reach out for the front tire's valve stem cap and twist it off slowly. I may not know Meredith as well as I thought I did, but I do know that she can't sit in the car on an August day without the air conditioning on full blast, which is the only reason I'm comfortable enough to press the pin inside the valve stem. I don't press as hard as I can, so the hissing stays at a minimal volume, but I hope I can make enough of a difference that it delays their plans long enough for Moreno to get here.

After a few minutes, I can see a dramatic change in the tire and decide that it's all I can risk right now. I leave the valve stop cap off and slowly scoot back.

Right into a solid surface.

"What do we have here?"

I slowly turn, finding the man standing over me, head cocked to the side, duffle on the ground, and a gun aimed directly at my head.

Shit.

"What the fuck do you think you're doing?" he asks.

I don't say anything. Hell, I can't even move my eyes from the gun. It's so similar to the day Lyla was born, reminding me how close my life had been to ending then.

The only peace I have is knowing my daughter is safe and sound at home.

"Who are you talking—" Meredith gasps, eyes widening in horror when she rounds the car to see my cowering frame under the man's gun.

"I told you this one would be a problem," he mutters.

"What the hell are you doing here?" Meredith asks in a strained voice like she actually gives a fuck.

I grit my teeth and lift my chin defiantly.

If I'm going to die, I won't do it begging these low lives for anything.

The barrel of the gun pressed to my forehead. "Answer the fucking question," he grates.

I look to Meredith. "I saw your car pull in when I was passing by. I knew you were supposed to be at work, so I followed to make sure you were okay."

The pressure of the gun leaves my skin, just to come down hard right above my left eye. My body slams against the ground, and my face meets the rough concrete, scrapping my cheek. The heat of the pain is blinding, and I gasp for breath as a hand grabs a fist full of my hair, dragging my head up to meet the man's cold eyes.

He's crouched to my level, and the scent of stale cigarettes hits with the need to throw up.

"Bullshit," he spits, and I can't even flinch away when his saliva hits my face.

"Vance, what are you doing?" Meredith asks, voice low and cautious.

"Getting the truth." He wrenches my head back, setting the gun directly under my chin.

"I'm only asking one more time before I let you bleed out. What *the fuck* are you doing here?"

I can barely see him from the position he's forcing me into, but I still do my best to glare as I whisper, "Ryder."

He laughs, and the cigarette scent fills my nostrils again. "Are you the knight in shining armor coming to save the damsel in distress?"

"I'm not leaving without him."

That makes him laugh even harder. He lets go of my hair and stands, giving me a chance to catch my breath before he, once again, aims the gun at my head.

"You're not leaving at all," he says, finger twitching for the trigger.

I expect countless memories to flash through my mind as I stare into the barrel of his gun, but my reeling mind is too overwhelmed, and I'm only left with three of the strongest emotions I've ever felt in my life.

The first, I'm ashamed to admit, is fear. I don't want to die, and I loathe that this man could force that fate upon me in the form of a bullet through my skull.

The second is grief, not for my own life, but for Lyla's. She'll have a lifetime of memories that I will have no part in. Her first day of school. Her first date. Her first heartbreak. Her first job. Her wedding day.

I'm going to miss it all.

The last feeling is regret. I regret leaving Ryder after Lyla's birth. I regret building walls that kept us apart for years. I regret every second of my life that I spent staying away when all I've ever wanted to be was *his*.

What I don't regret, however, is that my life will end, having done everything I could to save his.

"Wait!" Meredith's voice shakes with the command.

"I don't give a fuck if she's your friend," Vance huffs. "She's a loose end now."

"We'll take her with us."

Vance gives her a look, and I'm sure mine is just as bewildered.

"Ryder is in love with her. If she was in danger, he'd tell them anything they want to know."

The fury that boils in my veins is so violent that I can barely see straight. She'd save my life, only to sell me off as leverage over Ryder.

Friend of the year award over here.

The idea brings a glint of excitement to Vance's dark eyes. "I could jack up the price, too," he muses. "You'd be a good leash for the dog, wouldn't you?"

I glare at him with all the fury burning inside of me.

"I like this one," he says with another laugh, tapping the gun against my cheek, which is wet from the blood that glides down my face from the gash on my forehead.

"I have duct tape in the bed of my truck. Grab it," he says to Meredith, who scurries to do as he asks. "We'll need to move shit in there to your car, so we can throw them back there since your car is no longer drivable."

I don't have much of a choice but to let Meredith use the duct tape to bind my hands behind my back. I'm not naïve enough to think Vance's plan to sell me gives me any sort of immunity. He'll shoot me in the head the second he thinks I'm not worth the hassle. Though I'm not keen on the idea of being sold, this is buying time for Moreno to get here.

I'm kept on my knees by Meredith's car while they transfer multiple bags and boxes from Vance's car to Meredith's.

I think through every possible plan, but all I have is the hope that Moreno hurries. I have no idea how long it's been, but he can't be far now. It's just a matter of time before he pulls up and gets us the hell out of this situation.

Meredith comes over while Vance secures the cover over the truck bed and pulls me to stand.

"Why?" I ask under my breath. "What possible reason could you have for doing this?"

She turns my shoulders so I'm facing away from her. "Protecting my son."

"Protecting? If anything, you've risked his life by stealing from the Morenos. If you needed money, all you had to do was—"

"You have no idea what you're talking about." Her words cut

through mine as she pushes me forward. "No idea what I've had to do to keep him safe from them."

I resist her, turning on my heels to search her expression. "From who?"

I think about the envelope that I stashed in my glove box and wonder if I should've read it before coming here.

Meredith's eyes are wide, panicked, and I realize with overwhelming grief that I'm not facing a mastermind villain but a desperate mother.

She doesn't say anything, and I'm about to press when Vance calls, "We don't have all day, Mary. Throw her in the back."

Did he just call her Mary?

The color drains from her face, and she shoots him a lethal glare. "What the fuck, Vance?"

He feigns ignorance. "Oh, my bad. Did I blow your cover? Well, now I know you won't be trying to help her escape."

Cover? What cover?

And why does that name sound so familiar...

I stumble when a hand shoves me from behind, but I'm too preoccupied with the pieces of the warped puzzle coming together. The timing. The features. The lack of information about the past.

I'm pushed against the truck and turn just in time to see Meredith's horrified gaze as the pieces fall into place.

"You're Mary Anderson," I whisper. "You're the woman Mason Consoli was in love with...and he's Dominic's father."

CHAPTER FORTY-ONE

Ryder

Please be a figment of my imagination. Please, don't be real.

Because the alternative means accepting that Rachel is restrained in the back of the truck bed that I'm being dragged toward.

A man I vaguely recognize holds my upper arm, shoving me forward until I stumble into the truck. I'm barely able to catch myself with my hands bound in front of me, and I mostly end up collapsed over the hitch, fighting my blurry mess of a mind for clarity.

"Fight me, and I'll kill her," he says, flicking his head in Rachel's direction.

I want to curse him to hell and back, but it's all I can do to locate my arms and legs as I'm maneuvered into the small space that is the truck bed.

He slams the door closed, and the only light we're left with comes from each of the top corners, where the cover has a few small tears. It's not enough to signal for help, but it is enough to illuminate Rachel's bleeding face.

"Ryder," she says in a broken whisper. "What did they do to you?"

I have no idea when the last time I said a single word was, so it takes a while to connect my brain and mouth. When I try, I end up in a coughing fit.

"It's okay, it's okay," she murmurs.

When I finally can speak, the words burn and come out in a low rasp. "Tell me this isn't real. Please, don't be real."

The skin next to her eyes crease with sadness. "I'm so sorry."

"How did you get here? What-what the hell is going on?" I ask,

285

slowly processing that Rachel probably knows a lot more about what's happening than I do.

I don't know if it's my question or the answer to it that opens the floodgates, but Rachel's eyes shut as streams of tears pour down her cheeks, which twist with her pain.

The sight hurts worse than being crammed back here.

I spend more energy than I have to raise my bound hands and gently brush her tears away. "Don't cry, Rebel. I hate it when you cry."

But my words only make the tears come harder.

"This is all my fault," she gasps. "I never should've let you leave. When you were gone, I thought you were too mad about our fight to call, but I should've known something was wrong. You've never gone that long without talking to Lyla before."

My mind whirls, struggling to remember the fight she's talking about. Flashes of a heated conversation come back to me, and though I can't recall the exact words said by either of us, my subconscious accompanies the memory with a weighty regret.

It must have been bad.

"How long?"

"Ryder, you've been missing for eight days."

Fuck.

I knew it had been a while, but I thought a few days at most.

Over a week?

"I am so sorry," she heaves. "This never would've happened if—"

"Shh." I brush the tears away again, glad to see them slowing. "Does anyone know we're missing?"

She nods, looking marginally hopeful for the first time. "Moreno was a few minutes from the parking garage when we left. I gave him this truck's license plate."

We were at a parking garage?

"Moreno is here?"

"He and all the L.A. capos came into town yesterday."

Somewhere beneath the haze, I'm pissed about that.

"He involved you in all of this?"

"Actually, he threatened me several times, but once I figured out where you were, I couldn't just stay home. Everyone else was traveling to nearby bases, so I was the closest one."

"And how exactly did you know where I was?"

"Kade figured out that no one was hacking our IP address. The embezzling really was coming from our house. There was only one other person who's had access to our house all this time."

"Meredith." I spit her name.

"That's the best part," she says with a pained laugh. "Her name isn't Meredith. It's Mary Anderson."

Recognition flashes in my head at the information, seeming to know the significance before I can form the actual thought to connect the dots.

When I do, I can barely believe it.

"Mary Anderson, as in—"

"The mother of Mason Consoli's child."

"But that would mean Dominic—"

"Is a Consoli," she finishes for me.

For fuck's sake...

I shake my head, trying to clear it of the muddiness. "You shouldn't have come here, Rachel."

"You would've done the same."

"That's different."

"No," she whispers. "It isn't. Besides, I'm the reason you're in this position in the first place."

"Stop saying that. This isn't your fault."

"I should've known something was wrong when you weren't reaching out to talk to Lyla."

More and more flashes from that night come back to me.

"You had every right to be angry after how I left things."

"You remember?"

"I remember enough," I tell her. "I remember leaving you when I shouldn't have. Again."

"Again?"

I nod but stop when blurriness clouds my vision. "I kept replaying the day Lyla was born. Back then, it felt like the only way to protect you was to go stop Mason. But now..." I shake my head. "I never should've left your side. I'm so sorry, Rebel."

And there goes another tear.

"I never told you just how hard I'd fallen in love with you," she whispers, voice breaking on the last word. "Leaving you was the hardest thing I have ever done."

"And it won't ever happen again. We're done leaving each other." I stare into her beautiful eyes, willing her to feel the honesty in my words. "You're too important to walk away from. Fuck my job, fuck everything else. You are the only reason my life has an ounce of meaning, and I refuse to live without you for another second."

I don't have a warning before her lips take mine in the most heartbreaking, desperate kiss we've shared. My mind is still clearing, but I don't push through the fog in this moment. I let this kiss consume all working brain cells and lose myself in the only woman I've ever wanted.

What the fuck was I thinking all those years ago? How did I let her walk away? Forcing her hand had seemed like the only way to keep her, but I should've begged on my knees and groveled until she gave me another chance. I should've done *whatever* it took to keep her.

It's a mistake I won't make twice.

The truck hits a pothole, and our lips are wrenched apart as our heads bang against the sides. Both of us hiss in pain, and I briefly feel a pull toward unconsciousness but fight with all my might against it. I can't leave Rachel to fend for herself.

"Do you know where they're taking us?"

She's cringing, whether, from my question or the pain, I'm not sure. "They said something about a trade-off. Moreno thinks they're selling you to another family. When Vance caught me letting the air out of Meredith—Mary's—tire, he almost killed me. Mary proposed the idea of selling me to them, too, as a way to control you."

The answer is so much to process that it takes me a moment to speak again, and even then, all I can come up with is, "Who the fuck is Vance?"

"Mary called the man Vance. I'd never seen him before, but I'm almost positive he was the one who was stalking me. Do you know who he is?"

I picture his face. Something about it stirs a level of recognition, but not enough for my foggy brain to locate right now.

"I'm not sure," I tell her. "Look, Rachel, if all of that is true, we are in a *very* bad situation."

"You think I don't know that?"

"I think that if another family gets their hands on you, you will be assaulted, murdered, or both."

I hate the look of sheer terror staring back at me, but she needs to know what we're up against.

"If you have any chance to run, I need you to swear to me you'll take it."

"I'm not leaving you," she says without hesitation.

I lift my hand to gently brush the blood and tears off her cheek. "I know you don't want to, but we have to think of Lyla. We can't leave her alone."

"B-but I can't just—"

"You need to. She'll need someone to protect her."

Tears *again*. What wouldn't I do to make sure she never cries again? Those beautiful eyes weren't made for tears.

"Please," I whisper when she still doesn't answer. "Promise me."

With a soft shudder, she gives me a jerky nod.

"Words, Rebel," I whisper.

"I-I promise," she manages between hiccups.

I kiss her forehead, leaving my lips there as I savor the feeling of having her close. "Thank you."

We lay like that for a while, and I wonder if she's thinking the same thing that I am: that we wasted so much time. It shouldn't have taken being abducted for us to come to the realization that we can't be apart.

"I love you," she says, and though I've never asked for them, they're the words I always wanted most.

"I wish those words could properly express the level of my affection for you, but they can't. So, just know that every time I tell you that I love you—and Rebel, I fucking love you with everything that I am—I mean it more than you will ever know, and I plan to show you that every day for the rest of our lives."

It's then that the car pulls to a stop.

Her wide eyes land on mine, and at that moment, we both accept that we will do whatever it takes to get out of this alive.

For our daughter.

For each other.

For all the time we have to make up for.

I take her lips again, swearing to myself that this is not our last kiss but only one of the first compared to what's ahead of us.

CHAPTER FORTY-TWO

Rachel

Neither of us speaks when we hear the truck doors open and slam shut. Ryder lays his head against the back, eyes closing and face going slack. I wonder why he'd make himself so vulnerable in a time when he should be vigilant, but the answer comes as soon as the truck bed opens, casting sunlight on his peaceful face.

If they still think he's still unconscious, they may let their guard down.

Vance takes hold of my ankle, roughly dragging me to sit on the truck bed door before getting Mary's help to do the same to Ryder.

I squint as my eyes adjust and process our surroundings, a giant field with a wide road that looks more like a runway of sorts.

An airstrip.

Sure enough, a small, luxury plane is parked several yards away from us, and the airstrip is otherwise abandoned.

The plane's door slides open, and four men armed with large guns exit. They descend the stairs, standing at the base of the plane expectantly.

Vance does an inconspicuous check of his handgun—which looks like a kid's toy compared to what the soldiers are carrying—before looking at Mary. "I'll go make sure everything is in order." He glares at me and Ryder's figure, which is slumped with his head in my lap, then nods to Meredith's side, where I'm sure another gun is strapped. "Kill her if she starts causing trouble."

If I wasn't restrained, I would've flipped him off.

We watch Vance stride to the group with a confidence I doubt he's earned, and once he's out of earshot, I send a cutting look to Mary.

"Why are you doing this? How does *this* protect Dominic?" At the mention of her son's name, Mary's calm facade starts to crumble.

She looks between Vance and me, checking he's far enough away before lowering her voice. "I didn't have a choice. Vance found out who we were and has been blackmailing me for years." Her eyes trail to Ryder, and I lean forward as if I could use my body to protect him, though I can't in our current position. "Doing this...it's my ticket out."

"Why didn't you ask me for help?"

"By the time we were friends, it was too late." She casts a nervous look to where Vance is talking to the soldiers. "It was only some office supplies. I never thought it'd go on this long..."

She gets this lost look in her eyes, and a part of me actually feels bad for her. But not enough to erase what she put Ryder through.

"Moreno knows you're behind this. You won't be able to just go pick Dominic up like nothing happened. They'll never stop hunting you down."

That lost look sharpens like a blade before my eyes, and I feel the cut of it like a physical blow. "I didn't survive years on the run just to have my son taken from me. I ran once. I can do it again. You have *no idea* the lengths I'd go for him."

"I think I'm starting to get it," I bite.

Ryder presses his head into my leg in a warning that I lovingly ignore.

"I met him, you know. Dominic's father."

Mary looks away from me, toward the men who are caught up in conversation and paying us no mind.

"I met him the day Lyla was born. He sat beside me on a bench and told me about how he'd lost the love of his life and their unborn child."

"Shut up," she grates, and Ryder presses into me even harder.

"I wonder," I say, blatantly ignoring them both. "Did you know that he kidnapped Lyla and I? Did you know that he was the accident that Lyla's been scarred from for weeks now?"

"Of course, I knew." She twists to look at me with eyes that shine with anguish. "What do you want from me? An apology for being his dirty backstory? Because you won't get it. I loved Mason, but he was power hungry, even back then, and if I hadn't left, he would've destroyed Dominic and me."

I lean forward, meeting her crazed eyes with my glare. "You did a bang-up job all on your own."

Her hand comes out of nowhere, connecting with my cheek with a smack that rings in the field. Ryder goes rigid on my lap, but Mary doesn't notice. She steps forward, taking my chin between her sharp nails.

"I have had to beg, scrape, and fight every fucking day of my life, and I'm not about to stop now. I liked you, Rachel. I really did. I wish you'd taken my advice and left Ryder alone so you didn't have to get caught up in this, but you didn't, and now you'll be a means to an end just like him."

Her nails dig in so deep that my skin breaks, and I can't help my pained wince.

Ryder twitches in my lap, and I know he's about to interfere.

"No!" I rasp, eyes still locked on Mary, but Ryder heeds the warning, remaining where he is.

Thankfully, Mary takes my outburst as a plea and releases my face with a shove.

"Ladies," Vance practically spits, coming up to Mary's side. "Let's be civil in front of our guests."

Two of the armed men have followed Vance to us, and they take hold of Ryder's arms on either side. The urge to fight when Vance takes hold of me is strong, but I don't. I won't be able to overpower him, and trying will only minimize my chances of getting out of this.

Moreno, you better be fucking close.

We get to the base of the plane, and the door opens again, extending the stairs to make way for a man in a fitted suit to descend.

He's clad in black head-to-toe, with dark hair cropped short and a tidy beard to match. He wears sunglasses that cover half his face, but the other half is set in a stern frown that reminds me a lot of Briggs.

Confidence, authority, and something far more nefarious radiate off this man like a danger sign blinking in neon lights.

"Who the fuck is this?" he asks with a razor-sharp tone and a head jerk in my direction.

Vance's hold on me tightens. "Your ticket to controlling Bates. The mother of his child. He'd do anything to protect her."

"Is that right?" He looks from me to Ryder's limp body and back again.

I can feel Vance's nod. "For thirty-five percent more, she's all yours."

The silence that settles over the airstrip is lethal like it alone can suck the life from each one of us. After what feels like an eternity, the man nods to one of the soldiers at Vance's side.

One gunshot sounds.

Two voices shout at deafening volumes.

"Rachel!" Ryder jerks in his captor's hold, eyes flying open as he inspects me for injuries.

Vance wails in my ear, releasing me with a shove as he cowers to look at the bullet in his foot.

The man looks between Ryder and me with interest, and I know he's just realized the truth in Vance's claim. Ryder surrendered his surprise element to ensure I was okay.

He slides off his sunglasses to show his cold, cobalt-blue eyes and tucks them in the pocket of his coat with calculated movements. Though his face remains as hard as granite, his brows lift as though whatever he sees pleases him.

"What the fuck?" Vance hisses through tightly gritted teeth.

"Mr. Vance." The man steps closer to me, but his focus is trained on Vance. "Do you take me for an idiot?"

"N-no, sir. Of course n-not," he stutters.

"Then I suggest you stop treating me like one. Or should I tell the boss that you're no longer an ally?"

Vance grunts as he pushes to stand, leaning his full weight on this good foot. "Of course not, Mr. Diaz. My apologies."

My stomach drops.

I never paid much attention to how Mafia families operated when I lived in L.A., but the research I did on Mason over these last few weeks taught me a lot. Like how Leon Diaz is the boss of the Diaz Mafia family and owns the southeast part of the country. All I know of his character is that when debating which families to reach out to if they'd been approached by Mason, Leon Diaz was the only boss Moreno refused to see.

This man isn't Leon Diaz—according to the few pictures I've seen of him—but he looks similar enough that they have to be closely related.

The moment Diaz's snake-like eyes slide to me, I shudder. There's something horribly unsettling about the way they rake up, and down my body, like he's inspecting a car he'd like to buy.

If another family gets their hands on you, you will be assaulted, murdered, or both.

I'm about to be sold off like an object, and yet I cannot bring myself to regret coming for Ryder.

That familiar slither of anxiety crawls through my mind, but I don't let the thought settle before I combat it with my mantra.

I can do this. I am strong. I am capable. I am not a victim.

I lift my chin, showing this man that I am not afraid of him, even if it isn't completely true.

His lip twitches at that.

"I think I will be taking the girl." He takes slow, leisurely steps toward me, and I try to back up, but Vance shoves me forward into the man's hold.

Diaz catches my hips in a bruising grip and looks down at me with countless twisted fantasies openly written in those chilling eyes.

"Let her go!" Ryder calls, and though I can hear him struggling, I can't see him past Diaz's body.

"Huh," he mutters, "maybe you will be good for controlling the beast."

"Perhaps we can come up with a more reasonable price, then," Vance suggests, tone edged with well-concealed hysteria. "Twenty percent? Fifteen?"

"Mr. Vance, I pay for business, not toys," he says, eyes never leaving mine, and I feel so sick that a part of me actually *hopes* I can throw up all over his pristine suit.

"If you touch her, I will fucking kill you," Ryder's deadly threat is accompanied by the sounds of the soldiers struggling to keep him in their hold.

In a quick turn, Diaz has my back against his front, and I feel a blade digging into my throat as his other arm wraps around my middle, holding me in place. My hands are still restrained behind my back, and I wince when this position forces them to his groin.

Only weeks ago the mere sight of a knife would've been enough to break me, but now, I barely register the one pressing to my throat as I take in the scene in front of me.

I have a full view of Ryder thrashing in the hold of two soldiers, and I have no choice but to watch in horrified silence as he goes rigid in their grasp, eyes so full of conflict that my heart aches for him.

"Ryder, don't."

The blade digs in deeper, cutting my words as well as my chin.

"Yes, Ryder, don't struggle, or your girl is the one who will suffer for it."

I can do nothing but helplessly watch as Ryder lets the soldiers regain control of him.

Diaz laughs, and the sound might be charming if it wasn't laced with venom. His lips lower to my ear, and he bucks his hips, pressing himself into my hands suggestively. "I think we'll be having lots of fun together."

"Wait," Mary's voice cuts the suffocating tension with Diaz, and though it's brief, I'm grateful for the reprieve.

He turns us toward her, and the knife leaves my throat, though it's quickly replaced by an arm wrapped around my neck. It's not tight, but the threat of his strength looms over me, warning me not to fight against him.

"A problem?" he asks, leisurely stroking his free hand up and down my torso.

Mary steps forward, clearly terrified but trying to disguise it. "We change our minds. You can't take them both."

What the hell?

Mary's eyes flash to mine, and I want to think the regret there is fake, but it can't be. She wouldn't be putting her life on the line if it was.

"Yes, you can," Vance snaps, looking murderously at his partner. "What the fuck are you doing?"

Mary and Diaz ignore him.

"Is that so?" he asks, letting the arm around my neck lower, trailing crudely down my body and inspiring a shudder.

Mary nods sharply.

"And why exactly should I listen to you?"

I watch how her shoulders stiffen but don't cower. How her eyes flash with a burst of confidence. How her mouth opens to answer him.

And how she collapses to the ground as a gun at my side fires, hitting her square between the eyes.

My shriek is instant and ear-splitting, but Diaz only chuckles, tucking his gun back in its holster.

He clicks his tongue, returning the arm around my throat like it doesn't have the blood of my former best friend splattered across it. "Turns out I don't give a fuck."

Vance watches Mary's body with wide eyes like he just realized the guns aren't for show.

"I suggest playing your next move wisely, Mr. Vance," Diaz clips. "I have half a mind to give you the same treatment and leave here with the money, brute, *and* my new toy. So, what will it be?"

Vance visibly swallows, sliding his gaze to Diaz with a forced smile. "No issues here."

"Then I believe we'll be on our way." I feel the jerk of his nod as he signals one of his soldiers to drop the duffle in front of Vance.

Vance wastes no time taking the money and limping to his car without a single look back at the lives he's ruined.

As Vance drives away, Diaz pulls me back, and I look expectantly to the airstrip entrance. If Moreno doesn't get here before we're on that plane, any hope Ryder and I have of escaping is gone.

Step.

Step.

Step.

With each one, my eyes stay locked on the entrance, waiting, hoping, *praying* that cars will speed to our rescue.

Step.

Step.

Step.

Nothing.

No one is coming. I cast one look over my shoulder to where Ryder is already being dragged up the steps, and I'm only a few feet from the same fate.

If no one is coming to help us, then I'm already as good as dead. Which means I have absolutely nothing to lose.

With a deep breath, I accept that I may face a world of pain or even death, but it's better than going willingly.

Pulling from every defense lesson Ryder gave me, I thrash in Diaz's grasp, wrenching my arms from his hold with a swift jerk.

"Fuck," he mutters when I crash to the ground, unable to catch myself with my arms still restrained behind me. My back hits the ground, all the air in my lungs leaving in a *whoosh*.

"Rachel!" Ryder calls, his voice thick with dread.

When Diaz gets close, I kick my legs out wildly, reveling in the grunt when one lands on his shin and another gets his stomach.

The click of a gun is what forces me to snap my eyes to his deadly somber ones. He takes advantage of my hesitation, stepping in too close for me to kick him again.

He grips a fistful of my hair and uses it to drag me to a standing position as a whimper is forced from me. As soon as my lips part, the barrel of his gun is shoved between my lips, pressing so far back that it triggers my gag reflex. My eyes fill with tears, and I stare wildly into

Diaz's unrelenting stare.

I realize that, while I'm huffing and barely able to catch my breath, the struggle didn't have any physical effect on him whatsoever, and that fills me with so much hopelessness that the tears fall.

"You know," he says in a tone that's edging on amused, "you're lucky the idea of choking you with my dick is more appealing than seeing your head on a stick. I'll enjoy breaking you and using you to break him." He nods to Ryder behind us, who I can barely see frozen on the steps, watching this exchange with horror. "Then, and *only* then, will I let you beg me to take your life, and, being the gentleman that I am, I'll grant you that wish. Understand?"

He stares at me expectantly, and I give as much of a nod as I can manage since I can barely move with his grip on my hair and a gun in my mouth.

Diaz releases my hair, but the gun remains in place as he lifts a finger and brushes away my tears with terrifying care.

"I can't wait to see more of these," he whispers and finally pulls the weapon from between my lips. I'm gasping for breath when he takes hold of my upper arm, ready to pull me up the stairs.

Then I hear the sweet sound of screeching tires.

CHAPTER FORTY-THREE

Rachel

The relief that floods my veins at the sight of those two black cars would bring me to my knees if Diaz didn't have a death grip on me.

"You've got to be fucking kidding me," Diaz growls.

He drags me backward, the gun in his hand, and holds it to my forehead. I brace myself to fight against him when we reach the base of the steps, but he doesn't attempt to pull me up, and I'm sure it's only because he doesn't want to risk dividing his attention.

I want, more than anything, to turn to see if Ryder was forced inside the plane, but my current position doesn't allow me that ability.

Diaz's body tenses as he focuses on the cars, or rather, the people climbing out of them and aiming their weapons at our captors.

And, consequently, us.

Moreno leads the group, weapon pointed at Diaz and the signature no-bullshit expression on his face. Donovan and Kade follow, standing at his side. Harris and Knox wordlessly join their group.

"Ethan Diaz," Moreno spits. "Always a displeasure. I suggest you release my family before things get out of hand."

"How do you see this going? Because from where I'm standing, we're five-to-five, and I'm the one with leverage," he says, leaning in so close that his cheek presses to mine.

He's right. Moreno might be here, but Diaz has just as many men, leverage, and a plane.

Unless I can do something about it.

Any distraction could help give Moreno the upper hand.

The knife Diaz held to my throat only minutes ago isn't in either of his hands. He'd had it on his right side, and I'm willing to bet it's strapped to his waist there now.

I stretch my fingers as far as I can in my compromised position and start feeling around as inconspicuously as I can manage.

"You're in *my* territory. Abducting my underboss is an act of war, and I *will* retaliate with the support of every other family. Let them go, now," Moreno orders, and I don't miss the gravitational pull laced in his words, like some kind of hypnosis that people can't help but fall into.

"Former underboss." Diaz flicks a quick look over his shoulder to Ryder. "Isn't that right?"

The twist of his body, as slight as it is, gives me the room I need, and I'm able to reach far enough to feel the strap holding the knife in place.

Only a little closer, and I'll be able to get it...

"Let Rachel go with Moreno," Ryder calls, a steadfast conviction in each word, "and I'll go with you."

I jerk in Diaz's hold, barely able to see Ryder's sure expression directed at the man who holds me.

"Ryder, don't," Moreno clips, but Ryder doesn't even look to his boss.

"You let her go, and you take me. Everyone walks away from this."

"No!" I shout, the mere idea sounding like a new form of torture altogether. I writhe in Diaz's arms, and he retaliates by knocking the barrel of the gun against my temple in a warning, though we both know he can't shoot. If he did, there'd be nothing stopping Moreno from taking him out.

"Let her go," Ryder hisses, the hold over his control wavering. "Release her, and Moreno will let us leave."

"No!" I ignore my throbbing head and use all the force I have to jerk against Diaz as I reach around him.

I need this knife now more than ever.

But when I catch Ryder's gaze in my struggle, the look there gives me pause. The admiration, awe, and...*love* that stares back at me feels far too much like a goodbye.

"I didn't agree to that," Moreno states.

Ryder rips his gaze away from mine and looks to Moreno. I have no idea what sort of silent conversation passes between them, but the hope I had that Moreno wouldn't allow this slowly dissipates as his stony features lock on Diaz. With a firm nod, he confirms his acceptance of Ryder's conditions.

No. No. *No.*

"Fine," Diaz grates. "You can have the toy, but Bates is mine."

The gun trails slowly down my body, but I barely recognize the danger of the weapon.

"Ryder," I say through the thick lump climbing up my throat, "please, don't do this. I can't do it alone."

"You can, Rebel," he says in a tight voice, eyes glazed with something that twists my heart into a million knots. "You're the strongest person I've ever met."

"Well, isn't this sweet," Diaz mocks. I feel his eyes ravish my body like he can commit it to memory, and the idea sickens me. The only upside is that he finally removes the gun from my body.

"I do regret that we won't have our fun together."

When I look up at Diaz, I let all the confidence that Ryder has helped me build in the last few weeks shine through my gaze.

"Who says it has to end?" I ask and wish I had the time to appreciate the bewilderment on his face.

But I don't because I swing my hands, still bound behind my back but now armed with Diaz's knife, upward until I feel the resistance of the blade digging into his wrist.

That's when all hell breaks loose.

Guns fire, and since a brief glance assures me that Ryder wasn't a target—but is currently fighting against the soldiers that hold him—I focus on my own attacker.

I dive for the gun Diaz drops with his pained howl, and he dives with me. At first, I think his only goal is to get the gun, and, though he certainly tries, he's really mimicking my movements to use me as a shield between him and Moreno.

With my wrists still restrained, I'm at a severe disadvantage, and Diaz knows it. I inch toward the gun, using the knife to try to cut my bonds loose as I do. Luckily, Diaz is more focused on reaching for the gun than he is attacking me.

From where we lay on the ground, he reaches up past my head to reach the weapon that lies a few feet away. The sound of a ricocheting bullet resonates far too close, and Diaz draws his hand back fast as lightning.

"Fuck," he grates through bared teeth, clutching his bloodied hand just as I start to feel the blade slicing the tape.

The failed attempt to reach the gun prompts Diaz to try a new tactic. His newly marred hand reaches over my waist to pull me to him. I cry out as my skin scrapes against the concrete, breaking in a half dozen places. What's even worse than the pain is the fact that, as I'm tugged forward, I lose my grip on the knife. I tug at my wrists, trying desperately to force the tape off, but I can't get the momentum I need while lying on my side.

Diaz's face goes rigid with fury, but without the knife or gun, his only option is to use me as a human shield.

"Give up now," I tell him with a heaved breath. "You won't win this."

Dead eyes lock on mine long enough for a horrific fear to hit me soul-deep. "You better start praying that *you* don't make it out of this alive because *I will*, and I won't be killing you after all. I will use you until you're nothing but a lifeless shell. Then, I'll let my men have a go at it."

Footsteps come from behind, and I know it's help coming for me. Diaz realizes it too, because he uses his grip on my waist, and another around my throat, to drag my body upward against the concrete.

My open wounds scrape against the ground with each tug, and the white-hot burn steals the breath from my lungs, but the same inhumane strength that possessed me the day Lyla was born hits me with incredible force. I rock my head forward, nailing Diaz's nose with the motion and relishing in his anguished wail.

In the same moment, I kick my foot up behind me and hit the half-broken duct-tape twice before it finally breaks, then extend my arm as far up as I can. I don't grab the gun when my fingers meet the cool metal and instead shove it as hard as I can. A moment later, a bullet flies through the air, hitting the weapon and sending it hopelessly out of Diaz's reach.

"That's it," Diaz growls in a feral voice that doesn't sound human. One hand squeezes my throat with deadly force, and the hand on my waist reaches back until it locates the knife.

He squeezes so tight I can't bring a single breath to my lungs, let alone fight, as Diaz slings one leg over my stomach, then climbs on top of me. My body screams for breath so violently that black spots form in my vision, and I feel consciousness slipping away from me.

That's when I notice the knife digging into the tender skin over my heart.

"Stop!" Diaz roars.

I let myself take a second to look around me. Moreno, Donovan, and Kade are closer but still several yards away from us. Knox lays by the car, Harris at his side assessing some injury.

Then there's Ryder.

He has single-handedly taken care of one of the men that held him in place, and the other—who seems to be the only remaining Diaz soldier—looks on the brink of unconsciousness with his gun aimed at Ryder, who stopped fighting to lock eyes with me.

Though it's the last thing I want to do, I force my eyes from the man I love and look to his boss.

"Kill. Him," I grunt, still barely able to breathe from the weight of Diaz's body covering mine.

"If they kill me, this knife goes into your pretty little heart, and we go out together," he sneers.

"Do it," I grit, sending my pleading gaze to Moreno.

I can't read whatever emotions hide behind his blank features, but there's a sinking in my heart when I realize, for the second time, that he won't listen to me.

Diaz nods to his only remaining soldier. "Take him inside the plane."

"Please," I beg Moreno with all the desperation I have left. "Kill him, Moreno!"

But he doesn't so much as lift his gun.

"Here's how this is going to work," Diaz grits. "We're going to stand, walk to the plane, and climb up the steps. If you behave yourself, I'll consider releasing you."

He doesn't wait for an answer and instead hauls me to my feet with his grip on my throat. When we're standing, he has to readjust his hold on me so the arm that holds the knife is briefly wrapped around my waist.

The idea hits me with such clarity that I don't consider other options. I don't consider consequences. I don't consider *anything* except the fact that this is the very last shot I have at saving Ryder.

I look to the only man I've ever loved, and a million unsaid words pass between us in this fleeting moment.

We should've had more time. We should've told each other how we felt from the beginning. We should've tried harder, given everything we had to protect the once-in-a-lifetime love we share.

I know the exact moment when Ryder realizes what I'm about to do, and his admiration turns to horror.

Because this moment isn't about soaking in memories.
It's goodbye.
My hands take hold of the knife, but instead of wrenching it away from Diaz, I stab the blade into my own stomach.

CHAPTER FORTY-FOUR

Ryder

I take it back.

I take it fucking back.

I would rather live in a state of physical paralysis and mental nothingness than watch the scene in front of me play out.

The love of my life stabs herself in the stomach, catching everyone off guard, including Diaz, who stands in shock as she collapses to the ground. Moreno takes the shot as soon as Rachel is out of the line of fire, and the Diaz capo falls limply to the ground.

"Rachel!" I yell, and disarm the wide-eyed soldier before I lodge a bullet from his own gun into his skull.

I speed past the fallen soldiers and Diaz to get to where my girl is lying on the concrete, hands at her side, the knife lodged just below her belly button.

"I'm—I'm okay," she says on a shaky breath, but anguish contorts her delicate features.

"Kade is getting an ambulance here," Moreno says, rushing to kneel on her other side. He inspects the wound, tearing Diaz's shirt off and using it to apply pressure around it. "Keep her talking, Ryder."

She blinks rapidly like she can't figure out if she's in a dream or reality, and her hands shake uncontrollably. I take one in my own, squeezing gently.

"Rachel, stay with me, okay?" I pant, relishing the small contact I can have with her. "Help is on the way."

Her eyes meet mine, filling with tears again.

Those fucking tears.

"F-for some reason, I didn't think it'd hurt this bad," she rasps, shaking with a laugh that quickly turns into a wince. "You said it wouldn't do deadly damage."

She repeats the words I said to her during one of the training sessions we had. Though it's true, I'd meant it in relation to men, and *only* men.

Moreno briefly meets my eye, and I know he's thinking the exact same thing.

Rachel very likely punctured her uterus, which can cause very deadly bleeding.

My chest constricts, and pulling in the air takes more strength than it should at the mere prospect of watching Rachel bleed out here in front of me.

No. Please, no.

"Why did you do that?" I ask, unashamed, when my voice breaks on the last word.

She manages a wry smile. "He's dead, isn't he?"

"That's not how this works. *I* protect *you*."

"We protect each other." That faint smile fades, and her eyes start to flutter.

"Hey, eyes on me, Rebel. You're not going anywhere, okay? You're stuck with me."

"I was wrong," she says in a breathy voice, and the pain creasing her face shifts to an eerie peace that will haunt me until the day I die. "I-I thought a life without you was better than never coming first, but it isn't true."

I let her guide our joined hands to her lips, and she places a feeble kiss there.

"I would take the time we had—short as it was—over an-and over again before regretting a single second of our time together."

I swallow hard, but the lump in my throat goes nowhere. "Don't give me your goodbyes, Rachel. You're staying right here with me."

"Tell Lyla I love her," she whispers, eyes glossing over and growing distant.

Droplets from my eyes hit her cheeks, rolling down like they were her own.

"Please, Rebel. Don't leave me. We said we were done leaving each other."

I practically choke on the words.

A small smile tilts her pale lips. "We never really left each other,

Ryder. You know that."

"That's not enough for me!"

"I love you."

I bite my tongue. If I say it back, that's admitting this is goodbye, and this is *not* goodbye.

"Please, say it back," she breathes, energy visibly draining from her.

I don't want to. I really don't fucking want to.

But even now, I can't deny her.

"Rachel, with all my heart, and all that I am, I love you. I have loved you from the moment I met you, every moment you were with me, every moment we were apart, and I will spend the rest of my life loving you."

Then I watch her breathing stop as the sound of sirens blares in the distance.

My elbows rest on my knees, which just means that my entire body moves with the shaking of my leg, but I can't sit still.

"You should wash up," Moreno says from my side, where he's been since we got to the hospital an hour ago. We're in a private room, one of the many perks of being the biggest donor of the hospital and paying off half the building to keep quiet about what they treat for us.

I look down at my hands, which are covered in blood. It's morbid, I know, but the idea of washing it off feels a lot like washing *her* off, and I can't do that.

I can't lose her.

"I should go get an update," I say, abruptly pushing to my feet and taking hold of the IV pole that's currently shooting fluids and vitamins into my malnourished body.

Moreno grabs my arm. "It's been less than five minutes since the nurse left," he reminds me. "It'll be a few more hours until she's out of surgery."

Fuck, it feels like it's been hours already.

"Go home, man."

I rip my arm out of his hold. "I'm not going anywhere."

"She's not going to want to see you like this when she wakes up. You look like shit."

I glare at him. "I'd like to see how you fair after being drugged for a fucking week."

Still, I drop into my seat.

I hadn't wanted to see a doctor, but Moreno didn't give me a choice. They said exactly what I expected, that I was malnourished and overexerted. The amounts of propofol in my system were walking the line of life-threatening had I been on it much longer. The doctor said they'll run tests but expect that I'll get back to full strength with little to no permanent damage.

I just hope the same can be said for my Rebel.

"How do you feel?"

"Exactly how I look," I answer, and I swear I see him shake with a laugh out of the corner of my eye.

The door opens, and a nurse steps inside. I'm on my feet so fast the world spins, but she puts out a halting hand. "I have an update regarding Mr. Knox."

Moreno stands, listening to the nurse tell him how Knox is in stable condition and should be ready for discharge in the next few hours. His arm caught a bullet during the shoot-out and it hit a vein that caused a lot of blood loss before Harris could get to him. He was unconscious by the time the ambulance arrived, but his breathing never stopped.

Not like Rachel's did.

Almost every responder needed to tend to Rachel, so I wasn't permitted to ride in the ambulance and didn't push to. The more people helping her, the better. To occupy my reeling mind on the drive to the hospital, Moreno and Donovan fill me in on everything I missed and the blank spots of my memory that haven't come back yet.

They tell me how the perfect storm of events led to my disappearance not being discovered for a whole week, and I can't even blame them for it.

If I'd gotten my head out of my ass, I never would've left Rachel's side. I can't say Meredith wouldn't have found a way, but I would've been noticed a hell of a lot sooner.

I'm also filled in on all Kade learned about Clayton Vance in the few minutes he dug into his past. Vance is a former soldier for the Consoli family and ran off when allegations of embezzlement came to light. We still have no idea how he's connected to Mary Anderson, but figuring it out is a top priority. It's assumed that he conducted the embezzling from our family through Mary, but we'll know more after his interrogation, which I will gladly be leading.

Something about the information nags in the back of my mind, and I can't quite pinpoint why I have the feeling I've forgotten something important. I did spend a week on drugs that fuck with the mind in a million different ways, so I suppose that's to be expected.

Kade, Donovan, and Harris are currently on damage control to keep today's events out of the public eye. Vance was found almost immediately by Briggs and is currently in custody at the Sacramento base, but there was a lot of covering up to do since medical professionals showed up on a scene with several dead bodies.

Moreno should be with them, leading the clean-up efforts since he has the most authority, but he doesn't so much as glance at his phone. He just sits beside me in companionable silence once the nurse leaves.

"Why are you here?" I finally ask. It's not like Moreno and me to beat around the bush. "Don't you want to kill me?"

"Actually, no," he answers, expression somber. "It's the first time in a while that's been the case. It's kind of nice."

I eye him, waiting for the snarky comment to follow, but it doesn't. "What changed?"

His lip lifts in a small smile that's more pained than amused. "You were abducted by someone you trusted."

"Guess I deserved that."

"No, you didn't." Moreno shakes his head. "A fucking week, Ryder. That must've been hell."

"Definitely wasn't pleasant, but I wasn't conscious for most of it."

"I'm just glad we got to you in time. We might not have if it weren't for her."

And now it may cost her her life.

"You should've stopped her," I tell him.

"Trust me, I tried. Even threatened to put a hit out on her."

"You did what?" My hands shake with the desire to hit him just for thinking about harming Rachel.

But Moreno shrugs. "Would've been deserved after she slapped me across the face."

My eyes nearly burst out of their sockets.

What. The. Fuck.

I've never seen anyone lay a hand on Moreno and walk away alive. I suspect Elli could pull it off, but I've never confirmed the theory.

"She wasn't thinking straight," I assure him, though I clearly wasn't there to know. "It won't ever—"

"I might've deserved it," he admits with a dismissive wave and reads the question on my face before I ask it. "What you heard from

Briggs at the gala, that was me on the phone with him."

My head pounds from all that's happened in the last few hours, and processing this information only adds to that ache. "But he was delivering a package."

He nods. "An account of your whereabouts since you left Los Angeles. I had him keeping an eye on you to ensure loyalty."

Any offense I might've taken doesn't even register in light of everything else going on. "You thought I was still betraying the family?"

"No, but at least I would know what you were up to."

I stare at him for a long moment, reading between the lines of his fucked up words. "Joshua fucking Moreno, did you have me trailed *because you missed me?*"

"I had you trailed because you abducted my fiancée," he snaps with a deadly glare usually reserved for our enemies, then mumbles, "Bastard."

When I manage to crack a smile, he does, too.

An unspoken truce.

"As much as I dislike my orders being ignored, even I have to admit there's no way we would've found you in time without her."

"It's not worth it if she loses her life," I say, the words echoing in my chest and reverberating pain.

It's true. I'd rather be sold and gone than be without her.

Yes, we have Lyla, and for her, I will pick up the pieces of my life and give her everything I have, but without Rachel, there will always be a gaping hole in the core of who I am.

Joshua nods, and I'm sure he's imagining Elli in the same place.

As if my thoughts conjure her, Moreno's phone buzzes, and Elli's name lights up his screen.

"How are things?"

I can't hear what she says, but Moreno nods along to whatever it is.

"Still in surgery. Knox is going to be fine, too."

He listens for another moment, eyes flicking to me.

"I think he'd like that," Moreno says, holding out the phone to me.

I eye him but take it, bringing the device to my ear. "Hey, Elli. What's—"

"Daddy?" the little voice on the line says hopefully.

The sound of my daughter's voice hits me square in the chest, stealing my breath and filling me with a peace that feels undeserved.

There was a moment on that airstrip when I had to accept that I'd never hear her voice again.

"Tiger," I manage, sounding as emotional as I feel. "Sweetie, I miss you so much."

She sniffles on the other end. "Where did you go?"

"Daddy had some business to take care of, but don't worry. I'll be home soon, okay?"

"Promise?" she asks in a shaky voice like she's on the brink of tears.

I am, too.

"I promise. I'll be home, and I won't be going anywhere anytime soon," I tell her, imagining how holding her is exactly what I need right now.

"I love you, Daddy!" Lyla says, sounding much calmer now.

"I love you too, Tiger. See you soon, okay?"

"Okay!"

I hear her pass off the phone, and Elli's voice comes through next. "She's okay here. You don't need to worry about a thing."

"Thank you," I whisper.

"Of course. I'm just so glad you're safe."

"You and me both," I say with a weak laugh. "Are your brothers still coming into town?"

She pauses, and Moreno gives me a questioning look. "They're on a flight now, but I was going to send them home once they got here since the worst of it's over."

"Don't send them away. There are some things they'll need to know."

I hand the phone back to Moreno, who ends the call. "What's that all about?"

"Later," I tell him with a shake of my head, and he doesn't push.

He clasps a hand on my shoulder. "Your family has your back. Whatever happens, I'm here for you."

All I can manage is a nod.

It feels damn good to know my family is at my back, even if I'd give it all up to have Rachel at my side.

CHAPTER FORTY-FIVE
Ryder

I have no idea how Moreno managed to convince me to come to the base for a shower, but I stand under the stream of steaming hot water like it can burn away each shitty part of the last week from my body. He'd first suggested that I go home, but having Lyla see me blood-covered and disheveled sounded like a less-than-genius plan, so the base was a better choice.

The entire time, I never lose the nagging sensation that's been bothering me since Moreno filled me in on everything I missed. I try to reason that I'm only worried for Rachel or that my mind is a muddled mess from my propofol kick, but this feels different. Since I still can't place where the nagging is coming from, I force myself to play everything I remember on a loop over and over in my head, but all I end up repeating is the peaceful look on Rachel's face right before she stabbed herself.

I thought she, like me, was soaking in the memory of our last time seeing each other before I was taken, but she decided she'd be the one to go instead.

For fuck's sake.

If I lose her, there will be no moving on. There will be no other women, just as there has been no one since I met her.

She's it for me.

It killed me to see the way Ethan fucking Diaz touched her in ways that only *I* was meant to. Seeing the notoriously violent Diaz capo with his hands on my Rachel was its own form of torture. It will forever be one of my greatest regrets that he died a quick death. If I'd had it my way, he would've spent the rest of his life groveling for mercy I never would've granted.

Fuck, just the thought of what I would've done to him fills me with an intoxicating bloodlust that I have no intention of quenching through anything aside from the acts themselves.

I guess Clayton Vance will have to take the torture for both of them.

Pity.

Only when my skin is near boiling do I finally turn the water off and climb out of the shower. I'm barely dressed before I can't wait a second longer and pull out my phone.

"No, there's no update on Rachel," Joshua says by way of greeting.

"When was the last update?"

Instead of answering me, his voice is distant. "You're sure? Show me any security footage."

"What's going on?" I ask in a tight voice. "Is Rachel okay?"

"I haven't had an update on Rachel since before you left, but there's something else."

"What?"

"Knox is gone. He wasn't officially discharged, but he's nowhere in the hospital."

That nagging sensation comes back with jarring force, begging me to remember *something,* but I can't sort through what exactly it is that's so important.

"Any idea why?"

"None," Joshua answers. "Can you think of anything?"

"He's always been quiet. I barely know a thing about him, let alone his habits."

Moreno mutters a curse under his breath, and something about the lowered tenor of his voice takes me back to the airstrip.

I see Rachel's face above mine as she antagonized Mary for answers while Vance talked to the Diaz soldiers. From the small slit that I had my eyes open, I'd caught a distorted image of Mary's face.

What had they been talking about?

"You okay?" Moreno's voice sounds far away, but this time it's due to my racing thoughts.

I ignore him, focusing all my willpower on replaying the memory. Each time I play it back, more of it comes into view. At first, it's only Mary's distorted features, then it's a look of desperation, followed by pinched brows.

Finally, Mary's statement comes back to me.

It was only some office supplies. I never thought it'd go on this long…

There'd been too much going on for me to decipher what the confession implied at the time, but it hits me now like a punch to the gut and almost as painful.

"I'll call you back," I tell Moreno, racing from the locker room bathroom, across the base, and down three flights of stairs to an old bunker-turned-torture-chamber.

Unlike what should be the case, it isn't just Vance in the room.

Vance hangs from the ceiling by chains on his wrists, but the fearful, pleading look that almost always accompanies the entrance of a capo in an interrogation room, is missing.

In fact, there's no gaze at all in his droopy, lifeless eyes.

"You really shouldn't have come here," Knox tsks as he pulls the needle with an empty vial from Vance's arm.

"I'll give you thirty seconds to explain yourself."

The boy—and he really isn't much older than a boy—finally turns to look at me, and the most sinister, condescending look gleams those usually bland eyes.

"Don't act all high and mighty, Bates. You're just as much a traitor as I am. Do you really think being abducted will make Moreno forget that you traded his bride-to-be for your kid?"

"That's not an explanation."

"I mean, come on, Bates. Moreno might pity you, but he sure as fuck doesn't trust you."

Since he's clearly not intent on filling in the blanks, I do it myself. "Mary only stole from office supply funds. The Rohypnol was all you."

He taunts me with a bored expression.

"You knew they were stealing, but you let it happen so you could hide your own embezzling with theirs. You even knew it would be traced to my I.P. address, giving you plenty of people to pin the blame on if someone caught you." I take one menacing step forward. "You were contributing to Mason Consoli's funding."

"*Contributing*?" He barks a laugh, and anger taints his features. "You want an explanation, Bates? I organized every base's *contribution* to Mason. The Rohypnol shipments have been a mess since the prostitution rings came down, so no one noticed a fucking thing when I rigged them. Mason's entire army was built on what *I* gave him. I told him over and over to instigate in-fighting instead of going for brute force, but the only time he listened was when he took your bitch and kid.

I take another step toward him, feeling all sanity drain from my body and mind.

Knox takes a step back, eyes going wide with a frenzied panic that I *delight* in.

"I'm leaving, and you're going to let me," he blurts, squaring his shoulders though his tone is slowly deflating of confidence. "If something happens to me, Moreno gets evidence of every time money was stolen from the base that will tie directly to you. You think he'll believe—"

My fist connects with his mouth with a sweet crunch, and two of his teeth fall to the ground. Knox stumbles back, the realization dawning in his dull eyes that I couldn't give a single fuck about consequences right now.

It doesn't matter if Moreno thinks I stole from the base. It doesn't matter if this man is the reason Mason had the funds to nearly overthrow the family. It doesn't matter that he's the most vital tool in eradicating the rest of Mason's followers from the Moreno and Consoli families.

None of that matters.

All that matters is the euphoria that flows through my veins when the first droplets of blood flow down Knox's face.

My second punch knocks him to the ground, and I take my time towering over him.

"I should really thank you," I say, in a saccharine sweet tone. "I've had a week from hell, and since everyone responsible is dead, I'll get my pound of flesh from you."

My fists rain down on Knox's face until my hands go numb, and I mean potential-nerve-damage numb, and I don't give a single fuck. In fact, I marvel at the sight of the unrecognizable, smashed-in skull of a man I used to trust.

He loses consciousness far too soon, and there's no telling which of the blows actually ended his life, but I don't slow even when I know he's long gone.

All I can see is my Rebel driving the blade into her stomach, and every time the brutal image replays, I'm filled with a renewed fury. She could be dead. Our daughter might have to live without her mother.

All because I didn't stand by her when I should've.

So, I vow, in this moment, while I heave deep breaths over a lifeless, mangled body, that if my Rachel does make it through this, I

will never, *ever*, leave her side again.
And like an answer to my unrighteous vow, my phone rings.

CHAPTER FORTY-SIX

The Note

My Dearest Dominic,

I'm afraid you may never forgive me for the things I've done—the things I am about to do—but you have to know that it was all to protect you.

If you're reading this, it means I didn't come home tonight, and if that is the case, I feel you deserve to hear the entire truth from me.

My name is not Meredith Ashford, it is Mary Anderson, and your rightful name is Dominic Consoli. You are the only son of Mason Consoli, of the Consoli Mafia family.

I wished to hide you away, protect you, and give you a life ignorant of this fact, but I'm not sure that was ever truly an option.

I promise that you were the product of love, but when I told your father we were pregnant, he wanted to tell your grandfather, and I knew your only chance at a normal life was if I took you away. Your father was power-hungry, and his father was even more so. They would've used you as a pawn to secure their lineage, and I was terrified of what you'd become under their influence.

So, I left a note for Mason, took enough belongings to fit into a backpack, and moved across the country.

For months I went from women's shelter to women's shelter, looking for jobs and any sort of stability, all while pregnant and fearful of Mason following, but by the time you were eighteen months, I'd made a modest life for us with the job I got at a local daycare.

Meeting Rachel Lance was one of the best and worst things to ever happen to us.

I don't know what twisted luck streak brought her into the daycare I worked at over every other one in Sacramento, but I recognized Ryder's name as soon as I saw it on the paperwork.

As a form of protection, I'd learned to keep tabs on the Consoli family, and since I'd moved to California, I kept tabs on the Marsollo and Moreno families, too. I knew Ryder worked closely with Moreno and that Rachel and Lyla were extensions of that family. Back then, Moreno wasn't even a big name, but I knew better than to let my guard down.

Later, I'd come to learn that Mason believed his father killed us, so he betrayed his family and worked undercover for Moreno for years. Not so long ago, he attempted a coup of both families that cost him his life.

Of course, all I knew when I met Rachel was that I was far closer to being discovered than I ever wanted to be, so I made a plan for us to start somewhere new.

This time I had money, so the first thing I did was go to the most highly recommended man for false identification. That was how I found the true bane of my existence and the reason I am in the situation I am today.

Clayton Vance.

Vance was previously employed by the Consoli family and ran off when they started to suspect his embezzling. When I came to him for passports, he did what no one else had and figured out who we were.

He showed up at our home in the middle of the night, held me at gunpoint, and told me we'd be his ticket back to the Consoli family.

I did the only thing I could think of.

I told him I had a connection to the Morenos and that we could use it to make more money than the Consoli's would ever pay him for turning us over.

Vance agreed, and that's how I've supported us these last two years.

I thought it was temporary, that I had things under control, but Vance got greedy. He kept increasing the amount I needed to take and threatening our safety if I didn't comply.

I understand if you can't forgive me for this last part, but when I saw a way out, I had to take it.

When Ryder moved to Sacramento, I proposed to Vance that we sell Moreno's former right hand to another rival family, the Diazes.

Vance would get the full payout, and we'd be free of him.

By this point, Rachel and Lyla were more than simple pawns. The four of us had a family of sorts, and hurting them was never something I wanted to do, but I had little choice.

Vance didn't trust I wouldn't spill everything to Rachel, so he took it upon himself to keep tabs on her to keep me compliant, as if threatening our lives wasn't enough.

I've spent weeks planning this trade-off, so the entire plan goes off without a hitch, and I hope it does.

I hope I burn this letter before you ever get the chance to read it. I hope we live the rest of our lives free of the criminals who want to separate us, but I can't promise that future.

What I can promise is that I love you more than anything in the entire world, and if this plan works and we're free, it'll all be worth it.

I know I'm not a perfect, or even good, person, but I did it all for you.

You bring meaning to my life and light to my world.

Mom.

CHAPTER FORTY-SEVEN

Rachel

I reach to place the letter on the coffee table, but Ryder takes it from me before I've fully extended my arm.

I was discharged from the hospital this morning, less than twenty-four hours after my surgery, and Ryder's been doting on me obsessively. It took a lot of convincing to get him to believe I'm able to be in the living room with everyone else.

Normally, I wouldn't have fought the doctor who wanted me to stay to ensure my steady recovery, but with everything that happened, and everything that still needs to happen, I couldn't stay cooped up in a hospital room. The compromise Ryder and I come to was that I'll use a wheelchair to get around, and have a nurse on call around the clock.

It's worth it to not miss this unofficial meeting.

Elli and Moreno take the other side of the couch, but the one adjacent is occupied by James and Damon Consoli, Elli's older brothers. Logan Consoli, James's twin, and the family boss, doesn't sit with them and instead stares out the window to where Dominic and Lyla play on the swing set.

Dom still doesn't know about his mother, and though it's not something we can push off much longer, we're trying to prolong his normalcy by letting him believe he's having an extended sleepover here, at least until some things are sorted out.

Several decisions were made last night in a heated conversation with Ryder as we went over all that's happened in the last few days, and I'd be lying if I said the news the doctor told me as soon as I gained consciousness after my procedure has nothing to do with the emotions that I'm struggling to keep under control.

"I still can't believe it," Damon mutters. He's the oldest Consoli, but due to a history of addiction, it's his younger brother who leads the family. "How is this possible?"

Elli shakes her head. "Mason was convinced the note Mary left was faked by Dad. I wonder if he ever even considered that it was real."

"I doubt it," James mutters. "He was blinded by his anger."

"What are the odds she would've met Rachel by chance?" Damon asks. "That should be almost impossible, right?"

Ryder shrugs. "I'd guess she moved into our territory on purpose. If she knew enough to keep tabs on Mason, she probably knew where he did and didn't have reach. Sacramento is a big city in Moreno territory. Still, the odds they met are astounding."

I think back to the days I first met Mary. Back then, it had felt like a breath of fresh air to find a friend, someone I could rant to and share the struggles of single motherhood with. I thought I'd finally had some good luck in the midst of my heartbreak.

I don't realize I've tensed until Ryder squeezes my hand gently.

That's another thing, ever since I woke up in the recovery room, he's constantly touching me.

I could get used to that.

"She was doing what she thought was best for her child," Ryder says, only to me, though the others hear it.

"By stealing us from ours," I remind him.

His expression is unchanging. "I'd have sacrificed her in a second if I thought it was best for Lyla. Besides, you were never a part of her plan. In her head, she was ridding both kids of mafia influence."

We all stare at him with shared confusion.

He lifts his hands. "I'm not excusing her actions, just explaining them."

"He looks just like him," Logan mutters, eyes still locked on the kids outside.

It's the first time the Consoli boss has spoken since I read Meredith's note.

James, Damon, Elli, and Moreno all make their way to the window, watching along with Logan.

"I thought there was something familiar about him," Elli whispers. "Now that we know he's Mason's son, the resemblance is uncanny."

"He seems like a good kid," Logan notes.

"He is," I agree. "A bit of a wild child, but a great kid."

Logan nods sharply. "I'm sure he'll adjust to Chicago in no time."

"Excuse me?"

Logan's expression is purely diplomatic. "He's a Consoli, so he'll come live at the manor."

The statement inspires fear that leaves me speechless.

"Logan, you can't just take Dominic back to Chicago with you. You know nothing about kids."

He shrugs. "That's what nannies are for."

Elli shakes her head. "No offense, but you're not exactly *father material*."

"I don't need to be a father. I'm a boss, and this is my nephew," he says the last word like it tastes strange in his mouth. "I need to raise him around the base the same way we all were."

"Dominic deserves a semi-normal life at the very least," she insists.

James, who is ranked as his twin's underboss, shakes his head at his sister.

"That's not how this works."

"Then he'll come live with us," Elli declares.

"What?" Logan and Moreno say in unison, then proceed to glare at each other.

"He'll have a stable home and still be raised among family."

"He's a Consoli, not a Moreno," Damon states. "That's not fair to him."

Elli drops her hands to her side. "Well, I don't see how moving him across the country and throwing him at nannies is a better solution."

"He's not going to Chicago," Ryder says from my side, drawing every eye to us. "Or anywhere, for that matter."

"He's staying here with us," I finish.

Logan shakes his head. "Absolutely not. Out of the question."

"With all due respect, Mr. Consoli, I don't take orders from you. Dominic's life is here, so he's staying here."

He glares at me. "I'm not giving orders. I'm stating facts. He has Consoli blood, so he'll stay with his family."

"I have Consoli blood, and I'm a Moreno capo," Elli counters.

"Yes, something else that pisses me the fuck off. Thank you, Elise," Logan practically snarls.

"You're not his family," I tell him. "Not in a way that matters. He doesn't even know that his mother is gone. You expect a four-year-old to learn his mother is dead, pick up his entire life, and move across the country with men he's never met just so he can be thrown at nannies and expected to grow into some killer? No, it's not happening."

Logan steps away from the window and toward me. "Raising him ignorant of who he is isn't a better solution. It's a dangerous as fuck one."

I plant my hands on either side of me to stand, but Ryder's halting palm on my shoulder stops me. I throw a vicious glare at him, but he just shakes his head. "Glare all you want, but you're not moving unless it's to get in bed."

I stop trying to stand and instead turn my glare to Logan. "I'm not saying we never tell him, but moving him now is just cruel, and I refuse to let it happen."

"I don't remember asking for your permission," Logan bites. "If you're suggesting that I'd have to go through you, you should know I wouldn't break a sweat."

Ryder is by my side one second and then fisting Logan's shirt the next. They're the same height, but Ryder's build is bigger than Logan, not that it seems to bother the boss in the slightest.

"Threaten her one more time, and it'll be the last thing you fucking do," he grates.

Elli pushes herself between them with a look of complete and utter exasperation. "Can we have one conversation where no one is threatening to kill each other?"

I wish I could stand to match their confident stances, but all I can do is lift my chin. "Mr. Consoli, I won't let you take him. Threaten me, follow through if you must, but I have known that child most of his life, and I will fight for him if it is the last thing that I do."

It's the first thing Ryder and I decided last night when we talked over this situation. The idea of Dominic going with people who are strangers to him, or worse, into the foster care system, simply isn't something we can allow. As it is, I feel as though he's my own.

And according to my surgeon, I won't be having any more children of my own due to the damage the knife did to my uterus.

Logan stares me down like he's waiting for me to crumble beneath his gaze, but I don't. Mary might've hurt me, but her friendship got me through some of the hardest times of my life. In a way, we were a little family, and I don't take that lightly.

"This is only a temporary solution," Logan grits through bared teeth. "Hiding him away will make him more vulnerable the older he gets."

Elli nods. "It's true. I don't think he needs to know soon, but hiding it from him forever isn't going to protect him."

As much as I hate to admit it, I know they're right. If the wrong person finds out who Dominic is, he'd never be safe again. Knowing his own identity and how to protect himself isn't a choice but a necessity.

"Eighteen," I grant. "We'll let him live a normal life until he's eighteen. Then we tell him the truth."

"Thirteen," Logan counters.

"Sixteen." The word feels like spitting up shards of glass.

Logan and I stare unblinkingly at one another for long moments before he finally nods. "Sixteen."

"We should all get to know him," James adds. "He doesn't need to know that we're blood-related until he's older, but growing up knowing us as family will make the news a little less traumatic when the time comes."

Elli nods enthusiastically. "That's a really great idea. We'll do holidays together and take trips to visit. Lyla calls the L.A. capos uncles, right? We'll introduce ourselves as Dominic's aunts and uncles."

This is a condition I can easily agree to. The more love and support this boy can have, the better.

"Okay," I say. "He'll know you all as family, and when he's sixteen, we'll tell him the truth and let him choose if he'd like to stay with us or go to Chicago."

"That's not part of the deal," Logan says with narrowed eyes. "He's a Consoli, and he has a duty. Not to mention that he'll need training."

"I'm not forcing him to join the mafia, regardless of whose blood he is. He'll stay in martial arts classes, and Ryder can train him beyond that."

"She's right. He deserves a choice," Elli says and comes to sit at my side. "Part of why Mason turned on us was because no one ever gave him one."

Logan looks like he wants to argue, but his twin puts a hand on his shoulder, and they share a look I can't decipher.

Logan's lip curls in frustration, but his argument never comes. "Fine. At sixteen, he'll choose."

There's a silence that settles in the room, one that feels a lot like an understanding.

The sense of victory that buzzes through my veins is almost tangible. I may not be able to protect Dominic from everything—the grief of his mother's death or the truth about his father's identity—but I will do whatever I can to protect his innocence.

I reach out for Ryder, but there's only the cool fabric of the sheets where his warm body usually lays at my side.

My eyes flutter open, seeing no signs that Ryder was ever lying beside me.

Did he not come to bed?

Now that I'm awake, my throat burns with the need for water, and I take my time inching from the bed to maneuver myself into the wheelchair. Ryder will be mad that I didn't call for help, but if my hunch is correct, I don't want to interrupt him. As quietly as I can manage, I roll the chair to the kitchen and take a bottled water from the fridge, downing almost the entire thing in one gulp.

My eyes trail to the living room and the makeshift tent that takes up half of it, or rather, the two kids soundly sleeping inside it. I soaked in the time I spent putting them to sleep tonight, watching them make a fort, giggling, picking out a movie, sharing a bowl of popcorn, and finally giving in to their need to sleep.

I don't know how exactly things will change once Dominic knows about his mother, but I figure I can give him one more night of normalcy before that happens.

They enjoyed their sleepover, barely caring to ask why three men were sleeping in the pool house and why Uncle Moreno and Aunt Elli took over Lyla's room for the night.

Tomorrow, the capos of the Consoli and Moreno families will meet at the Sacramento base to review all the evidence of embezzlement and tie up any loose ends. I wasn't invited to that meeting, but that's fine by me.

Once everyone returns to their designated bases, Ryder and I will sit Dominic down and tell him that his mother has passed away.

It's a conversation that I'm dreading horribly but can't avoid.

It's almost three in the morning, and though I opted for an early night due to my overly exhausted body, the others stayed up late. Elli seemed to enjoy spending time with her brothers, despite the deadly glares her fiancé was shooting them the whole time.

Just when I wonder who all is still awake, hardy laughter comes from the back porch. I hadn't heard the voices before, but their laughter is so loud it's a miracle the kids sleep through it. With slow movements, I maneuver the chair to where I can see through the window to the back deck.

The only two sitting out there are Moreno and Ryder, both reclining in porch chairs, cradling a whiskey glass with the half-empty bottle on the table between them.

"Sounds like he did exactly what you told him to do," Ryder says around another sip.

"He should've known that I was bluffing, and I wanted him to do the opposite," Moreno huffs.

"How the fuck would he have known that?"

"You would've."

"That's because I have the unfortunate ability to know how your fucked up head works."

They share another laugh, and Moreno sets his glass down.

"It's not as easy as I thought it'd be. Donovan is good, but he isn't you."

Ryder smirks. "According to Elli, you don't help your own situation. I'd start by avoiding reverse psychology when asking him to complete simple tasks."

"Or you could come back."

My stomach drops, and goosebumps rise across my arms as I wrap them around myself.

I just got him back.

Ryder's laughter fades as he studies his friend. After a long moment, he seems to realize Moreno is being serious. "I thought you needed time."

"I thought so, too. Turns out I just needed you to get abducted," Moreno says with a half-hearted shrug.

I study Ryder's unreadable face like my life depends on it, waiting for the confirmation that he's bound to give. After all, this is what he's been hoping for since he moved here.

I just thought we had more time.

"As for Rachel and the kids, bring them," Moreno adds.

Ryder's lips part in a smile, and it's so beautifully effortless, lighting his handsome face. "Thank you, Joshua, but I don't think I'm ready yet."

My mouth falls open.

"What do you mean?" Moreno asks, echoing my thoughts.

"I mean, Lyla is still recovering from the factory night, and Dominic's world is about to fall apart. I don't think I can be the parent they need and the underboss you need."

Moreno eyes him speculatively. "And?"

"And the man that Rachel needs," he says with a ghost of a smile. "I won't ask her to leave everything behind. Maybe once things settle down, we can revisit the idea."

He nods. "I miss having you around. This has been nice."

"Yeah," Ryder says, looking more at peace than I've seen in a long time. "It has been."

Moreno pushes to his feet. "I should get inside. Elise doesn't sleep well without me."

Ryder follows, and I roll the chair toward where the kids sleep in the living room. This far away, he shouldn't suspect I heard anything.

"Rachel, what the hell are you doing awake and out of bed?" Ryder whisper-hisses, shoving his glass into Moreno's hand and rushing to my side. "You shouldn't be getting up without help. Do you *want* me to take you back to the hospital?"

I wave him off. "I just got restless, is all. I'm fine."

Moreno sets the glasses and whiskey gently on the counter, giving Ryder a *good luck with this* look before heading up the steps.

Ryder gives me a chastising look. "If you wanted to get up, you should've called me. If you were to fall—"

"I'm fine, Ryder. Really. I was just..." I drift off, mood going somber when my eyes land on the peacefully sleeping boy.

He sighs, nodding at my unspoken dread. "It won't be easy, but he's a good kid, and we'll support him every step of the way." Ryder takes both my hands in his, lowering himself to place kisses on each one. "Telling him is going to be rough, but we'll do it together."

Together.

He lowers to his knees in front of me, taking my face between his warm hands and leaning in to place the slowest, sweetest kiss on my lips, and the message is loud and clear.

We have all the time in the world.

Epilogue 1

Rachel
Six months later

"Slow down!" I call for what feels like the hundredth time, but Lyla and Dominic don't acknowledge me.

"Don't worry, Rebel. They know better than to run into the street," Ryder assures me, wrapping an arm over my shoulder and pulling me to him. I can count on one hand the number of times I've been in the same room with Ryder, and his hands *haven't* been on me.

When I asked him why he's so adamant about having his hands on me, he said he's making up for lost time, and I have no objections to that.

We finally arrive at the ice cream shop, located on one of the more populated streets in our area, to find the kids already waiting in line. We join them, pissing off a few parents as we do, but a glare from Ryder shuts them up before they even think about calling us out.

He takes "scary boyfriend privilege" to an entirely new level. I suspect I could get away with just about anything with him at my side.

"You guys are super slow," Dominic states with a chuckle, and I know without even looking at Ryder that we're both relishing in the moment of playfulness.

Things haven't been the smoothest since Dominic found out about his mom.

The week following the news, he didn't leave the windows by the front door, convinced his mom would pull up in her gray van like she always did before. The next week, he hit Ryder a few times, getting unreasonably angry about things that never would've bothered him before. When Ryder caught him trying to climb out the window of his newly renovated Cars-themed bedroom to "go home," we knew it was time for us to do something more.

I've been taking him to see Dr. Danver twice a week for a few months now. At first, he refused to talk to her, but a few sessions in, she told me they were starting to make progress.

Since then, he's traded violent tendencies for destructive ones, which Dr. Danver said is normal for his age, and she's hopeful it's only a phase.

Dominic isn't the only one getting help. A few weeks after things settled down, I found myself a therapist to help me work through my anxiety all on my own so I don't have to rely on—in her words—*toxic coping mechanisms*. I went weekly in the beginning, but now I only go once a month since I've responded so well to the techniques she taught me.

"Well, that's what happens when you're old. You get slow," I tease, and Dom scrunches his nose.

"We're never getting old," he declares, looking to Lyla for confirmation.

She nods, seeming content with that idea.

Even through his life changes, Dominic still adores Lyla and, though my daughter is trying to understand why Dominic lives with us now, she enjoys always having him around. They still get along like they always have, but these light-hearted, playful moments are few and far between.

"Is that right?" Ryder asks with a lifted brow.

"Yup," Dominic confirms.

"You know," Ryder says, lowering to their level, "if you never grow up, you'll never get to drive a car like Lightning McQueen."

Dominic's eyes go wide for only a second before he composes himself and defiantly crosses his arms over his chest. "I don't want a car like Lightning McQueen. I want a car like Uncle Logan!"

Uncle Logan.

It's still strange to hear, but there's no denying that it's for the best. Both Dominic and Lyla have taken to calling the Consoli's their uncles.

We took the kids to Elli and Moreno's wedding a few months ago, then we all went to stay at their new house in Los Angeles for Thanksgiving. This has given everyone a chance to form a relationship with Dominic, and it's been nothing short of heart-warming to witness.

Damon isn't like the capos I've met in either the Moreno or Consoli families. The more I'm around him—which, admittedly, isn't a lot—the more I see why Logan stepped into the boss role of their family. Damon's good at what he does, but he's a smart ass and, quite frankly, a goofball. From what I can tell, Dominic seems to like Damon the most since he's the only one who will wrestle with him and pretend to lose.

James is nice but more reserved than his older brother. He's taken to teaching Lyla and Dominic how to play different board games, though both of them really just like Jenga, and only because Dominic *tries* to make the tower fall over.

Logan found his way into Dominic's good graces through their mutual love for cars. When we took a weekend trip to Chicago with Elli to see her brothers a few weeks ago, Logan took Dominic for a drive in every single one of his dozen sports cars. In the most vulnerable moment I've ever caught Logan in, he actually let Dominic pick out a new car for him, and they went to pick it up together.

Elli and Moreno even volunteered to take the kids for a weekend to Disneyland, so Ryder and I could have some alone time.

"You definitely can't drive Uncle Logan's cars unless you grow up," Ryder tells him.

"Fine," he huffs, looping his arm around Lyla's. "We'll only grow up to drive, but that's it."

"Right, of course," I say with a chuckle, and we step up to the front of the line.

I go to lift Lyla, but Ryder shakes his head, lifting Dominic in one arm and Lyla in his other to help them order. It's not necessary since I've been fully cleared by the doctor for all physical activity for months now, but Ryder still treats me like I'm recovering from my knife wound. He doesn't let me do any heavy lifting if he can help it.

Once the kids have placed their order, they squirm out of Ryder's hold and race to the pick-up window.

"I swear keeping up with these two is a full-time gig," Ryder mutters.

"Actually, I was thinking the opposite," I tell him. "I'm ready to start working again."

After my abrupt extended leave and putting Mrs. Caster on thin ice for vouching for a no-show employee, she found herself a new assistant. I didn't blame her and barely felt the loss when I officially turned in my resignation. In the weeks following Mary's death, taking care of Lyla and Dominic had been a handful, but things have calmed down recently. Now that both kids are in school for half the day, it's time for me to start working again.

Ryder stops abruptly. "Wait, really?"

I nod. "The kids have been doing great, and I need something to fill my time when they're at school. Something to make me feel productive."

He leans in to kiss my temple. "What would you like to do? I'll get you a job anywhere you want."

I laugh at the ridiculous—and no doubt genuine—offer. "Actually...I was wondering if the base had any openings."

"What would you do at the base?" he asks with pinched brows, far calmer than I'd expected him to be at that request.

"Something in finance...I mean, nothing crazy. I just thought—"

His thumb brushes my bottom lip. "I'll talk to Moreno, but I don't see why not. I think it's a great idea."

"Yeah?" I sigh with relief. I've never been interested in working for the Moreno family before, but now it doesn't feel like such a crazy idea. Working on my own schedule, as much or as little as I want, all while doing my part to protect our family. Somehow, it's become the most logical option.

The server hands Dominic and Lyla their ice cream, which they accept with mumbled thanks, and race off behind the building.

My heart drops.

"Dom! Lyla!" I call after them. "Fuck, they know better than to run off like this! We need to talk to them."

Usually, he's the one going crazy about the kids safety, so I have no idea why I'm dragging him and not the other way around.

We weave through people, going to the back patio where customers can enjoy their ice cream, but the usual tables and chairs aren't spread out across the space tonight. Instead, they're pushed against the edges, overflowing with more floral bouquets than I've ever seen before.

But that's not all.

The kids turn to look at Ryder and me with wild excitement as they stand by Elli and Moreno. My eyes scan the line of people who accompany them, Alec, Donovan, Kade, Harris, Ava, Briggs, Donna, Logan, James, and Damon. Even my parents stand with the group.

What the...

My feet are frozen until a soft pull on my arm from Ryder encourages me to walk with him.

"What on earth is going on?" I ask, scanning the entire group until my eyes fall on the man I love, who has stopped to kneel in front of me.

My breath catches, more at his dazzling smile than anything, as he reaches into his jacket pocket and pulls out a little black box.

"I had this very ring in my pocket the day Lyla was born," he tells me. "I thought I was ready to call you mine forever, but then you told me you wanted to move back to Sacramento, and I told myself it was for the best, but I don't think I ever believed that."

"Ryder," I whisper.

He places a gentle kiss on my knuckles. "I didn't realize what it meant to really put you first, but I do now. If I could go back in time, I'd choose you over and over again, but since I can't do that, I promise to spend every day of forever choosing you."

He opens the ring box, showing off the pear-shaped diamond inside in all its glittering glory.

"Rachel Anne Lance, my Rebel, will you do me the honor of becoming my wife?"

"Yes." I say breathlessly and nod furiously. "Yes, of course, Ryder." His smile turns drop-dead-gorgeous, and he slides the ring on my finger, standing to take me in his arms as our family applauds.

"Can we do it now?"

His brows knit together. "Like, now? Now?"

"Why not? Everyone we love is here."

"Don't you want to plan a wedding? Isn't that the dream?"

I shake my head, feeling light-headed in the best possible way.

"*You* are my dream," I tell him. "Let's not wait any longer than we already have."

Ryder nods slowly, the look in his eyes almost...disbelieving.

"Any chance someone here is ordained?" Ryder asks.

Everyone looks at each other with wide eyes. None of them had expected this turn of events.

Hell, I just thought we were out for ice cream, and now it's my wedding day.

It's Damon who raises his hand.

Everyone turns their questioning gazes to him, and he shrugs.

"Got ordained on a dare one *very* drunken night a few years ago," he admits, not looking at all ashamed by that fact.

"That works for me," I say, and everyone murmurs in agreement.

"Mommy, what's happening?" Lyla asks, and she and Dominic

come to stand with us.

I crouch down to their level. "Daddy and I are going to get married."

Dominic's eyes go wide, and he looks at Lyla. "Can we get married, too?"

Everyone laughs at that, but his question is a dead serious one.

"That's another thing you'll have to grow up to do," Ryder answers, lowering beside me.

Dominic's brow furrows, but he nods. "Fine. I'll grow up, but only to drive Uncle Logan's cars and marry Lyla."

The Consoli brothers—who no doubt came into town more to see their nephew than for this occasion—laugh at that.

"Lyla, do you want to help me pick out some flowers for your mom?" Elli prompts, and Lyla nods enthusiastically, taking her hand as they go.

The next ten minutes must set some kind of wedding-planning record as we transform the small space into a functioning venue.

And as quickly as that, we get married.

My father walks me down the aisle, smiling wide like this is exactly how he pictured this day going, though, of course, none of us did.

Damon makes up a script as he goes, even going off on a tangent about the divorce rates in the country, though he clarifies that his bet is on us *making it*.

Somehow he nails the vows.

Ryder and I say *I do*, and we spend the entire evening celebrating with ice cream and drinks back at the house.

It's the strangest Thursday night of my life, but I wouldn't trade it for the world.

I spent years waiting for Ryder, and now, I'll never have to wait again.

From today until forever, we will belong to each other.

We will love each other.

And we will *always* choose each other.

Epilogue 2

Ryder
Eight months later

I heave a deep breath, and I shut the bedroom door behind me, massaging my temple to relieve the unrelenting headache there. Though, I'd take a million headaches over the hopeless feeling that stabs me in the gut when I picture my son's solemn features on the other side of this door.

That's what Dominic is to me, my son. It doesn't matter that he isn't my blood or that I've only known him for a year now. I love him just as fiercely as I love my daughter.

And it kills me that he isn't doing well.

Most of the time, he loves seeing his aunts and uncles, but since they came to town late last night to celebrate Thanksgiving, he's been in a black mood. We went to Moreno's last year but didn't do much celebrating because the loss of his mother was so fresh, but my now-six-year-old isn't taking the holiday season well.

He's developed anger issues throughout the year and, though martial arts has helped to some degree, there's not a lot we can do but be patient, work with him, and take him to Dr. Danver.

Today was a particularly rough day, complete with him throwing a toy straight through the living room window.

He felt guilty afterward and offered several apologies to Rachel. We were mostly able to de-escalate the situation and have a pleasant remainder of the evening, but this isn't the type of progress we've been hoping for.

Dr. Danver says his ability to recognize his actions and apologize is a good sign, but that doesn't make the situations any less exhausting, so I try to handle them to give Rachel a break. On days like these, guilt weighs on her as if it's *her* fault Dominic's mother isn't here anymore.

Now that Dominic and Lyla are sound asleep, I make my way down the steps of our house to where Joshua, Elli, and all her brothers are already sitting around the living room with their drinks of choice.

My rebel sits on the edge of the couch, vodka martini in hand, and an empty spot beside her that I'm sure is reserved for me. I plant a kiss on her forehead before moving into the kitchen to make myself a drink.

I could use one.

I'm deciding what I want when soft hands wrap around my waist from behind. I hadn't noticed how rigid I've been since tucking the kids in, but just her touch is enough to ease the tension.

She pulls me closer, pressing her cheek to my back. "Thank you," she murmurs.

I gently turn, so I can hold her in my arms, too. "For what?"

"Handling everything with Dom today," she says, dropping her eyes to the floor. "Sometimes I wonder if we're doing the right thing."

I lift her chin so I can stare into the eyes I fall in love with more every day. "We are. His other options were the foster care system or moving away with people he barely knew. We're doing everything we can."

She nods. "I know you're right. It's just hard some days."

I can agree with that.

"Do you ever wonder if being here is too much for him?"

"What do you mean?" I ask, trailing my fingers over her delicate cheekbones.

"I mean, he seems to do alright when we spend holidays in L.A. or Chicago, and I wonder if Sacramento reminds him too much of his mother."

I'd never thought about that, but now that she mentions it, it seems like a likely possibility.

"That would make a lot of sense."

"Then, so would moving to Los Angeles."

At first, I think I haven't heard her right.

Could she be saying what I think she's saying?

"You mean—"

"I think it's time to say yes."

I stare into her eyes, searching for any sign of hesitation or wariness, but there is none. She means it.

Every time I see or talk to Joshua, he always accompanies his goodbye with an offer to take back my position as his underboss.

Every time, I thank him and decline since Rachel and the kids need me the most.

In the year it's been since I made that decision, I haven't regretted it once. It feels right to be in Sacramento, especially now that I've taken over all of Knox's responsibilities.

But if Rachel is right, and moving the kids to give Dominic a fresh start is what's best for him—for all of us—then I'm sold.

"Are you sure about this?" I ask. "Because if any part of you isn't absolutely sure, then we shouldn't—"

She cradles my face between her small hands, looking up at me with firm sincerity. "I'm positive. It's time for us to move to Los Angeles. I mean, think about it, we can move into Elli and Moreno's neighborhood, put the kids in a new school system, and find them a martial arts studio. We can make new memories and—"

I cut her off by lifting her into my arms and spinning her around. Rachel's laughs draw attention from the others but I couldn't care less.

"I love you so much, Rebel."

She dips her head down to take my lips with hers as she murmurs, "I love you, too."

THE END

Made in the USA
Monee, IL
02 September 2023

42019936R00198